Praise for *The Neighbors in Apartment 3D*

Mysterious sounds on the other side of a borrowed bedroom wall had me hooked from the get-go. Compelling characters, an unusual diagnosis, and a tightly-woven plot kept me glued to the story.

   Twiles does an excellent job of balancing relationships, insights, and suspense, making *The Neighbors in Apartment 3D* one to read with your lights on and your doors locked.

Susan Crawford, international bestselling author of *The Pocket Wife* and *The Other Widow*

PRAISE FOR THE BEST MAN ON THE PLANET: A MODERN GOTHIC ROMANTIC THRILLER

An absolute corker of a read and one that left me twisting around in circles.

Booksprout Reviewer

This is a beautifully written book with complicated questions at the core. It's also really sexy.

The New Gothic classic!

# THE NEIGHBORS IN APARTMENT 3D

A Tale of Domestic Suspense

C.G. TWILES

## Chapter One

"**W**elcome to the building," Cintra said.

It sounded a little presumptuous. She was a newcomer herself, having arrived three weeks ago. The new neighbors must have moved in last week, judging by when a smiley-face doormat made its appearance in front of apartment 3D. In a city that thrived on neighborly indifference, there was something a little off-putting about a grinning doormat.

In Brooklyn, neighbors tended to ignore each other. But this was the New Cintra. Might as well add a dash of suburban-esque cheeriness to her New Self by welcoming the couple. At least, she presumed they were a couple.

"Thank you. We're happy to be here." The woman smiled, then turned and pointed a small black square at their door. The thing in her hand (remote controlled door lock?) went *bluup*.

Now the man looked at Cintra. He had round, dark

eyes, like woodland ponds that hid their unexpected depths. They flared at her with a hateful intensity.

Geez, what was *his* problem?

Cintra let the couple pass by her down the stairs. The woman was petite and fleshy, with an ashy-blonde braid twisted between her shoulders. Her skin was vampire pale, as if she hadn't been outside all summer, or any summer. By contrast, the man looked as if he loved the sun, or the sun loved him. A few steps above them, Cintra noted the top of the man's shaved head was two shades lighter than the back of his sunburn-tinged neck. Must be a hat wearer.

In their forties, she guessed. Good. Cintra's hearing was sharp, her sleep surface-light. Sedate, well-behaved, middle-aged neighbors with a smiley-face doormat would be ideal.

On the first floor, she veered off to the mailboxes. The new neighbors' footsteps tapped lightly behind her down the porcelain tile to the lobby, which was patterned with Art Deco-style fans and cubes. Still no mail for her. The few pieces inside the metal box were addressed to her roommate, Pedro, or to Occupant Apt. 3C. Perhaps her change of address form had vanished into the abyss of her old neighborhood's dysfunctional post office.

She'd ask her husband to bring her mail tomorrow. But who knew if he would. He was not yet convinced of New Cintra, and asking her to move out wasn't his only way of showing it. There was his passive aggressiveness as well. Taking several hours to return communications.

Telling her he was "too busy" to join her in therapy. Yes, she wouldn't put it past Elliot to "forget" to bring her mail tomorrow. But she couldn't blame him.

She was lucky he hadn't insisted on a divorce that very night.

## Chapter Two

"*I* saw the neighbors today," said Pedro from the kitchen as he poured a glass of red wine. The waft of ripe tomatoes in the air let Cintra know he was cooking.

"I did too. Coming out in the morning." She plunked her tote bag on the granite kitchen island that separated the kitchen from the living room.

"Wine?" he asked.

Shaking her head, she reached into the fridge for cranberry juice. She didn't want to get into the habit of drinking alcohol after work. She had enough problems.

"I guess the mystery is solved," he said.

Pedro was invested in the identity of the new neighbors. After all, it was his sublet. Apartment 3C had pre-war details, arched doorways, an open kitchen, two bathrooms with original black and white tiles, double windows, and was located two blocks from Prospect Park, the borough's five-hundred-twenty-six acres of wild, green refuge. A horse barn that served the park was so close that certain breezes delivered the musky smell of horse dung through the open windows.

The building was five stories of red brick with winged lions leering down from a stone archway over the front walk. A DANGER sign on the sidewalk hailed a mini-excavation of unknown intent, but the dig's tremoring *whurrs* and *pongs* didn't reach apartment 3C, in the back. Cintra was only here until she could sort out her marriage. Elliot had asked for a six-month trial separation, but she was fiercely hoping that time could be shortened once she proved herself.

"At least they *look* normal," Pedro said of the neighbors. "You never know in this town."

"They seemed in their forties. Probably not partiers." Recalling the female neighbor's spritely greeting, Cintra was oddly eager to defend her. "She was nice. But the guy glared at me."

"Glared?" A dubious smile slid over Pedro's face. Cintra knew the look. *Are you sure you mean GLARED, Cin? Are you sure you aren't EXAGGERATING?*

"Maybe not *glared*," she clarified. "He seemed grumpy, though."

"Not everyone's a morning person," Pedro offered. "He's decent looking." He wiggled his black brows under a tassel of short dreadlocks, indicating he thought the neighbor was more than "decent."

Cintra thought back to the man's looks. Sly-dark eyes round as nickels, sun-bronzed skin with a bone-white shaved head. He'd be more attractive without that surly look. She'd strongly felt his glower was personal, as if she'd wronged him in some way. Impossible, of course. She'd never met him before.

Anyway, no man seemed attractive these days. She was too consumed with thoughts of her husband and the possibility that she'd lost him. They'd married when she was twenty-four and he was twenty-five, an early marriage for New Yorkers. At thirty-eight, she couldn't imagine being with anyone else.

"Maybe we should try to get to know them," she told Pedro. "That way, if there's any noise issues, we can ask them to pipe down and they might actually listen."

Pedro had mentioned that his previous neighbors had played thumping music late at night, and their copious marijuana usage had seeped through the walls despite their pre-war thickness. He shrugged noncommittally at her suggestion, turning his attention to whatever was simmering on the stove, probably pasta sauce.

Maybe she should do it. Try to make friends with the neighbors. Why was there an unwritten rule that city folk didn't get to know their neighbors? It would be nice to have some nearby friends. Besides, she sensed her friends didn't want to be around her much anymore. She hadn't heard from Poppy, her closest female friend, in a few months. Out of everyone, Pedro was the most understanding of her problem—perhaps because he made his living spinning stories on stage. They'd met at a state college two decades ago, where both were active in the theater department. Pedro had been The Star who snagged every lead role. Cintra, at five-feet-eight-inches, was usually cast as Someone Tall.

Pedro had been offered the apartment 3C sublet by

a fan, an opera singer named Callie, who'd seen him in an off-Broadway show, a musical version of *Taxi Driver*. Yes, his big solo number was "You Talkin' To Me?"

"Maybe I'll do it," she said as she peeked over Pedro's arm at the—so it was—pasta sauce. "Try to make friends with them."

He added a double pinch of a spice he bought from a Jamaican store—his "secret ingredient"—to the sauce. "You want to have friends who won't know?" he asked.

She backed away from him as if the stove had scorched her. "No! I hadn't even thought of that."

"Cin," he sighed. "You asked me to help you practice, to call you on stuff. So I am."

He was right. Dr. Grace had said it would be good if she had an "accountability partner." Pedro fit the bill. For one, he was here. For two, he was the least judgmental person she knew.

"All right. It would be nice to have friends who don't know about me. Good?"

"You get an A-plus," he said, putting a wooden spoon with a dab of sauce on it up to her mouth. She tasted and gave a thumbs up.

"And you?" she asked, gingerly placing her palm on his back. "How you feeling these days?"

"I'm stupendous," he said, as a flare of blue flame hugged a pot of water.

He didn't sound stupendous. The only reason Cintra was here—besides Elliot kicking her out—was that Pedro had also kicked out his boyfriend of six years, Liam. Pedro hadn't wanted to discuss it much. She only knew that after he and Liam had moved into the sublet,

Pedro had discovered his boyfriend cheating. Discovered it through a trail of X-rated and, he swore, nauseatingly juvenile text messages.

Cintra felt guilty at her gratitude that she had a nice place to live, but only because of Pedro's breakup. Renting a place by herself would have been a financial strain as she was still paying her share of rent in her and Elliot's apartment. She'd agreed that was fair, given that the separation was because of her.

"If you want to talk," she told Pedro, but he only smiled wanly.

AROUND MIDNIGHT, something woke Cintra up out of a deep dream. At first, she thought she was hearing whatever had been in her dream, a long, low whine—a perverse sound, almost otherworldly. Groping towards consciousness, she became dimly aware the sound was outside. A stray cat in heat? No, the sound was inside. Pedro playing music or listening to the TV this late?

Pushing away sleep, she lay trying to pinpoint the location of the sound. It was eerie, low but keen. All at once, she realized the noise was coming through the wall behind her headboard, coming from apartment 3D. A dog whimpering to be let out?

Her hearing was too sharp for city living. Any old sound could jar her out of sleep. She fumbled in the dark to open a bedside drawer that contained a small plastic jar of foam ear plugs. Not finding it, she sat up and reached for the small lamp on the paneled headboard.

The sound was a little louder. Sex? Ugh.

She hoped this wouldn't be her new nightly reality, having to listen to strangers having sex. Irritating, especially as she herself hadn't had sex in—what? Four months? She buried the thought, as it would lead to one big, repulsive thought, and she'd be awake all night, writhing with shame.

Light on, bare feet planted on the parquet wood floor, she swept her palm around the contents of the drawer. Finding the earplugs, she was about to twist a pair deep into her ear canals when the sound stopped.

Her skin cooled and a conviction came over her: the sound wasn't sex or the whimpers of a dog. It was the sound of someone crying.

## Chapter Three

------------------------

*L*ate Saturday morning, Cintra met Elliot and Boston at The Tea Spot, an upscale brunch bistro with thirty different kinds of tea and almost as many different variations of avocado toast. Cintra and Elliot put in their brunch orders at the crowded counter while Boston saved them a table. Elliot kept his head down, staring at the oversized menu. He always ordered the same thing, custard style eggs with ginger garlic and Jalapeno cilantro, so she knew his being consumed by the menu was to avoid talking to her.

At the rustic table, she wanted to barrage Boston with questions. How was camp going? Had his soccer game improved? Had he finished his essay on rites of passage? But it wasn't Boston under the microscope these days. She wished she'd gotten to the table first and slid in next to her son, but Elliot had done so. A nugget of rejection sat forlornly in her stomach. He'd allied the two of them together on the opposite side of the table.

"How are you guys doing?" she asked.

"Good." Boston's brown hair was getting too long, falling into his eyes. At thirteen, he was all elbows and hair. If she were home, she would have insisted it was haircut time.

"That's great," she said, forcibly upbeat. "How's Dumps?"

She missed their cat, Dumpling aka Dumps. He was a fat, funny creature, who didn't so much as walk as waddle. Who would clip his nails while she was away? Dumps could be feisty about it, and she doubted either Elliot or Boston could succeed at the task. Dumps couldn't live with her as Pedro was allergic.

"He's good, but he's licking his ass a lot," said Boston.

She wanted to tell her son not to use the word "ass," that it could get him in trouble at school, but it was not the time for her to issue directives about what and what not to say. Given what had happened, the hypocrisy would be off the charts.

"Maybe Dumps needs to see a vet," she told Elliot, who nodded.

Their brunches—eggs for her and Elliot, chocolate chip waffles for Boston—were delivered, and they ate in silence for what seemed a long time. Was Elliot going to even ask her anything?

"How's the novel coming?" he ventured. Guess he wasn't going to waste any time with baseline questions.

The spicy mayo omelet went rubbery in her throat, and she took several sips of green tea, trying to wash its stickiness down. A tendril of nausea uncoiled in her belly and fizzed ominously upwards.

*The novel is going fantastic. The twists and turns are incredible. It's writing itself. This will be a HUGE hit.*

All those things she'd said.

Elliot was testing her. No one else would have registered the spark of challenge in his blue-gray eyes, but she did.

Managing to swallow, she took a few deep breaths, as Dr. Grace had advised her to do, even though it must look strange, her sitting there taking deep breaths. *What you say is more important than how fast you say it,* Dr. Grace had told her.

"I haven't written a word a month." It came out a mumble-whisper. The admission was a blunt, hacking instrument. The part of her that was so powerful felt betrayed. Elliot reached over and squeezed the top of her hand.

"Thank you, Cin."

The gesture gave her the courage to plow forward. "I've emailed my agent twice but she ignores me. I don't even know if she's my agent anymore."

"There you go!" chirped Boston. His blue-gray eyes, Elliot's eyes exactly, snapped with approval as he chewed his waffles.

"And the therapist?" Elliot asked.

"I had two sessions last week, back to back. Now we'll go to one session a week. I know she'll be really helpful."

Wait, she didn't *know* if Dr. Grace would be helpful. She *hoped* Dr. Grace would be helpful. Is this what normal people did all day? Told every last shade and gradation of truth? How was that even possible?

"I'm glad to hear it," Elliot said, nodding officiously.

Cintra's throat swelled, threatening tears. Her and her damn tears. She cried so easily. "Any more bad news you want to hear?" she asked, remaining composed. "I'm game."

"We want to see progress, that's all," Elliot said.

"Yeah, Mom, progress," Boston parroted.

"Well, there you have it." She put down her fork, the nausea settling into a low ache. "I'm not writing, and it sucks. I don't know what made me think I could write a thriller in a bog. At the time it seemed atmospheric."

"It will get easier," Elliot said.

"The thriller?"

"No, not that. Thriller in a bog sounds hopeless. Sorry."

Boston laughed with his characteristic snorting, and she wanted to flick a piece of omelet at her husband.

"The other stuff," Elliot said. "It will get easier."

That's what Dr. Grace said too. She needed to *feel her feelings*. The more she felt them, marinated in them, the more comfortable she would get with them. Eventually, they would not only be second nature, but preferable to those other feelings, the edgy, exciting ones.

"Did you finish your essay?" she asked Boston. She felt her honesty gave her credits she could cash in.

"Yep. Dad helped me."

Elliot grinned proudly and she wanted to lean over and kiss him, but didn't dare. He wasn't classically hand-some. At thirty-nine, his brown hair was thinning on top, and he was a little paunchy around the middle. Now that she'd moved out, he'd felt free to start growing that beard he'd been threatening for years. The long scruff sprouted gray hairs. Cintra didn't think the scruff suited him, but even so, his was the face she loved looking at more than any other face besides her son's.

"Did you bring the mail?" she asked.

"It was only a few junk things so I didn't bother," Elliot said, and went back to his eggs, forking out bits of cilantro and shifting them to the side of his plate. He always forgot to ask for less cilantro.

As much as she adored seeing her family, she was fighting the urge to get up and walk out. Self-scrutinizing her every word to them was stressful and exhausting. Or maybe she was just exhausted. It had taken her at least half an hour to fall back asleep after the crying sound behind the wall had woken her up. Though she could no longer hold onto the certainty that the sound had been crying—at least, human crying. Maybe, like she'd originally thought, it had been a dog whining.

Thinking of the neighbors, she wrestled with a familiar urge, as strong as the urge to take a breath: to tell Elliot and Boston something about them—that the man was a ballet dancer or TV actor, that the woman was a professional wrestler. Anything about them that would liven up the conversation, give it that familiar hum of electricity.

Or she could go even further than that. Tell them something dark. Like that she'd heard the man yelling at the woman through their shared wall and that she would befriend the woman to find out if she needed help. That would give herself a tinge of the heroic.

She stared at her barely-eaten omelet, rooting deep into her brain for any other motives for why she would want to say all this, probing around in a way she ordinarily would not have done.

Telling Elliot and Boston something interesting about the neighbors would... what?

Distract them. Pull them away a little bit farther from what was happening between the three of them. If Cintra could come up with something—anything—to grab their attention, then she wouldn't have to sit in this pit of shame.

"Guys, I want you to know, I'm going to work very hard. I'm going to do this," she said.

"You *have* to," said Boston, a flap of hair over one eye. "And you *will*."

## Chapter Four

*The bog was hung with white mist, thick as a blanket of smoke over the emerald trails that glittered with silvery quartz monzonite. The air was sappy wet, drenching her clothes. There was only about another hour of daylight. Lisa shook off her rucksack and dug around for her Lumen flashlight, wanting to make sure it worked.*

*"Charlie?" she called, voice ringing through the wetlands. "Where are you? This isn't funny anymore."*

*Lisa's boots made sucking noises on the silver mud as she trudged…*

Trudged? Is that the word she wanted? Cintra pulled up a thesaurus, plugged in "trudged."

*Clump, slog, wade, plug.*

Hmm, maybe she did want "trudge." Spooning yogurt into her mouth, she thought about checking her stocks. No, no. She'd be there for an hour. At least she had written a little today. She could genuinely tell Elliot she'd written, what? Half a chapter?

Laundry. It must be finished. She'd get that and then watch some YouTube videos about bogs. What did they sound like, smell like? Perhaps she should go to a bog. She could hike through the wetlands in New Hampshire.

Forget that, what she needed was a plot. Who was stalking Lisa in the bog? Why was she still named Lisa? It was a placer name, inspired by a childhood friend. The heroine of a thriller needed a snazzier name, yet one that wouldn't give her finger cramps.

Laundry.

In the laundry room adjacent to the basement, she took her clothes out of the dryer and piled them onto the long folding table, enjoying the clean scent and warm feel of the freshly dried fabrics.

Instinctively, she patted around for something that belonged to Boston, as she liked to give his pants and shirts an extra whiff to make sure they were clean, but of course, nothing of his was there, and her heart contracted with pain. She'd heard of ghost limbs and ghost pregnancy, but never ghost laundry.

Finger-drawn in layers of city sediment coating the windows above the washing machines were various symbols and words: Bye, Kill, Clean Me! Salsa music, staticky with poor radio reception, drifted to her from elsewhere in the basement. Along one wall, a folding table was strewn with tenants' cast-offs: tattered paper-backs, board games, old clothes, naked dolls.

Her book was going nowhere. In six months, she'd written only about twenty-thousand words. Her first book, *Woman on the Subway*, had come to her at lightning speed. She'd finished the first draft in eight weeks and pitched it as *The Warriors* meets *Rear Window*. Within a year, she'd secured her agent, and a year later, the book was in stores.

But a bestselling book with a similar title had overwhelmed it. Sales were mediocre. Her agent had slowly receded into the ether.

She had to face the facts: her future as a novelist was as uncertain as it could get. Facing facts wasn't anything she'd ever been particularly good at.

"Afternoon."

Cintra turned to see a soap-pale, plumpish blonde woman entering the laundry with a basket of clothes: her new neighbor.

"Hi," Cintra said. "3D, right?"

"That's right." The woman scattered the clothes onto the folding table and began separating darks from lights. She had a pleasantly bland face. So bland that Cintra had the odd feeling she would forget what the woman looked like as soon as she walked away, as if the woman's features had arranged themselves into something as uneventful as possible.

"You all settled in?" Cintra asked.

"Oh, sure. It's a nice building. We were lucky to get it. A large two bedroom, two-bathroom around here at a decent price is like gold. There's even an office."

An office? Cintra was jealous.

"Don't I know it," she said. "I'm new myself. Three weeks ago."

"June," the woman said, stretching out her hand, smiling. "My name, not the month we got here."

"Cintra. Nice to meet you."

"What an interesting name. With an 'S'?"

"A 'C.' It's a town in Portugal, where my grandfather went to college. My mother thought it was a good idea to give me the name to honor him. But she misspelled it. It's supposed to be with an 'S.'"

June stared off past Cintra's shoulder. "I feel like I've seen that name once before. An author. I read her book, ah… " Her fingers wagged around. "Something about the subway…"

"*Woman on the Subway.* I wrote that."

June's eyes widened. Cintra noticed her orbs were almost gray, similar in color to Boston's and Elliot's eyes. Cintra's eyes were a vivid cobalt blue. People complimented them as an attractive contrast to her black hair, miraculously still without any grays.

"You wrote that?" The neighbor seemed impressed. "I loved it. Really. The way the woman, um…" She paused, and Cintra could tell that she remembered none of the plot. "Well, she solved that crime, didn't she? On the subway?"

"Yep, yep. With the help of the train conductor."

"Right. She sees the murder in the other train while looking out the window." The woman checked the pockets of a pair of green-brown cargo pants. "Good for you. I always thought about being a writer, but I'm not that talented. Do you have a new book?"

The words were out in a flash. "Yes. It'll be out end of the year."

"I'll pick it up. What's it called?"

Cintra folded a blue and white striped towel, then shook it apart, and refolded it. It was frayed. She'd taken the towels in the worst shape, leaving the good ones for Elliot and Boston.

"Actually, I'm trying to write it. It won't be out end of the year. I'm not sure why I said that."

"Oh."

Cintra looked up in time to see the woman turning down her small, pink mouth slightly. What was her name again? Joan?

No, June. *Not the month I got here.*

June stopped checking pockets and moved one pile of clothes to a washer. Cintra noted the cargo pants on top of the other pile. They looked small, a boy's size. Boston had a similar pair.

"You have a kid?" Cintra asked, then wondered if the question was intrusive.

June shoved all the clothes in the washer, and uncapped her bottle of laundry detergent, a "natural" brand that promised not to pollute the water supply. (Did water from washing machines all over the world actually go into the water supply?)

"Leo. He's eleven next month. Hey, is there a good restaurant around here that has a kids' menu too? All I can seem to find are takeout places."

"I don't know the area too well myself, but there's Hamilton's." She waved towards the wall of dryers, not sure if she was waving in the correct direction. "I've only been there once, but I think they have mac n' cheese and pizza. I'm sure you can find it online."

June put a second load in the washer. "Great, thanks. Leo loves mac n' cheese."

She placed her hands on her hips and smiled again. Cintra noticed her wedding ring. So the couple were married, not boyfriend and girlfriend. Seemed like an odd pairing. June was perky, sociable. From Cintra's brief glimpse of the husband, he'd seemed dour and unfriendly.

But they say opposites attract. Her own choice of husband had certainly proven that. Elliot was dry and practical, Cintra was imaginative and creative—*too* creative. Maybe June's husband had been having a bad day that morning when she'd seen him in the hallway.

"Nice to meet you, Cintra," said June, pushing the cap down on her laundry detergent. "Good luck with the book."

Cintra laughed awkwardly. "Nice to meet you too. Hopefully we'll see you around. By the way, dryer number four is on its last legs. Avoid."

"Thanks for the tip. And yes, I saw your husband this morning. It might be nice if we all got together. Niko and I don't know anyone in the area yet."

Cintra laughed even more awkwardly. "He's not my husband."

June looked down at Cintra's ring finger, at her wedding ring. Cintra rubbed it self-consciously. "You must have seen my roommate. Pedro." She shrugged. "It's complicated."

"I get it," June said, leaning over the table and lowering her voice conspiratorially. "I've been in *compli-*

*cated*." She winked and was out of the room, fingers swinging her jug of detergent.

Cintra had slowed down her folding so she wouldn't finish at the same time as June, then have to walk out to the elevator with her, making small talk. But she regretted that she hadn't. She liked the way June had winked at her "it's complicated" line. Maybe they *could* be friends. What a relief it would be to make friends with someone who didn't know about her problem, who couldn't judge her.

Look how she'd slipped up telling June her new book would be out end of the year. It had been a slip-up, and she'd corrected it. Done. Over. Elliot would have given her the deep freeze for an hour. Pedro would have teased her with goofy titles, made her feel small, even though that wouldn't have been his intention. Like that time she'd told him she'd seen Daniel Day Lewis reading her book on the subway. Pedro later informed her he'd read in a gossip rag that the actor was in Paris. For months, he would tack onto various anecdotes of hers, "And was Daniel Day Lewis there?"

And June had an eleven-year-old son. Remembering Boston at that age—such a sweet, open age—Cintra grew warm with nostalgia, yet felt poison-shame churning in her gut. She may not have killed his love, but she'd killed his trust, or at least wounded it severely. And it wasn't only that one night.

How was she only now realizing the damage she'd caused? It was as if she'd sleepwalked onto a highway and awoke to see a truck barreling down on her. How had she got here? Could she still save herself?

*Stop, breathe.*

She saw Dr. Grace on Tuesday. Two more days. Every session got her closer to moving back home.

* * *

LATER THAT AFTERNOON, an alert came in that a stock Cintra was watching had dipped to her buy price, so she bought twenty shares, then decided that her main character, Lisa (Mila?), wasn't being stalked in the bog by her hiking partner, Charlie, but by her ex-boyfriend. Now she had to figure out when to get Charlie back into the picture.

Stalker ex-boyfriend. Too obvious. What about a crazy grandmother?

In despair, she spent half an hour researching the current most popular thrillers, and saw at least half of them involved a kidnapped child. On a whim, she emailed her agent, Alexis, asking if she should insert a kidnapped child into her bog thriller. To her shock, Alexis replied within twenty minutes. "Love it!" she wrote. "Sorry I've been MIA, Damien's book, as you've probably seen, has hit it out of the ballpark and it's nuts over here. Haven't forgotten you, Cintra. Kidnapped kid. Yes!"

For several minutes, Cintra was elated that she'd figured out the trick to getting Alexis to answer one of her emails, but then came the sinking realization she had no idea how to work a kidnapped kid into a bog. And who the hell was Damien?

The doorbell buzzed. She wasn't expecting any

package deliveries. Maybe it was one of those religious types who managed to sneak into buildings, spreading flyers for their church meetings. They were always getting into her old building, ringing doors and wanting recruits. But through the peephole, she saw June, looking up expectedly.

"Hey, there," Cintra said, opening the door, keeping one foot plugged behind it, so she could shut it fast if needed: the habit of a longtime city dweller. Realizing what she was doing, she pulled her foot back and opened the door wide. June, in a pink summer dress cluttered with geometric patterns, was holding a few envelopes.

"I believe these are yours," she said, handing the envelopes over.

"Ah! They were… ?"

"In my box. The mailman must have gotten confused. We don't have a name tab up yet. Waiting for maintenance to give it to us."

"I'd thought it hadn't forwarded yet. Thanks." She glanced through the mail. "Though I guess I didn't need it. Just junk."

"Don't you hate that? With the Internet there's no excuse to cut down all of those trees."

"You have a point there. Why is Spectrum still sending me stuff? No, Spectrum, I don't want to come back. You had your chance."

June laughed. "Exes should remain exes! Also, Niko and I wanted to invite you over this week for dinner. At your convenience; and your roommate, of course, if he'd like."

Cintra put her hand over her heart, as if the invite had startled her, which maybe it had. Brooklyn neighbors didn't tend to do this kind of thing. "Sure, that would be fun. Can I bring anything?"

"Whatever wine you like. Do you both eat fish?"

"That sounds great. Will be nice to have something other than pasta; that's basically the only thing Pedro can cook and I'm not exactly a cook myself."

"Want to say Friday?"

"Works for me, but I'll ask Pedro."

"If that's not good, maybe Saturday afternoon for brunch."

"Oh." Cintra put on a crestfallen face. "That's when I'm meeting my husband and kid. You should try the place, The Tea Spot. On Cortelyou."

"Thanks for the recommendation. If Pedro's a no go, slip a note under the door. We'll come up with something else. Or come yourself."

Cintra thanked her and closed the door.

Dinner with the neighbors. For the first time in months, Cintra was kind of excited. Her vague fear of a neglected dog locked in a room became ridiculous. June, the woman who bought natural laundry detergent and worried about cutting down trees, wasn't the type to do that, or allow her husband to do that.

She supposed she'd know for certain once she was inside the apartment.

## Chapter Five

"How are things going?" Dr. Grace asked. "You saw Elliot and Boston over the weekend?"

Cintra sat in a wood chair with a crimson cushion in a small room with off-white walls. Cintra had found the doctor by randomly calling psychologists who came up in a Google search and who had nearby offices. Her full name was Dr. Grace Dareczek, but she had told Cintra to call her Dr. Grace. She had eyeglasses with retro thick frames, crazily cropped dark hair, and was young, twenty-nine, which she'd revealed on the first session to make sure Cintra was comfortable with it.

At first, Cintra was nervous that someone so young wouldn't be qualified to help her. But by the end of the session, she'd felt in good hands; Dr. Grace seemed to have an awareness and insight into her issue. And importantly, because she had been in practice for only a year, she was willing to charge sixty dollars an hour, half of what the others wanted. With Cintra's True Crime

TV blogging gig only three days a week, her second novel stalled perhaps permanently, and paying rent on two places, she wasn't exactly raking in the cash.

"Yes. And I told them," Cintra said. "About the novel. Or rather the non-novel."

"I'm happy to hear that."

"Well, I think they knew it wasn't going anywhere. Or at least Elliot knew. I usually let him read a bit here and there and I wasn't, so he knew."

"But you'd been telling them it was almost finished."

"Yes." Sighing in self-disappointment, she stared at a black and white print of a woman in a skirt suit with wide shoulder pads, who was hanging from a trolley car. The picture appeared to be from the 1940s.

"How did it feel to tell them the truth?"

"Awful. Afterwards, I was glad. That night, I slept so much better. But in the moment…" She tried to stop her leg from rocking, and managed it for a few seconds before it popped up and rocked again. "It felt so alien."

Dr. Grace's look was part dry clinician, part sympathetic friend. "That's because you're not used to it. Your neurons have a very well worn path they like to travel, and you're trying to— " She made a driving motion with her hands, as if they were on a wheel. "— maneuver around that path. It's going to feel uncomfortable. That's the way most of us feel when we lie. Your brain has it backwards."

Cintra propped the side of her cheek into her palm, squeezing the flesh, not caring that she was contributing to new wrinkles. "I don't understand it. How did I get this way?"

"We were talking about that last week. You mentioned that your mother wasn't around a lot after your parents' divorce."

"I don't want to blame my mom. That's so cliché. So Freudian."

"We're not blaming anyone. But our habits are often formed in childhood."

Cintra really did not want to get into her mother. Their relationship was okay these days and it hurt to dredge up all that past. But she had to get to the bottom of things. If rummaging around in her painful childhood would do that, then fine.

"She wasn't. But I don't… I don't think this is her fault. I'm the one who chose to live with Dad and stay in my school."

"I'm not saying it's her fault. But we need to get a better sense of when and how this all started."

Cintra spent several moments wrestling with thoughts, rubbing the flesh around her mouth and cheeks. "When she would come visit or call, I had this feeling as if she didn't want to be there. As if there was something more exciting out there that I was keeping her from. So I—" She shrugged. "I would tell her things. Tell her I'd been voted prettiest girl in class. Tell her I made the basketball team. Tell her I'd found a kitten and saved it from dying."

"And none of it was true."

"No."

"She never knew?"

"She was busy with her new husband and their business in Maine. He had two kids, her stepkids. From what she'd tell me, the kids were… perfect. Straight-A students. Athletic. Student council. I met them a few times on holidays. They were both gorgeous."

"Sounds like you were competing with them. On some level, you felt you were being replaced."

The words cut straight through her in a way that only the pure truth can. As an adult, it seemed so obvious to her.

"Ugh." She squeezed her arms tight around her ribcage. "I think you're right. When I'd tell Mom something exciting, she'd act so proud or interested. She and Dad didn't speak that much, so they didn't compare a lot of notes."

A memory surfaced. It was so embarrassing, her stomach ached, as if she'd eaten a terrible meal.

"One time I told her I'd been in a car accident. I hadn't heard from her for awhile and was panicked, as if she was forgetting me. That one made its way back to Dad, and he asked me about it. I can't even remember what I told him. I think I broke down and admitted I'd lied. I remember the look on his face, so disappointed."

The image of Cintra's brawny, good-natured father looking so bewildered—so hurt—that his daughter would say such a horrible thing for no discernible reason came to her as vividly as if it had recently happened. She clutched her stomach, unable to speak for several long moments, wishing desperately that she could go back in time and tell her father how sorry she was for causing him distress.

She looked around for another print she could focus on. The only other one was of a beach, startlingly blue water and a bended palm tree plunked in white sand in the corner.

"And Elliot? Was it always like that with him?" Dr. Grace asked.

"We met in college. By then, I was saying all kinds of things to people. When people would find out something wasn't true and get mad at me, I couldn't understand it. Why couldn't people invent their own reality? I kind of thought everyone did it. He knew I had a penchant to… say things. Sometimes he'd confront me."

"What would you do when he confronted you?"

"Lots of times I kept lying. Sometimes I'd act like I was confused. But we loved each other. It's hard to explain."

"I understand. People love each other through all kinds of things."

"Other than that, it was a good relationship. We laughed a lot, talked easily. But I was oblivious to how much it was affecting him. Then we decided to get pregnant. After Boston was born, it was like he didn't want those fun and games anymore, that dramatic side of me. We were supposed to settle down and be serious."

"Is that what you think the lying was? Drama?"

"Up until what happened with Boston, that's what I thought. Just exaggerations, or a harmless altering of reality. But I'm telling you, I didn't do this stuff as much when I was younger. I had a penchant, yes. But it became worse a few years ago. Maybe the pressure of the novel coming out, trying to seem like I was a success, even though it was clear I wasn't."

"Are you ready to talk about what happened with Boston?"

She tightened her grasp on her chest, over her knot-tied lungs. "I'm not ready. When I think about it..." She shook her head slowly, feeling in a trance. "When I think about it, I— " Her brain became overwhelmed with the enormity of it and she couldn't speak.

Dr. Grace handed her the box of tissues that was looming on her side table. Cintra took a few sheets and balled them tight in her hand, uncertain if she was going to cry or not.

"It's okay. We don't need to get into it today," Dr. Grace said. "Let's focus on what's going right. You're seeing this behavior no longer serves your best interests, as you truly believed it did for a long time. You told them the truth about the novel."

"Yes, but I'm so nervous. Elliot said if he catches me in a lie, big or small, any time in six months, he's filing. I don't know if he meant this, but that night, he said he'd fight for full custody of Boston. That my son shouldn't live with someone like me." The tears burst out. "He's ruh-right."

She cried for several minutes, wondering if anyone in the other offices could hear her. But they were probably used to the sound of blubbering therapy-goers.

"Cintra, you may slide back once in a while. Elliot needs to realize this."

"He doesn't care!" she wailed. "He's so fuh-fed up. That was the last straw, what I suh-said to Boston." She was gasping, hardly able to speak. Dr. Grace handed her the tissue box again and she took several more sheets and pressed them up against her runny nose. "Huh-he'll divorce me."

She took a long, gulping breath, then expelled it back out. She could be a real crier, a cry-at-commercials crier. Animal rescue videos, feel good news stories, crafts that Boston made for her at school, they all triggered waterworks. Crying wasn't exactly a skill that was prized in this world unless you could do it on demand in front of a film camera, but it was what it was.

"Hopefully, he'll join some sessions in the near future," Dr. Grace said. "He can learn more about this disorder. That you're not doing this to deliberately hurt anyone."

Cintra sat sucking in air. Her shoulders sagged, as if she'd been deflated. That had been quite a jag and she was relieved it was over. "I don't know if he'll do that," she whispered, and hiccuped. "He says it's too crazy busy at work right now. But I think he thinks it's my problem."

"I'd like you to do a little homework." Dr. Grace wrote on her notepad, tore off a piece of paper and handed it to her. "There's some exercises in there to help. The author is pretty well known."

Cintra dabbed at her bleary eyes and took in the print. *Tell Me No Lies: How to Stop Lying to Those You Love, the Complete Self-Help Guide for Compulsive and Pathological Liars.*

*Compulsive and pathological liar.* Was this what she was? It sounded so evil.

"Don't let the title make you feel bad," Dr. Grace said, catching her dismayed expression. "'Compulsive' is what we like to call it, 'pathological' has a negative connotation. There's a spectrum of habitual lying. I haven't treated you long enough to know how deep your issue goes, but the fact that you're here of your own volition is a good sign, even if it was sparked by a crisis in your marriage. This isn't going to happen overnight. It took years for this habit to form, and it could take years to gain control of it."

Cintra nodded, her throat burning. "I don't have years. My time has run out with Elliot. I don't want to lose my guys."

"You have a powerful incentive for change. But don't put so much pressure on yourself. That's bound to make you anxious, and can trigger your instinct to lie."

Sopping up her runny nose with tissue, Cintra gazed longingly at the print's sharp blue expanse of tropical water, at the palm frond waving carefree in the wind.

THAT NIGHT, Cintra sat with pillows propped up behind her back, against the bed's headboard. She opened her Kindle, swiping through the table of contents and foreword.

*For most people, telling a lie is accompanied by a sense of guilt. But for some people, telling a lie is easier than telling the truth. The person may not consciously be aware of why he or she is lying. Eventually, lying becomes second nature, something that makes him or her feel better than telling—*

She skipped forward a few pages. The next chapter was titled, "Lying Begins in Childhood."

Not that again. Maybe it did start in childhood, but the thing had upticked a few years ago. From lies every few weeks to at least every few days, or even hours. And there were the nonsensical lies that weren't rooted in trying to please, impress, or grab attention.

*Where are you?*

*In the garden. Getting some fresh air.*

*Good, Cin. You're inside too much.*

*The garden is beautiful. We should come out here more.*

In reality, she was in the grocery store, looking at cans of soup and wondering why, why she was telling her husband she was in their building's garden, and coming up with no answer except that it gave her some sense of something, something she couldn't explain but needed. Like those hoarders on TV, how they couldn't throw away a piece of junk. Some day, some way, that piece of junk might be needed. The junk wouldn't leave, betray, or reject. No one else understood this, but the hoarder did.

Cintra felt a similar connection with her lies. They gave her a sense of control even as they spun her life out of control.

That night, Elliot informed her that he'd realized the little key to the back garden's gate was on his key chain. *Where were you really?* he'd wanted to know.

Rather than admit the ridiculous truth, which she doubted he would believe anyway, Cintra told him a neighbor had let her into the garden. Nor did she appreciate his tone, and the insinuation that she wasn't where she'd said.

It made no sense to double down. By then, both of

them knew she had a problem. But the problem was so out of their frame of reference that neither had a way of understanding it, let alone naming it. So they did what they usually did: acted like the incident hadn't happened.

*A child may start out lying to please or placate his or her parents—*

A low, keening sound disrupted her reading. Cintra sat utterly still, her eyes darting back and forth past her reading material.

Putting her Kindle aside, she went to the open window and leaned on the windowsill, her ear pressed almost up against the screen. It was completely dark outside. For a few moments, the sound disappeared under the clanking tumble of a can windblown down the street.

All she could see was a few peach-colored lights in the windows of the condo building next door. The condo had a large deck catty-corner and one floor below Cintra's bedroom window. She wondered if a low-howling cat was prowling around on it.

The sound started again. Slowly, Cintra turned from the window, orienting towards the noise, listening so hard she could almost feel her ear canals dilating.

She moved back to the bed. The wall was blocked not only with the bed and its headboard, but a small cherrywood bedside table, and a desk with her laptop and a printer, where she did her work. She'd brought her printer from home, but the rest of the room's furniture, including the storage bed frame and its matching headboard with sliding panels, belonged to the woman who owned the apartment. Pedro had said her name was Callie, an opera singer who was traveling Europe.

Gingerly, she slid out the side table from between the bed and the desk, making sure its ornate legs didn't scrape along the parquet wood floor. She wedged her body sideways into the resulting space. With her cheek flush against the silver and blue vine-patterned wallpaper, she listened. The sound continued for maybe ten seconds, then abruptly stopped.

It was definitely coming from 3D. She had no idea how that apartment was laid out, if it was identical to 3C. Was the sound coming from the entryway or a bedroom? It was too isolated, too unaccompanied by other sounds, to be coming from a TV. And the sound was different this time. Lower, more monotonous. Like a low hum.

"You!" A voice cracked.

Instinctively, Cintra yanked back from the wall, as if the person on the other side could see straight through to her. She pressed her ear up again, but there was only silence.

Perhaps June's son had been playing a video game. The register of the voice, distilled through the thick wall, was somewhere between male and female. Picking up her phone from the desk, she glanced at the time. 10:36 p.m. Kind of late for a child of eleven to be awake? And the last time she'd heard a noise, it had to have been sometime after midnight.

She didn't like the harsh crack of the voice, though she guessed it was understandable if Leo had gone over a strictly enforced amount of tablet time. She couldn't imagine the perky, winky June cracking out that one word silencer: "You."

Him. Him, she could imagine it, what with that cold, dour look he'd given her in the hallway.

*I've been in complicated.*

Maybe June had meant she was in complicated *now*.

## Chapter Six

June's apartment was a shabby-chic lover's wet dream. The long foyer had purple walls running to the expansive combined living and dining area, which had alternating turquoise and beige walls with bright white trim. A large dark wood dining table sat under a starburst chandelier that brought to mind a giant gold porcupine.

Cintra was surprised to see that the apartment, larger than 3C, looked as if it had been lived in for a while, no sign of boxes. There were already various knickknacks and gleaming books filling up a pinewood shelf unit that stretched from floor to ceiling. She and Pedro made noises of approval as June, in a paisley Boho dress wrapped around plush hips, a braid falling between her shoulder blades, led them around.

The lighting was soft and Cintra noticed a framed print of Sergeant Pepper's Lonely Hearts Club Band over a wooden media console. Another print was an astrology wheel, with the sun signs and their corresponding animal figurines surrounding a Yin-Yang symbol inside a wavy yellow sun. She gradually came to identify the circus-like twang floating through the air as The Doors' "Alabama Song (Whiskey Bar)."

Cintra handed a bottle of rosé wine to June. She hoped it was okay. She'd bought it at a nearby deli. It had been the rainiest summer she ever remembered, and today was no different. She hadn't felt like taking a rather long walk in the muggy rain to the nearest wine store.

"The apartment is beautiful, June," Cintra told her.

"I love what you've done with the place!" Pedro pronounced in his "uptight white guy in a 1970's movie" voice.

June practically blushed. "Thanks. I bought most of it on Etsy. Other stuff came with us." She waved towards the sunshine yellow chaise sofa, with turquoise and beige pillows to match the walls. Cintra sat and glanced to the end table at her side. On it was a row of six short, squat peg dolls with different color dresses and varying skin tones. It took her a few moments to register that the peg dolls' red flat arms, crossed in front, were each giving the viewer a tiny middle finger.

"Let me go open this," June said. "I'll get Niko out here. He's been prepping."

A few minutes later, Niko emerged, wiping his hands on a floral dish towel. "No, no, don't get up," he said.

Cintra was tempted to take a peek at Pedro, because Niko was more handsome than she remembered. Despite his directive, the two of them stood, and Cintra saw that Niko was about her height exactly, maybe an inch or two taller. Definitely handsome, with dark, oval-shaped eyes, full, sensuous lips, and an effortless aura of masculinity, bordering on machismo.

June was back with four flower-etched wine glasses. She spread them around the low coffee table in front of the couch, and made introductions. "Cintra with a 'C,' this is Niko with a 'k.' And Pedro."

"With a 'P,'" Pedro said, shaking Niko's hand.

Niko was wearing a gray button down shirt and black dress pants. As his shirt rose from his wrist during handshakes, Cintra noticed he had on the largest black watch she'd ever seen, one of those new watches that were more like computers, she imagined.

"Honey, can you get the wine and the Brie?" June asked Niko, who said, "Duty calls," and disappeared. There had been no sign of that malignant glint Cintra had thought he'd directed at her in the hallway the first time she'd seen him. He'd either been having a bad morning or she'd attributed something to him that wasn't there. Now she felt foolish that she'd mentioned his supposed glare to Pedro.

"I hope you like salmon?" June asked. "It's wild. They don't have a good fish store around here that I could find, so I went to Soho. I always get wild, sustainable. We're destroying the oceans."

"June, could you wait until dessert before bringing up the destruction of the oceans?" Niko said, returning with the rosé bottle and a tray.

"To neighbors," June said, and they all clinked glasses. Cintra again noted June's wedding ring, but there was no engagement ring. From the sound of her, she probably objected to "blood diamonds."

"You have great style," said Cintra. "And work much quicker than I do. I still have unpacked boxes, and I only have one room's worth of stuff."

"The tenants before us left it a bit of a mess, so I went whole hog." June pinched her nostrils. "The *stench* in this place. I had to vinegar spray everywhere."

Cintra indeed detected the very slight whiff of vinegar in the air.

"I told my sister about it," June said, then lowered her voice. "They were quite the pot smokers."

"Sister?" Cintra asked.

"Oh yes, Callie. That's my sister. She owns this apartment too. When she didn't renew the last tenants' lease, Niko and I were interested in coming to the city for awhile. We're up in Cold Springs, and it's beautiful, but not a lot to do. Then Barton's opened an office here and Leo was accepted to The Science Center, a great alternative middle school."

"What's Barton's?" Pedro asked.

"Real estate," June and Cintra said in unison.

"Oh, that's where the money is," Pedro said as June lifted a tea tray and offered him the wedge of gooey Brie with wheat crackers, a small cheese knife to the side.

Cintra noticed that one of Niko's legs was jiggling up and down, and although he hadn't said anything, his dark eyes were shifting intensely from her to Pedro and back again. She tried to bring him into the conversation. "What do you do, Niko?"

"Ahh," he said, looking down at his bouncing leg.

"He sold computers, and is hoping for something around here in that area," filled in June.

Cintra couldn't reconcile the jittery man who followed June's orders like an obedient soldier with one who would have yelled at his wife or their son. In fact, Cintra got the feeling Niko had some kind of social anxiety issue. Should she not speak to him? This was going to be an awkward meal if not. But then he looked straight at her. "What do you do?" he asked.

"She's a writer," said June, putting her hand on his bouncing knee, which stilled it. "The *Woman on the Subway* book. Didn't I tell you? I could have sworn I did."

"Right, right." He put his hand over June's but almost instantly moved it back to his thigh.

Cintra was glad Pedro was there, because she felt the eager churn at the base of her throat, the threat of an intoxicating rush of words that would tell them about her book, the one that had been on the *New York Times* bestseller list for several weeks. Maybe she would have even mentioned a movie deal. With Daniel Day Lewis!

"Trying to write a new one, but these days I mostly trade stocks and do blogging," Cintra said. "Unlike real estate and computers, not much money in thrillers. Or at least there hasn't been for me."

In the periphery of her vision, she saw Pedro turn to her. She knew him so well that she could feel that his look was one of pride at her somewhat humiliating honesty. "Real talk," he would have said. His look of approval tamped down that thing inside of her that was annoyed she'd exposed her failure to this good-looking couple who had grown-up type jobs and apartment decor out of an interior design magazine.

"Thrillers," Niko said. "Like mysteries?"

Cintra spread a chunk of Brie on a cracker and tried to take a graceful bite, but the gooey cheese wasn't conducive to grace. She finally popped it all in her mouth, then held up her hand, clumsily chewing while everyone waited for her to continue. She swallowed, looked around for a napkin and, not finding one, resumed her thread.

"You could call them mysteries, sort of updated Agatha Christie. There's usually no detective."

"The woman solved the crime in her book. On the subway," June told Niko.

"Did she?" A spark of approval animated his dark eyes, as if Cintra herself had solved the crime. "Regular people going around solving crimes? Does that really happen?"

"Probably not," Cintra said, laughing. "That's why people want to read about it. Imagining they could do the same thing, when, of course, they couldn't. Or wouldn't. We all have enough to do, am I right?"

Niko laughed too, more like a guffaw, and grabbed June's bare knee. For the first time, he seemed happy. "Maybe they could though," he said, bobbing his shaved head. "Like me, I think I could. A crime is like a puzzle. I'm good at puzzles."

"You couldn't solve any crimes." June shook her head, then looked to Cintra and Pedro as if her husband was being daft. "He can barely remember where his socks are, and he's supposed to solve a crime?"

Cintra watched as Niko's grip tightened on June's knee. Then he made a low *humph* noise and moved his hand to his wine glass, taking a long sip. Cintra was alert to the subtle shift in the atmosphere between them.

"Crimes go on all of the time, underneath everyone's noses," June said to Niko. "No one even notices."

"That's too bad," Niko said, then put down his wine glass and wiped at his mouth and neck as if he was hot.

"A few years ago, there was a man on our street who turned out to be a drug kingpin. That's what the news called him, kingpin. He looked like a regular guy. Mild mannered. No one knew." She turned to Cintra and Pedro. "None of us knew."

"I suppose not," Niko said. "People mind their own business. Especially in cities."

"So true," said Cintra. "You take someone like Jeffrey Dahmer. The serial killer?" She gave them a "Do you know him?" look and they nodded tentatively. "He lived in an apartment in Milwaukee. His neighbors would hear sawing noises all through the night, but no one thought to report it. He was sawing up bodies."

"Cin, my appetite!" yelped Pedro.

"See? No one solved the crime," said June. "Except the police."

"Only after two of them returned a victim to Dahmer's apartment and handed him over to his killer," said Cintra. "They'd believed Dahmer's story that he was a drunk boyfriend who was lost. After the police walked him into Dahmer's apartment, he was killed."

"Cops," Pedro said, shaking his head.

"That's terrible!" said June. "Imagine being so… oh, what's the word?"

"Obtuse?" Cintra offered.

"That's a good word," she said, reaching for the cheese knife. Niko got to it first, made her a Brie cracker, and handed it to her. She smiled at him, then returned her attention to the couch. "Do you know I wanted to be a police officer when I was in my early twenties?"

"I could see that," Pedro said, and Cintra had no idea whether he was joking.

June waved her hand. "It wasn't for me. I looked into it, but more money in real estate. Still, Niko and I enjoyed the gun range up in Cold Springs. You don't know the shoulder power it takes to hold a gun properly for more than a minute until you try it." She stuck both arms straight out, pointing an invisible gun at Cintra. "One hand doesn't go *under* the gun, like you see on TV. Both stay on the *sides*, or when the gun kicks back, you miss." She folded her hands on her lap and looked at Niko. "I'm a pretty good shot, wouldn't you say?"

Niko pushed a cracker into his mouth. He chewed for a few moments, then said, "What about you, Cintra? Would you have figured out a serial killer was next door?" His tone was a little challenging.

"I'd like to think I would have. As a writer, I hope I'd pay attention to the little signs."

"Or the big ones," said Niko, then to June, "Sawing noises are pretty big signs," and she looked back at him as if to say, *You would think so.*

"I will say my hearing is very sharp, so the sawing noises would have bugged the hell out of me," Cintra said. An awkward silence ensued and she punctured it with, "So how's the real estate business?"

* * *

Two HOURS LATER, after the salmon, the rosemary mini-potatoes, the steamed asparagus, two more bottles of wine, and slices of apple pie ("Ugh, ooh, a small one, June, very, very small, please," begged Cintra) at the large dining room table, the four of them had moved to the couch area for espresso. Cintra noticed it was Niko who had cleared the dishes, Niko who had served the espresso. He might not be the social butterfly that June was, but he clearly had his good points.

They had all spoken fairly easily through dinner, though Niko was definitely the quiet one of the group. Conversation had turned to real estate, which New Yorkers could talk about for infinity, and how prescient Callie was to buy in the neighborhood when prices were good; and how her investment, which couldn't have been more than $500,000 for the two apartments, 3D and 3C, ten years ago, were worth at least two million dollars today. June had described their old farmhouse in Cold Springs, which was two hours north up the Hudson River.

Finishing her espresso, Cintra was stuffed, rapidly losing energy, and thinking about how to wrap things up. During dinner, she'd inquired whether the couple had any pets (without mentioning the sound through the wall) and June said they did not, but were considering adopting a dog at some point. Cintra had vaguely wondered where June's son was, but figured he must be at a sleepover.

That's when a small boy came into the room, carrying a tablet. He had shaggy blonde hair a few inches past his ears, with a blue swath on one side, delicate features with a little turned up nose, long eyelashes, and sparkly hazel eyes.

"June, can I use your charger? Something is wrong with mine," he asked in a wispy voice.

"It should be on the writing desk in my bedroom," she said. "Cintra, Pedro, this is Leo."

The three of them waved at each other. Cintra had been a bit taken aback by his use of "June" instead of "Mom," but it wasn't the first time she'd heard a child using a parent's first name. One of Boston's friends did the same, and Cintra had always found it unusual.

The tablet was making loud hums and whirrs. Cintra decided that the noise she'd heard through the wall must have been coming from Leo's tablet.

"What are you playing?" Cintra asked him.

"Strike It." He grinned shyly. "I like your hair," he said to Pedro.

Pedro touched his hair, looking touchingly bashful. "Thanks, pal. Yours too."

"Leo ate earlier," said June, as he left the room. "All I can get him to eat is carbs. So he was allowed to sit this one out and play his games. Adult time!" She raised her wine glass; she was the only one still drinking wine.

"He's a gorgeous boy," Cintra said. "Looks like you too, June."

This time, June did blush. "Well, he looks more like Callie. Which makes sense."

Cintra was confused. She had noticed that the boy's pale skin, so like June's, had nothing of the darker complexion of Niko mixed in it. Was Leo—not theirs? Or maybe not Niko's? She didn't want to ask.

Pedro had no such compunction. "That's Callie's kid?" he asked. Pedro seemed quite surprised. Cintra remembered that Pedro had told her he'd only met Callie once in person, when he'd come to pick up the key. Apparently a billionaire had offered Callie the chance to make excellent money singing at private events throughout Europe.

"Oh, yes. I'm sorry. Did you think he was mine?" June pressed her hand to her large bosom. "I probably gave that impression in the laundry room."

They all laughed awkwardly.

"Excuse the confusion. Yes, he's Callie's boy, my nephew," she said. "He'll stay with us while she's touring Europe, but will go visit her during school breaks. She didn't want to give up the opportunity to have him in The Science Center, which is perfect for him."

"That's great," said Cintra. "Best of both worlds."

Despite what she'd said, Cintra couldn't imagine being separated for so long from her son. Seeing Boston only once a week left her with chronic heartburn. But it was probably better to have Leo in a stable environment than being dragged all over Europe. Who knew what Callie's schedule was like? Besides, from the age of fourteen, Cintra hadn't lived with her mom, and she'd survived, hadn't she? Well, she'd apparently picked up a compulsive lying disorder as a result, but… anyway, it was none of her business.

Cintra looked at Niko, who had steadily grown mute again, and was staring off into space. Maybe he was tired. Cintra was getting tired too.

"I'm sorry," she said to him. "But I like to call my son before he beds down. Do you have the time?"

"I'll start the dishes," he said, and got up and walked out of the room.

Pedro had his cell phone out of his pocket. "It's almost ten, Cin."

"Oh, I should probably—"

"Of course. Go call your son," June smiled.

Within a few minutes, the three were crowded into the foyer, and when June turned to the door, Cintra heard little popping sounds. When June moved aside, Cintra caught a glimpse of a black pad with silver key numbers on the door handle.

For a moment, her mind rewound to when she first saw June in the hallway, and the black rectangle her new neighbor had pointed at the door of 3D, and its *bluup* sound. But Cintra's attention quickly reverted back to the couple as Niko rejoined them for a round of cheek kisses and hand clasps.

"We'll have to do this again," said June.

"We sure do," said Niko, putting his arm around June. "It's nice to have company."

# Chapter Seven

On Sunday afternoon, Cintra was at The Tea Spot with her friend Poppy. "Mind if I switch to booze?" Poppy asked, after draining her tea mug. "It's five o'clock somewhere."

"Be my guest. I'm going to try to get some writing done today or I'd join you."

The Tea Spot only had two types of wine, house red and white. Poppy was at the counter and back with a Mason jar half filled with white in a few minutes. She took a long sip and visibly relaxed.

"How did you do it?" she asked. "Get Elliot to want a kid in your twenties?"

"I didn't *do* it," Cintra said, taken aback. "We started talking about it, tried for it, and it happened pretty quickly. I mean, I was twenty-four."

Poppy propped her chin in her hand. Her curly light-brown hair was more tangled than usual, and her nails, normally salon pristine, showed chipped red polish, a few torn down to the nubs of her fingers.

"That's the thing," she said. "I'm thirty-five. I don't have forever."

Cintra nodded. She had heard this complaint from a few of her female friends: that they were ready for baby making, and the guys were dragging their collective feet.

All of Cintra's friends had been aghast at her pregnancy practically out of college. It was a time for career and city adventure, not diapers, emergency room visits at four a.m., and the continual hunt for reliable childcare.

When Boston was a baby, Cintra and Elliot had lived in Manhattan, in the Meatpacking District, when it was still a place most families avoided. Blood from slaughterhouses ran through the cracks of the cobblestone streets. Elliot had scored a good job with the city, working at public relations in the Department of Corrections, and Cintra was at her first editorial job. It hadn't been a life of luxury, but it had worked. Now she was a mother to a teen who did pretty well without her while her friends were on the baby track, or trying to get on it.

Cintra had met Poppy at their first publishing jobs, at a tiny literary press. Both had been assistant editors, and neither had stayed more than a year, but their friendship had continued. As part of her determination to clear the air with her friends, she'd called Poppy a week ago, and told her all about her issues with lying, her separation from Elliot, and her therapy.

"I did wonder about things," Poppy had said after a long pause. "To be honest, I'd started tuning it out. But yeah, it was always hard to know what was real and what wasn't. I mean, you told me Oprah had called you about your novel, but her show was already off the air."

Cintra had cringed; she'd forgotten that whopper. She'd apologized, and they made a time to meet up. Cintra had expected they would discuss her issue, but Poppy was more focused on her own problems. Primarily that her long-term boyfriend, Joseph, still wasn't ready to "settle down" after Poppy had issued him an ultimatum: marry her and start working on a family or she was out.

But two months after her own deadline, Poppy couldn't bring herself to make any moves, terrified of the difficult New York dating scene, and the odds of finding a man who'd want to settle down with her at thirty-five. She'd heard all the stories from her single friends about middle-aged men happy to live in perpetual adolescence, bed-hopping with twenty-somethings.

Cintra was actually relieved that her friend was so preoccupied with her stalled relationship with Joseph, as Cintra's acceptance of her diagnosis as compulsive liar was still so fresh and humiliating, she didn't look forward to its dissection with her friends.

"Joseph always said he wanted kids too, but now I wonder. Do you think I should go off the pill and not tell him?" Poppy asked. "I hate to do that, but I feel like he's forcing me. Maybe he'd be fine once it happened." She slugged more wine.

Cintra sighed. These were waters she'd never had to navigate. Once Boston had been born, she and Elliot had considered themselves "one and done."

"What if he's not fine, though? Do you want to be with a baby and he isn't enthusiastic about it, or even resentful? I couldn't have done it without a fifty-fifty partner."

Poppy looked at her with raw fear in her eyes.

"Fancy meeting you here."

June was standing at their table. She was wearing a long peach skirt, a navy blue peasant blouse with a twisty gold chain, makeup done and hair neatly pulled back into a low ponytail, as if she'd come from work.

"June, hi!" Cintra introduced her to Poppy and the two of them shook hands.

"I thought I'd check out this place you'd mentioned. Pick up some muffins," June said.

"Why don't you join us in some wine?" Poppy asked, seeming slightly tipsy. "Or me anyway."

Cintra was surprised at Poppy's invite to a stranger, given the topic of their conversation.

"Don't mind if I do. I showed a house in the neighborhood and am quite free."

"Oh, great," said Cintra.

"I'll be back," June said in an Arnold Schwarzenegger voice and went to the counter.

Cintra lowered her voice at Poppy. "Don't mention my issue."

Poppy made a key turning motion at her mouth.

"Organic," June said when she returned, holding up her Mason jar. "Nice they have it. Doesn't cause hangovers."

She slid in next to Cintra and talked about her listing, a gray-shingled Victorian in Ditmas Park with a wrap-around porch and castle-like turrets.

"How much?" Poppy asked.

"One point five. Not too bad when you consider there's five bedrooms, two baths and a pretty big backyard. You could pay close to that for a two bedroom in our building."

One point five million. Cintra quickly did the math. June would be bringing home $90,000 for one listing. More than Cintra would make all year. She regretted that she and Elliot had never managed to scrounge up enough money to buy an apartment. If they'd done it in the Meatpacking District before the area turned into an overpriced shopping mall, they'd have been set for life.

There was half an hour more conversation about real estate, and three more glasses of wine. Cintra caved in and joined them, accepting that no writing would get done this afternoon.

Poppy started to spill about her boyfriend problems, and June leaned over the table eagerly, a crackle of mutual interest passing between them.

"It's so unfair," said June. "Men take up all our fertile years with their indecision. Why shouldn't they? It doesn't affect *them*."

Cintra was surprised to hear the vehemence in June's voice. Was she having the same problem with Niko?

As if reading her thoughts, June looked at her. "I don't mean Niko. The one before him. They're called 'future fakers,' these types. Was with him for seven years, from thirty-three to forty. All along, he said he wanted to get married and to have kids. I'd start to think he didn't, break up with him, and then he'd do everything in his power to get me back, and the whole thing would start up all over again." She blew air out of her cheeks. "I could smack my younger self. I'd go off birth control, we'd try for a bit, then he'd come up with an excuse why it couldn't happen right then—his mother was sick, he lost his job."

"Yes, yes! Joseph always has an excuse too. You couldn't break it off?" Poppy asked. "I'm not judging. I've had the same problem. We live together and it's so difficult."

"I'd try," said June, offering them both cranberry wheat muffins she had in a bag. "He'd move out and when I'd recover a little and start dating, he'd come back around, pleading for another chance. He always sensed when I was on the brink of moving on. Then he'd charge at me, using every trick imaginable, saying he'd changed and couldn't live without me. A few times, he came over to my place, crying."

"Ugh," Poppy said. "That sounds very manipulative. Why do we put up with it?"

"Because love, I guess. Women can be stupid about love. We're more wired for it, as we're the ones taking on all of the risks of pregnancy." She raised her brows knowingly at them and split a muffin in half. "And the dating was pretty bad, and there he'd be, on my doorstep with flowers in hand. I even begged him to leave me alone because I apparently didn't have the willpower to resist him, but he didn't care. At one point, a long-ago love, one from college, came back around, but my ex ruined it. He told the man that he and I were together when we weren't. I didn't find that out until later. I could have had a real chance with that old college boyfriend. It was all a game to my ex."

"That's awful." Poppy drained her wine and looked around as if searching for a waitress, though orders were made at the counter. "I don't get why they do it. Why not go away if you don't want what we want?"

"Because they want both things," said June, adamantly. "The girlfriend and the freedom. They want an escape hatch in case something better comes along. If it does, they can leave and have a family, even in their fifties and sixties, but the time for the woman has passed. There's IVF, but that's expensive, difficult on the body, and not always successful. Of course, there's adoption."

They both nodded.

"But that can take years and most agencies prefer not to adopt to a single mother. And some of us would like biological children. There's no shame in that." June drank more wine and broke off a chunk of her muffin. "But it all worked out. I finally stood firm, and a year later, met Niko." She chewed, her grayish eyes lit up.

"Who's Niko?" Poppy looked at her ring. "Oh, you're married. I didn't notice."

"Niko is nice," Cintra told Poppy, feeling adrift from the conversation.

"It was a miracle, a fairytale," said June. "I was forty-one, living in a small town, and Niko moved nearby. He could have had his pick of the ladies, believe me."

"Are you going to have children?" Poppy asked.

June waved. "We'd like to, but I'm forty-two. He's said that's not important to him. If it happens, it happens." She grinned. "All I'm saying, Poppy honey, is that there are good men out there, but you have to be free to find them. You're still young. What are you, late twenties?"

"Thirty-five, but thank you."

"You look fabulous. And you have time, but not *his* kind of time. How much more of your ovaries' lifespan do you want to waste on this future faker? Let me tell you something." She leaned over the table. "Less than a year after I made the final break with my ex, he was married to some girl he'd just met, and she was pregnant."

Cintra and Poppy shook their heads, making "stop" and "no, just, no" exclamations of disapproval.

"Oh, yes. All that waffling because of *trauma* from his parents' divorce, *supposedly*, but he dove right in with the next one after me. Married and pregnant in a minute." She snapped her fingers. "Of course, she was ten years younger than me. Poppy, honey, wake up. If they *truly* want it, they do it fast."

Poppy had sullenly slunk down the wood bench and was rubbing the bulbous lip of her empty Mason jar with one finger, looking as if the world had caved in on her.

"Maybe June's right," Cintra said, gently. "Maybe it's time to break up. You gave him the ultimatum. That's come and gone."

"What about you, Cintra, honey?" June asked,

peering pointedly at her wedding ring. "I haven't wanted to pry, but… you're separated, I take it?"

Cintra squirmed on the bench. "Yes, for now. It's nothing he did. It's me."

"I see," said June, with a look in her eyes that indicated she was imagining some sordid drama.

"*Not* an affair," Cintra said, though she wasn't sure why she felt the need to clarify. "We needed time apart to sort things out. Our son is staying with him."

"How is he handling everything? Your son?" June asked sympathetically.

"He's thirteen, so he's fine without me for awhile, though I know it's affecting him. For now, it's the right thing for the family."

June nodded and swallowed a piece a muffin. "No need to explain further. I didn't mean to pry."

"No worries," Cintra said, downing the last inch of wine. "We all have our issues, don't we?"

June and Poppy nodded and laughed their assent. "I left my issue back in Cold Springs," said June. "Done with that issue. Should have been done with it years before!"

They all said, "Hear hear," and raised glasses, all of them empty or nearly so.

"One more round?" asked Poppy.

Half an hour later, they left, Poppy and June exchanging cell phone numbers on the sidewalk. June and Cintra made their half-drunken way down the shady Victorian-dotted streets of Ditmas Park towards their apartment building. June pointed out a few homes she hoped would get listed with Barton's.

When they made room on the sidewalk for a mother passing with a ringleted, chunky-cheeked toddler in a stroller, June said, "Wouldn't you like to snatch her up?" and balled her fists against her chest. Then she laughed, an odd gleam in her eyes as she looked to Cintra for confirmation that she too would want to snatch up a stranger's baby.

Cintra laughed with her, but inwardly cringed. She was glad to be long done with a toddler, but didn't want to say this to a woman who so clearly wanted one of her own.

## Chapter Eight

The next morning, around 7:30 a.m., on her way to work, Cintra came out of the door at the same time that June and Leo came out of theirs. June was in a bright yellow dress, her almost-as-yellow hair pinned back. Leo had on a t-shirt, jeans, and sneakers with red lights flashing on them. Cintra remembered when Boston had gone through the lighted-sneakers phase.

"Hi," Cintra said, and June said, "Oh, hi!" as Leo turned and started taping papers up on the door.

June came forward. "Cintra, I wanted to apologize. I realized I kind of inserted myself into your time with Poppy yesterday."

"Not at all. The more the merrier."

June looked back at Leo taping up the papers, and then turned and lowered her voice. "I feel as if I unburdened myself a bit too much about my ex. Wine can give me a loose tongue."

"Please don't feel like that. Poppy needed to hear another opinion besides mine."

"Thank you for understanding," she said, hoisting a sunset-hued messenger bag higher on her shoulder. "I just hate to see a woman fritter her time away like I did. If she truly wants children, she should do whatever is necessary to make that happen. It might cause her pain at first, but she'll regret it otherwise."

"That makes sense," Cintra said, her fingers tussling with the long wire of her earphones, which was tangled in the flap of her tote pocket. "You put it to her in a way I wouldn't have thought of."

June smiled appreciatively, then said, "Leo, come on. We're already running late." She looked at Cintra. "He had a toe stubbing accident this morning and ice was in order."

Leo turned from the door, said, "Hi," and got next to June. Cintra let them pass before her down the stairs and then her earphone wire, which she hadn't managed to unsnag from her tote pocket, snapped her earphones off. They stretched awkwardly inside of her long hair. She stopped to unravel everything, loosening the wire as if it was a string knotted up in a ball of yarn. Instinctively, her eyes were drawn towards the door of apartment 3D.

On it were three large pieces of white paper, taped horizontally. Over the past couple of weeks, she'd occasionally noticed various messages and drawings, but had only glanced at them, not quite remembering what they were, or what they said. She vaguely remembered a fire truck and a horse.

But this time, the papers were right in front of her. The top paper, written in purple Magic Marker, in the same underdeveloped, scrawly hand she'd seen before, said:

I'M BEING

The next paper down from that said,

HELD

And below that was a paper with a crude sketch of a boy with straight-up blond hair and arms jutting out from his sides. In the boy's hand was—what?

She inched closer, but not too close, not wanting June to come back up the stairs and see her staring busy-bodily at the door. In the boy's hand was a small brown blob. And there was a gray-black shape, about an inch wide, right near the boy's head. Cintra squinted and peered closer at the shape.

There was no mistaking it: A gun. Pointed at the boy.

Strange. Cintra was surprised that June, with her love of organics and non-polluting detergent and sustainable fish, would let her nephew draw something like that, or at least, once he had, wouldn't dissuade him from displaying it in the hallway.

She walked down the stairs. June and Leo must have taken the side door out of the hallway, as they were nowhere to be seen.

On the sidewalk, an unpleasant feeling fluttered

through her gut, an odd prickle of the familiar, of something clicking into place.

## I'M BEING HELD

Then she thought, *Impossible, impossible.* Leo walks around like he's fine. June would have seen him write a note like that, and taken it if it was true.

*Impossible!* She yelped out a laugh at herself, turned on some music, and fleetingly wondered if she should find a new line of work. Writing about crime had her imagining it everywhere.

## Chapter Nine

Three days a week, Cintra took the subway into Midtown, to the glass high rise of the Global Broadcast media conglomeration, where she blogged for True Crime TV. It wasn't a bad job. The pay was decent for the fairly easy work and it was flexible. Why she couldn't work at home like most other freelance jobs allowed, she didn't know. But it was nice to get out of the apartment and mingle with people.

Bloggers sat at a grid of white desks in front of large monitors, publishing articles instantaneously. Cintra could track her traffic numbers and which posts became popular as she worked. Sometimes she did original reporting, but mostly she gathered information from a large array of news sources, including True Crime TV and its dozens of shows dedicated to crime.

Her editor, Mavis, a forties-ish woman with a long face and the no-nonsense manner of a news editor juggling dozens of stories at a time, came over to her.

"Hey, Cin," she said. "You ever hear of a woman named Ettie Brightman?"

The name rattled around her memory as if it had been there before, but nothing concrete fell out. "Mm… Sounds familiar. Can't place it though."

"Mom of five who murdered her ex-husband and his new wife twenty-five years ago up in Belle Cove. They made a movie out of it."

"Oh, right. The actress who played her, she was—"

"Megan Walsh. The mom from *The Family Chronicles*."

"Right." She'd never seen the movie, but had heard of it. And *The Family Chronicles* had been huge when she was a child. She'd also heard of Belle Cove, a rich enclave somewhere north of the city, because it had been the setting for a short-lived reality show called *The Belles of Belle Cove.*

"Well, Ettie's out of prison," said Mavis. "She was granted parole. We're going to do a special and are trying to find her, but she's hiding out. A source tells us she's staying in Brooklyn."

"Get out of here."

"That's where you live, right?"

Cintra laughed. "You don't think I'm going to run into her, do you? Brooklyn's pretty big."

"Yeah, but the source says she's somewhere near the park. That's near you, right?"

"Still. It's a big area. I'll keep my eyes peeled. Any new pictures of her?"

"I'll have the photo desk send you whatever we can

dig up, but nothing since her parole that I'm aware of. Brush up on her. Be prepared."

"I will, but what should I say if the murder gods align and I happen to see her?"

"Tell her we'd love to talk to her and we'd be sympathetic. Give her your number. Try to get her info."

"Will do."

Mavis left and Cintra got down to researching Ettie Brightman.

After a savagely acrimonious divorce, Ettie's well-respected heart surgeon husband, Monty, was awarded most of their assets, as well as their five children, then remarried his twenty-four-year-old mistress, Paige. Less than a year after Monty's remarriage, Ettie, who was forty-five at the time, went to the couple's new house in tony Belle Cove and blew them both away.

Despite herself, Cintra felt sorry for the murderess. Ettie had held down three low-wage jobs to put her husband through medical school, borne him six children, one of which had been stillborn, and when the couple should have been at their apex of happiness and financial security, Monty left her for a young secretary who worked at his hospital. Monty's best friend, Stanley Steelman, was a fearsome divorce lawyer who knew every conceivable trick to hide or diminish Monty's assets, leaving his ex-wife with a pittance for alimony. Even worse, through a complicated series of legal maneuvers that used Ettie's increasingly volatile behavior against her, Monty was awarded full custody of their five children.

To pour acid into the wound, mistress-turned-second-wife Paige uncannily resembled Ettie in her youth. During the murder trial, young Ettie and Paige had to be labeled on photos, as witnesses and the jury were having trouble telling them apart.

Young Ettie had been quite attractive, with long, flat red hair in the seventies style and piercing green eyes. In her mug shot after the murders, she looked overweight and worn out, years older than her age, probably the stress of all of those kids and that no-good husband.

The murders had gotten colossal media attention at the time, culminating in the telemovie, *A Woman on the Verge: The Ettie Brightman Story*, starring Megan Walsh, who'd been nominated for an Emmy for the role. Back in the days when three networks ruled the airwaves, the telemovie had been enormously popular. The public was riveted by the story of a "scorned" suburban housewife —the media called her a "socialite"—snuffing out her former husband and his much younger new wife after a prolonged, bitter divorce. The story especially struck a nerve with older divorcees.

Ettie had claimed self-defense, saying that she went into the couple's new house to talk to her ex-husband about their teen daughter, Emily, who was spending too much time with an older boyfriend. She said she'd only had a gun in her purse because a week earlier, she'd been mugged. But there was no police report of the supposed incident.

Ettie had not rang the doorbell, but let herself in, saying she feared Monty wouldn't answer the door if he knew it was her. Finding Monty and Paige in their kitchen in the early evening, with all of the children out of the house doing various school activities, Ettie claimed an argument had broken out and Monty had become aggressive, threatening her with a carving knife. She'd testified she'd pointed the gun at Monty to scare him off, but accidentally pulled the trigger. Paige had jumped in front of Monty, taking a second bullet.

But Ettie was almost certainly lying. She knew the children's schedules and that none would be home that night. Her fingerprints were on the knife she'd claimed Monty wielded. And Monty and Paige had been shot point blank in the chest as they sat at the kitchen table, apparently having turned around as Ettie came into the room. Their half-eaten chicken dinners were still on the table, and Monty looked as if he'd tried to crawl underneath the table before he died. Hardly the body language of a man who moments before would have been standing away from the table and threatening Ettie with a knife.

And who "accidentally" pulls a trigger twice? On top of that, Ettie hadn't called 911. She'd driven around the neighborhood for hours before going home and ringing a friend. According to the friend, Ettie had crowed that Monty's last words were, "You win." The friend testified that Ettie sounded elated at his last words, which were burbled through blood.

Still, there was enough doubt about what exactly had happened, and enough jury dislike of Monty, that Ettie's lawyer managed to get second-degree murder convictions instead of first, and two concurrent sentences of twenty-five years to life with a chance of parole after twenty. Not too bad for killing two people in cold blood.

Monty's desire to rub Ettie's nose in his new marriage seemed to have sealed his and his new wife's fate. On December 17, the afternoon of the murders, Ettie had opened a Christmas card sent to her by Monty. The cover photo was of him and the children in their traditional Christmas attire, only Paige was standing in the spot that used to be occupied by Ettie. He'd signed the card, "Love, Dr. and Mrs. Brightman." It would be the last thing he'd ever send to Ettie. The last thing he'd ever send to anyone.

At seventy years old, after her second parole hearing, Ettie was a free woman. And living in Brooklyn of all places.

Cintra wondered what Ettie's life would be like. Did any of her children want anything to do with their murderer mother? Cintra couldn't find the children, even using the LexisNexis database. Lizette "Ettie" Brightman had last been in civilization twenty-five years ago, when databases that tracked virtually everyone who had a phone number didn't exist, so she wasn't listed as a "potential relative" under anyone with the same names as her children.

Ettie's urge to kill in her ex's kitchen must have been as strong and unstoppable as Cintra's urge to lie. Deep down, Cintra was a little uncomfortable at how much she related to Ettie in this moment. Both women's inability to control their baser impulses had hurt those they cared about most: their children.

## Chapter Ten

*W*alking back on Fifth Avenue with a sandwich in her tote on a muggy day wrapped in gray (the least sunny August she could ever remember), Cintra's phone pealed.

Poppy's number. Cintra wondered if everything was all right. Her friend was a busy editor at a finance website. It was unusual for her to call in the middle of the workday.

"Cin, are you at work today? I'm so sorry to be calling. I wanted to do it tonight but couldn't wait."

"It's fine," Cintra said. A cab's horn bleated, and she ducked into the cutaway of a building, where she could be more insulated from noise. "Are you okay?"

"I'm great! Get ready. I'm engaged."

"Wow! When?"

"Last night. At Celestine. A huge rock too."

"Oh my God. I'm happy for you." Another horn bleated and she burrowed deeper into the cutaway, poking one finger in her ear. "Joseph finally wised up."

"I was all set to end it. Maybe he sensed I was serious this time."

"You didn't have another talk with him?"

"Not really. A little. I mean, he knew I was upset. The last time I saw you, when I came home, I was so quiet. I think he knew it was put up or shut up time. It was a total surprise though. Well, not total. I figured if he wanted to go to Celestine, something was up. He insisted we dress up, which isn't like him. And he seemed kind of nervous. The restaurant clapped."

"Exciting, Pops."

"We're going to have a little engagement party. Neither one of us wants to do a big bachelor-bachelorette thing. It'll be casual. Save the Saturday after Labor Day."

"Of course."

"And… I didn't know whether to invite Elliot?"

"Well… " Cintra sighed. She and her husband had been separated for such a short amount of time, it hadn't occurred to her how they'd divvy up social events of mutual friends. "Joseph probably wants him there, right?"

"You've always been our friend more than him. Don't get me wrong, we like him, but if we have to make a choice…"

"You don't have to," Cintra said. "Go ahead and invite him. We're not enemies. We're only taking time apart."

Cintra wrapped up the conversation and walked through the revolving glass doors of the Global Broadcast building.

Joseph had certainly come around all of a sudden.

* * *

THE ENGAGEMENT PARTY was at Atrium, a cozy, wood-paneled restaurant overlooking the East River on the Brooklyn side. Immense windows framed downtown Manhattan's world famous view, so clearly limned against the night sky it appeared a skipped pebble would hit the jeweled spire of One World Trade Center.

Poppy looked beautiful, in a white, lacy summer dress, her brown hair rushing over her shoulders, her eyes lined with kohl liner, her lips purple-red, her nails back to perfection. She was flitting around, greeting everyone. In Cintra's ear, she said, "Elliot couldn't come."

"Or wouldn't because of me," Cintra said. "Don't take it personally."

Cintra grabbed her friend's hand to check out the diamond. It was bigger than she'd expected. An oval-cut gem of maybe four carats, with a rose-gold pavé diamond band. Joseph must be making serious money these days at his financial consultancy job. She vaguely remembered him complaining about his firm's penurious commission-based salary, but that had been a few years ago.

"Stunning," Cintra said, as Poppy smiled widely, seeming drunk with giddiness.

Cintra noted Joseph lounging near the bar with a couple of his friends, guys she recognized from various get togethers, but could never remember their names.

She made greetings with a couple of Poppy's friends, women she'd seen before but didn't know very well, and was about to head over to congratulate the groom-to-be (and get a drink) when she felt soft but firm fingers on her bare arm.

"Fancy meeting you here."

June. Her customary braid was gone, her blonde hair frizzed down to the tips of her shoulders. Cintra was surprised to see her at such a personal event. So far as she knew, June and Poppy had only met that one time at The Tea Spot.

"Nice to see you," Cintra said, as they exchanged a cheek kiss. "Where's Niko?"

"Afraid we don't have a trusted babysitter for Leo."

"Oh, June. I could have given you a few names."

June faux-slapped her forehead. "I hadn't thought of that. Next time."

At Leo's age, Cintra and Elliot had allowed Boston to stay home alone for a few hours, but he'd always been a mature child. Perhaps that wasn't the case with Leo. Who was she to judge?

She watched as June opened her mouth wide at something behind her. Poppy almost bowled Cintra over in her rush to get to June and hug her. Cintra was even more perplexed. How had these two become so chummy so fast?

"Uh-huh. *That's* a ring," June said, bending over Poppy's finger. "Just what you deserve. You earned it!"

June and Poppy clasped hands, as if they'd come through a trauma together and were deeply moved to have survived it. Cintra made small talk with Poppy's two friends, then weaved her way to the bar to get a drink.

"Congratulations, Mr. Groom," she said to Joseph, laying her hand on his back, which was hot and sticky through his blue dress shirt. He turned with a look of mild surprise, kissed her on the cheek.

"Thanks, long time coming, all that." He turned back to the bar and stood rocking against it, staring absently into the mirror lining the booze shelves.

Cintra tried to bury the feeling that he didn't seem excited or happy. She ordered a Prosecco, only finding out it was open bar for the party guests after she tried to pay.

In her side vision, she noted Joseph move away from the bar, disappearing into the crowd. He was always chatty, especially when he'd been drinking, so Cintra found it uncharacteristic he hadn't talked to her more. Maybe there were friends in the back he wanted to see.

An hour or so later, many of the guests were seated at a long wood table near the door, various food dishes spread out in front of them. Cintra was between two of the couple's friends she'd never met before, and was a little peeved that June was at the corner of the table, right near Poppy and Joseph.

Cintra didn't want to be petulant, but it was bizarre that she'd known the couple since they'd first started dating, yet June sat in a prime spot, while she herself was so far away she couldn't hear the couple over the din of the restaurant. One of Joseph's friends—a man named Gordon—was nice enough, but boring her nearly catatonic with his stories of antique collecting.

On her third glass of wine and pondering how to leave without insulting Poppy, she spotted an older woman with short gray hair making her way to the end of the table. She watched as June flew up from her seat, hugged the woman and introduced her to Poppy.

The older woman looked to be in her sixties, and was short and portly. She was wearing a bright red dress. Cintra excused herself in the middle of one of Gordon's stories about collecting antique eyeglasses and made her way to the end of the table.

"Cintra!" said June, all smiles. "This is my friend..."

"Sorry?" Cintra said, cupping her hand around her ear. She hadn't caught the woman's name over the restaurant's clamor.

"This is Liz!"

Cintra shook Liz's hand. It was rough, almost callused. The short gray hair was bobbed. Bright green eyes stared out from a pale face crisscrossed with lines.

"Hi, Liz," Cintra said, still shaking. She thought she heard the woman mouth, "Hello."

Those eyes. They were almond shaped, the green of them so pure they looked like emeralds. Quite pretty. Cintra felt a strange tug at her memory, as if she'd met the woman before.

"We don't know each other, do we?" she asked, leaning her long frame down to be closer to Liz's ears.

"That's doubtful," Liz said. "I've only moved here from Colorado."

"How do you two know each other?" Cintra asked, looking at June.

"She was a friend of my mother's. My mom passed away last year."

"Oh, sorry to hear."

June nodded jerkily, as if trying to hold back tears. "I mentioned to Poppy that Liz was new in town and she very graciously said to invite her along, so here she is." June insisted that Liz take her seat, and poured her a glass of wine from a table bottle.

"Welcome to civilization," June said, clinking Liz's glass.

"Indeed," Liz said. "Quite a refreshing change from Colorado."

"Was getting boring there, was it?" June asked.

"You said it." Liz sipped her wine, crinkling her nose at June.

As there was nowhere for her to sit, Cintra slunk back to Gordon and his antique collecting. For the rest of the evening, she felt almost like an intruder at Poppy's party, so preoccupied was her friend with Liz and June. A couple hours later, she pleaded exhaustion to Poppy, and made her round of goodbyes.

Outside, she waited for the car she'd called a few minutes earlier. Turning, she saw Joseph standing by himself, off to the side in the dark, a tendril of smoke curling up from a cigarette.

"Hey, buddy," she said, coming over.

"You leaving already?" he asked.

"Already?" She looked at her phone time. "Been here four hours. I'm exhausted. Besides, Poppy is distracted and I don't know the others too well."

He took a deep puff and blew out, staring off at the cars passing before them.

"It was a nice party," Cintra said.

"Yeah." He took another puff, offered her one. She waved her hand and said no thanks. She smoked occasionally, but it was another thing she was trying not do these days.

"You good, Joseph? You seem kind of…"

"Yeah, yeah, I'm good," he said, sucking on the cigarette, his profile inscrutable.

Cintra didn't dare ask him if he was having reservations about the engagement. That would be a betrayal to Poppy. But what if he was? What if he called it off tomorrow? Poppy would be devastated. Why had he proposed if he wasn't sure about it? A swell of anger gripped her before she realized she was jumping to unfounded conclusions. He could just have a migraine or something.

Glancing at her phone app, she saw the car was a block away. "You sure you're good?" she asked him.

He tossed the cigarette to the ground, somewhat violently. "I can't get into it, Cin," he said. "In some strange way, maybe it's all for the best. Thanks for coming."

She was about to ask him what was for the best, what couldn't he get into, but he was walking back into the bar, and her car was on the street.

Inside the car, her thoughts charged in manic circles. On her phone, she typed "Ettie Brightman" into an image search. Ettie's green eyes looked back at her. So like Liz's eyes. What would be the odds? But Ettie was in

Brooklyn, according to a mysterious source at True Crime. Still, there were over two million people in the borough. Cintra had never won any kind of lottery.

And "Liz." Ettie's full name was Lizette. The face Cintra had seen at the party was so much older, so much saggier, than the last photos of Ettie she could find, ones from her trial and her old mug shot, when she was at her heaviest, her face ballooned out round as a platter. Much had been made during the trial of Ettie's weight gain towards the end of her marriage, and Monty's alleged taunting her about it. Her defense attorney had gleefully latched onto that in another attempt to suggest Monty's cruelty was culpable in his own murder.

Ettie had done no media interviews during her incarceration and had managed to be released without any cameras capturing the moment, so Cintra had no recent pictures to examine.

That story about her moving from Colorado, being a friend of June's deceased mother. If Liz was lying, that meant June was lying too. Why would June know Ettie Brightman, if she did? Did Joseph know who Liz really was, and that's why he'd acted so out of sorts?

"I need to go back to Atrium," she told the driver. She would talk more to Liz. Study her features better. Only she couldn't think of a single reason to explain her return to Poppy and June. The party had been open bar, so there was no claiming she'd left behind her credit card.

Right before she left the car, she plucked out one earring and put it inside of her tote bag. She'd tell everyone she'd dropped it somewhere, then pretend to find it.

But inside, she discovered that June and Liz had already left. Cintra pantomimed scrutinizing the floors for her earring, as Poppy and a couple of her friends pointlessly helped.

## Chapter Eleven

The next morning, Pedro was drinking juice and getting the coffee machine going, looking hungover. "Hey, sis," he mumbled. "How was the party?"

"Good." She reached into the fridge for her own juice. "Though Joseph was acting kind of out of it." At this point, she couldn't quite remember what he'd said to her at the end of the evening. Something about everything being for the best.

"Maybe he's in shock." Pedro grinned. "I hope Poppy wasn't mad I couldn't come. That after-party for *Cabin in the Woods* had been set for ages."

"I don't think she would have noticed you anyway," Cintra said, a little grouchy. "She was totally engrossed with June."

"June was there?" Pedro looked surprised.

"Yeah, they're fast pals. So." She leaned against the counter. "I have to tell you something. I know what you're going to think, but…" She finished her juice, washed her glass, and placed it top down on a towel on the counter. "I've made up stuff in the past," she said, crossing her arms.

"Yeah?" His voice had a little "uh-oh" embedded in it as he put a filter into the coffee maker.

"But I'm not making this up. June might be friends with a woman named Ettie Brightman, who killed two people twenty-five years ago."

Pedro turned, his dark eyes went wide, he blinked several times, then burst into laughter. "Cin…"

"I'm serious. And I'm not lying."

"Okay." He rubbed at his forehead, then did the usual thing he did when he was thinking hard, twisted one of the dreads near the right side of his cheek. "And you think this why?"

"There was an older woman who came to the party last night. Said she moved from Colorado. Her eyes are bright green, very similar to the eyes of this woman named Ettie Brightman. And my editor told me that Ettie Brightman, who's been paroled from prison, is living in Brooklyn somewhere."

"Woman, green eyes, Brooklyn. Must be a murderer," Pedro said, spooning ground coffee into the filter.

"And she said her name is Liz, and Ettie's full name is Lizette."

"Green eyes, Brooklyn, Liz. Yep, sounds like a murderer," Pedro said, pouring water into the maker.

"You don't think I'm lying?" she asked, a little confrontationally.

"I don't know." The maker gurgled. "If you say

you're not, you're not. But you do remember that time you told me your grandmother used to date JFK."

Cintra looked down.

"And the time you told me that you were at a pool hall and Brad Pitt was there and he hit on you."

"I…" She squirmed up against the kitchen counter. "He looked like him."

"But it wasn't him."

"Probably not," she whispered.

"So, Cin. I don't know what to think exactly."

"I swear this happened. In fact," she said, bringing her phone out of her pocket and tapping at it. "Here's Ettie." She handed him the phone and he stared at it. "See the green eyes? If this woman shows up here, she's short and kind of heavy, with bobbed gray hair. You'll notice the eyes."

"Okay," he said, handing her phone back. "I'll keep a lookout. Will she try to kill us?"

"Of course not. She killed her ex and his new wife. She's not, like, a serial killer."

"Good, because not even a serial killer is making me give up this apartment," he laughed, waving his hand around. "But note to self: Be nice to any gray-haired, green-eyed old ladies wandering around the hallways."

"True Crime wants an interview with her. But there's no way to bring it up to June without sounding nuts if I'm wrong. And I take it you never heard Callie mention anything like this."

"Callie?" His lighthearted amusement vanished, his brows crossed under their fringe of dreads. "What's she got to do with it?"

"If June knows Ettie Brightman, maybe her sister does too."

"Never heard anything like that," he said, bringing down a mug out of the cherry wood cabinet. "And don't ask me to ask her. 'Hey, landlady, any chance you and your sister are pals with a double-murderer?' Yeah, that will fly."

"I'm not asking you to. I was just curious." Cintra looked at the time on her phone, she was meeting Elliot and Boston for brunch. "I better go meet my guys."

"Cin," Pedro called to her, and she turned around. "If I were you, wouldn't mention this to Elliot. I don't think he'll be as amused with it as I am. And, frankly, you're sounding a little obsessed with the neighbors."

She hiked her tote strap higher. "I don't plan on telling Elliot anything even remotely bizarre. Anyway, it's not the kind of thing he or Boston needs to know. I only find it interesting, that's all."

She waved and left.

IN THE LATE AFTERNOON, Cintra's stomach was still heavy with brunch despite having taken a dog from the nearby animal rescue group for a long walk in Prospect Park with Boston and Elliot. Boston had seen a kitten at the shelter that he wanted, and she and Elliot had to explain to him how it wasn't a good time to be adopting an animal, what with Mom "working on" herself. Then Elliot and Boston left to attend a Cyclones baseball game.

Cintra was in the middle of doing a biography on her protagonist, Lisa (who was close to being renamed Mila, as soon as Cintra could convince her index finger to get used to going one keyboard row down), when her phone rang.

"Hey, girl," said Poppy. "Thanks for coming last night. I apologize for not talking to you much."

"It's fine, you had a lot of people there," Cintra said, relieved to get away from Lisa/Mila. There was a gaping silence at the end of the line, and Cintra waited.

"I guess I feel kind of obligated to June," Poppy finally said. "Joseph might not have proposed if it wasn't for her. This isn't something I wanted to tell you earlier, because it sounds so strange."

"Well, you've heard some strange things from me over the years, so let's have it." Cintra put her laptop to sleep so she wouldn't be distracted, and turned away from her desk, looking out of the window to the condo next door. A couple lazed on their small terrace, a shaggy brown dog at their feet. Finally, it was a clear, sunny day.

"June is really into astrology," said Poppy.

"I thought you were about to say something important."

Poppy laughed. "It is, but it's also weird. Not long after we met at Tea Spot, she called and offered to do astrology charts for Joseph and me. She swore it would tell her everything about our relationship and whether we should even be married. And if we *should* be married, what I should say to him, and when I should say it."

"This is getting better."

"So I told June where and exactly when we were born. I had to look in Joseph's files where he keeps his birth certificate, because I didn't know the time of birth, of course. A few days later, she did the charts for both of us, saying we should be married, and that we *would* be married. But for it to happen, I had to say, 'I love you Joseph, and I'd like to be your wife, but if you don't want to be my husband, then we should go our separate ways, peacefully and with love.' I had to say this to him on a specific day and time."

Cintra was absently making half spins in her desk chair. Without thinking, she opened the desk's top drawer. Inside were household staples: scattered paper clips, a cell phone charger, a small dictionary, and a ponytail holder with a green-black winged butterfly. "I take it you told him all this," she said, stretching the ponytail holder's band with her fingers.

"Yes, that Tuesday at 9:01 p.m."

"Oh-one. Down to the minute." Cintra smirked.

"Whatever. I figured what harm could it do. If she'd asked me to say something stupid, I wouldn't have. The next day, he brought up going to dinner. Then he proposed."

"That's quite a story," Cintra said, putting the pony-tail holder back in the drawer and closing it. "I think he would have asked anyway, with you saying something like that. He didn't want to lose you."

"Maybe so, but it wasn't that far off from what I'd said months before, and he didn't care."

Cintra thought about Joseph's demeanor at the party; his quietness, what he'd said to her outside of the bar about everything being for the best. "Did he know about this astrology thing?" she asked.

"Absolutely not. It sounds pretty weird."

Cintra wondered if the astrology had sprinkled some kind of voodoo on Joseph, and he felt pushed into the proposal without even knowing why he felt pushed. But that made no sense.

"All that matters to me is that you're happy… and Joseph is, too," she said.

"I think he is. He's certainly being more attentive. Like a new man, really."

Hearing this, Cintra was relieved, but also felt a bit guilty that she'd interpreted his party behavior as being less than thrilled at his engagement.

"What did you think of that older woman, Liz?" she asked.

"Who? Oh, right. June's friend. She didn't say too much, but seemed nice enough."

"Did she say where she came from?"

"Erm, Colorado, I think? It was sweet how attentive June was to her, stood over her the whole time like a servant." She laughed. "Something the matter?"

There was no way Cintra was going to tell her friend her suspicion that Liz was a double murderer. Not when Poppy also knew Cintra's penchant to make up stories. Pedro's skepticism was enough for the day.

"Just curious," she said.

## Chapter Twelve

On Monday, Cintra didn't get home from work until around nine p.m. She'd reached Brooklyn at six-thirty, then went to the gym for an hour, then went grocery and pharmacy shopping. As she was putting her key into apartment 3C's lock, her arm was grabbed. She let out a tiny, startled scream.

A man was next to her in the hallway, a man she'd never seen before her in life. He had on a black cap with white lettering, but she didn't dare take her eyes off his, so she didn't know what the lettering said. He was a few inches taller than she was, which put him at about six feet. There was a sickly sweet smell oozing from him—alcohol. Oddly, her mind darted to the glass jar of olives in one of her grocery bags, and how she didn't want to drop the bag in her fright and smash the jar. Her mouth hung soundless and useless.

"I know who you are," the man said, lowly. "You're part of this. Shell company. But I have a friend who can get anything. You own that apartment. You must have known."

Cintra pulled her arm from his grip. "I have no idea what you're talking about," she said, trying to be calm. "I don't own anything."

She didn't want do or say something that would cause the man to lash out at her physically. Weighted down with bags and her tote, she was completely vulnerable. Even if she was able to get her bags unwound from her wrists, he was on the stairwell side, and there was no way she would get by him. She considered kicking him in the shins, but feared it wouldn't have much effect given her soft gym sneakers, and would only enrage him.

"You all thought I wouldn't know who was behind it, so clever," he sneered. "But that's some serious stuff, lady, breaking apart families. What did you get out of it?"

"Sir," Cintra said, hoping a sign of respect would make him go away. "You have the wrong person."

He came closer to her face and wheezed, "I shouldn't have gone along with it. I agreed to do it but I shouldn't have. You're twisted. You had me in a bad position. I should have fought harder."

Cintra was grappling with what to do, whether opening the apartment door would give the man an opportunity to barge in after her, when she heard, "What's going on?"

Pedro had opened the apartment door, was standing there.

The man looked at him and fled down the stairs.

Pedro grabbed her, pulled her through the doorway, shut the door and locked it.

"Who the hell was that?" Pedro asked, eyes wide.

"Jesus Christ." Cintra plunked all of her bags down on the foyer floor. Her heart was racing. "Some… guy! Out of nowhere."

"Could he live here?" Pedro asked.

"Did you lock it?" she asked, breathlessly, and not waiting for him to answer, checked to make sure the lock handle was turned. She'd heard the click of the bolt when Pedro had shut the door, but wanted to double check.

"Hell, yes," he said.

Cintra moved unsteadily into the living room. Too much adrenaline was coursing through her for her to sit, so she paced, pressing her palm into her crazily beating heart.

"That was messed up," she said, and laughed nervously. "I don't think he lives here. He seemed drunk, like he came off the street. He thought I was someone else. Or he was flat out nuts."

Pedro came over and touched her arms. "Are you okay?"

"I thought he was going to hit me." She sat down and rubbed her arms and thighs, her limbs on fire with adrenaline.

"I'm going to make sure he left." Pedro walked into the kitchen and came back with a big knife.

"Are you insane?" Cintra screeched. "You can't go out there. We need to call the cops."

Pedro, lean and sinuous, with a baby-pug nose and

cherub lips, didn't look threatening. But Cintra knew he could take care of himself. A longtime dancer, he was strong as an ox. He'd also taken Krav Maga for several years. But Cintra didn't want him to risk a confrontation.

"Cops won't be here for an hour. I have to make sure he's gone," Pedro said. "Don't call anyone until I get back. I'm a brown skinned man with a knife and that won't end well for me."

The door buzzed, and the pair locked eyes. Then there was an intense rapping on the door. "Cintra?" the voice called. Female.

Cintra and Pedro kept staring at each other, frozen, then Cintra stage-whispered, "I think it's June."

They walked to the door and Pedro looked through the peephole. "It is," he said, opening the door.

"Are you—" June said before Pedro pulled her inside, shut the door, and locked it again. June's nervous eyes shot to Pedro's knife, and then to Cintra. "Are you okay? I saw that guy with you."

"I'm okay. I have no idea who that was. Maybe he's still downstairs."

June held up Cintra's key. "It was in the lock," she said.

"Oh my God," Cintra said, hand over her mouth, taking the key. "He could have come right in."

"I heard voices and opened the door and saw him as he was running down the stairs. I tiptoed down, and watched him leave through the side entrance. What happened?"

Cintra shakily indicated that everyone should move

into the living room. "He came out of nowhere," she said, gesticulating wildly. "He must have been hiding in the stairwell. Babbling that I owned an apartment, something about a shell company." She clasped her hands at her chest. "Wait, June, could he have me confused with your sister and thinks I own 3D?"

June crossed her arms, frowning. "He said you owned the apartment?"

Cintra hesitated. She'd been so focused on the man's eyes and when they might flicker a warning that violence was imminent that she hadn't paid much attention to his words. But if she didn't commit to her lips what she thought he'd said, she feared the memory of it would fade forever.

"He said he had a friend who could get anything, and figured out who owned the apartment. He didn't specify which apartment. But the way he said 'that apartment,' made me think he meant 3D. And Callie owns both of them."

June sighed as if something she'd hoped to avoid had finally caught up with her. "He could be the guy who used to live in my apartment. I didn't want to tell you this and worry you, but the couple who lived there before us wasn't happy when Callie had the rental agency refuse to renew their lease. Someone in the building told her they were dealing drugs. That's why I have the combo lock."

"The what?" Cintra asked.

"On my door. It's stronger than regular locks, can't be picked. If I lock it from the inside with the combination, no one is getting in. Callie didn't want to risk anyone in their circle trying anything."

Combination lock. Now Cintra remembered catching a glimpse of it when she and Pedro had left dinner. And the black square that June had pointed at the door of 3D, the first time Cintra had ever laid eyes on her.

"Should we report him?" Cintra asked. "Callie would have his name."

"I can't say for sure the man was him," said June. "I've never seen him before. Have you, Pedro?"

Pedro shook his head, then rested the big knife on a nearby end table. "No, I saw the girlfriend a couple of times, but I was doing *Taxi Driver*. I was hardly home when they lived here."

"What else did he say to you?" June asked Cintra.

"I wish I could remember all of it. Something about breaking apart families. Something about he shouldn't have gone along with it."

"Yeah, Callie mentioned that he seemed really strange,"—she pointed to her head— "not all there."

Something about all of this teasingly disjointed. How could the man not know what Callie looked like, if he'd lived next door to her? But Cintra had to admit that in her old building, there were maybe a handful of neighbors she'd be able to pick out of a line-up.

There were Ryan and Ziad, but she only knew them because Boston was friends with their son, Max. There was the tall, sandy-haired man who had a dog Boston always stopped to pet. And there was the hunched old lady, but she only stuck out in Cintra's mind because she wore a red bathrobe in the hallways. If the woman ever bothered to put on clothes, Cintra likely wouldn't recognize her at all.

Five years in her old building, and most of her neighbors were a complete mystery to her. It wasn't out of the question that the former tenant in 3D might think Cintra was his former neighbor.

"You should call the police," said June. "I'll talk to Callie and get her to ask maintenance to change the lock downstairs."

"Maybe we need a combo lock too," Cintra said.

"This is a brand new double bolt lock," said Pedro. He rubbed the bolt lock's shiny steel. "He's not getting in here."

"Good thing Niko is out picking up dinner," said June. "He would have killed the guy, and then I'd have a husband in prison. And Pedro—" She looked over at the knife. "No sense you going to prison for a loon, either."

"I'd go to the clink for my girl," Pedro said.

Cintra gave him a squeeze around his waist. "My hero."

The three talked for another ten or so minutes, and Cintra gave June her phone number before she left. Then Cintra called the police and microwaved some food.

Pedro was correct in that it took about an hour for two officers to show up. One jotted on a notepad as Cintra ran through what had happened, and described the man as best as she could, and June's suspicion that the man had been a former neighbor.

As the man hadn't threatened her and Cintra had

seen no weapon, the officers didn't seem too concerned. As they left, she was certain there would be no investigation. This was Brooklyn, and they had bigger fish to fry. She'd tell Elliot about it. His job at the Department of Corrections meant he occasionally came into contact with cops. Maybe he'd know one who could look deeper into things.

\* \* \*

As she wouldn't be meeting Elliot and Boston for another two days, Cintra emailed her husband, asking if he could meet for a drink after work. She could have told him what had happened over email, but the truth was, she missed him. She wanted to see if the incident with the unhinged man would arouse his protective instincts enough that they could have a mini-reunion, maybe a kiss or two. She wanted to see that her husband still loved her.

He agreed, and around seven p.m., they met at a bar in Cintra's old neighborhood, Park Slope. They sat at a small wooden table close to a Foosball table, which no one was using. A pinball machine went *clang clang*.

It was abnormal and wretched that for the first time in almost two decades, Cintra couldn't reach over and rub Elliot's hands, couldn't lean over and kiss his soft lips, especially now that he'd shaved his long scruff.

First, they talked about Boston. He'd started high school and liked it. He was taking a math class that was advanced for his age. He was still a little behind in reading, and Elliot was going to take him to get his eyes checked.

As for Dumps, he'd been to the vet, and the vet couldn't find anything wrong with him. The vet thought Cintra's absence could be manifesting in the cat's stressed out butt licking, so Elliot agreed that on Saturday, Cintra would go to the apartment after brunch to hang out with Dumps for awhile.

Cintra waited until her vodka gimlet was half-drained, her mind relaxed, and she told Elliot what had happened with the strange man in the hallway. Threading through her words was a strong temptation: to tell Elliot that the man had threatened her with a gun. But now she recognized that for what it was: a cheap attempt to garner sympathy and attention, a cheap attempt to wrangle a display of love out of her husband. Now she knew it was unfair to drag concern out of him under false pretenses. She kept the story to what had really transpired.

"Geez," Elliot said once she'd finished. "Sorry that happened, Cin."

But he was looking past her shoulder. No real sign of alarm or concern. A flush of irritation spread through her.

"I suppose you think I'm lying," she said.

He took a long sip of his pint of dark beer. "That's the problem with lying. How am I supposed to know what's real and what's not?"

"For one, I have witnesses. Pedro saw him. So did my new neighbor."

"Should I start acting like Woodward and Bernstein? Calling around to verify your stories?"

Cintra took her phone out of her tote. "I could call Pedro. He'll tell you."

Elliot put up his palm. "Cin, if you say a man confronted you in the hallway, then fine. What do you want me to do about it?"

She couldn't believe the coldness in his voice. Had he really fallen completely out of love with her? Would he never understand that she had a disorder, and not something she was doing on purpose to hurt him? Never, ever would she forget the look on Elliot's face when Boston was born. Crying tears of ecstasy. Or how they had taken every step together in those first difficult years of parenting. Never, ever would she have said what she'd said unless she was dealing with something beyond her control.

"The cops didn't take it seriously," she said, putting her phone on the table. "I thought maybe you'd have a police contact who might."

"You said the guy didn't threaten you, so what do you want the cops to do? They've got murders and rapes to investigate. We don't live in Mayberry."

They sat in silence for at least a minute.

"Have I lost you forever, Elliot?" A heavy depression sat on Cintra's heart, and her fingers clawed at the cocktail napkin on the table, getting ready to use it if necessary.

"Cin, I—there was one thing I asked you to do. One thing. Live somewhere else for six months. See us once a week. Let me think, let us heal. Don't tell a lie. And here you are—"

"You agreed to see me."

"I thought something was really wrong. Like you'd been told you had cancer or something. Not this bullshit."

"Bullshit?!"

"So a drunk asshole thought you were someone else. Stuff happens in cities. I had a homeless guy try to hit me with his umbrella a couple of weeks ago, thought I was an uncle who'd taken all of his money."

"Wow," Cintra said. The tears retreated. "It's completely different. This guy was inside the building and grabbed me." They sat silently, but she could tell by his slumped posture that he regretted everything he'd said.

"I'm sorry, really, I am," he finally said. "But why are you acting so shocked that I might not believe it?" He kept his eyes on the table. "At this point, even if you'd told me you *had* cancer, I'd want to see proof. You told my son—"

She stopped him. "Please. I know what I told him. I can't hear it again." She didn't like that he'd said *my* son, not *our* son, but didn't correct him. "He knows I'm in therapy and he knows nothing like that will ever happen again."

"I wish I was as sure about that as you seem to be," Elliot sighed, then leaned forward and surprised her by touching her hand. The tender gesture, after so much coldness, brought the tears to the back of her eyes, and she clutched at her cocktail napkin.

"I love you, but I need no drama," he said. "I need to trust you can be a normal person, someone who, when she says a man came at her in the hallway, I don't have to call six people to get verification. Can you understand that?"

She stuffed the napkin into the corner of her right eye, but it was no use, as the left one was leaking too. Her nose clogged.

"I swear that's what you'll get, Elliot." Her voice was wavering. "I shouldn't have said anything. If he comes around again, maybe I can stay with Poppy."

Years ago, a man on the street had followed her into her apartment vestibule after she'd brushed off his come-ons, and threatened to kill her, actually *kill* her. She'd called police, and it had gone nowhere. Drunken ramblings she could make no sense of was not going to launch an investigation.

Maybe that previous experience was coloring her reaction to this one, because she couldn't shrug off the feeling that the strange man portended something larger, something more than just drunkenness and mistaken identity. As if she'd caught a quick glimpse of an iceberg's tip reaching out of the still, dark sea.

"If you think you're in danger, then move in with Poppy," said Elliot. "I'll help you with money. But I can't ask you to come back with us. I'm sorry. I can't. Not yet. Cin, after that night, do you know what I wanted to do?"

She said nothing, dreading whatever was coming.

"I wanted to lie to you," he said, so quietly she almost couldn't hear him over the *clang clang* of the pinball machine. "Something big. Just so we were even for once. You're turning me into a person I don't want to be."

She said nothing, nodding numbly. "I—I won't turn you into that person," she finally managed.

On the sidewalk outside of the subway, Elliot hugged her. Then he said, "There's an NYPD program, Neighborhood Community Officers. I can find out the ones for your precinct. Maybe you can ask them to get security footage for your building."

She nodded tightly, hugged him again, kissed him on the cheek, and said, "Tell Boston I'm calling him soon as I get home." Then she went down the smelly subway stairs and waited twenty agonizing minutes for a train.

Later that night, after getting off the phone with Boston, she came into the living room, and sat with Pedro on the couch. They were half an hour into a movie when Pedro's phone chirped. As he made his greeting, his eyes darted over to Cintra.

"Yeah, that's right, man. Some clown. We think he was drunk. Our neighbor said he might be the guy who used to live next door… uh huh. No, she's fine. Shook up, you know." He kept his eyes on Cintra. "Uh huh… no, man. I get it. Uh huh. Sure thing. You too."

He hung up.

"Elliot?" she asked.

"Yep. Checking your story."

*Good*, Cintra thought. How else was he supposed to know that she had stopped her lying habit if he didn't occasionally check things?

But she'd learned her lesson. No matter what

happened, she couldn't tell Elliot anything even remotely out of the ordinary. For the first time in her adulthood, her husband was not the person she could rely on to buffer her and support her through the stormier times of life.

\* \* \*

TWO DAYS LATER, June called. The downstairs locks had keys that couldn't be copied except through the maintenance company. There was no record of the company having made any extras for the couple who used to live in 3D. "He must have buzzed the door of someone who let him in," she said.

Nor did the building, which was small at only twenty units, with two apartments on each floor, front and back, have surveillance cameras. The maintenance company said it would address the question of whether they were needed at the next co-op board meeting, which wouldn't be until December 1.

Cintra was irritated, but there was nothing she could do short of moving, and that wasn't possible. She'd never get another room in as nice an apartment and as close to her son for as little money as she was paying.

A few days later, a memo was slipped under everyone's door, reminding them not to let anyone in the building that they didn't know. Additionally, as the police theorized that the man had slipped a credit card into one of the downstairs doors' locks to pop it open, a metal frame would be placed inside of them to prevent that happening again.

Elliot emailed her the name of a police officer in her precinct, but she thought it would be useless to contact him. There was no proof that the man in the hallway was the former neighbor, and she doubted the NYPD would put in the manpower to find and question him. Especially as he'd only said some bizarre things that, as she tried to recall them, were jumbling in her mind. Shell company? Breaking apart families? It made no sense. Like the homeless man who'd thought Elliot was his thieving uncle, maybe the building intruder had an emotional disorder and nothing he'd said had any bearing on reality.

She bought pepper spray from a nearby pharmacy, keeping it gripped in her hand as she came up the stairs. But as a longtime city dweller who'd had her share of oddball and borderline dangerous things happen, she grew weary of being high alert, and the pepper spray went to a permanent resting spot in her tote bag pocket.

## Chapter Thirteen

*a* few days after the incident in the hallway, Pedro looked downcast. "You all right?" Cintra asked him.

On a chair by the couch, he had his arms crunched up against his chest, his dark eyes staring off into nowhere. "Heard from my agent. Didn't get *Aladdin*."

"Ugh, I'm sorry."

"I nailed it. *Nailed* it. That's it. I'm old. No one wants me."

"Thirty-six is not old."

"In this business, it's ancient. You should see the guys at the callback, they were like twelve." His face was a mask of fearful anguish. "I knew this day would come, and I'd have to plan for it, but I didn't plan. Should I go back to school? I don't have the money. I used to waiter, but it almost ruined my knees. Could I teach?"

Cintra sat on the cushy arm of his chair, rubbing between his shoulder blades. She didn't want to give him advice; she didn't know what to tell him anyway. As a creative, she knew the heartbreak of creating and the very real possibility that no one would want those creations. All she could do was be there for support.

"This year has been brutal," he said. "I don't think I'm over Liam either."

"Of course not. You were with him for a long time. It will take awhile."

"I really trusted him," he said, sadly. "He was the first man—no, the first *person* I fully trusted."

"I'm so sorry, Ped. He ruined the best thing that ever happened to him. You deserve so much better."

"How is it you can be with someone for six years and not know him at all? Was it all a joke? A mirage? A way to spend his time?"

"He's an ass," Cintra said, then was silent. She wanted to take her friend's pain away as much as if he was Boston. But everything she was saying sounded so trite and pointless.

He put his hand on her knee. "Thank God for this apartment. It's the only thing keeping me from throwing myself off the Brooklyn Bridge. I'd be on the street without it. I can't move back home and my friends are all broke too."

"You'll never be on the street as long as I'm alive," she promised, and she meant it.

He smiled a little at her. "But it won't last forever. Callie will return, and then what? Maybe June and Niko can adopt me?"

"Maybe both of us. Who knows if Elliot will ever want me back."

"Of course he will. No offense, but Elliot isn't

exactly hunk of the century. You're way out of his league. Anyway, I'm gonna drown my sorrows in ice cream. You want anything?"

"I'll have a few bites. Whatever flavor. By the way, what is Callie's last name?"

Pedro was yanking his laceless sneakers on his bare feet. "Ah, hm. Can't quite remember. I can look it up. Why?"

"Since that guy in the hallway maybe thought I was her, I was curious if we looked alike."

"Cin, she's like ten years older than you."

"I'm curious."

He grabbed his phone off the kitchen island and tapped at it. "Bates. Like Norman."

He handed her his phone. She examined a Facebook profile photo of a woman in a white and blue summer dress on a boat who was so far away from the camera lens that Cintra couldn't make out any facial resemblance to her own; but the woman's hair, though pulled back in the photo, was black, as was Cintra's. Callie looked to be twenty pounds heavier though.

"Well, we both have dark hair." She handed Pedro his phone as he zipped out the door.

In her bedroom, she pulled up Facebook. She didn't have a personal account. She'd wanted to keep Boston off social media as long as possible. When he was eleven, he'd started bugging her and Elliot to get an account, so they'd decided to deactivate theirs. They figured that would mean less temptation for Boston, and it seemed unfair to deny him one when they had their own.

But she still had her professional account, the one she'd used when she was promoting her novel. It had about one thousand followers, the same amount it had had three years ago. From various comments, a quarter of her followers thought Cintra was the author of the more popular book that had a similar title to hers. Shamefully, a few times she'd answered people as if she *was* that more popular author, until someone called her out and she stopped.

She logged in to do a search for "Callie Bates Brooklyn" and a profile by the name of "Calista (Callie) Bates" came up. There was the profile photo she'd seen on Pedro's phone, the buxom woman with the pulled back dark hair, on a white boat, on unknown waters.

She clicked around into the various photos that were public. There weren't many, about a dozen, a few of them professional shots, a few of them what appeared to be her in opera performances. Callie looked to be in her late forties, with bouffy hair that ranged from dark black in some photos to reddish tinged in others, none of the ashy blonde color of June's hair.

Cintra scrolled down, down. The last public photo was of Callie standing on a city street, holding the hand of a young girl in a frilly green dress, who was blonde, and appeared to be five or six years old. There were a few comments to the side of the photo. "She's getting big!" "What a cutie" and "Hello Leonara!"

Cintra stared at the photo. Stared and stared. At the little girl's blonde hair, swirling around her shoulders. At her pretty little face. There was a slight resemblance to

Callie, mostly in the heart shape of the face. June hadn't mentioned having a niece too.

She didn't see any photos of Leo. Interesting that Callie had named her son Leo and named what appeared to be her daughter Leonara. But people did such things. Boston had come up in school with fraternal twins: Nolan and Nola. Kind of silly, if you asked her.

When Pedro returned, they had some ice cream in the living room, Cintra having more than she'd intended. Pedro was still mopey. Having run out of consoling things to say, she retired to her room.

She read a few chapters of the book on compulsive lying, more so she could honestly tell Dr. Grace she had done her homework than anything, and then hunkered down at midnight to sleep. She had to be up at seven a.m. to make it into work the next morning.

But she couldn't sleep. It was nearing October, yet unfathomably humid outside. She got up and turned on the AC, though she hated to increase their electric bills.

Back in bed, she tossed onto her stomach. It was her preferred sleeping position, but one she tried not to do anymore, as she'd noticed her right eye had more crow's feet than the left, probably a result of keeping her right cheek scrunched into a pillow for so many years.

In the past, she would have had her leg hoisted over Elliot's leg, but now there was only the lump of the blanket. Until Boston was about six, he'd occasionally slept in the middle of them, using their bodies as a fortress against various ghosts, monsters, and nightmares.

Dumps usually took up residence on top of Cintra's feet, or between Elliot's legs.

Now it was only her. Cintra hadn't felt lonely in ages, not since she'd met Elliot, really. She had forgotten the cold grip of it. She wasn't close to her mother, who was still living in Maine with her husband. She barely knew her step-siblings. Her father was dead. Her guys, Elliot and Boston, were the only real family she had.

She hadn't heard the sound from behind the wall since she'd thought she'd heard a voice say, "You." Had that been enough to make Leo stop using his tablet late at night? Maybe he'd turned down the sound or was using headphones.

She drifted into a dream that seemed to be inside of a cave; she was wandering around it, trying to locate something important. She reached for a hand, Boston but not Boston. Another child.

She drifted upwards, back out of sleep, or somewhere between sleep and wake. She was in the hallway of the apartment building, and the drunk man's face was before her again, clear as anything. More clear than he'd been in real life. The pinched brown eyes, the thin nose listing slightly to the right side. The smell of unidentifiable liquor.

*That's some serious stuff, lady, breaking apart families.*

She heard his voice in a way she hadn't since the incident. Exact. Precise. As if his words had been in a little box in her memory, one that she had sealed off, but was now wide open.

*I agreed to do it but I shouldn't have. You're twisted. You had me in a bad position. I should have fought harder.*

In the cave, she reached down to grab the little hand so the child wouldn't slip on the rocks. Boston but not Boston. Boston but Leo. Little blond Leo, with his delicate upturned nose, his perfect rosebud lips. Girl's lips.

"She's getting big!"

"Hello Leonara!"

"Leonara," Cintra said. "Be careful. The rocks are slippery."

They were looking for quartz. The trails were glittery, silvery. Like the trails in the bog, the silvery quartz monzonite of the bog.

"Is Callie your mother?" she asked Leonara.

But Leonara wasn't there anymore. It was Leo.

*I'm being held.*

She was shivering, clutching the blanket around her neck, and groggily got up to turn off the AC. The room was dark and chilly.

She got back into bed, and before she drifted off again, she thought, "They've kidnapped her. The man in the hallway did it for them. They dressed her up like a boy and called her Leo. Leonara was trying to tell me, with the sign on the door."

## Chapter Fourteen

*A*ll through the long subway ride to work, it seemed like an incoherent jumble of a nightmare. Caused by her loneliness. Caused by Pedro's anguish over his uncertain future. Caused by her own uncertain future. Caused by too much chocolate ice cream?

That's what the dream had been, a bizarre commingling of nightmare and reality. Too many crime stories. Too much going on in her life with the bog thriller, with Elliot and Boston, and with her disorder. Even the stock market. It was tanking.

There could be other explanations for the blonde girl in the photo. Another relative of Callie's. Maybe even a friend's child or the child of a fan. (No, not with those comments. "She's getting big!")

But it weighed on her. Weighed and weighed. The man in the hallway. *Breaking apart families.* The sound behind the wall, a child crying for her mother? The message on the door. *I'm being held.* The boy in the picture, a gun at his head.

At work, she went to the list of Callie's Facebook friends. She searched for "June" and a profile came up of a "June Garcia," but the profile photo was of a flower. She clicked into the profile and searched its public photos. Most were of bucolic scenes, countryscapes. Cintra had never been to Cold Springs, but imagined the place was filled with trees and flowers.

It wasn't until Cintra got to the very last photo that she realized this was definitely the June she knew, for the last photo was of a couple, and the woman was June. She was in a chunky, white, turtleneck sweater with red and blue ribbons stitched on the front. The couple was far away from the camera, but the man with June looked like Niko. Only he had a full head of glorious black hair.

She couldn't tell the date of the photo, but June didn't look much younger, though a bit thinner, even under the bulky sweater. Niko was in a dark coat, and the colorful explosions of red and orange leaves behind them said the picture had been taken some autumn. Since it was autumn now, the photo was at least a year old.

Niko's mass of wavy black locks struck her. She wouldn't have thought a man with such impressive tresses would have shaved them all. She knew from Elliot's fretting about his thinning hair that men were generally pretty vain about having hair. Could this photo be old enough that he'd started to lose his hair from then to now?

She did a search for "Niko" and "Nikolas" in June's friends' list but nothing came up.

"Any luck with our mom killer?" asked Mavis, coming up from behind her, grinning, as if checking in about Ettie Brightman was more of a joke. Cintra smoothly clicked back to her content management system, embarrassed at having been caught snooping around Facebook pages.

She was momentarily at a loss. Would it be a lie to say no, no luck? But if she told Mavis she'd seen a woman who had green eyes like Ettie's, but who had a different name and who'd said she was from Colorado, she'd seem crazy. Or worse, like she was trying to curry favor with her editor. She went with somewhere in the middle.

"Not yet," she said, grinning back. "Keeping my eyes peeled though."

Mavis touched her on the shoulder and left.

Cintra went back to the story she was writing, slowly pecking out words as her mind rewound to the get-together at The Tea Spot, with June and Poppy. The vehemence in June's voice when she talked about her ex-boyfriend, the one who'd taken up so many of her fertile years with no real intention of marrying her and having a family. How she'd said to Poppy, "How much more of your ovaries' lifespan do you want to waste on this future faker?" about Joseph. She remembered what June had said to her in the hallway about Poppy.

*If she truly wants children, she should do whatever is necessary to make that happen.*

Had June wanted a child so badly that she would… steal one? Steal her sister's child?

And Niko went along with it? Or helped? Or even planned it?

*What about you, Cintra? Would you have figured out a serial killer was next door?* The edge in Niko's tone, the flicker of a dare in his sly-dark eyes.

Was Callie *really* in Europe?

That would be simple enough to verify. Pedro could write to Callie, ask her something mundane about the apartment. But how would they know if whoever answered was really Callie?

## Chapter Fifteen

On Saturday, Cintra went with Elliot and Boston to play Frisbee in Prospect Park, but despite the grueling humidity of the day before, it was cold and unbearably windy. The Frisbee kept flailing off course like a boat in a storm. (Callie on the boat. Where had the boat been?)

After about forty minutes, they gave up and went to get pizza at the old school Italian place on Prospect Park Southwest. With week-long gaps between seeing her son, Cintra felt like he was growing up rapidly. He used to come up to her shoulders, but was now nearing eye level. He also looked like he'd gained five pounds in the past week alone. She could clearly see the impending man-shape of him, a shape that hadn't been as obvious when she saw him every day.

She didn't want her son to grow up this fast, without her there to guide and shape his journey to manhood. There were so many things she wanted her son to know and feel in his heart, things she felt were her responsibility, not Elliot's, to embed there. This meant she had to be on her absolute best behavior; no telling Elliot her far-out speculations about the neighbors and the child in their apartment.

When she separated from them at the subway entrance, she hugged Boston tight, and it was like her soul was ripped out of her body as he murmured, "I miss you. Keep working on it, Mom." She didn't know if she could take four and a half more months of this.

Elliot's birthday was coming up on October 28. They'd always done a combined birthday-Halloween celebration. She supposed they wouldn't be spending the holiday together this year, for the first time since, what, junior year of college? Would she even get to see Boston in his costume (he was deciding between a zombie and Chewbacca)? Soon, it would be December. She *would* spend Christmas with her son, and that was that. Her understanding and desire to please Elliot went only so far.

But what would happen at the end of this trial separation? How would her husband know for certain that she'd changed? She'd have to talk him into seeing Dr. Grace with her.

At the apartment, the sounds of Pedro doing vocal exercises floated from his bedroom. He was gearing up for another audition. What a heartbreaking profession he had chosen, but she supposed one didn't have a choice in creative callings. They were more like curses.

Knowing she wouldn't get much work done with his *ahhh ahhh*s and *wahh wahh*s vibrating through the apartment, she sat with her legs stretched out on the living room couch, reading another book on compulsive lying, different from the book Dr. Grace had recommended, which she'd finished. This one wasn't as good as the first.

When Pedro was done, he came into the living room, and they made small talk. His audition was for a musical version of *Scarface*. He was up for the lead role of Tony Montana.

"*Scarface*," Cinta smirked. "Geez, what's next? *Jaws*?"

"You're gonna need a bigger boooaaat!" Pedro crooned. Grabbing her socked feet, he shook them and plopped next to her. "How'd it go with the hubby?"

"It was good. Only I feel like I can't tell him anything. Anything could be perceived as a lie, even though it's not."

"That's true." He made a grave face. "You're in kind of a bind. Until you get his trust back."

She put her Kindle on her lap and squirmed. Knowing she should keep her mouth shut. Unable to do so. "Can I tell you something, Ped? I looked up Callie on Facebook. I saw a picture of her with a young girl, and I'm pretty sure the girl's name is Leonara."

"Aaaand?" he asked, in an ominous movie-narrator voice.

"The boy next door is named Leo. He looks a lot like the girl in the photo. Here's the thing, a couple of weeks ago, I saw Leo put up some papers on their door. They spelled out, 'I'm being held' and there was a drawing of boy with a gun to his head. I also found an elastic band with a butterfly on it in Callie's desk. Like something a little girl would wear. Add in that weirdo in the hallway who told me I'm breaking apart families, and who might think I'm Callie, and who knows Callie owns the apartment next door…"

"Where you going with this?"

She shrugged and squeezed her arms tight around her chest. "What if… Leo is kidnapped? And he's really a little girl named Leonara."

Pedro stared at her for a few moments, as if he couldn't believe his eyes or ears. Then he shook his head and looked at the floor. "Cintra…"

"Pedro, if I can't tell you this stuff, then I've got no one!"

He patted her feet again, and shook his head more, slowly. Whatever was going to come out of his mouth wouldn't be good. "I'm going to be honest. You're starting to scare me. First, June is hanging out with a murderer, now she's a kidnapper? Are you testing me with this stuff or something?"

Hot tingles ran along her spine, and she shrugged out of her jogging sweater. "I'm not testing you. But this is a lot of bizarre stuff."

"So Callie has a daughter. Maybe? Maybe the little girl is in Europe with her."

"If Callie is only gone temporarily, and she has a daughter, there would be more girl stuff around the apartment. She wouldn't take *everything* with her."

"Her stuff is probably in storage. That's usually what happens when people sublet. Or maybe the little girl *died*, Cin. And why would June, if she kidnapped a kid, let the kid draw something to alert you to this supposed kidnapping?"

"When Leo put up the papers, she was distracted, talking to me about Poppy. I don't think she saw them until she got home, because then they were gone. What kid draws something like that?"

"I don't know much about kids," Pedro said, plucking at his lower lip. "But don't they draw all kinds of weird stuff? And why would June kidnap her sister's kid, knowing we're in her sister's apartment? Wouldn't that be kind of stupid?"

"I pay the rent to you by PayPal. Who do you pay?"

"Callie. I send it to her by PayPal too."

"When was the last time you heard from her?"

His mouth dropped open, he thrust an open palm at her. "Wait, woah. What are you saying? June off'd her sister? *Girl...* you're reading too many crime stories. Why would she invite us over there for dinner? So we can see the kidnapped kid?" He laughed. "Sorry, I don't mean to make light of this."

"It's not like I've figured it all out. But what better way to commit a crime? Do it in plain sight. Act like everything is normal."

He got up and began pacing a little. "I'm no sleuth. I'm an entertainer. But why... why would they dress her up like a boy?" he asked, looking at her quizzically, getting into the role of sleuth.

She slung her feet over the couch and to the floor. "Maybe to disguise her for a while, in case relatives reported her missing."

"And these relatives wouldn't, like, come look here?" He swung his arms, taking in the living room.

Cintra propped her elbows on her knees, contemplating the kink in her theory. "Like I said, I haven't figured it all out. But you should have heard June at this brunch spot, when I was there with Poppy. Going on about an ex who took up years of her life, might have ruined her chances of having kids. She even said if Poppy wants a child, then she should do whatever it takes to make sure that happens." She put a finger to her mouth, a buried memory resurfacing. "On the sidewalk, she said something about wanting to snatch up a toddler who was in a stroller. The look in her eyes was downright creepy."

Pedro crossed his arms, stared down at her as if he was humoring her. "And what does the former neighbor in the hallway have to do with everything?"

"Maybe he wasn't the former neighbor. Maybe he's a guy that June and Niko hired to get Leonara. He brought the girl to 3D, later had regrets, got drunk, and broke into the building. I remember him saying he shouldn't have gone along with it. And that I—or the person he thought I was—was twisted."

"And why would he confront you instead of June and Niko?"

"He was waiting in the upstairs stairwell. He saw me instead of them, and thought I was Callie, who he'd figured out owned 3D. He doesn't know Callie is Leo's mother."

"I think what this is…" Pedro said, walking slowly towards her, and squatting down. "I really think… one, you're missing Boston. Your mothering mind is going haywire. And two, didn't you say your agent told you to make your book about a missing kid? A kidnapped kid?"

Cintra sighed heavily. So that's where he was going. She hadn't even considered that angle.

"Maybe your mind is… " He twirled one finger around his forehead. "Making up scenarios. That would be a good one for your book. Though you might want to tone it down, kind of complicated."

"But what if it's true? And we ignore it? Remember at dinner how June was talking about crimes right under everyone's noses? How in cities, no one pays attention to their neighbors."

"*You* brought that up, Cin."

"No, no. *She* brought it up. And Niko looked very uncomfortable, as if he knew something, and she was saying too much. Shortly after they moved in, I heard what sounded like crying coming from their apartment. At first, I thought it was a dog whimpering, or them having sex, or even June crying. But now I think it was Leo crying."

"I hate to break this to you," Pedro said, "but kids cry."

Cintra barely heard him, her mind was too preoccupied trying to recollect everything she'd noticed that had led to her dream, and this startling conclusion of a kidnapping right next door.

"I saw a picture of Niko on Facebook. He used to have this really thick black hair. Why would he shave that? Maybe to disguise himself?"

"He probably started going bald and wanted to get ahead of the situation." He laughed again. "I really can't believe all of this."

Looking into Pedro's eyes, Cintra could feel her

desperation contorting her face. She must look half-crazed. "Can't you send a message to Callie? Ask her something. Tell her the dishwasher isn't working. Anything. To see if you get a response."

"Fine. I'll send her a message." He stood up, looking down at her as if she was someone he didn't quite know after all. "Here's the thing, though. I love you, and you're one of my best friends, maybe my *best* friend. But I can't let you make me lose this apartment. You can't go around accusing the sister of the woman who owns it of being a kidnapper and sister killer." He looked sterner than she'd ever seen him look. "Are we clear on that?"

"We're clear. I would never do that. I'm asking one tiny favor. Send a message to Callie, ask her something mundane. See if you get a reply."

"Okay," he said. "But I'm serious. If you do something to mess this up for me, it will not be good. And I can't be your backup for Elliot, making him think you've changed, when in reality you've gone off the rails."

He walked out of the room, to his bedroom, and shut the door.

Cintra lay her head back on the couch cushion. Her breath was quickly rising and falling. Right then she knew she couldn't do one thing she'd been considering —sending a Facebook message to the woman who'd written "Hello Leonara" on the photo of Callie and the girl, and asking her what she knew about the little girl. If that got back to Callie, and to then Pedro, he would be furious.

It had been a dream. A bizarre, bad dream. Why could she invent these dramatic situations in real life, but had such a hard time making them up for fiction, which might, instead of alienating the people she loved, actually make her money?

She crimped her knees up to her stomach. If Callie responded to Pedro's message, she would forget this whole thing. Kids draw weird stuff. A drunk dude said nonsensical things to her in the hallway. If he was the former neighbor, he probably meant that getting kicked out of the apartment could break apart his family (perhaps he considered his girlfriend to be family, or maybe they'd been married). Perhaps getting kicked out of 3D meant the couple would have to move back in with their parents, separately. Saying he should have fought harder meant he should have taken Callie to court for not renewing the lease. Or, like June said, he was "not all there" in the head.

And Liz. She was a woman from Colorado who happened to have green eyes similar to those of Ettie. Leonara—simply another relative or, God forbid like Pedro had said, maybe Callie's daughter who had died. That was it, and Cintra would get on with her life, get on with the business of earning back Elliot's trust and keeping her fantastical imagination to the page.

## Chapter Sixteen

———————————

*C*intra told Dr. Grace the whole story. How, over the past few days, she'd managed to convince herself, through a series of small and disconnected events, that the couple next door had kidnapped a little girl and were passing her off as a boy. She watched Dr. Grace's face for a reaction, but it was impressively blank.

Then the denouement, proof that her theory was wrong: Pedro had showed her Callie's Facebook reply, which he'd received in the morning. Callie had finished singing at several private events in Athens, and was about to tour various islands. Wifi could be spotty, and she wouldn't always be available over the Internet. But yes, things were fine, thank you for asking, and she hoped the apartment was suiting his needs.

Cintra kneaded the end of one sleeve of her cardigan. "It definitely seemed to be her replying," she said, explaining that Callie had mentioned the name of a theater producer both she and Pedro knew and that she'd "put in a good word" for him. "She also warned him not to use the microwave and coffee machine at the same time, that it will trip the electrical wires. And we'd already figured that out." She laughed, hoping Dr. Grace would laugh with her. "I think Pedro thinks I'm losing it."

Dr. Grace sat completely still, saying nothing for several seconds, tapping her pen against her notepad. It was strange to think she was only twenty-nine. She had the bearing of a woman in her forties or even fifties. "Now you don't think this child was kidnapped?" Dr. Grace finally asked, somberly. "Because I would be required to report a crime in progress."

The breath caught in Cintra's throat. She hadn't even considered that. "No, no!" She held up both hands. "You can't do that. Elliot knows cops. It would get back to him in no time that this came through me. If I'm wrong, he'd think I was lying, and he'd divorce me and—"

"I need to make sure, Cintra. Kidnapping a child is an extremely serious offense."

"I'm sorry. I—I thought I had patient confidentiality. I wouldn't have told you all this otherwise." She couldn't believe Dr. Grace might betray her confidence. Then she remembered that Dr. Grace had no way of reporting anything, as she didn't even know Cintra's address. Cintra paid the doctor by check after each session, and the checks only had her name on them. There would be no record of her new address anywhere online. Even so, she figured she better pile on to make sure Dr. Grace knew she did not believe this outrageous theory anymore.

"I only told you all of this to get a sense of what happened here. Why I took these small things and weaved them together into something so… *out there*. I might be a writer, but I've never become convinced my fiction was real before."

Dr. Grace nodded slowly, seriously. "You've been under a lot of stress. Stress can have a wide array of negative effects. How many lies have you told since you've started seeing me, can you estimate?"

"None. Well, a small one to my neighbor about my book, but that was in August. I've been really, really good."

"Then I suspect what might be happening is that your brain, accustomed to lying and now being told it can't, has replaced lying to the ones you love with lying to *you*."

Cintra gave a breathy, nervous laugh. "You talk about my brain like it's not part of me."

Behind her retro glasses, Dr. Grace blinked her big brown eyes. "In some ways, it's not. Think about the drug addict who desperately wants to quit drugs, but the brain has other ideas, and rebels. The brain tells the addict, one more hit, one more drink, one more snort, whatever it may be. Think of the addict who, when trying to quit heroin, turns to drinking. Or when trying to quit drinking, turns to marijuana. Or trying to quit marijuana, turns to gambling."

"So I…"

"You turned to the neighbors."

Cintra hadn't considered any of this. But it all made so much sense. She had replaced one addiction, lying, with another form of making things up. She told Dr. Grace about her thriller-in-progress, and how she needed to add a kidnapped kid into it.

"There's another incentive," Dr. Grace said, folding her hands over her notepad.

Cintra looked over the doctor's head to the framed print of the woman on the trolley, at her porcelain white face, her black hair swept into a forties chignon, at the sepia-tinted red trolley car. Then her gaze roved to the other print, its sapphire water and the palm tree's thick, curved trunk and green fronds. She wondered if she should buy Dr. Grace another print.

"The good news is I didn't tell Elliot anything. Thank *God*. He'd probably try to have me committed."

"Oh, the bar is rather high for that," Dr. Grace reassured her. "But it's probably wise that you find another person you can confide in for the time being."

"I feel like I've run out of people," Cintra said, tucking some hair behind her ear. "Pedro is totally fed up with me. My other friend, Poppy, thinks my neighbor is the greatest, so there's no going to her."

"There's me. That's what I get paid for."

"I'm done with all of it," Cintra said. "I feel like I woke up from a fever or a dream or a hallucination."

"Cintra." Dr. Grace leaned forward confidentially. "I called a colleague who has more experience with pseudologia fantastica than I do. He said there have been studies, involving brain scans, showing that people who compulsively lie can have physiological abnormalities. Have you had any head trauma?"

"Head trauma?" Cintra asked, alarmed.

"You mentioned a couple of times that you felt the lying had worsened a few years ago, after your book came out. I'm wondering if anything happened. Car accident? Fall?"

"Car accident, definitely not. Fall? No, I'd remember something like that. I— "

Then it came back to her. In a flash.

Having to get a last minute babysitter. Going to the hospital. The MRI. Elliot at the hospital, his face a stretched mask of worry.

"There's one thing," she said, quietly. "I was at the gym, and there was a machine..." She made a motion with her arms, trying to simulate the machine. "With pulldown cords so you can exercise your arms. And flat weights. I pulled a little metal pin out of the flats to bring it up so the weight be lighter. That made the metal handle bar on one of the pulleys crash down, and it fell onto my head. I haven't thought about that in ages." She stared at Dr. Grace, eyes wide. "It hurt for a bit, but I continued to work out, thinking nothing of it. But later that night, I got a bad headache. Elliot was worried I had a concussion, so we went to the emergency room. They did an MRI to check for bleeding, but didn't find anything. They told me to keep ice on it, take Tylenol, and gave me a printout of symptoms to watch for in case of concussion. But I felt better."

"Um hmmm," Dr. Grace said, scratching out notes on her yellow notepad. "This was around the time the book came out?"

"Yes, because a concern of mine was that I had a podcast interview the next day, and wanted to keep it. I wasn't sure if I would be able to. But I did. Do you think this all has something to do with my lying?"

"Could be," Dr. Grace said, noncommittally. "The studies on compulsive lying and brain trauma are rather new."

Cintra was overwhelmed. On the one hand, there was something to blame for her lying—besides her mother. On the other hand, if she had some kind of permanent brain damage that had intensified her lying, how could she ever stop?

"Does this mean I'll be like this forever?" she said hoarsely, eyeing the tissue box.

"Not necessarily," Dr. Grace said. "The brain is malleable. It can be retrained. But you're going to have to work hard to retrain it."

Cintra nodded vigorously. She'd train the bastard, all right. Train it like for a brain marathon.

"I'll ask my colleague for more reading recommendations. I'll email them to you," Dr. Grace said. "Since you already had an MRI, and you've been functioning normally since the incident, it doesn't sound there is any physiological emergency. But I definitely advise that if you start entertaining other ideas you feel are out of the norm, you don't take any action you might regret."

"Of course not," Cintra said.

"If you find yourself getting a little— *dramatic* in your thinking, slow it down. Take a bubble bath. Get a massage. Drink some herbal tea. Do you meditate?"

"No. I've thought about it, but— " She clamped her teeth. "Sorry, I've never thought about it. I think that was a lie."

Dr. Grace grinned. "A small one. Most of us tell insignificant lies occasionally, but you need to be vigilant about them in a way most of us don't, so you can learn to feel comfortable with the truth. Thank you for correcting yourself. You might want to start meditating. You can find meditations online. I do them myself. They're helpful and calming."

Yes, meditation. That's what she needed to do.

She also needed to email her agent. There was no way she was going to write about a kidnapped child. In fact, she would pitch the idea of a romantic comedy.

## Chapter Seventeen

*E*lliot had been unreachable all day. Cintra had called him twice, on her lunch break, and when she'd left the office. She'd also emailed him. No responses.

But his job at the Department of Corrections could get mind-bogglingly busy. In the past, if she couldn't reach him, she would let it go, unless it was an emergency. But she felt possessed. She wanted to see him after work.

Elliot commuted by car to Queens (a commute he complained about endlessly), and Cintra took the subway into Midtown. She had usually been the one to pick up Boston from school and walk him home. For the past few years, he'd been old enough to do that for himself, especially as his school was only five short blocks from their building.

On the subway ride home, she decided she would go straight to their apartment. She wouldn't let herself inside, that would be disregarding Elliot's boundaries.

But looking at the time on her phone, she thought she might be able to catch him as he parked in the building's outdoor lot. She wanted to tell him what Dr. Grace had said about her potential head trauma and how it had—maybe?—contributed to her lying.

She had debated it. If any damage to her brain had caused her lying to intensify, then Elliot might think she would never change. On the other hand, it would excuse so much. Not *excuse*, that was the wrong word. She wasn't excusing herself. But maybe it would help him understand what she'd been up against, and how she hadn't done anything on purpose to tear apart their family. And it was perfect because Elliot could call Dr. Grace to verify everything. Perhaps he'd even want to join their sessions now.

She didn't want to bother him—*bother* her own husband—but she would tell him the news and be on her way. They could discuss later about how much to tell Boston.

OUT OF THE SUBWAY STOP, she walked down the tree-lined street to her old apartment building. The tail end of autumn was coming on strong and fast. Some warmth lingered, but there was a snappy under-chill in the air, and the brownish-orange leaves littering the side-walk smelled burnt and earthy. Her feet were buoyant as she rounded the corner to her old building. This new information could be a new start for her and Elliot.

There was a laugh, a woman's tinkling laugh, then a

man's voice. The voice and the laugh struck her like lightning. Her body processed this stimuli before her brain did. She came to a sudden stop, her ears pricked, each hair on her neck going straight up.

"Aw, that's sweet of you," she heard. It was Elliot's voice, the voice he'd used on her in the early days of their courtship, soft and playful.

The laugh again, female. As a woman, Cintra understood the laugh. It was the breathy *ha ha* of flirtation. "And don't forget it," the woman said, pretending to punch his arm.

They were walking down the sidewalk in front of her, their backs to her, having come out of her old apartment building. Their sides bumped into each other, teasingly. She knew the back of Elliot's head, every line and curve of his body, but she didn't recognize his brown leather bomber jacket, it must be new. Elliot in leather?! The woman she didn't know, but Cintra could tell from the bouncy walk, from the glossy flip of brown hair, and the hip design of the high-heeled brown boots, that the woman was younger than Cintra.

Her heart sped up rapidly, and she followed them, waiting for Elliot to sense her and turn around. But he was completely engaged with the woman. Cintra could feel the energy between them, could tell by the deliberate bumping of their sides that they were… what?

Involved somehow. Romantically.

No, no, it couldn't be. Not Elliot! Not him! Not her love, her husband, the father of her child.

And then she saw it. He casually turned to the woman, slipped his hand to the back of her hair, and swished a handful of tendrils out of the underlining of her coat. An intimate gesture, too intimate for just friends.

A frighteningly strong impulse to rush upon them and hammer her fists at their heads engulfed her. Should she do it? She had every right to!

But then another impulse overwhelmed that one, an impulse to throw up. Bile surged upwards from her gut. She backtracked several feet, entered the parking area where Elliot kept his car, and ran until she was blocked by the side of the building. Thrusting her knees on the gravel, she gagged as whitish foam drizzled from her throat.

*  *  *

BACK AT APARTMENT 3C, she was trembling so badly she had trouble getting her key in the lock. Pedro wasn't in the living room, thank God, because she could not deal with seeing anyone.

She shook off her coat, absently dropping it to the floor of her bedroom, and went to her computer. Her hands were too shaky to type so she went to her bathroom and ran them under warm water for a few minutes. Back at her computer, she pulled up the Department of Corrections website and went to the bios of the executives and office staff.

She had a pretty good idea where the woman with Elliot had come from. Elliot never took a day off work unless he was almost dead, so he wouldn't have taken a day off for a woman, any woman. It was possible the woman had met him at the building when he came home from work, but it seemed too early for a date. That meant the woman had most likely driven back with him from Queens, and that meant she was a coworker.

Kneading her hands as if she had a ball of clay in them, Cintra scanned the site's staff bios for any new faces. At one time or another, she'd met most of Elliot's coworkers, and the woman hadn't looked like any of them.

Cintra finally came to a picture of a smiling woman named Brittany Barstow, a DOC investigator. She looked to be in her early twenties, with soft brown eyes, wavy brown hair to the cusp of her shoulders, and dimples. The glossy wave of her chestnut hair made Cintra positive this was the same woman she'd seen on the sidewalk.

More searching around brought up the woman's LinkedIn profile. She'd graduated from NYU three years ago, and had started working at the Department of Corrections in June.

Months this had been going on. Months!

No wonder Elliot had been acting so distant before she'd moved out. So edgy and grumpy. No wonder he hadn't wanted to have sex. And him telling her it was all about her lying, when it was all about *his* lying!

The night she had told Boston that terrible thing, that horrible thing that got her banished from the family. She'd been tense and feeling rejected over Elliot's distance, his grumpiness, his lack of sex drive.

Stress at work, he'd said. Not feeling well, he'd said.

Then she'd blurted it out to Boston, not even believing it had come from her mouth. Blurted it out as if it was a dumb joke she could take back. "He's not your father, you know."

Boston had said something. No, he hadn't. Yes, he had.

"Who isn't?"

"Elliot. Dad. He's not really your father."

*He's not your father.*

She didn't remember what Boston had looked like when she said this, had blocked it from her mind. Had blocked it all from her mind, until later that night, when Elliot shut the door of the bedroom, and snapped the top of her laptop down, almost shearing off her fingertips.

"You bitch," he'd said, his face completely red. "You've gone too far this time."

Then she'd remembered what she'd said. Had she really said it? It was like someone else had said it. Boston had been talking about something banal, something she could hardly recall, and it had slipped out of a mouth that wasn't her mouth. But slipped out with such *authority*.

She'd dissolved into tears. Begged and pleaded with him. Of course he's yours, look at him. He looks exactly like you! He *sounds* like you! He *walks* like you!

Please forgive me, please, please. I have a problem.

"You're goddamn right you do," he'd said, his face all red and rage.

This woman, Brittany.

What had all of this been the last few months?

Cintra, in therapy. Cintra, groveling to be let back into the family. Cintra, on her absolute best behavior, thinking of nothing but getting back to Elliot and their son. And him, doing this thing behind her back. Probably not wanting to repair their marriage at all.

No wonder he wouldn't go to therapy with her. No wonder he'd been so unaffected at the bar when she'd told him about the strange man in the hallway. No wonder he'd acted like he thought she was lying again— he didn't *want* to believe she'd changed. Then he could stay with this Brittany woman.

She clenched her fists, got up, and collapsed on the bed, curling up tight. She waited for the gush of tears, but they didn't come.

SHE GOT in a good workout at the gym, almost two hours. Sparring with boxing gloves for forty minutes with another woman. Punching, punching, and after that, flailing at the punching bag for another twenty minutes until her arms felt like they would drain out of their sockets. Running on the treadmill for half an hour.

Outside, sweaty, hot and buzzing with adrenaline, she bummed a cigarette off a man who'd walked by smoking. She sucked smoke into her lungs and got light-headed, it had been so long since she'd smoked. The spicy smell of Indian food wafted down on her from the overhead vent of a takeout place. She walked until she found a brownstone stoop, sat, and called Boston.

"Hey, Mom," he said.

"Hey, bunny bear. Is your father home?"

"Yeah, he just got here. Want to talk to him?"

"Is anyone with him?"

"Uhh. No."

"Okay, I'm coming over. Don't tell him, I want to surprise him."

She took a car service to the building, and let herself in, and up the elevator, and into the apartment. Boston was writing at the kitchen table, and Elliot was across from him, looking at his laptop. Her husband's eyes went big when he saw her.

"Boss, I need to speak with your father alone," she said in the *I'm-your-mother* tone she hadn't used since before that terrible night. "Go to your room."

Boston grabbed several workbooks in front of him and scampered off. Elliot sat looking as if a burglar had burst in. Even Dumps, whom she spied lounging on his favorite chair, popped his head up at her presence.

"What's going on?" Elliot asked.

She pointed to their bedroom and stalked into it. It was a bit of a mess. She stared at the rumpled bed, wondering if Brittany had been in it.

"Close the door," she said when Elliot came in, his mouth slack.

"I saw you today with your coworker," she said, her body betraying her by starting to tremble. "Since when do you wear leather?"

"What?" he asked, running his hand through his hair. It was thinning even more than she'd realized.

"I saw you. You're screwing her, aren't you?"

"Cin, what the—?"

136

"Don't you dare try to tell me this is me lying, or all in my head. I *saw* you."

"She's my *coworker*," he blew out of his mouth. "Her car is on the fritz and she lives in the neighborhood, so we've been commuting together. We had a drink; it's been a hellish week. Are you spying on me?"

"Spying!" she spat. "I'd come here to tell you some news. Then I saw that!" She tried to lower her voice to a *don't-want-Boston-to-hear-we're-arguing* voice but wasn't quite managing it. Their disagreements were usually pretty civil; they rarely raised voices with each other. But despite their various marital glitches over the years— most of it due to her lies—she'd never confronted with him with anything this enormous.

Elliot walked to the bed and plopped down. "I'm not sleeping with her," he said, but the way he said it made Cintra think he wanted to.

"I saw the way you walked together, and how you touched her hair. *Something* is going on. I'm not stupid."

He held up one hand, defeatedly. "I'm not sleeping with her."

"Did you kiss her?"

"No!" He hung his head. "Cin, I'm gonna be honest. I've wondered what it would be like to… be with someone I can trust. Who doesn't lie."

"Don't put this on *me*!" she yelled, far above the voice that wouldn't reach Boston.

"Nothing has happened between us, absolutely nothing. But yeah, yeah…" He looked back up, a little defiant. "I'll admit I've thought about it. I don't know about us anymore. You tell my son I'm not his father? What the hell else are you going to tell him when I'm not around?"

"I get it, Elliot. But if the goal is to heal the family, I don't see how flitting around with another woman is going do that. And let me tell you something. You were acting distant for weeks before that. Something was going on with this girl, and I felt it. You denied anything was wrong and tried to put everything on me. I snapped with that stupid lie."

"Now it's my fault?"

"No, it isn't. But you didn't tell me the truth either. So *you're* not so special!"

"Okay, okay," he said, his posture softening, the defiance receding. "I have a little crush, I guess. It's been so easy to talk to someone who, when she says something, my mind doesn't go in twenty directions wondering if what she's saying is truth or fiction. She has no interest in me."

"With that laugh?" Cintra did a bitter impression of the woman's flirtatious laugh.

"Whatever," he said. "Are we done with this?"

She jabbed her finger in his direction. "If this is your game plan, kicking me out so you can get custody of Boston, it's not going to work. I'll fight you. You're not taking my son from me so you can shack up with a twenty-something and tell him it was all my fault."

"All right, you've said enough," he growled. She could tell that she'd pushed him into that angry place he didn't go often.

"And she has an overbite and is plain," Cintra said. "*Basic*, as the kids would say."

She opened the door and stalked out of the room. "Boss!" she called, opening his bedroom door. "Want to go get pizza with your mom?"

He looked at his watch. "It's nine-thirty."

"Ice cream?"

"Yeah!"

## Chapter Eighteen

The ice cream shop on Park Slope's Fifth Avenue was still open, even at almost ten in the middle of October. They ordered, a double chocolate cone for Boston, a small cup of vanilla toffee swirl for Cintra. It was colder than it had been when she'd come out of the gym, so she dug her workout hoodie from her tote bag, slipped it on, and put her arm around Boston.

"You cold?" she asked. His height was such that she could barely tuck him into her underarm.

"Nah," he said. He had his hoodie wide open, with only a t-shirt underneath. He'd always run hot; she'd long since stopped demanding he put on heavy coats or hats. But she still liked to ask him if he was cold, just in case.

They walked up the street, the shops lining it shutting down, but there was still a decent amount of people strolling about. At a small park adjacent to the middle school, there was a lone bench that faced the sidewalk. They sat and ate their ice cream.

"What was that with Dad?" he asked, dully.

"We had an argument," she said. Ironically, despite her various lies over the years, she'd always tried to be honest with Boston about the things that really mattered. Except that one horrible night.

"You know that none of this is your fault, right?" she asked, wiping a smear of brown ice cream off the corner of his mouth with her napkin. A couple of times, Boston had expressed that he thought everything was his fault.

"Yes, I know," he sighed. "You said that before."

"You did right asking your Dad about what I'd said to you. You know it's not true, right? You're his mini-me."

"Yeah," he said. "You said that before too. Plenty of times. But Mom, it really made me mad when you said that. Dad too. And you've told *me* not to lie, but you said that about Dad. It's so hard to know anything for sure. I just wish you'd be normal."

Her nose tingled harshly and her bottom lip quivered. She couldn't cry, she had to remain parental. A deep, steadying inhale of night air tamped down the nasal tingles.

"I know, baby. And that's why I'm so careful what I say now. I want you to know that I will never, ever lie to you again. It was sort of good what happened, because I'm figuring out why I say things that aren't true. I'm actually proud of myself because I haven't told one lie since that night. Well, one tiny one to my neighbor about my book. But that was it. I'm like an alcoholic hitting rock bottom."

"That's awesome, Mom," he said, switching his cone to one hand and patting her back with the other.

"Yesterday I found out… Remember the time Dad and I went to the hospital a few years ago? Dad thought I might have a concussion after that metal bar at the gym fell on my head."

"Mmmm… That night you and Dad had the big fight?" he asked.

"No, not that night. The time I came home from the gym. A few years ago."

"Yeahhhh… " he said, seeming uncertain.

"Well, it's possible that did something to my brain. The lying got worse."

"Really?" He looked at her, his blue-gray eyes reflecting shock in the streetlights. But perhaps it wasn't shock, perhaps he thought she was lying. No matter how much she reassured him, the only way for her to prove herself was to continue to tell the truth.

"It can't be proven. But there have been studies," she said.

He stared at his toes for a few moments. "Can I write about it for English class?" he asked.

"Well, no. Not right now. Someday."

He looked disappointed. "Cause I never know what to write."

"You're great at English. You're great at math. What else is going on with you these days?"

"Look," he said, bringing up his phone, which was tucked in his pocket. "Do you know this band?" He showed her the phone. On it was a picture of five young men with soulful eyes, gelled hair, and black, boxy-shoul-dered linen jackets, the look of the eighties. Above their faces was the title: "Don't You Forget About Me - Simple Minds."

"Sure, I know them. Is that what you're listening to?"

"Yeah, and Led Zeppelin and Janis Joplin, and uh… " He scrolled through his phone. "Depeche Mode."

"Impressively eclectic mix," she said. "Eclectic meaning varied." Where did he learn all of that music? Elliot tended towards jazz and weird European techno. Cintra's choices leaned towards the fluffiest chart toppers with "you go, girl" vibes.

"Kenny knows all the good stuff," Boston said.

Ah, Kenny. His best friend of the past couple of years. "I'm glad he's schooling you right in the music department," Cintra said.

"He is." He stared off wistfully off into the haze of a streetlight. "I like him."

Something jumped in Cintra's gut. An intuition. "Like him? Like as in… a friend, or… " she trailed off, awkwardly.

He shrugged. "I'm not sure."

"Maybe more than a friend?" she ventured, cautiously.

She and Boston had not discussed sex, or romantic feelings towards either girls or boys. Well, he knew how babies were made, but that was about it. The times she'd tried to bring up whether he was developing feelings towards the opposite sex, he'd reacted so uncomfortably that she'd stopped.

"I don't know," he said. "Sometimes I think maybe more than a friend, but then I'm not sure. I think about him a lot, though."

Hmmm, was her son coming out to her? And Elliot wasn't here to help with this?

"If that's the way you feel, that's fine," she said, her voice a couple of octaves above its usual. "If it's not, that's fine too. You have plenty of time to figure that out. I'm sorry I haven't been around to talk more. You can call me anytime. Day, night, whenever. You can tell me anything. Dad feels the same."

She'd been so consumed with her own issues that she'd completely overlooked the fact that her son was going through puberty and must have issues too. In the past week, she'd thought more about the neighbors' kid than her own. Guilt gnawed at her.

"It's okay," he said, diving back into his ice cream, which was starting to trickle down his cone. She handed him more napkins. "I just want you to come home soon. I don't like you not being there. I keep thinking I hear you, but it's not you. It's no one."

"I believe I will be home soon," she said, rubbing his back. "Dad and I still have things to work out, but I'm hopeful."

"Dad has punished you enough, I think," he said, judge-like.

"It's not about punishment, Boss. It's about healing."

"Nah. It's like Dad sent you to your room, but the

room is across town. *Let me out, let me out,*" he croaked, scratching at an invisible door.

She had to laugh. Her son may have his father's looks, but the droll humor was his own.

This was what everything was about, Boston. He wanted both his mother and father under the same roof. If she could give it to him, she would. And she wanted her son to see that while marriage could be difficult, two people who were committed to each other could work through their problems.

"He's not with that girl," Boston said. "She came up to the apartment so Dad could get a coat, but I've never seen her before."

Damn, kids were good. Of course, he must have heard all of the argument, or enough of it. "Don't you worry about that, bunny bear," she said.

"Ugh, don't call me that." He rolled his eyes as she fluffed his hair, which was now almost to his shoulders.

"Let's get you home to bed. And tell Kenny I approve of the music choices."

AT THE APARTMENT, Pedro was doing lunges in the living room. "Were you at an audition today?" she asked, setting down her tote on the nearest chair.

"Yep. Killed it," he said, a little breathless. "But it's a long shot. So many talented people. So *young*."

"I think my son came out to me tonight."

Pedro stopped lunging, and looked at her. Then he

walked over with his hand held high. "High five, mama!"

She slapped his hand. "Oh, and my husband is in the process of falling for his twenty-something coworker. *Brittany*." She spat the name out.

"Damn, girl. Do you need a drink?" He started for the kitchen. "It's been quite a day for you."

"All the more reasons I need to get back home. My son and husband need me. I want to make sure I'm there in case Boston wants to talk more."

"Drink," Pedro said, handing her a glass of red wine.

She tipped her glass to his own. "No more crazy stuff with the neighbors," she said. "I need to focus on my own life."

"Right on," Pedro said.

## Chapter Nineteen

*N*iko was at the door, staring at her with those round, dark, impenetrable eyes.

"Niko, hi," Cintra said, surprised. She rubbed at her eyes, which were dry from staring at her computer non-stop since late morning. It was now sometime in the late afternoon. She'd been desperately trying to come up with story ideas she could run by Alexis to get out of having to write about a kidnapped kid, reading anything that might spark an idea for an alternative—romantic stories, feel-good stories, even crime stories as long as they didn't involve a kid.

"June is sick," Niko said, not bothering to return her greeting.

"Oh, that's… is she okay?"

"She aches all over and is shivering. Maybe the flu."

"Has she been to the doctor?"

"She doesn't feel well enough to go outside."

Cintra was at a loss. Was he expecting her to do something about this? Hopefully, he wasn't going to ask her to come to their apartment, where she might pick up June's bug. She found herself sneaking a long peek his hairline, wondering whether he'd shaved his head because he was starting to go bald, as Pedro had suggested, and quickly looked back to his dark eyes.

"I'm sorry. Is there anything I can do for her?"

"I have to do laundry." His voice was eerily devoid of fluctuations. Cintra again had the odd feeling that Niko had a social disorder of some kind; he seemed lost without June to prop him up. "Leo's clothes are all dirty, he has nothing," he continued. "But I went to the laundry room, and the card machine… I can't figure it out."

"Yeah, sometimes it's a little wonky."

"If you could show me how to use it, that would be great."

"Sure, do you have money?"

He took a twenty-dollar bill out of his pocket and showed it to her. She grabbed the keys that were hanging on a hook right by the door and closed the door after her. There was a basket of clothes sitting by the elevator, the same "natural" brand of detergent that June used placed on top. Niko stood looking at the elevator, as if it would magically open on its own. Cintra pressed the down button.

On the short ride, he still said nothing, staring at the lighted floors as they descended. They walked down the long hall, which took two turns, past rows of grime-coated gas meters making ominous tick-tick sounds, as if they might blow up any minute, and past a half-gutted, abandoned stove that Cintra wondered if anyone would ever collect.

One of the light fixtures above their heads was flickering in its death throes, casting the hallway in an eerie grayish glow.

"How long has she been sick?" Cintra asked, trying to penetrate the thick air of silence between them.

"Since last night."

In the laundry room, she showed him how to work the laundry card machine. "Put the money here, and here's the message asking if you want a card, and here's the lever to decide how much money to put on," she said as he watched. "And here we go."

The card slid out of the machine. She handed it to him. "Thanks," he said, staring at her intensely, as if he was trying to read her mind, burrow into the depths of her thoughts. She had the sudden urge to get away from him.

"Well, tell June I hope she feels better," she said, walking away.

"I will. Wait a second, where does this card go?"

Cintra turned and gave a fake little laugh. "Here, I'll show you." Could he be this useless with laundry? This was a man who had figured out an espresso machine.

She walked with him to a machine and showed him where to put in the card, hoping her discomfort wasn't obvious, for she had the awkward suspicion that he was inventing reasons to spend time with her.

"Ah, that's easy," he said. "Sorry to be a pain. I'm distracted hoping June is okay. Anything that affects her, affects me."

At that, Cintra was embarrassed about her suspicion. He was only worried about his wife. A dejected lump formed in her chest as she realized how long it had been since she'd felt that kind of concern from Elliot.

Niko plopped the laundry basket on the big folding table and began to take clothes out of it. She saw the brownish-green cargo pants that she'd seen before, ones that belonged to Leo.

"It's flu season," said Cintra. "Does June need anything? I could go out and get medicine. Or soup."

"Could you? Maybe flu meds? I'm sorry, I don't want to leave her for too long."

"That's sweet of you," she said, not adding that it was also impractical.

He reached inside of a pocket of the cargo pants, brought out a piece of paper folded up into a pocket-sized square, and began unfolding it. "Gotta always check Leo's pockets," he said.

"I know the feeling. My kid leaves all kinds of stuff in them. Gum, pens, twice I found his phone."

Niko unfolded the piece of paper and set it down on the folding table. On the paper, the word UP was written with purple Magic Marker in large block letters, written in the same child-scrawl Cintra had seen previously, Leo's scrawl. The bottom of the letters faced towards her, so she could read it clearly. Niko's knuckle brushed the edge of the paper as he put the cargo pants back on the pile with his other hand.

"Yep," he said. "Kids will be kids, won't they?"

"Especially boys," she said, watching him.

"I suppose so. Not that I know anything about girls."

He folded the paper back up, rather carefully, walked to the garbage can and dropped it inside. "Thanks for your help," he said, turning and staring at her so pointedly that she averted her eyes to her thumbnail, and began twisting off a tiny stub of skin.

"What kind of flu meds should I get for June?"

"I'm sure she'd be happy with anything."

"Will do." She waved at him and walked out of the laundry room. At the elevator, she watched the light that indicated it was dropping floors, willing it to hurry.

The light stopped on the fourth floor, stayed there for a minute. Someone on that floor must have the door held. She glanced over her shoulder, back down the dimly lighted hallway, which had cobwebs dribbling around pipes running the length of the ceiling, and fluorescent light fixtures pooled with the silhouettes of dead flies. Her thumb hit the elevator button again, hard, as if that could speed it up.

"Come on," she said behind her teeth, thumb still pushing. There was no other way to get upstairs except to head back to the laundry and take a right towards the basement door, which would send her past where Niko was.

His last laser stare had reignited her discomfort. She didn't want to be alone with him again, not here in this dim, isolated basement. Maybe it was wrong to feel that way, but she couldn't help it, and she wasn't going to ignore her instinct to get away from him any longer.

The elevator light began its descent. Four, three, two...

"Still here?" asked Niko, causing her to startle.

Her laugh was breathless and airy, her smile too wide. "Unfortunately."

"Fortunately for me. Here it comes."

The elevator groaned deeply as it came level to the floor. Cintra opened the outer door, holding out her arm to let him go in first, but he said, "After you." Inside, she was closer to the Art Deco button panel, and him closer to the door, hemming her in. She pushed the button for three.

"Kids," he said, jamming his free hand inside the front pocket of his black sweatpants, eyeing her with that look that was too intense for chit-chat. "They go through a lot of laundry."

"They do."

"The crazy things we'll do to get a kid, eh?"

"I'm sorry?"

He took his hand from his pocket and wiped his forehead, which had a glowing sheen in the light of the elevator. "What am I saying? *For*. The things we do *for* a kid." He blew air out of his mouth. "I haven't slept much."

The doors opened and he didn't move. She inched forward, ready to push by him if necessary. "It's us," she said, smiling without teeth.

"So it is. I really need a nap." He stepped out and Cintra moved swiftly past him, towards her door.

"I'll bring the meds soon and leave it on your mat," she called. "Sorry, but I can't afford to get sick, so I better not go inside. See ya!"

"Thanks, Cintra. See ya."

Behind her door, she gave an exaggerated shiver and bolted the lock.

*The crazy things we'll do to get a kid.* Had she really heard that? Yes, she'd heard it. He'd even corrected himself.

In her bedroom, she turned off the light, searched for "ten minute meditation" on YouTube. On a pillow on the floor, her breath rose in and out to the gentle drone of the female narrator.

"Relax and close your eyes. Bring your attention to your breath. Become aware of how you're feeling in this moment… "

*The crazy things we'll do…*

"Feel the breath in your toes, moving up to your stomach… "

*… to get a kid.*

## Chapter Twenty

The next day, Cintra met Poppy for lunch in Midtown. While both of them worked near Herald Square, they'd rarely meet for lunch, given that both were normally busy and eating at their desks.

So it was unexpected when, in the morning, Poppy sent an email asking if Cintra could meet at Jooni's, a cheap but good Thai diner. Cintra said yes. True Crime TV owed her a long lunch, given all of the times she'd worked straight through them.

At Jooni's, they put in their orders. Cintra wasn't sure if Poppy had asked to meet because she wanted to talk about something specific or just because. But once the white wines and appetizers arrived, it became apparent that Poppy wanted to unload.

"It's Joseph," she said.

Cintra hadn't thought much about Joseph since the engagement party, but it came back to her, how unsociable and out of sorts he'd acted that night. She hoped he hadn't called things off.

"Things are… unusual," Poppy said.

"In what way?"

Poppy took a steadying long sip of wine and leaned back against the intricately detailed red pillows lining the booth. "This is going to sound crazy, but he's buying me flowers, he cooks, he cleans, he wants sex every couple of nights."

Cintra grinned. "Sounds terrible," she said.

"But he does it with such… I can't explain it. It's like he's not there. He seems empty. Like he's doing it for a role he's playing. It doesn't feel *organic*."

"Hm," Cintra said, her glass up to her mouth. She wondered whether she should tell Poppy about his behavior the night of the party, but it had probably been nothing. Engagement jitters. Poppy was on edge already. Cintra didn't want to perturb her more with vague observations. "Are you sure you're not feeling this way because you're not used to him doing nice stuff?"

A waiter came over to clear their appetizer plates. Poppy pointed at her half-filled wine glass, indicating she wanted another. "I can do my job drunk," she told Cintra.

Cintra couldn't, so she baby-sipped at her wine, not intending to finish it. "Have you asked him about everything? Maybe he's stressed at work."

"I have, but he says nothing is wrong. He says I should be happy that he's doing all of the things I'd always wanted him to do."

"He's got a point there."

"You know how Joseph is—he doesn't listen. Not really. I'll tell him something and half an hour later, he's telling me the same thing, acting like he came up with it. Or he asks me a question I already answered."

"You've mentioned that a few thousand times."

"Well, now he listens. He sits there with this expression on like he's Oprah." She tilted her head, nodding oozy-eyed at Cintra. "*I hear you, Pops. I'm listening.*"

Cintra had to laugh. Poppy must be exaggerating. "Is he on drugs?" she asked. Then, realizing her friend was serious, "I don't see how this is a problem."

Poppy leaned back, exasperated. "He doesn't laugh anymore. One of the things I used to love about him was his sense of humor, but it's like it's disappeared. In his place is some sensitive guy, but he's an *empty* sensitive guy."

"Maybe he needs to see a doctor," Cintra said, and when Poppy looked distressed, she added, "It's probably nothing physical, but it couldn't hurt to check. Or he could have depression."

"True, but I hope, well, I hope this isn't what marriage with him is going to be like. I put pressure on him to get married, but I didn't want it like this. I'd rather have the jolly old commitment-phobic Joseph back and not be engaged."

"Poppy, you said you want kids and you're thirty-five. You've got to start trying soon if you want them. Besides, sounds like he'll be a great father if he's cooking and cleaning and acting like Oprah."

Their lunches came and they turned to work topics for a while. Cintra didn't want to tell Poppy about her husband being romantically intrigued in his coworker, as it seemed like her friend was dealing with enough. When

Poppy asked how things were going in Cintra's marriage, rather than lie and say they were good, she shrugged and tried to change the topic. But Poppy didn't want to discuss the movie everyone else was talking about. So Cintra switched back to Joseph.

"When's the wedding?"

"We're planning a beach ceremony in St. Thomas. My friend is a planner at the Marriott down there and offered us a good deal. It would be too much to ask a bunch of people to come, so it'll be us, and our parents and family." She put her hand on Cintra's. "I hope you don't mind. We're going to have a big reception when we get back."

"Of course not. So June's not going?" she asked, teasingly.

"No, but that reminds me. Do you mind if I tell her your birthday?"

Cintra almost choked on her wine. "What for?"

"She called and wanted to do your astrology chart, and Elliot's. I guess I shouldn't be telling you this because she wanted it to be a surprise for you. She left a message but I haven't returned it because I'm terrible with birthdays and don't remember yours. Sometime in April?"

"May."

"Elliot's birthday I have no clue."

"Listen," Cintra said, putting down her wine glass. "I'd rather you not give June that information."

"Oh?"

"It's not like I know her very well. That's kind of

private. I mean, with my name and birthdate, she could figure out pretty much anything about me."

"I hadn't thought of that. But I thought charts might help, like they helped me and Joseph."

"Did they really?" Cintra asked, raising a brow. "You're complaining he's giving you too much sex and too many flowers and listening too hard."

"Ha!" Poppy said, but her eyes didn't light up. "Okay, I'll tell her I don't know your birthdays, which is true."

Walking back through the throng of people towards her office building, Cintra had an uneasy feeling that kept expanding until it edged into anger. She couldn't shake the idea that June was trying to snoop around, trying to find out things about her.

June only had her first name. She wouldn't be able to find out much with only that. Then she remembered how June had once brought Cintra's mail, when it had been left in the wrong mailbox. June must have seen her last name, Coutinho. She'd kept her family name after her marriage to Elliot. But with that information, June could find out Elliot's name, as well as Boston's. Could she find out about Cintra's compulsive lying?

She stopped in the middle of the sidewalk, causing a guy in a suit behind her to bump into her. "Watch it!" he sniped, angling around her.

What was June's game?

Feeling her thoughts running away from her, Cintra took a few deep breaths. Even if June managed to find out about her disorder, so what? It was personal and embarrassing, but there wasn't much she could do with knowing about it. And why would she want to?

In the office, Mavis made an appearance as Cintra was tucking her tote under her desk with her foot. "Haven't seen Ettie yet," she offered, hoping to disarm her editor before she was confronted with her longish lunch.

"Yes, I figured," Mavis said. "But we're starting deep research for the special and I'd love for you to be on the team."

"Great," Cintra said, excited to do something besides blog.

"These high profile killers usually have fandoms. Hell, there are people who make fan videos about Ted Bundy. Pretty sick. Ettie's not on Ted level, but my gut tells me she's got fans out there. Must be lots of suburban housewives who'd love to blow away their exes and the younger replacement wives. We want to have one on the special, as a balance. A sympathetic voice for Ettie."

"You think someone will go on TV and cheer on what she did?"

Mavis looked at her as if she was an imbecile. "Most people will do anything to be on TV. Besides, twenty-five years ago, Ettie was a feminist folk hero. Plenty of women were on TV cheering on what she did. Some could be hanging around online."

"I don't doubt it. When do you need this?"

"Let me know what you find in a week or so," Mavis said. She smiled her efficient smile and sauntered away.

As Cintra pulled up a search engine, she remembered the overpowering anger that had flooded through her when she saw Elliot walking with Brittany, and how only a rebellious stomach stopped her from pouncing on them. As she started her research on Ettie, she had even more insight into what Ettie must have been feeling as she blasted bullets into her ex-husband and his new wife.

* * *

Although Mavis was right, and Cintra expected her to be right, she was still shocked at what she found. An Ettie Brightman Fan Club. Actually calling itself "fan club." On the forums section, the fans were delighted with Ettie's parole. Horror mingled with fascination as Cintra read the comments.

"Thank GOD Ettie is finally free! Does anyone know where she is? If she needs a place to stay, I've got a bedroom. You took one for the team, Ettie!" This from Kara009.

"A lot of women have been through what Ettie has. We didn't do what she did, but we wanted to. Those bullets were well deserved. They BEGGED to be blown away," wrote Lulu05.

"I hope Monty is rotted in hell, the bastard," wrote BetteDavisEyes. "Stay Strong, Ettie. Show No Remorse."

"She had to show remorse," said Lulu05. "Or they wouldn't have given her parole."

"As long as she doesn't mean it," countered Bette-DavisEyes, with a string of laughing emojis.

"The best day of my life was the day my beautiful

son was born but a close second is the day Ettie was RELEASED. She won!" wrote JoBethLovesDogs.

"My husband did the same thing to me. Left me with the kids, two, three, and four, and went on vacation with his nineteen-year-old slut, got the child support down to almost zero. I nearly snapped like Ettie. All the respect in the world for this fearless female," wrote Ettie-IsABadass.

"Me too, Badass. I didn't kill them but I wanted to. Ettie had the balls," said Lulu05. "Why should emotional torture be legal?"

"Exactly, Lulu. Why is cheating, lying, gaslighting, and emotional abuse legal and we as a society are supposed to turn away from it and accept it??!! Why can't they be punished too?" wrote JoBeth.

A few of the posters claimed to have spent time with Ettie in the women's correctional facility.

"She was always warm and positive," wrote Mabel77. "Like a mother hen to us. Everyone loved her, even the guards. She bought us things when we couldn't afford it ourselves."

Ettie's address at the prison was prominently posted in several areas. Many of the women claimed to have sent her money and care packages over the years. Others, for some reason, had sent her thank you cards.

In the months up to her parole hearing, the fan club had organized a letter writing campaign. Tips on what to say and what not to say to the parole board were posted. ("Letter should be positive, short, and not personal. Focus on the age factor, how she has been a model inmate, and can help others with volunteering when she's released.")

Cintra estimated that ninety-five percent of the fans were women, though there were a few vocal supporters claiming to be men who admired Ettie for being "a good wife and mother." A couple of them sounded in love with Ettie. "My special lady will soon know what it's like to be treated like the princess she is by a gentleman who understands her true heart and loyal soul," a poster named ShiningKnight rather scarily promised.

"Anyone know where she is?" asked EttieIsMyShero. "I really want to meet My Queen and tell her how important she is in my life."

No one seemed to know, or weren't telling.

One commenter, EttieWON, was worried that Ettie wouldn't be able to survive on the outside. But another frequent commenter, EttieNeedstobeFREE, calmed her. "I know for a fact that she has support on the outside. Ettie will live the rest of her life in comfort and peace."

Another commenter intimated that Ettie's children were not part of that support. "It's so sad that her children don't understand," she wrote. Several commenters agreed.

Surveying the fan site commentary, Cintra realized Mavis would have her pick of fans to invite on the special. Perhaps an entire room full of women—a *large* room. Far from these women being leftovers from when the case was big in the early nineties, many of them seemed young. Ettie remained a folk hero for a new generation of pissed off women.

Cintra decided to focus on the most vociferous of

the bunch, and the ones who'd said they'd been in prison with Ettie. Hopefully, she'd also snag EttieAdmin, who often waded into the scene with a tone of authority, correcting misinformation and quelling disputes. She appeared to be the president of this unusual fan club.

Cintra was still on the fence as to whether the Liz she'd met at Poppy's party was Ettie Brightman. Pedro was right, green eyes and a similar name didn't make a double murderer. Nor did a strange kid drawing and a drunk man make a kidnapping. Stress and her lying disorder must be behind her unsettled state of mind, as Dr. Grace had said.

But it couldn't hurt to stay alert to any other unusual happenings in apartment 3D.

## Chapter Twenty-One

"*C*intra!"

Cintra turned towards the voice on the opposite side of the street. June was waving at her; then she watched the street for cars, and crossed. She was wearing a sage double-breasted pea coat, her blonde hair gathered in a wind-strewn bun, her plump cheeks flushed with the crisp air. Cintra, in thick black yoga leggings and a teal blue polyester jogging jacket, was taking her favorite way back from the gym, through the historic district of Ditmas Park.

Though plopped in the midst of the city, the area was known for its free-standing family homes in Victorian, Queen Anne, and Colonial styles. With its lacquered lawns, towering oaks, broad porches, and bird-tweeting, pastoral quiet, the area had a Southern feel while retaining the vibrant multiculturalism of mid-Brooklyn.

She waited as June crossed to her.

"Thanks for the flu meds the other day," June said.

"No problem. You feeling better?"

"Oh yes. Twenty-four-hour thing. But I was out of it for awhile."

"Good thing you had Niko."

"Yes," June smiled. "He was very devoted. He said you helped him with the laundry machine."

Cintra nodded and pushed her hands deep into her sweater pockets. She suddenly had an intense chill, even heated from her workout. She wondered if she was going to have to walk all the way home with June.

"I'm so glad I ran into you, because there's something I want to tell you," June said. "Do you have a few minutes to see a house? It's right up here."

Cintra didn't really want to hang out with June, but she loved the sprawling homes in Ditmas Park and was curious. Besides, it would give her a chance to ask June about this birthdate thing. Cintra agreed and the two took a turn onto one of the loveliest streets in the area, Rugby Road.

Halloween was seventeen days away, and the homes lining the street were bursting with bright orange pumpkins, white cobwebs spun around iron banisters, white-sheeted ghosts and skeletons, open coffins, gravestones, devils and goblins. A few of the homes had so much paraphernalia they were nearly invisible behind yards tangled with flying monsters, hanging bodies, and plasticized depictions of torture and mayhem.

The weather was back to being almost mild, fine for a light coat, though a few hardy souls jogged around in shorts and t-shirts.

"This is the one." June led Cintra up a porch with

fluted white columns, past a two-seater swing bench, and to the door of a slate blue Victorian with periwinkle and white detailing. "Want to go inside?" she asked, dangling a keychain.

The house was bare, the slightly-warped blond oak floors swept shiny. A staircase lay right ahead of them, two large rooms winged out on either side.

"You have to see this," said June.

Cintra followed her through an empty living area with windows all along on one side and a red brick wood-burning fireplace. At the back was a glass-walled room that jutted out into a yard that was fiery with orange and red leaved trees. The beveled windows of the enclosure were rounded at the top.

"A greenroom," said June. "Isn't it precious?"

"It certainly is. Love the yard too."

June led her through the dining room, her low pumps echoing along the wood, and into a fairly large country kitchen with a deep ceramic sink with Italianate ceramic backsplash, brass faucets and hardware, distressed white cabinets along three walls, and a thick-slatted wooden kitchen island. "They're original," said June of the cabinets. "And look," she said, opening a door to a deep closet space with shelves, "A butler's pantry. The house was built in 1913. It needs a bit of work, the appliances could stand an upgrade, but nothing too terrible that I'm aware of."

"It's darling," said Cintra. She couldn't ever remember having used the word "darling" before.

Through the dining room that looked out over a small side yard and onto the house next door, they went up the creaky stairs. The master bedroom was level with the yard's trees, the windows overlooking explosive reds, yellows, and oranges. "Imagine waking up to that view," June said.

"I'd never get out of bed," Cintra laughed.

They went into the bathroom, with its ceramic claw-foot tub, and the second bedroom, about half the size of the master, with another en suite bathroom. Greenery peeked in all the windows and every room had the same woodsy, country look. Cintra felt at peace in the house.

"There's another bedroom downstairs, and a small room down the hallway," June said. "Could be a guest room or office. And there's a large attic, could be a studio or playroom area. There's plumbing up there for a bathroom, though one hasn't been built yet. And a garage."

A garage!

June clasped her hands together and turned. "So. What would you think about living in a place like this?"

"I'd love it, of course. But there's no sense imagining things like that. I haven't got a million bucks lying around."

"What if I told you this house was in foreclosure," June said. "And hasn't been listed anywhere yet?"

"Foreclosure?" Cintra dragged her eyes away from the hypnotic view of the outdoors.

"Yes, the house will be up at auction. Likely it will get about half of what it's worth on the open market."

"I'm not sure what you're saying. You think I should bid?" She laughed. "I don't have even half of a million."

"I'll tell you what," June said. "I have some inside information. The bank is eager to have houses off its books. A lot of them aren't selling and the taxes pile up, and the shareholders aren't happy. I'm pretty sure the bank would take a lowball offer as long as it wasn't insulting low. Somewhere in the range of maybe three-hundred-fifty thousand? You couldn't even get a one-bedroom for that in our building."

Cintra's breath was having a hard time budging out of her chest. Visions of living in a house like this—with Elliot and Boston—crowded her mind. A house like this could be a fresh start for them; the lingering dark memories of their apartment left behind.

Her and Elliot cooking breakfast in the country kitchen. Growing vegetables and herbs in the greenroom. Summer on the porch, drinking iced tea while swinging on the two-seater bench. It would be the kind of life Cintra had always secretly yearned for, except that she couldn't bear the thought of leaving the city. The nearby Q line offered a direct path to Brighton Beach in the summer. Boston wouldn't even have to switch schools...

Coming out of her reverie, she said, "June, I appreciate the heads-up, but there's no way I could do something like this now. My husband and I... you know we're in limbo. I've got this part-time blogging gig that wouldn't impress any mortgage lender in the world."

June's sunless hand was on her shoulder. "I understand. Think about it. We may be able to go lower. I could make it so your bid is the only one that looks viable."

"You could do that?"

June winked. "I have my ways."

Cintra looked out a window, onto a blazing red and orange tree. Had she really been so down on June, to the point where she'd believed June had kidnapped a child and killed her own sister? Where she thought that June, who'd only wanted to do her astrology chart, was trying to dig up information on her?

Cintra's cheeks flushed warm. She was thankful she hadn't confronted June about the astrology charts. What had this woman ever done to her that she would continually entertain such deranged thoughts about her? "If you don't mind my asking, why don't you and Niko take the house?"

"Oh, I couldn't do that." June smiled, sweetly. "Agents can't snap up their foreclosure listings. Besides, Niko and I will probably move next year. He's not having much luck with the job market here, and we miss having open space. This is open space for here, but not what we're accustomed to. Heck, we're thinking Utah or Arizona, the middle of nowhere. I wouldn't mind living 'off the grid' for a while."

Cintra sighed longingly, taking another look around the master bedroom. Her heart swelled with visions of Boston and his friends playing outside; of her and Elliot waking up to that glorious tree-burst view; of a spitting fire warming their toes on a winter night. They could get one of those cat enclosures and put it in the yard for Dumps. Wouldn't he love that? When it was nice out, he could sit looking at squirrels and—

June touched her arm again. "We've got some time.

The listing won't be for a few weeks. Things might change between you and Elliot by then."

"Maybe," Cintra said, doubtfully. "I really appreciate this. I'll definitely think about it." She'd buy it herself if she had the money, but she wouldn't be able to afford the taxes on her own.

June looked at her watch. "I have to go show a place. But I wanted you to see this."

After they parted on the street, Cintra resolved to change. No more unkind thoughts about June. She walked dreamily down the quaint street, spinning homey fantasies in the Victorian, imagining having Christmas there: the dense, heady sap smell of a pine tree; apple cider in front of the snapping and crackling fireplace. She leapt to scenarios that, realistically, wouldn't happen: Elliot splitting wood logs; Boston camping in the backyard; a hen house for fresh eggs.

At some point, it occurred to her that June had mentioned Elliot by name. And yet Cintra had never used his name in conversation with her, not that she remembered.

## Chapter Twenty-Two

*C*intra had just come into work when her phone rang and she saw Elliot's number. Her heart dashed into her throat, imagining bad news about Boston.

"Elliot?" she said, dangling her coat halfway to her chair.

"Cin, you need to tell me what is going on," he said, catching her off guard with his angry tone. "Did you really call Brittany and threaten her?"

Cintra thought her husband was playing a strange joke on her, that's how bizarre his question sounded. "I —" She draped her coat over the chair, plugged one finger in her ear, and walked towards the kitchen, trying to get to a more private area. "Threaten? What are you talking about?"

"This isn't funny. She's my colleague. I told you nothing is going on between us. I don't appreciate this."

Standing at the large island that separated the kitchen area from a row of desks by the windows, Cintra watched people linger around the coffee maker and put their lunches in the oversized stainless steel refrigerator. Morning was the worst time to try to get privacy in the kitchen, but the bathroom wouldn't be any better. Half a dozen women would be inside applying makeup and doing their hair.

"I have no idea what you're going on about," she said.

"Someone called Brittany and told her to stay away from me or she'd live to regret it. She's very upset."

"Why in the hell do you think it's me?" she asked, tone rising.

A colleague glanced sidelong at her, and she pivoted out of the kitchen area, towards the bank of floor-to-ceiling windows overlooking high rises.

"Who else would do that?" he asked.

"I don't know! It wasn't me. You can check my phone."

"She said it came from a caller marked 'private.' She only picked up because the number had called a few times."

"And it was a woman who did this? I'm so confused, I—"

"She said the voice was like a recorder. An inhuman voice."

"Sounds like a bunch of bullshit," she scoffed, looking behind her to make sure no one was near.

"She wouldn't make this up. Unlike some people, she's not a liar."

"All right, Elliot," she snapped. "I don't have time for this. I'm at work."

"Don't do crap like this, Cin. This is my place of business. I have to work with these people."

"I don't need these ridiculous accusations," she hissed, pressing her mouth flat to the phone. "I didn't call her. And why would I do that knowing she would cry about it to you, and you'd blame me?"

"I don't know. But if you did do it, stop. And if you didn't, you have some messed up friends."

"It doesn't occur to you she's making this up to get attention from you?"

"No, it doesn't."

He hung up.

"Unbe*liev*able!" she burst out, as a coworker walked by and eyed her warily.

* * *

"GIRL, this is all too *Melrose Place* for me," drawled Pedro, stretching out one long leg on the kitchen island, his impromptu ballet barre.

"Right? Like I would call her? It's not high school." Cintra had come in the door not ten minutes earlier and told Pedro the whole story.

"Do you think she's lying?" he asked, dipping his long form over his perfectly straight leg, every blunt-cut muscle visible through tight leggings.

"Or *he* is. Maybe he doesn't want to get back together." She sniffed, nose tingling, a warning sign that tears weren't far off. "This could be his excuse to break it off permanently. Why doesn't he say he duh-doesn't…"

"Aw, Cin," said Pedro, swinging his leg off the island,

and coming over to rub her shoulders. "Could anyone else have done it? Poppy?"

"She doesn't even *know* about this woman. And making a threatening phone call? Using a voice disguising thing? That's not Poppy. Besides, she has her own problems."

Pedro led her to the couch and sat her down. "What's up with her?"

"Joseph acting strange. I don't think he really wants to marry her, but doesn't want to tell her. Only, he's doing it in the most bizarre way—cooking, cleaning, bringing her flowers."

"Flowers? Uh-oh. That's guilt over something."

"Pedro," she sniffed, using the bottom of his shirt to dab at the corner of one tear-submerged eye, "I feel like the minute I stopped lying, everyone else started."

"That's some irony shit right there," he said.

"Or I'm only noticing it now. Oh!" She stopped sniffing. "June showed me this gorgeous house in Ditmas Park. Said she could get it for me cheap. Still not cheap enough if it's going to be only me paying for it, but wasn't that nice of her?"

"So you don't think she's a kidnapper sister-killer anymore?" he snorted.

"I was wrong about her, Ped. Even Niko. I went down to the laundry room with him a few days ago, and he made me nervous the way he stared at me so intensely. But it was because he was tired and distracted since June was sick. I even went out to get her meds because he didn't want to leave her." Her nose stopped tingling, the threat of tears retreated.

"You know what? We should do dinner with them again."

"Might as well," he said.

She let go of his shirt and slouched low on the couch. "I wish I could get another book deal, then I could afford the down payment on the house. Even if I sold all my stock, it wouldn't be enough. I'd lose money with the market in a panic."

"Wish I could help," he sighed. "I'm broke too. Even broker since *Scarface* didn't happen."

"Didn't get it? Oh, I'm sorry."

"Yeah." He ran his fingers over his dreadlocks, got up, and went back to stretching on the island.

"You don't seem very upset," she said.

He shrugged, leaning over one leg. "I'm getting used to it."

Definitely not the melodramatic reaction she was accustomed to when he didn't get a role, but perhaps he was making peace with aging out of Broadway.

"Anyway," she said, standing and patting the side of one eye with a knuckle. "If this is Elliot's new game, then fine. I didn't make a phone call to his crush, and if he's going to believe her over me, maybe we have no future after all."

She walked into her bedroom and shut the door.

SHE THOUGHT about calling Elliot to hash out his accusation. But it was a bad idea. She clung to hope the family would be reunited. Every time she spoke to

Boston, he made it clear he wanted her home. And she wanted to be home. Back with her son and cat. Even back with her husband, if he'd let her.

Although Elliot was severely testing her patience these days, her therapy was showing her for the first time how she'd severely tested *his* patience with her lies. Up until that terrible night, the lies were always small, weird lies. Dumb things, like that she'd had lunch at a place where she hadn't had it; like that she was writing a great book when she wasn't.

She'd tell him untrue things to add drama to anecdotes, to prop up some sense of her not being interesting enough. She couldn't say she'd talked to an old friend. She'd have to say she talked to an old friend who'd become an astronaut. How could she have not seen that her lies, far from being inconsequential, had eroded his trust completely?

Now, she didn't want to tell him about the metal bar crashing on her head and how that might have contributed to her disorder. That would be *drama*. She hoped Boston hadn't told him already. Elliot would probably think she was lying to her son. Calling him to argue about a threatening phone call to Brittany would be drama. If Brittany was the one lying now, he'd figure it out eventually. There was only so much she could control.

An email message slid into the top corner of her monitor. It had caught her unaware, so she didn't see the name. She clicked into the email.

"Hi, I'm the administrator of the Ettie Brightman website. Thank you for your interest in interviewing me, but I'd prefer to keep my relationship with Ettie private. She doesn't want to do any press or attract any attention to herself these days, and I wouldn't want to betray our friendship.

I hope you understand. Good luck with the special. I hope it will be fair to Ettie. She's already served her time and has been through so much!

Best wishes, EttieAdmin."

Cintra looked at the email address. A generic one with EttieAdmin as the name. Well, that was a shame. She wrote back, thanking her and saying she hoped the special would be fair, and to please tell Ettie if she ever felt like talking, to get in touch.

Back to her marriage...

It occurred to her that Elliot would know about voice disguisers; he'd probably heard about them on his job. She plugged "voice disguiser" into a search engine and saw they were everywhere—all kinds of apps and gadgets, some as cheap as ten dollars.

Was Elliot the one who'd called Brittany, hoping to scare her right into his arms? He'd said she had no interest in him. Maybe he hoped a threat would spark it; they could bond over his crazy, possessive wife, Cintra, the liar.

On the floor, she adjusted her pillow, and crossed her legs into the lotus position. The soothing hum of the meditation narrator began. *Listen to your breathing. Feel it in your body. Start in your toes. Ummmmmmmmmmm.*

She stopped umm'ing and opened her eyes. That sound.

It came again from her computer, from the meditation video. *Ummmmmmmmmm.*

That was it! The sound she'd heard from behind her bed wall, at least the second time. Someone in apartment 3D had been meditating. Laughing, she rocked on her lotus-crossed legs. Probably June. (Why had the meditating stopped? Why had Niko said, "The crazy things we'll do to *get* a kid"? He was tired, that's all, tired. An innocent word slip-up.)

There was nothing wrong with June and Niko. It was *Elliot* who was the problem.

# Chapter Twenty-Three

"That was delicious, June," said Cintra, stretching back into a wishbone chair, holding her stomach full of roasted chicken with red wine sauce, garlic mashed potatoes, steamed spinach, and Caesar salad.

"Thank Niko," June said. "He did all the cooking. I only did the salad."

"Thank you, Niko," Cintra said, nodding at him. He nodded back from across the dining table, and she heard Pedro, sounding equally as food-comatose, saying thank you, and she thought of Joseph, who also was a cook —suddenly.

"Does he bring you flowers too?" Cintra asked, smiling at June, who pursed her small, pink bud-mouth.

"Flowers?"

"Sorry," Cintra said, laughing. "I didn't mean a man couldn't be the one who cooks. My husband never did much of it, but then neither did I…" She felt like she was babbling incoherently, and sipped from her wine glass, though there was only a few drops left.

"It was delicious, both of you," said Pedro, raising his also-empty wine glass.

"And *really*, next time, it's on us." Cintra had invited June to dinner when she saw her in the hallway with Leo in the morning. But June had insisted that she and Niko host. They got so little use of their dining set, and they loved entertaining. She'd said Cintra and Pedro would be doing them a favor. Besides, she only had one listing to show that day, and would have most of the afternoon free to prepare. Cintra, happy to have the burden of cooking off her, agreed. She and Pedro brought the wine, three bottles of rich red.

"Would anyone like mousse?" Niko asked. "Strawberry. I confess I didn't make it. June picked it up… where?"

"I found a beautiful dessert place on Church." She snapped her fingers. "Morty's Gourmet?"

Cintra shook her head, she hadn't heard of it. She was too stuffed to eat mousse but didn't feel she could turn it down. Niko disappeared into the kitchen.

"You have a keeper there, June," said Pedro.

June burst out with a short laugh, coughed. "I sure do," she said, and sipped her wine.

Within a few minutes, Niko was back and spreading petite dessert bowls of mousse around the table.

"Why don't you tell Leo he can have dessert when he's ready?" June said to him, and he nodded officiously and walked off. "Once again, Leo only wanted pizza for dinner. Any tips how to stop this, Cintra?"

"My son was always a good eater," she said. "I had him eating sushi as a toddler. He's always liked vegetables too. Nothing I did."

She realized that she'd made a concerted effort not to use Boston's name, though she didn't know why. Pushing aside whatever lingering wariness she had about June, she volunteered, "Boston. That's my son."

"For the city?" asked June.

"Yes, my hus—*Elliot* and I were there when we got pregnant. We're pretty sure that's where it was. We like to think it was."

Cintra had earlier decided that June must have known Elliot's name because she'd heard it from Poppy.

"Honey," June said to Niko as he walked back in and started placing dessert spoons next to everyone's bowls, "if we got pregnant here, we could name the baby Brooklyn, but that name is too popular now, isn't it?"

Niko said nothing as he walked around the table, finished handing out spoons, then sat. Finally, he took a quick glance at June, and said, "Probably too popular. How about Staten for the island."

"Staten? Oh, you're hilarious."

"Or maybe the street we're on," he said.

June pursed her lips and stared at him for a few moments with an even, unnerving stare. An uncomfortable tension rustled the atmosphere. Cintra wondered if these two were cut out for each other.

"Prospect," suggested Cintra, diving in to save Niko from June's deathray stare. "For the park. Considering it's so close."

She expected a few laughs, but there was only

silence. Niko's arm froze with his spoon almost to his mouth. Then he swallowed a spoonful of mousse without any sign of pleasure. June pressed her cloth napkin up to her mouth.

These two really had no senses of humor when it came to baby names. It occurred to Cintra the couple could be having trouble conceiving, and the topic of baby names was a sensitive one. But June had started it.

"If it happens, perhaps go with Nikolas if it's a boy," June said, turning to rub Niko's arm. "Something charmingly old-fashioned about naming a son after his father."

For a moment, Niko looked ill. The combination of wine and mousse must have had a squeamish effect on him. Or could he not want a child with June after all? But then he shook off whatever had overcome him and tapped his spoon on the side of his little bowl.

"There's time to decide that, sweetie," he said. "Names aren't as important as having loving parents."

"So true," June perkily agreed, then asked one in particular, "How's the mousse?"

"Delicious," Pedro said, nodding enthusiastically.

Seeing Niko's big black watch peeking out of his long shirt sleeve, Cintra leaned forward, and pointed. "Is that one of those computer watches?" she asked.

He looked down at the watch. "Yep. You name it, it does it."

"I can't imagine," said Cintra. "Like what?"

"To be honest," he smiled, "I only use it for the time. I got a good deal on one at the computer shop I used to work at, but was still a waste of money. What are you working on?" He gave a long stretch, then his arms went down behind the table.

"Right now, this mousse," she said, taking another spoonful. It was quite rich, but yes, quite delicious. She didn't think she would be able to move around freely after she finished. "I suppose you mean my book."

He shrugged, a sly smile sliding over his handsome face.

"The book isn't going anywhere, I'm afraid." She was astonished how easily the truth about her writer's block came out of her mouth these days. Maybe she *could* learn to be a normal person.

"No one solving the crime?" he asked.

"Not yet. But work is interesting. I'm doing research on a woman—" She stopped, remembering that she had suspected Ettie Brightman was June's friend. Now it seemed comical.

Everyone was staring at her intently, waiting for her to finish.

"A woman named Ettie Brightman. Have you heard of her?"

"Brightman, you say?" asked June.

"Yes, she killed her ex-husband and his new wife twenty-five years ago. Shot them in their home upstate in Belle Cove."

"Belle Cove," said June, looking at Niko. "That's not far from Cold Springs." Then, back at Cintra, her blue-gray eyes reflecting the table's candle flame, two pinpoints of orange where her pupils used to be. "I hadn't heard of this. Is it important?"

"Not important, no. But a lot of women identify

183

with her. You know, the man getting older, taking up with a younger woman and dumping his wife, often with young kids."

"Oh sure," June nodded. "That happens. So, this woman, Brightman, killed her husband?"

"Her ex-husband. They'd had five kids and a very bitter divorce. The husband was a heart surgeon who had judges and lawyers for friends. He gamed the system, and ended up with most of their assets, and the kids too."

"That doesn't seem fair," Niko said, flatly.

"No, and Ettie snapped. Long story short, she was paroled from prison recently. I'm researching her, and found a fan club of hers."

"Fan club?" asked Pedro.

Cintra searched out the wine bottle with her eyes. Would she seem like she drank too much if she poured a little more? Niko, noticing the direction of her eyes, reached over and poured for her.

"Yes, they literally call themselves a fan club. They relate to her, feel bad for her. A lot of them think she shouldn't have been put in prison. That Monty and Paige—that's Ettie's ex and his new wife—deserved what they got."

"Seems a bit harsh," said Pedro.

June touched a bit of soft wax that was dripping down the candle, rubbed it between her fingers, and deposited the tiny ball on the side of her plate. "Murdering your ex because he leaves you. That's—" she shook her head, dazedly, "unconscionable."

Given her reaction, Cintra was doubly embarrassed

that she'd once suspected that Liz, who was only June's late mom's friend, was the infamous double murderer. Her brain sure could conjure up some doozies.

"I'm trying to get a fan to agree to appear on the special True Crime is doing, but so far no one has emailed me back. Except the president of the fan club, and she—I assume it's a she— said she didn't want to betray Ettie's friendship." Sipping her wine, her mind tumbled happily into drunkenness. "Oh. And we think Ettie might be in Brooklyn."

"What?" said Pedro, his hand over his heart in mock fright. "Here? Among us? Maybe we'll see her in the hallway."

If he'd been closer, Cintra would have given him a hard prod to his shin under the table.

"In Brooklyn," said June, eyes wide. "What are the odds."

Cintra scraped her dessert dish clean and put down her spoon. "I can't move," she groaned.

"That's quite something," said Niko. "But I guess there's all kinds walking about. We probably pass a murderer on the street all the time without knowing it."

"Or a future one," said Cintra, trying to loosen the band around her black satin pants.

Niko stood and picked up the emptied dessert dishes. Leo came into the room. Cintra couldn't help but smile at him, such a beautiful little boy. She did wonder what had happened to Leonara, and hoped that the little girl hadn't been Leo's sister who'd died. She hoped the little girl was, for whatever reason, in Europe with Callie while Leo stayed behind. It was none of her business. As June hadn't mentioned a niece, she would stay out of it.

"Where's my mousse?" Leo asked, craning his head towards the table.

"Leo, say hello to company," said June. "You remember Cintra and Pedro?"

"Hi," Leo said, and the three waved at each other. "Can I eat out here?" he asked.

"It's adult time," said June. "You can eat on the desk in your room."

He pouted as Niko came back into the room, handed him his mousse, a spoon, and cloth napkin. Cintra wondered why June didn't let him stay. But perhaps it was for the best, considering their conversation often veered to murderers.

"But I'm bored," he complained.

"Come on, Leonara," said Niko, gently. "I want to hear you've improved your Strike It score."

The second she heard it, Cintra went rigid and she gripped the sides of the chair under the table.

Niko turned, laughed lowly. "That's my little pet name for him when he's being dramatic."

Leo stood holding his mousse, napkin, and spoon, staring straight ahead. Suddenly June was up from the table, her hand on Leo's back, moving him out of the dining room.

Cintra sat with a cold pit in her stomach. The effects of the alcohol had instantly vanished. She wanted to leave, but her bladder was so painfully full she didn't think she would make it out of the apartment in the time it would take to do goodbyes and thank yous.

186

"Can I use your bathroom?" she asked, her voice quavering a fraction.

"Of course." Niko held his arm out. "Do you… ?"

"I remember where it is."

In the bathroom, she stared at herself in the mirror, drew her hand down one cheek. She was flushed, her cheeks bright pink, her teeth tinged light purple from the wine. Her blue eyes glittered in their sockets. She ran her hands under the tap, washed them, found a hand towel hanging on a silver towel bar, and dried them.

Leonara.

Leo was Leonara.

Hunched over the sink, she clutched the sides, as if she might get sick. Leo had to be the little girl in the photo. Where was Callie? Had Callie really answered Pedro's Facebook message?

Realizing she wouldn't be sick, she leaned into her reflection, the effects of the alcohol resurfacing, the world woozy. The sides of the sink felt putty-soft under her palms. "You're going crazy," she whispered.

At the door, the four of them did cheek kisses and goodbyes and thank yous and let's do this agains.

"Have you thought more about the house?" June asked, her hand on Cintra's arm. The touch sent saliva gushing through her mouth and she had to stop herself from shrugging away.

"I think about it all the time. I just don't think it's possible. Not without my husband."

"He'll come around," June said. "I know it."

A thin line of sweat trickled down Cintra's back, and

a swarm of heat rushed her face and neck. "I'm sorry, all," she said. "Not feeling well. I need to go lie down."

"Of course, of course. Niko, could you get Cintra a cool cloth?"

Niko turned straight around and walked off.

"I really need to lie down," Cintra said, as Pedro looked into her eyes with concern, asking, "You okay?"

As she'd done at the last dinner, June stood in front of the door as little popping sounds came from it. This time, the pops seemed to ricochet through Cintra's head.

Niko was back with a damp cloth and put it to her forehead, despite her feeble protests. "I feel better, really," she said. "Thank you, Niko, and June, thank you."

She gave Niko back the cloth and walked into the hallway with Pedro, hearing June call behind her, "Get some rest, Cintra."

* * *

INSIDE THE APARTMENT, Cintra sank onto the couch. Pedro walked to the kitchen, running tap water into a glass.

"Did you hear it?" she asked him. "He called her Leonara."

Pedro didn't respond, gulping water. Then he said, "What?"

"He called her *Leonara*."

"Who?"

"Niko!"

Pedro turned and ran more tap water. "I didn't hear that," he said.

"Well, I did. Just like I told you. Leo is that little girl in Callie's Facebook photo."

"Oh God," he said, leaning against the kitchen counter. "Are we back to the kidnapping thing?"

She pushed to the end of the couch and pointed towards the far wall. "Something is going on over there!"

"Ssh, Cin," he said. "Are you nuts?"

"I'm telling you! I've felt it all along. A mother's intuition. Leo is a little girl, and she wrote 'I'm being held' and put it on the door. And that combination lock? Who has that?"

"Someone worried about a druggie ex-tenant?"

"Someone who wants to keep control of someone. And when I was in the elevator with Niko, he said, 'Crazy the things we do to *get* a kid.' It was a slip-up. Like tonight was a slip-up when he called her Leonara. He said it was his pet name for her—when she's being dramatic. You didn't hear it?"

"Hm. I checked my email at some point, so maybe it was then, but I didn't hear it. And now he's a 'she'? Does that kid look like he's been kidnapped? He's eating mousse and playing video games, happy as a clam."

"She's a *kid*. And if June is really Callie's sister, then Leonara knows her, and wouldn't be frightened."

"And she'd be cool with being dressed up like a boy, being called 'him'?"

"Maybe they've given her a reason."

"Cin," Pedro said, with a disbelieving chuckle. "Didn't your therapist tell you to meditate when you got like this? I suggest you start about now."

She stood up and whisper-shouted, "Something is wrong over there!"

"All right, fine." He brought his cell phone out of his pocket, walked to the living room, and thrust it at her. "If you think that kid is kidnapped, call the cops. Lose this apartment. Lose your husband and son. If you really believe this, isn't that what you should do?"

"Look," she said. "I'm going to show you."

She lurched into her bedroom, grabbed her laptop and brought it into the living room. Pedro was on the couch, shaking his head slightly, staring off into the middle of the room.

She sat next to him and opened her laptop on her knees, went to Facebook and Callie's profile. She found the pictures section and began scrolling. The picture of Callie on the boat. Pictures of her in operas. Pictures of New York landmarks and what appeared to be a couple of vacation photos, a beach, a forest.

"Where is it?" She urgently traced her finger over the pictures. "Where'd it go?"

"Oh, man, Cin," said Pedro, still shaking his head.

"It was here! A picture of Callie on a street, it looked like the city. She was with a little girl. The girl's dress was, um, green. It was definitely a girl. There were comments. 'She's getting big,' and, um, 'Hello Leonara.' It can't be gone."

She kept looking, expecting the picture to appear any moment.

Pedro finished his water and stood up, his phone in his hand. He opened his palm towards her. "Are you calling or not?"

"I—" Her eyes darted over all of the pictures. It was gone, gone. "I don't understand," she said, weakly.

"I'm going to bed," said Pedro, walking away.

"Ped!" she called. "It was here. I swear it."

Pedro was silent for a few moments, looking serious. "That woman just served us the best meal I've had since the last one she gave us. She offered to get you a deal on a freaking *house*. She was right here the night you got confronted by that drunk dude. And this—*this* is your thanks?"

He walked out, shut his door.

Cintra looked through the pictures, though she knew it was hopeless. She slowly closed her laptop, collapsed back onto the couch.

There were no thoughts for a minute, only a drunken, fuzzy blankness. Then she allowed herself to think it. The metal bar crashing onto her head at the gym. Had the impact done something terrible to her brain? Something that not only made her want to lie, but made her see things and hear things? If Pedro hadn't heard Niko say "Leonara," maybe he hadn't?

## Chapter Twenty-Four

*T*he wind cut a blade across Cintra's face. She pulled the zipper on the collar of her jogging sweater stiff under her chin. She should have worn something warmer. Across the street, an empty playground sat behind wire fencing.

If the school worked like Boston's old middle school, the kids would be coming out after lunch, around 12:30 p.m. She hoped she'd be able to recognize Leo from this far away. She also hoped she was remembering the name of Leo's school correctly, almost certain that at the first dinner, June had said he went to The Science Center.

She was peeking over the hood of a bakery delivery truck, but when a man got in it and drove off, she slithered up to a streetlight post. A few signs hung on the post: a missing Cattle dog, a flea market, a community board meeting. She pretended to study them. Then she killed more time by walking to the end of the block, turning around, and walking back. She did that twice.

On the second time, she noticed kids scrambling out of a side door and into the playground, which contained a multi-colored jungle gym and two basketball hoops on either end. She ducked behind another light post, the wind whipping into her eyes.

The kids split off into various groups and pairs, chasing each other, climbing the jungle gym, and kicking balls around. A few sat on the pavement by the fence, reading. A woman, presumably a teacher, threaded between the kids, occasionally talking to them. It was a diverse array of children, but not too many blondes. Cintra thought she'd be able to pick out Leo if she got closer. After waiting for a line of cars to pass, she crossed the street.

A yellow-haired kid was atop the jungle gym, waving an arm, spinning around. When the child turned, Cintra saw it wasn't Leo. Tightening her arms around her chest, she moved to a closer light post, acting as if the signs on that one had drawn her attention: a missing elderly woman; the same missing Cattle dog; a pet sitter ad.

Her gaze switched back to the playground and focused in on a blond child in a blue and red windbreaker, kicking a ball between two other kids. The child yelled something, and as the ball shot towards the fence and bounced against it, the child ran to it and Cintra spotted Leo's dyed blue stripe of hair. She swiftly approached the fence.

"Hey, Leo!" she called.

Leo swiveled his head up, as if the sound had come from the sky.

"Leo!" she called again.

He looked at her, recognition dawning on his face. "Oh, hi," he said, picking up the ball and tossing it back towards another child.

"Cintra. Remember me?"

"Yeahhhh…." he said.

"I'm June's friend. I saw you last night at dinner."

"Yeah, sure," he said, with a "gotcha" flick of his finger and thumb. "I remember."

"Cool. I had an appointment near here and happened to see you. How are you doing?"

"Good." He looked over his shoulder for his friends. She could tell he was itching to get back to his game.

"Hey, listen." She'd mentally rehearsed what to say, but it still sounded squirmingly awkward. Leaning towards the fence, she bounced on her feet, trying to seem casual. "I was curious. Niko called you Leonara last night. I've always liked that name."

He squinted at her in the lambent autumn light, as if she was speaking a language he didn't understand.

"Is that your name?" she asked, bluntly.

"No."

"No? Sorry, maybe I'm confused. He called you Leonara, right?"

He shrugged. "I don't know." Looked back towards his friends, who were now staring at Cintra too. Behind them, the woman whom Cintra assumed was a teacher was also eyeing her.

"So that was never your name?" she asked, trying not to seem out of her mind, and feeling she wasn't succeeding.

"It's not my name!" he shouted, bounding off towards the other end of the playground.

Heart hammering, Cintra shoved her hands inside of her sweater pockets and walked quickly up the sidewalk past the school.

\* \* \*

It was 5:07 p.m. when the buzz came at the door. Cintra opened it, and saw June standing with Leo, who was in a Mets t-shirt. So he'd done it. He'd told June what had happened. Cintra had her story ready. It meant lying. But with a child potentially in danger, she had no choice.

"Hey, guys," she said.

June's face was impassive. "Cintra, may we come in?"

"Of course." She opened the door wider and let them pass. "What's up?"

"Is Pedro here?" June asked.

"Yes, he's in his bedroom." In fact, Pedro seemed to be nowhere these days except the apartment. It was as if he'd given up his dancing career completely.

"It might save some time if he hears this as well," said June.

Cintra acted confused. "Okay… I'll get him." She knocked on Pedro's door and asked him to come out. He waded into the living room sleepy-eyed, as if Cintra had interrupted a nap.

"Please, sit," Cintra said to June and Leo, indicating

the couch. Cintra took one chair and Pedro, after saying his hello's, backed into another.

"Leo mentioned that you came to his school today," said June.

"I didn't come to his school. I happened to walk by it. Is there a problem?"

"You asked me my name," said Leo.

"Oh, right," said Cintra, as if remembering. "When I heard that name last night, Leonara, it was so pretty. I'm thinking of naming a character that, and was going to ask Leo if he knew its origin, since I saw him. Is something the matter?"

June folded her hands in her lap, locked her blue-gray eyes on Cintra. "Cintra, I think we've made you concerned. Or confused."

Cintra kept a face on like the entire conversation was bewildering her. June looked down at Leo. "You are okay with this?" she asked.

Leo shrugged. "Sure."

"You see," June said, looking from Leo to Cintra. "Leo is a boy. However, at birth, it appeared he was a girl. But he knows he's a boy. He's always been a boy. He's a transgender boy."

"Yep," said Leo. "I used to have to dress like a girl. Not even cool dresses either. Like ones with ribbons." He made a vomit motion with his finger in his mouth.

"That's past," June said, patting his knee. Then she turned her attention back to Cintra. "Callie had given him the name Leonara. But when he knew he was a boy, he wanted to be called Leo. So now he is. Callie couldn't risk bringing him to other parts of the world where people, schools, doctors, administrators, might not be as understanding." She looked at him and smiled.

Cintra's mouth went completely dry. "June, I'm—"

June held up her hand. "I worried you thought something unusual was happening."

"No," Cintra said. "I... well, that's... of course!" she blurted. "It's great!"

Pedro sat utterly still, deadly silent.

"We don't go around telling everyone because it isn't everyone's business," said June, pointedly. "Niko knew Leo when he was called Leonara, and he made a mistake."

"That's... of course," Cintra said, nodding.

"We thought you should know. Leo wanted you to know."

"Thank you, Leo," said Cintra, each word sounding as if it was the wrong word.

"I had one more thing for you, if you have another minute." June brought out her cell phone from her sunset-hued bag. In a few moments, June was saying hello to someone, and then she was crouching towards Cintra, the phone half-outwards in her hand.

"Yes, I hear you!" a female voice said from the phone. "Hello?"

"Yes, Callie, I'm here, and this is our neighbor, Cintra, Pedro's roommate." June turned the phone full out in her palm.

On the screen was a tawny-cheeked forties-ish woman with dramatically-defined black eyebrows, black hair with a widow's peak, and cushiony lips. "Hello,

Cintra!" said the woman. She had an open, amiable manner.

"Hi, hi!" Cintra said, speaking louder than was necessary.

"Hi, Mom!" Leo called from the couch.

"Are you enjoying the apartment?" Callie asked.

"Yes, thank you."

"I'm so glad we got a chance to meet. I'll be on a boat soon with no wifi. June said you wanted to introduce yourself."

"Have… have fun on the boat," Cintra offered, smiling stiffly.

June walked back to the couch, staring into the phone. "We'll call again as soon as we get into the apartment, Leo definitely wants to speak with you. I know it's late there, we'll be right back on from the computer."

"Hi, Mom!" said Leo again, wriggling upwards and poking his face into the phone. "Mom, I got a spelling trophy at school."

"Terrific, darling," Cintra heard.

"When we get home," June said to Leo, holding him back with one hand, then, "Yes, stand by, just a couple of minutes."

The phone was back in her bag. "I don't want to take up more of your time," June said, heading with Leo towards the door. Cintra walked with them and opened it.

"June, I want to apologize. I didn't mean to make anyone uncomfortable. You've been… a good friend…"

"Don't worry about it." June put her hand on Leo's shoulder.

"Bye!" Leo said.

"Bye now," Cintra whispered.

She closed the door and stood with her head hung for a few moments. When she turned, Pedro was staring at her with wide, unblinking eyes. "So there you have it," he said.

Cintra put her hand up to her mouth. "I'm so *embarrassed*."

Pedro waved his hands, shook his head. "Cin, it's—"

"I could die. What was I thinking? Of *course* he's trans."

"Hey, Cin. That thing on the door. 'I'm being held,' with a gun? I admit it. It was weird. No wonder your mind went in that direction. Don't beat yourself up. I didn't figure it out either."

"Why didn't I even *think* of that?" She bent over, gave an *ugh* sound.

"And that dude in the hallway? Saying something about breaking up families? Then whatever it was Niko said to you about getting a child. The combo lock. It all added up to something strange. You did the right thing. I shouldn't have made you feel so bad about it."

"Do you think June hates me?"

"No, no." He waved his hands more. "I'm sure she gets it."

"All right, I need to… " She started for her bedroom, but realized she was going in the opposite direction. "I need to… "

"Why don't you sit?"

"No, I'm fine. I need to go lie down for a few. I'm so

*stupid.*" She clasped her forehead and staggered off to her bedroom. Shut the door. Lay down. Closed her eyes.

What was going on here? She needed to be ruthlessly honest with herself. She'd never been good at that. A meditation video with the soft rolling roar of an ocean played in the background as she delved into the depths of her mind, trying to root out the source of her animosity towards June.

June had an intact marriage. Niko, as much as he gave Cintra an uncomfortable vibe sometimes, was devoted to her. June got to live with her nephew; wasn't separated from him like Cintra was from Boston. June was in real estate and made great money and never had to write about kidnapped kids and other ridiculous things.

June had it together. Cintra did not. She'd become jealous of her. That's what this was about. Pure jealousy. Her mind, unable to admit it, had gone berserk. She needed to worry about herself, not June and Niko. She was the one who needed help, not Leo.

And yet there was something about the video call that nagged at her. A dark undertow. She resisted its pull. Leo had acted very obviously like the woman on the phone was his mother. And the woman looked like the Calista Bates on Facebook.

Whatever the nagging sensation was signaling, it wasn't coherent for her.

* * *

AFTER ABOUT FIFTEEN MINUTES, she went to the Ettie

Brightman fan club site and checked the inbox of the profile she'd set up to email the fans.

"Sure, I'd love to chat about Ettie," EttieWON had written a couple of days ago. "She was really railroaded! Call me anytime but early evening is best. Janet."

Finally. Mavis had asked her to do preliminary interviews to see who might have something interesting to say and who would be dead air. But far from her previous idea that she'd get to pick and choose, so far Janet was the only one to respond. And it was early evening. Better get her while she was willing. She dialed the phone number Janet had left in the inbox.

A woman picked up and Cintra confirmed that the woman was Janet and introduced herself.

"Thanks for agreeing to speak with me about Ettie," she said. "Is this a good time for you?"

"Oh," Janet said and there was a long pause. Cintra immediately had a sinking feeling. "I'm afraid I can't do the interview," she said. "I'd thought there would be no problem but…"

More silence. Cintra couldn't tell much about the woman from her voice, though she guessed her to be somewhere in her thirties, with perhaps a slight Midwestern inflection.

"Can you tell me why?" Cintra asked. "We'd love to have some support for Ettie on the special."

"Well, it's just that she—I—well, I didn't realize. I'd thought…"

She trailed off again and Cintra didn't press. Years of reporting had taught her people couldn't stay silent for long. What sounded like children chittered in the background and a dog barked.

"Janet?" she finally asked.

"Yes, I'm here, it's just that…" She seemed to be moving into another room, the noise faded. The woman lowered her voice. "It's my husband. He'd be embarrassed if I was on TV defending a woman who murdered her husband."

"But he was Ettie's *ex*-husband." Splitting hairs, Cintra realized, but she could think of nothing else to say.

"I know, but… I didn't realize. I didn't know. I mean, I'd assumed I could…"

"Can you speak off the record? Tell me a little background on the club?"

Janet was quiet again, and then she practically whispered, "I was told not to. My husband. I can't. Don't say you talked to me, please? Don't put me in danger."

"Danger?" Cintra was alarmed. Was Janet's husband abusive? "Of course not, but can you… are you all right? Do you… Janet? Hello?"

The woman had hung up. Cintra went to her recent sent calls and called back but got no ring and went to voicemail. She left a message asking Janet to call if she ever changed her mind, but knew she'd never hear from the woman again. Cintra had been blocked.

## Chapter Twenty-Five

*O*n Sunday, Cintra took her first yoga class.

She'd decided that yoga might help her calm her mind more than the meditation, which apparently wasn't stopping her from inventing bizarre scenarios involving her neighbors.

The yoga studio was on the corner across the street from Hamilton's restaurant, and as she came out of class about noon, she saw June and Leo, in a green and white soccer uniform, exit the restaurant's door and turn the corner in the direction of their building. They must have just come from brunch, as Hamilton's was a popular spot for it.

Cintra opened her mouth to call to them, but something stopped her, and before she knew it, she had opened the door to the restaurant, scurried past the short line of brunch-goers waiting for a table, and was making a beeline to the only two-seat table she saw that was cluttered with food dishes, but empty of people.

She sat and pretended to wipe a spot of liquid on

the table with one of the discarded white cloth napkins, while her other hand reached under the cloth and palmed the credit card slip sitting between a coffee cup and a plate greasy with egg remnants. She stuffed the receipt inside of her hoodie front pocket.

A waitress appeared from behind the bar area, looking a bit annoyed. Cintra smiled innocently at her.

"I need to clear this," the waitress said, her tone in between a scold and an apology. "And there's people waiting…"

"Oh! I'm so sorry! What was I thinking? I'll get in line."

Cintra got up and promptly walked out. Around the corner, under the scaffolding of a building on a street parallel to the restaurant, and across from an animal rescue group with an assortment of dogs and volunteers outside, she pulled out the slip, hoping she'd gotten the right table. Below the last four digits of the credit card account number on the slip was:

Customer: JUNE CROSS

Cross. Not Garcia, as was on June's Facebook profile. Garcia must be Niko's last name, and June hadn't gotten around to switching her credit cards to her married name. *Supposedly.*

Hopefully, "Server Zoe B" had June's credit card information somewhere, or she was out $31.27. Cintra vowed to generously tip Zoe the next few times she was in Hamilton's.

At home, she plugged "June Cross, Cold Springs, New York" into a people search database and paid to get a report.

The June Cross in the report lived at 52 Pine Ridge Drive in Cold Springs. Niko wasn't listed as a potential relative, but if they'd gotten married in the past year or so, the database likely hadn't caught up yet. What intrigued her more was that there was no Calista Bates listed as a potential relative either.

Calista Bates, American mezzo-soprano, had a spare biography on Wikipedia. Listed were her roles and seasons at various opera houses, going back several years. In the "Early life" section was the sentence, "Calista Dauro Bates was born in Manhattan, New York." There was no information about her personal life, no mention of her having a child. Calista Bates clearly wasn't famous enough for the full Wikipedia rundown.

But also nowhere was the name "Cross." Cintra paid for another people search report, this time on Calista Dauro Bates. Several people with the last name Dauro came up as "potential relatives," meaning Dauro had to be Callie's maiden name. There could be various explanations as to why June's last name wasn't Dauro, the most obvious one being that the two women had different fathers. But Cintra felt this confirmed what she'd suspected for awhile.

June and Callie weren't really sisters.

## Chapter Twenty-Six

On Thursday, Poppy asked to meet for drinks, so they met at an Irish bar near Herald Square. Poppy ran late, and it was almost seven p.m. by the time she arrived. Cintra was halfway through her second white wine.

Without saying hello, Poppy tossed her big wrinkled purse onto the wooden bar and leaned over to get the bartender's attention. "I need a drink before I can get into this," she said, then ordered a gin gimlet when the bartender arrived. She waited, staring at her reflection in the long mirror behind the bar. When her drink came, she gingerly took a few sips holding the glass over the bar in case it spilled, then put down it and shook her head at Cintra. The look said she had gloomy news, her face drawn and pinched in the amber light of the bar.

"Geez, what is it? Joseph?" Cintra asked.

"I don't think we're getting married."

"Oh, Pops," Cintra gasped. "What happened?"

"Apparently he's been… he calls it 'shifting money

around' from clients. I think most people would call it stealing."

"Stealing?" Cintra screeched, then eyeballed the other people at the bar, to see if anyone was staring.

"He swears it was all innocent, blah blah. But he started getting emails about it. Someone knew. He says then the emails would… disappear. Self-destruct."

Cintra stared at her friend. She downed some wine to help her process this, then asked, "The emails would self destruct?" feeling as if she'd stepped into another, much stranger world, one where she had to repeat Poppy's words to make sure she hadn't misheard her.

Poppy nodded, gulped more gimlet.

"Do his bosses know about all of this?"

"I doubt it. I didn't ask him since he was acting like whatever he was doing wasn't as bad as it sounded. I suspect they would have fired him if they did. But that's not even half of it. He claims—*claims*—that the emailer told him to start treating me right."

"The—I'm sorry, what? The person emailing him about his 'shifting around money' said this? About *you*?"

"That's what he says. That the emails said he better treat me right or proof of his 'shifting around money' would be sent to people."

Cintra laughed, out of shock. "Wait, wait," she said. "Someone was blackmailing him to marry you?"

"That's what he says!" Poppy drained her gimlet and signaled to the bartender for another.

"And it's not you?"

"Of course not," she sputtered. "But he thinks, of *course*, I must be behind it. Only he doesn't know how.

And I don't know *what* to believe. Maybe he's making this whole thing up to get out of marrying me and doesn't want to just call it off."

"Wow," Cintra said, draining her own glass. She was going to need another too, but wanted to pace herself, so she traced the stem of the empty glass. "That's quite a story if he's making it up."

"*That's* why he was suddenly so attentive. He was scared to death of me. Can you imagine? I told him, forget the whole thing. If this is the way we're going to be married, I don't want it. He says he *does* want to marry me, but not like this, with him being blackmailed. But honestly?" She looked at Cintra, her expression sad and fragile. "I don't know if I want it. Whatever he's doing with his clients' money, I don't want to be involved. And I didn't send those emails and for him to think I'd do something like that—"

"Oh my God," Cintra said, remembering. "Last week, Elliot accused me of crazy stuff too. Said I called a coworker of his and threatened her, using a voice disguiser."

"Excuse me?" Poppy said, sliding her new gimlet closer.

"I didn't tell you this before, but we got into a big argument about his coworker. *Brittany.*" She made a face as the name settled sourly on her tongue; something about it goaded her with a disproportionate weight, as if it held the echo of a darker time and place. "I saw them together and thought they were having an affair. He swears they're not. Then he said someone called her and ordered her to stay away from him. Naturally, he thinks it was me."

"And it wasn't."

"Hell no."

"You're not… ?"

"No. I'm not lying." She rubbed at her suddenly-itchy neck. "I've been having strange thoughts, but not those."

"Strange thoughts?"

"I can't get into it," she sighed. "I want to forget it all."

"What's up with these guys?" Poppy cried. "What is their problem?" She opened her purse, took out lip gloss, and absently applied a layer.

"How does Joseph think you'd even know that he's embezzling… or whatever he's doing?"

"That's the thing. Like I'm a hacker all of a sudden? I've complained about him to a lot of people. Maybe someone took it upon themselves. I have friends in IT. My sister is married to a PI."

They sat silent, absorbing these dramatic shockwaves. "He could be making it up," Cintra said, quietly. "Elliot too. They don't want to seem like bad guys by breaking up in a clean way. I could see Joseph preferring to seem like a criminal than a guy who broke off an engagement. The first one, you wouldn't tell. The second, you'd tell everyone."

"I told him he's free to move out. I don't need to blackmail anyone into wanting to be with me."

Cintra rubbed Poppy's wrist. "Of course not. He'd be lucky to have you."

"Damn straight. Sometimes I think, though… this is going to sound bizarre."

"More bizarre than everything you told me?"

For the first time, Poppy smiled a little. "Sometimes I think… remember when June did the astrology charts?"

Cintra stiffened at her neighbor's name. "Yes?"

"Everything started with that. Joseph got strange right after. Could that have done something to him?"

"*Done* something? An astrology chart? Like how?"

Poppy gave a huff of bafflement, said, "You got me," and drained half her gimlet.

"Pops, that's when the whole marriage thing came up. The chart happened to be right before it. It's the idea of marriage that made him weird, not the astrology. Besides, don't get me started on June. Ever since she came into my life, it's been one thing after another."

"Do tell."

Cintra reached out and patted her friend's arm. "I can't get into it. I need to focus on one thing. Getting my family back. Or at least Boston. That means no drama, and especially no June drama."

What she didn't volunteer was having spent two months obsessing on the idea that her neighbor had kidnapped a child, and that it hadn't even occurred to her the child was transgender. Or that yesterday, she'd stolen June's credit card slip off a restaurant table.

Why June might lie about Callie being her sister, she didn't know. The most important thing was that Leo seemed fine. He would have to be one hell of a child actor to so convincingly have pulled off the spontaneous, loving behavior she'd seen from him during the video-call with Callie.

Poppy drank in silence for several long moments, tapping one red nail on the bar. "You know, Cin," she said, not looking at her. "This whole thing. With you, I mean. I'm sorry I haven't discussed it with you more. I've been so preoccupied with work and this stuff with Joseph. But… it's…"

"What?" Cintra didn't like the look on her friend's face. She had a feeling what was coming.

"Let me ask you, when you say you're not lying… couldn't you *be* lying? I've never been so aware of it before, now that you've told me."

Cintra was tempted to leave money on the bar and walk out. Find someone outside from whom she could bum a cigarette, then smoke and seethe. But she knew her friend had a right to ask this. "I'm telling the truth about Elliot's accusation, and that I didn't call his coworker. I understand if you can't believe me, but there it is."

"Okay." Poppy grabbed her hand sloppily, her gimlets having taken hold. "Sorry. I had to ask."

Poppy suggested one more drink, but Cintra no longer had the heart to talk to her friend, knowing every word could be doubted.

# Chapter Twenty-Seven

*S*he didn't get home until almost eleven p.m.
From the mess in the kitchen, it was apparent
Pedro had been cooking. And hadn't bothered to clean.
But he was a generally clean roommate, so Cintra
figured he'd get to it in the morning.

Besides, what else did he have to do? He never
seemed to go anywhere anymore. Hadn't told her about
any other auditions. Hadn't, so far as she could tell, even
gone out with friends. She worried he was depressed,
but didn't know what to do about it. When the time was
right, she'd try to have another a talk with him.

In her bedroom, she undressed, slipped on her usual
sleeping attire, loose shorts and a sleeveless shirt, and
turned on a meditation video. The videos helped her fall
asleep, especially the ones with an ocean roiling softly in
the background, though she preferred the videos
without seagulls squawking. Too much distraction.

Normally she would have spoken to Boston by now,
but as he'd told her he was going to see a movie with

Elliot and she herself had plans with Poppy, the call had been waived. It would be the first night she hadn't spoken to her son since she'd moved out, and she wondered if she'd be able to fall asleep without his voice being the last one she heard. Even if they only spoke for ten minutes, it eased the permanent ache in her chest.

Not quite ready to sleep, she kept the bedside light on a dim setting, and lay on top of her comforter. The booze had mostly worn off on the ride back to Brooklyn. Her stomach gurgled and she remembered she hadn't eaten dinner. The whole thing with Poppy had been too surreal to think about food.

Joseph, embezzling from his clients? Thankfully, she'd never invested money with him, as Poppy had once suggested she do. The couple had a duplex apartment in Dumbo with a breathtaking Brooklyn Bridge view. Had Joseph's clients paid for it with money meant to be invested? Poppy's gorgeous engagement ring—had they paid for that as well?

The ocean roared and a seagull squawked. She'd chosen the wrong video, but was too lazy to get up and change it.

All of this time, Joseph had been doing so many things for Poppy. Cooking, cleaning, the flowers. When Pedro had said, "Uh oh, that's guilt about something," regarding the flowers, how right he'd been. Only it wasn't guilt but... *fear.* Fear that Poppy was behind the mysterious emails and would alert his bosses or his clients, or both, to his deception. End his career. Maybe send him to prison. That is, if this "shifting around" of funds wasn't as innocent as he'd claimed. How *could* it be if he was willing to be blackmailed into a marriage he didn't want?

She rolled over, stared at the windows' rectangles of black night.

What an odd thing for a blackmailer to say. To treat Poppy right. Had that been the person's exact words? Who talks like that, except a woman who wants to be treated right?

Could Poppy be behind it after all? Not the Poppy she knew. None of this made any sense. How bizarre that both she and Poppy had been accused of retaliatory messages by the men in their lives within a week of each other.

A rapping came at the door and she turned over. "Are you up?" Pedro asked, poking his head in. "I saw the light but wasn't sure. Sorry about the mess. I made lasagna."

"Was it good?"

"Pretty good, I think. There's a bunch left in the stove if you're hungry. Was keeping it warm."

She pushed up, sat on the edge of the bed, and blinked at him. Was too tired to get into the whole Poppy story with him tonight. "I'll come out and grab some, thanks."

He blew her a kiss and closed the door.

But she lay back down. Heard the roar of the ocean, and another seagull cawing. Smirking, she thought about Joseph madly cooking, cleaning, buying flowers, and giving Poppy orgasms, all in an attempt to keep her from ratting him out. Maybe that was the key to keeping your man in line. Have something to hold over him. She giggled, relishing her mind's deviousness. If she ever used this scenario for a novel, Poppy would kill her.

Pedro knocked on her door again, poked his head in. "You sure you're up? Cause otherwise I'm going to put the rest in the fridge."

She groaned, pushed up again. "Yeah, I'm up. I'll put it in the fridge when I'm done."

He winked, and walked away. This time leaving the door open.

"I'm up," she grumbled, and stood.

Up.

She remembered the piece of paper that Niko had taken out of Leo's cargo pants. The word "UP" written in purple Magic Marker. She stood rooted, her mouth working silently as her brain herded various memories and images and began to arrange them into something. Something not yet formed.

UP.

The way Niko had stared at her so intently in the laundry room. The way his knuckle brushed against the paper, edging it closer to her, as if he'd wanted to make sure she read it.

The way he'd folded up the paper, carefully, and dropped it in the garbage can, then stared at her again. As if trying to read her mind. As if trying to… tell her something.

She put on her jogging sweater and flip-flops and went to the kitchen. Pedro was gone. In bed. Grabbing her keys, she walked out of the apartment, and took the elevator to the basement.

In the laundry room, she peered inside of the garbage

can. It wasn't emptied regularly as it was only used for the sheets of soft gray lint scraped out of the dryers' filters. A few empty jugs of laundry detergent were inside the garbage can too. She dug below the lint sheets and the jugs, found the folded piece of paper, and took it out.

She unfolded it and stared at it. UP. In Leo's purple scrawl.

I'm being held…

UP.

I'm being held… up.

The gun at the sketched boy's head. The little blob near one hand. Had that been… a bag of money?

It rushed on her with complete certainty. Leo hadn't written "I'm being held" but "I'm being held *up.*" As in a robbery. That explained the gun and the little bag of money.

He wasn't trying to communicate that he'd been kidnapped. He was playing a role! A boy being held up in a robbery. It had been an innocent note, completely innocent!

Good lord, what an idiot she'd been all along. Thinking he was trying to draw her attention to his kidnapping. A boy of eleven would have written something obvious like "I'm kidnapped" and June would have pocketed it.

She let the paper fall from her hand and into the garbage can. In the elevator, she watched the light as it ascended to her floor.

*The crazy things we'll do to get a kid.*

Had Niko said that on purpose? If she didn't know

better, she'd think Niko had deliberately taken the "UP" portion of the papers out of their sequence, to make the message menacing instead of innocent.

If she didn't know better, she'd think Niko had been deliberately trying to make her think Leo had been kidnapped.

In the kitchen, she cut a square of lasagna, and put it on a plate and into the microwave.

*What about you, Cintra? Would you have figured out a serial killer was next door?*

*Regular people going around solving crimes? Does that really happen?*

*Come on, Leonara. That's my little pet name for him when he's being dramatic.*

If she didn't know better, she'd think Niko was playing games with her. Calling Leo "Leonara" on purpose. Trying to let her know that Leo had once had another name.

She took the lasagna out of the microwave and stood eating at the kitchen counter. Very good. Pedro was becoming a real cook. She got juice out of the refrigerator and poured herself a glass.

Yes, if she didn't know better, she'd think Niko was testing her. A little game of his—seeing if Cintra could figure out a crime next door, only the crime was a non-existent one.

She finished the lasagna, washed her plate (one less for Pedro) and went to bed. Turned off the meditation video. Wanted silence tonight. Flicked off the light. Closed her eyes.

Her brain churned with thoughts of June, Poppy, Joseph, Elliot. Of Niko.

*I'm being held up.*

Why would the last paper be folded in Leo's pants pocket? Leo wouldn't have put it there, he would have hung the paper up on the door. Niko is the one who could have put it in Leo's pocket. If he'd wanted, for some insane reason, to make her believe Leo had been kidnapped, why would he then take the "UP" portion of the paper out of Leo's pants and make sure she saw it? That would ruin "the game."

Stop, breathe. Go to sleep.

He'd put the paper so deliberately into the garbage can. As if he'd wanted her to know he'd taken the "UP" paper. As if he'd wanted her to puzzle together that he was trying to fake a kidnapping. Was he just a horribly twisted man?

Stop it, you're insane.

Unless he was the one. Unless he was the one.

Go to sleep.

Unless Niko was the one in trouble.

## Chapter Twenty-Eight

*I*t was the most outlandish idea she'd had yet, and she couldn't stop thinking it. The possibility hounded her all through the long subway ride to work.

Niko. Niko could be held hostage, not Leo.

Insane!

She and Pedro had had dinner with the couple twice. Niko could have stood up and announced, "This bitch is holding me hostage!"

Had he been worried no one would believe him? Cintra had to admit that if Niko had said something like that, she would have thought there was something seriously mentally wrong with him. June could have told her he had mental health issues, and that's why they'd moved to a place with a combo lock—that he had fits, that he needed to be kept inside when he was "acting up." Cintra would have believed it.

If he was being held against his will, there had to be something keeping him there. Did June have a gun and so he didn't dare try to alert anyone to what was happening? With June's talk of the gun range and the proper way to hold a gun, Cintra wouldn't be surprised if June owned one.

At work, she shoved her tote underneath the desk, took off her cardigan, and powered on her monitor. The computer always took several annoying minutes to boot up, so her imagination had more time to seethe with questions.

When she and Niko had been alone together in the laundry room, he could have said something to her. Was he afraid she wouldn't believe him? Hell, there was a door by the laundry room. He could have walked out of the building.

Then she thought of Joseph, who'd been acting like the perfect fiancé for two months, with full freedom to roam, only because he worried Poppy might identify him as an embezzler. June could be holding something similar over Niko. But if he'd committed some sort of crime in the past, and June was using that as her leverage, Cintra couldn't solve the situation.

Leo. Could June be using threat of harm to Leo to keep Niko in check? But Leo went to school. Cintra had seen him on the playground. Niko could wait until Leo was at school, then overpower June. There was no way he couldn't overpower her. Punch her in the face! Even if June had a gun, she couldn't possibly have it cocked and ready every moment of every hour.

Cintra's monitor finally lit up with her CMS system and she logged in.

Her mind went back to the laundry room. How

intense Niko had seemed, staring right through her with those dark eyes while making small talk. If he needed help, he could have said something to her then.

"Maybe she was listening in," Cintra said aloud.

"Sorry, what?" said the twenty-something sitting next to her, leaning sideways.

"Oh. Nothing." Cintra waved, and the young woman made a "whatever" face and looked back to her computer.

How could June have been listening in?

"He's wired somehow," she said aloud.

"What was that?" Mavis asked, standing over her.

Cintra erupted in nervous laughter. "When I'm thinking, I sometimes talk to myself."

"Glad I'm not the only one," Mavis drawled. "How we doing with the Tribe of Ettie?"

Cintra rubbed her lower lip with her thumb. "It's strange. I've emailed seventy-five of them and not one emailed back." She shook her head. "Sorry, sorry. I emailed about twenty. One emailed back, the president of the club, but she—I assume it's a 'she'—declined an interview. And another woman agreed but changed her mind. Claimed her husband wouldn't like it and she sounded scared of him. As for the others, I don't understand. They don't seem ashamed of being supporters."

Mavis nodded, and glanced towards the opposite row of bloggers, as if she had somewhere else to be. "Any more you can try? We only need one."

"Sure, I'll get on it."

Mavis smiled and left. Cintra walked to the kitchen,

wanting coffee. A man was using the machine and she got behind him, waiting.

Niko wired. June listening in. How?

A feeling of ice melting diffused through her stomach. The watch. She remembered during the first dinner when she'd asked Niko for the time, he'd ignored her and left to start the dishes. No one is that eager to wash dishes, especially with guests still in the apartment. And even if he had been, within minutes, he was back to say goodbyes at the door.

The man in front of the coffee machine left and she got a tiny tin of ground coffee and put it in, and pressed the start button. The maker came to life with a loud gurgle.

Back at her desk, she couldn't concentrate. A woman holding a grown man hostage inside of an apartment. She'd read hundreds, probably thousands, of crime stories, and never seen that one. A search on "woman holds man hostage" only brought up the movie *Misery*. A search on the FBI's missing persons database using Niko and varying spellings of his name came to a dead end. "Missing man Cold Springs New York" also led nowhere.

This was absolutely nuts. She should make an emergency session with Dr. Grace. But it was the Friday before Halloween. Dr. Grace had said she wasn't available that Tuesday, so they'd agreed to meet after the holidays. She needed to go home and meditate these preposterous speculations out of her system.

But the little pieces kept swarming together, forming a picture.

Niko's shaved head. Maybe he hadn't shaved it to disguise himself from anyone looking for a man with thick black hair who'd taken "Leonara." Maybe June had shaved it to disguise Niko as the man *she* had taken!

The combination lock. How both times June had walked Cintra and Pedro to the door after dinner, Niko had not been there when she opened it. The first time, he'd gone to the kitchen to "start the dishes." The second, he'd been getting Cintra a cool cloth for her forehead. He could be under instructions not to be by the door when June tapped in the combination.

Let's say he overcame June with a punch or something else, and was locked inside the apartment. He could still use June's phone to call 911. Even with password protection, you can call 911 without using it, unless June deactivated that feature somehow. Or he could scream his bloody head off. Cintra or Pedro would eventually hear him. Perhaps he was worried no one would believe a story of his kidnapping, and he'd only be arrested for assaulting or even killing June.

She went to the Ettie Brightman Fan Club site, and clicked into the forums section. All the same old stuff. Ettie is a shero! Ettie, my queen! Blah blah.

*Hi, I'm a researcher for True Crime TV. We're doing a special on Ettie, and we'd love to hear your take on things. Any chance you could speak to us on camera?*

She sent the same email to several new fans.

Clicking around more, she saw a post from EttieAdmin. It was an old one she'd seen before: EttieAdmin's instructions on how to send money to Ettie through PrisonPay. There were multiple appeals for donations leading up to Ettie's parole date.

Only there was something different about EttieAdmin's old post. The avatar. It used to be a picture of Ettie from the trial. Cintra was sure of that. Now it was a small square of bright teal blue. She clicked into the avatar, and then hit the zoom button on her keyboard. Water. Bright blue water. And a small white boat in the distance.

A hand was on her shoulder and she jumped.

"Sorry to keep startling you," said Mavis. "I should announce myself."

"No problem," Cintra said, breathless. "This stuff puts me on edge."

"No doubt," Mavis smiled. "I wanted to tell you we can use a silhouette screen if they prefer. No names. Of course, we'd rather get their faces, but if it means no one will talk, we'll do it the other way."

"Good to know."

Mavis walked away, and Cintra opened Facebook. She plugged in "Calista Bates." Up came Callie's Facebook page. She clicked around the photos section. There it was. Callie on a white boat with bright blue water.

She was only faintly aware of her mouth hanging open as she went back to EttieAdmin's avatar. The white boat there certainly looked similar to the one on Callie's page. But white boats, blue water… it all looked the same. But combine that with the "Liz" she'd met at Poppy's party. The Liz with Ettie-like green eyes.

She clicked into EttieAdmin's profile and up came all of her posts. She scrolled down, down, and found one that said, "I'm out of the country Lulu, and my wifi isn't very reliable. But as soon as I get a better connection I'll look that up for you." The date of the forum post was after Callie had left for Europe.

Callie was EttieAdmin. She was certain of it. What did that make June?

How to get Niko to tell her what's going on, and if he needed help. How to do it without telling a soul, because she couldn't afford to be wrong about June one more time. Pedro already thought she was insane and was probably on the verge of calling Elliot and telling him she was insane.

There was no calling police. She had no proof of anything, nothing except some wild theories based on gut instinct and a bunch of small events she'd already misread several times before. Elliot? Forget it.

She needed to get to Niko in a way that wouldn't make her look out of her mind if she was wrong, like she'd looked out of her mind when she'd confronted Leo at his school. And to do it in a way that didn't put either Niko or herself in danger.

She sat for several minutes, typing out random letters so it would appear she was working.

She had an idea.

## Chapter Twenty-Nine

*A*fter work, Cintra walked three blocks in the chilly dusk to the brightly-lit streets and teeming crowds of Herald Square. Riding up the escalator in Macy's, she found the boys' department and looked through the autumn jackets hanging inside of the activewear section.

She tried to picture Leo exactly, his form, his weight, his height. She needed something two sizes smaller, not wanting to risk that he would fit into the jacket, even snugly. If she got the size wrong, her plan would not only not work, but could put herself and Niko in harm's way.

Her phone rang inside of her bag. She ignored it, intending to let it go to voicemail, but a last second intuition made her look at the caller. Elliot.

"Hi," she said, distractedly, opening jackets and checking the inside linings for pockets.

"Boss and I are in the city looking at costumes. Did you want to join us?"

Even with Halloween paraphernalia everywhere, she kept forgetting how close the holiday was. And Elliot inviting her to spend extra time with them? This was new.

"Where are you?" she asked.

"Halloween Haven in Greenwich Village."

Way downtown. She had so much to do. Giving up on finding the perfect jacket in this section, she looked around, wondering which section to try next. There were no employees nearby. "I'm kind of busy," she said. "How long will you be there?"

"An hour? He's pretty sure what he wants, so…"

"Can you do this tomorrow?"

"No, Cin. There's a party he wants to go to Saturday night. He needs it now." He sounded irritated.

"Couldn't you have told me this earlier?"

"I did. I left you a message last night."

Damn, as she'd been out with Poppy and hadn't spoken to Boston, she hadn't checked her phone or even heard it ring.

"He'd like you here," said Elliot.

"It's that I'm—busy right now."

"Doing what?" Elliot asked, starting to sound… suspicious. Did he think she was on a date?

"I'm…" What could she say? She didn't want to lie to him. Today, she'd felt it so strongly, the urge to start spewing lies. She'd even told Mavis she'd emailed seventy-five Ettie fans, when it had been not even close to that amount. She couldn't start lying to her family now, it might open up something in her brain, and she'd never stop. "I can't say. I'm sorry, but it's private."

"So whatever this is, it's more important than seeing your son?"

"Please. I don't need this guilt trip."

"Hi, Mom!" Boston.

"Hey, bunny bear. Oops, not supposed to call you that."

"Can you come down? I can't decide this year. I thought Chewbacca but now I'm thinking a Velociraptor."

"A what?"

"*Dinosaur*. Awesome!" he exclaimed, obviously looking at something. "The costumes are really cool here. Come on, it's not as fun without you."

She had moved to another section of the store and was pawing through more jackets, checking their linings. Why did none have inside pockets?

"Mom?"

"Yeah, I'm here," she said.

What was she doing? Ignoring her son while he picked out his Halloween costume so she could go down this wacky path of trying to find out if a grown man was being held hostage by his wife... or whoever June was. Hadn't she promised Dr. Grace that when her thoughts became abnormal and irrational, she would take a bath, drink some herbal tea, and meditate?

Elliot was softening in his stance on seeing her only once a week. He was offering a chance, a way back into the family. And her son wanted to see her. What, what was she doing in Macy's desperately inspecting boys' jackets? All for a plan that would likely lead nowhere. All for a man she hardly knew.

But she couldn't get it out of her mind—that if Elliot or Boston were in trouble, and the only person who'd figured it out was a nosy, half-crazed neighbor, she'd want that nosy, half-crazed neighbor to do everything in her power to try to help.

She blew air out of her mouth, looking around the vast store. "I'm sorry, baby. I'm really busy."

"Doing what?"

"Honey, I've promised never to lie to you or your Dad again. That means I can't answer you, because it's private."

"Okay," he said, sounding disappointed. "I'll survive. I'll take pictures for you."

Her son. He was so good. He deserved so much more than she was giving him. "I love you, baby."

"Love you too, Mom." He hung up.

She went back to checking jackets. Several other stores were in the same mall. She could try them.

A COUPLE HOURS LATER, what she needed was wrapped snugly in thin white paper in a shopping bag. She walked down the mobbed sidewalk towards the subway.

It was dark out, but lit up brightly everywhere, and a tall man passed on the street whom she knew somehow. Automatically, she stopped and turned, catching the powerful scent of roasted chestnuts from a nearby food cart. The man was at the corner, waiting for the light. She walked several feet, winding through the seething

humanity until she was next to him, and touched
his arm.

"Liam?"

He turned and gaped at her for a moment before his
eyes registered recognition. "Cintra!" he said. They gave
each other half-hugs.

A woman was next to him. She was almost as tall as
Liam was, and blonde. Both of them wore long, dark
coats, hers accompanied by a plaid pink scarf and pink
fur hat. The blonde woman turned as Liam turned, her
pretty face peeking around his shoulder. Cintra didn't
pay much attention to the woman.

In fact, she wasn't sure why she'd stopped Pedro's ex-
boyfriend. It had happened without input from the
rational side of her brain, which didn't want to speak
with him, not after he'd betrayed Pedro. But she and
Liam had always gotten along and she'd known him for
years, so she'd reacted. But now she didn't know what
to say.

"How are you?" she asked.

"Great. You?"

The blonde woman seemed to be sniffing the chill
air, and she tipped forward, as if to hear their conversation. Liam had his eyes focused on Cintra, focused hard,
as if he was trying to ignore the woman.

His dark hair, with swoops of silver-gray along his
temples, was longer than she remembered, and slicked
back, a style she'd never seen on him. He was a theater
director and producer and had always dressed neat, but
casual. In his expensive-looking dark overcoat, with his
gelled-up hair, he looked like an eighties yuppie.

"I'm good." Cintra held up her shopping bag. "Doing a little shopping."

"How's the novel coming?"

She waved one hand. "Finished it," she said. "Got a great deal."

Feeling she didn't owe Liam honesty, she didn't correct herself. She'd confess her slip-up to Dr. Grace next week.

The blonde woman smiled in a bit of a pushy way and said, "Oh, novel? That's wonderful." She had an Eastern-European accent.

"Sorry, this is Elena." Liam looked at the woman. "Elena, this is an old friend of mine, Cintra."

"Hi," Cintra said, shaking the woman's hand. An antennae went up, the way the woman was chafing against Liam almost possessively, the way he'd subtly seemed as if he was trying to avoid introducing her. Then Cintra noticed it: the woman's coat popped straight out from her stomach. She was pregnant. Heavily so.

"My wife," Liam said, and seemed to clear his throat.

"*Wife?*" Cintra blurted, then pulled the bleat of her voice down a notch. "Oh, hi. Congratulations."

"We're here doing some shopping too. And to see auditions for a new play," Liam said.

"Uh huh," Cintra said, hating herself for nodding so vigorously.

"*Scarface,*" the woman added.

"Yes, I'd—I'd heard that was coming. Are you? An actress?" Cintra ventured.

"No, investor." The woman looked at Liam. His eyes roamed over Cintra's head and she thought he might dart off into the crowd of people.

"I live in Santa Barbara now," he said, bringing his eyes back to hers. "*We* do." He put his arm around the woman's waist, and she pressed the side of her huge round belly against him.

Cintra could say nothing, and hoped she wasn't gaping too badly.

"Well, it was nice seeing you," he said.

"You too, you too. Nice meeting you," she said to the woman. The couple disappeared into the throng of people crossing the street.

Cintra walked away in such a daze that she crashed into a group of teens, and murmured apologizes as she maneuvered around their wall of bodies.

Liam. Married. To a woman. And she was pregnant!

Cintra stared at the shimmering black glass walls of a bank, her reflection showing her biting her thumb knuckle. She couldn't tell Pedro. It would destroy him. Judging by the size of the belly, the woman had been pregnant before Pedro had kicked him out of the apartment. Had Liam ever planned to come clean about this?

And *Scarface* auditions. *Now*? Pedro had said he'd gone to an audition for that over a month ago.

At the subway entrance, she took the noxious-smelling stairs with care, aware of being distracted to the point where if she didn't pay close attention to where her feet were landing, she could fall. She opened her wallet and gave a dollar to a homeless man, his lower half plugged into a sleeping bag.

Thank goodness Pedro hadn't been cast in the show. He would have found this whole thing out. Finding out the love of his life was married—and so soon after their breakup!—would be bad enough, but to a *woman*? Had Elena been the one he'd caught Liam cheating with? Cintra had assumed Liam had been cheating with a man. Given everything she'd heard from Liam over the years, she'd thought women weren't his jam.

She hoped Pedro wasn't cyberstalking him. What if the happy pregnant couple had pictures on social media? Poor Pedro. Maybe he already knew about the marriage and that's why he was acting so depressed and not leaving the apartment. Maybe he couldn't bring himself to tell her about it.

\* \* \*

"Rawrr!"

Cintra flinched, grasping at her chest. Fanged white teeth and claws several inches long reared at her.

"Sowwy," Pedro warbled, plucking the fake teeth out of his mouth. "Testing out my costume."

Cintra pressed her hand up against her racing heart. "Don't do that, Pedro."

"Sorry. You dressing up this year?"

"I don't know."

"You all right?" He pressed his clawed hand on her arm. "Didn't mean to scare you."

"It's fine. I need to do some things." She walked from the door straight into her bedroom, wanting to get away from Pedro before he asked her anything that would force her to have to lie to him. She couldn't tell him about seeing Liam with his pregnant wife tonight, was not emotionally prepared for his potential reaction with everything else on her mind. If he already knew, he'd mention it when he was ready.

She dug the rolled boy's jacket out of the shopping bag, peeled off the thin, crackly paper. Got the reporter's notebook and pen she'd taken from work, slipped the pen's tong down the small metal rings of the notebook, and put the notebook inside of the jacket's interior pocket.

## Chapter Thirty

"*P*lease, Ped?" she begged, scrunching her eyes, massaging her thumb into one temple. "I think you caused it with that scare of yours, you owe me."

"Sure, I'll go to the deli."

"No, the pharmacy. The deli doesn't have Aleve. Only Aleve works."

He looked at his watch. "It's almost nine."

"They're open. I beg you. I won't get anything done until this headache is gone." She squinted pleadingly. The pharmacy was a longer walk away than the deli, and she needed time to put her plan into action.

"Okay," he said, hesitantly.

She gave him the ten dollar bill she had folded in her hand. "Only Aleve."

He went back to his room, and came out with light coat on.

"Thank you, sweets," she said, pouting at him.

She waited about five minutes after he'd left, until

she was fairly certain he wouldn't re-appear unexpectedly. Then she went to June's door and pushed the buzzer.

Within a minute, she heard the soft tapping sounds of a finger on the door's combo lock.

"Cintra," said June, surprised. She had on a black tunic shirt with a twisty gold chain hanging down between her breasts.

"Sorry to bother you, but could I borrow Niko for a minute? I have to move the fridge so I can put a roach motel behind there, but I can't budge it."

"Ohhh…." said June, something flickering behind her blue-gray eyes.

"Pedro went out," Cintra explained. "I need to do this now, they're really skeeving me out. It'll only take a minute." If June said Niko wasn't home, she wasn't sure what she would do.

"Well…" June said, glancing over her shoulder. "He's doing some… okay, well… let me get him."

"Thank you so much."

June closed the door. Cintra stood staring at it. Who would close the door before getting her husband for a quick errand? Someone up to no good, that's who. Looking down at the grinning doormat, she crushed its smile with the sole of her sneaker.

It seemed like a long time before she heard the soft popping of the combination being put into the lock and the door opened. Niko was down the foyer, almost to the living room. As Cintra suspected, he wasn't allowed to get near the lock. She knew it.

Niko walked—hesitantly, she felt—out of the door, shooting a quick glance at June.

"Roaches?" said June. "Callie is so clean."

"It can happen anywhere. It will only take a minute," Cintra said. "Thanks so much, Niko. I really needed a man." She laughed, hoping the laugh sounded natural.

Niko walked with her down the hallway and Cintra opened her door. He came into the apartment with her, looking—did he?—nervous. She was closing the door when suddenly it jammed. June's hand was on it.

"I've always wanted to see your apartment. May I?" June asked, smiling.

"You've been in here," Cintra said, smiling back. "Remember?"

"Oh, I hardly paid attention those few minutes I was here with Leo."

"But hadn't you seen it before? I mean, with your sister living here."

June laughed. "I haven't seen it in ages. I'm curious what you've done with it."

"Nothing, really."

June stood there. Refusing to leave. Damn it! Cintra should have seen this one coming. That smile on her face!

"Come on in," Cintra said, opening the door wide. June stood in the foyer, looking to the left, towards the living room. Like a hawk.

"Here," Cintra said, leading Niko to the kitchen, showing him the refrigerator. "If you could pull it out a few inches, that would be great. I tried, but…" She shrugged, helplessly.

Niko bent and grasped the sides of the refrigerator. Grunted and pulled. Stood back and went at it again with a better grip. He bent lower, one hand on the fridge's bottom, the other on its side, grunted again, and shook it from side to side, waddling it outward.

Cintra looked at June. Her gaze was lasered on Niko.

"Good?" Niko asked, unfurling.

"A little more," Cintra said. "June, look at those prints over the couch." She pointed towards the living room. "Can you tell me where that middle one is from? It was here when I got here. I don't think it's Pedro's."

June wandered slowly into the living room until she blocked by the short archway that separated the kitchen from the living room. Cintra couldn't see her, but had directed her to a large glossy print of a glowing red fire shooting out of a dark, hulking mass, the sky stained pink and violet.

"I'm not sure," June called. "I don't remember it. Hawaii?"

Cintra firmly touched the back of Niko's bicep, almost pinching it, to draw his attention away from the fridge, grabbed the boy's jacket off the kitchen island and held it open in front of her chest, so it was only a few inches from him. It was a slim-cut fleece jacket, beige color, so he could see the notebook.

"This is my son's old jacket," she said. "Cost me two hundred dollars but he's outgrown it. Could you give it to Leo, see if it fits him?"

She slipped her hand to the left inside lining, slid her finger across the metal rings of the notebook poking out of the interior pocket. "It's got an inside pocket for a phone," she said. "But where in Hawaii?" she called back to June.

Niko looked at her, looked down at the coat, looked at her. Took the coat. "It's nice," he said. "Hopefully it will fit him."

"Hopefully it will *help* him stay warm." She stressed the word "help," searing her gaze into his eyes. "It's washable. Make sure to check the pockets before you do, of course. Don't forget that."

"I don't know where it's from," June called. "Looks like a volcano. Could be anywhere, I guess."

"Oh, June," said Cintra. "Come in my room for a second, I want your opinion."

"Now?" June said, coming back to the kitchen.

"Yes, for a minute. You wanted to see the place, didn't you?"

"Well, of course."

Cintra moved past Niko and took June by the elbow, leading her down the small hallway to the threshold of her bedroom. Did she feel June resisting?

"Do you think turquoise would look good in here? It's so stunning in your place, but I don't know if it would work for a whole room. Callie might not be on board, so I could do one section. That color is so cheery."

"Maybe one wall." June looked over her shoulder, back down the hallway.

"Which wall?" Cintra asked, increasing her grip on

June's elbow, trying to lead her farther into the room. "By the window?"

"Yes, that, or over the bed might be nice. A pop of color for when you enter."

"That's what I thought, thanks, I—"

But June had slid out of her grasp and was headed back to the kitchen. Cintra followed her. Niko was standing at the kitchen island, the boy's jacket draped over his arm.

"What's this?" June asked, eyeing the jacket.

"It was Boston's," Cintra said. "He's hardly ever worn it; he prefers dark colors, and he's outgrown it. It's like new." She suddenly and horribly wondered if she'd remembered to cut off the price tag. Wait, she'd ripped it off with her hand. "Elliot gave it to me last time I saw him, wondering if I knew any moms who'd want it. I thought of Leo."

"It's gorgeous." June took the jacket from Niko, and held it before her, eyeing it up and down. Cintra could swear her heart stopped. "Might be a bit small though." June folded the jacket over her arm.

Niko's black cotton shirt was hanging past his belt-line in the front. Had it been that way before? Or had the shirt come out of the front of his pants when he'd moved the fridge? Or had he gotten the notebook and stashed it down front of his pants?

There was nothing Cintra could do. It was all up to him. If the notebook was still in the jacket pocket and June saw it, it could easily be explained away as something Boston had put inside and forgotten about. While at work, Cintra had added text to the first page, using only her thumb and forefinger on the pen to make the writing look like a kid's scrawl. "Today we learned about dinosaurs. They roamed the planet millions of years ago. The Velociraptor has claws and big teeth. It eats meat. It weighs 300 pounds and is very cool looking!!! In the movie Jurassic Park, the Raptor is cloned and **BEING HELD ON AN ISLAND**. But that's just pretend! Or is it? Haha JK!"

Cintra walked them to the door. "If the jacket doesn't fit Leo, could you do me a favor and drop it in front of my door? I'd like to try someone else. It's too expensive for the Goodwill. But not until tomorrow at earliest. I have a raging headache and am going to bed early. I wouldn't want it left in the hallway too long. Not sure when Pedro is returning. You know sometimes crazy people get in the hallway and I wouldn't want it disappearing." She laughed, aware that her mouth was far too open, her laugh too airy.

"Where's Pedro?" June asked, a sharp edge to her tone.

"Oh, I don't know. Thanks again, Niko." She awkwardly shook his hand. "I'm sure I can get the fridge back in place, or Pedro can."

"No problem," he said. "Hope that takes care of the roaches."

Cintra made a "gross" face, tongue peeping out between her lips.

They left, and she closed the door, her heart thumping.

Would he be able to get the notebook back inside of the jacket before it came back around to her? Would

June return the jacket and see or feel the notebook inside and open it? She trusted that if Niko couldn't replace it safely, he wouldn't.

Or was all of this in her mind and she was truly headed to crazytown? Or was she already living there?

In her bedroom, she lay down, her body electric with adrenaline, a vein throbbing in her neck. About twenty minutes later, Pedro knocked on the door, handed her a small plastic bag from the pharmacy and her change.

*       *       *

THERE WAS nothing in front of the door at eight a.m. Or at eight thirty. Nothing at quarter to nine. Or at nine thirty. Or at quarter to ten. Nothing at ten either.

"What the hell?" asked Pedro, eyeing her as he stood in the kitchen with a mug of coffee in hand. He'd only emerged out of his room half an hour ago, but had seen her open their door three times.

"I gave June a boy's jacket yesterday to see if it fits Leo. If not, she's returning it."

"Maybe it fit him," he said, eyebrows raised.

Cintra went to the kitchen, and took the mug that Pedro had poured for her. She added almond milk, took a sip.

"Important jacket?" he snorted.

"I don't want it getting stolen if she drops it off."

"Stolen?" He raised his brows again, sifting through some mail on the kitchen counter. "Why don't you go ask her about it, if it's that critical?"

The doorbell buzzed and her coffee sloshed as she hurried to place the mug on the counter, leaving a few nickel-sized smatterings of liquid behind.

Leo, in a Mets cap, stood at the door, holding out the jacket. "Thank you," he said. "But it's too small."

"Oh, that's a shame." Cintra took the jacket, frowning sadly. "Would have looked great on you."

"June said you're both invited to her Halloween party if you want to come. Mostly her real estate friends. But *I'm* going trick or treating with my friend Alfie and his mom and having a sleepover. So you'll be denied my charming presence," he said, deadpan.

"That's unfortunate. When is the party?"

"On Halloween." He looked at her as if she was dumb.

"Okay, sweetie. I wasn't sure if it was earlier. What are you wearing?"

"Spiderman!" he said, shooting his arms out, hands flicking an invisible spider web.

"Good choice. Tell June I'll try to make it, but not sure of my plans yet."

"I'll pass on the message," he saluted, then bounced off down the hallway.

Cintra shut the door. Pedro was staring at a piece of mail he'd opened. "So you can stop checking," he said.

"Guess so," she said, breezily. "I'll find someone else for it."

Pedro nodded distractedly, and she went into her room and closed the door. Locked it.

Spreading the jacket on her bed, she saw the inside pocket had been zipped shut. Judging by the shape under the fleece, the notebook was inside. Her hands trembled slightly as she unzipped the pocket and slid out the notebook. She sat on her bed, took a deep breath, and opened it.

The first page was her attempt at kid writing, the stuff about the dinosaur. She wet her thumb and slid the first page up. The second page was blank.

But someone had zipped the pocket shut. Then she noticed it. The second page had a tiny fold on its bottom corner. She lifted the pages from the back, tumbling them down with her thumb, feeling as if the almost-imperceptible fold was a sign telling her to keep going.

Her thumb stopped. The middle of the notebook was filled with handwriting she didn't recognize. She began to read.

## Chapter Thirty-One

*C*intra,
        If you're reading this, then congratulations. You've solved the crime.

There's a chance your son left the notebook and pen in the coat by mistake. In that case, you may never read this. But if this is intercepted, horrible things will happen.

Every minute I wonder. Every night I have nightmares from which I wake up stifling screams. There is nothing worse than not knowing. Can you help me find out about my daughter???

I can write all night, but I'm not used to writing in longhand, so forgive my handwriting. I'm also writing with my left hand wrapped in a blanket to smother the watch, so any scratch of the pen across paper won't be detected.

Cintra, as you probably guessed, June is holding me hostage. How is this possible?

Let me give you some background, because before

you risk yourself, I want you to be fully informed. You would be within your rights to toss this notebook in the trash and forget about me. I brought most of this on myself.

June and I dated for seven years. I loved her. We lived together for long periods, but every couple of years, she would throw me out for months at a time. She wanted marriage and children. She'd been honest with me about that from the beginning.

I didn't know what I wanted. I was in my mid-thirties and still felt like a boy, and acted like one. I had plenty of time, and didn't take into consideration June's time. I figured if she was serious about not wanting to be with me, then it was up to her to break it off. But, after she did so, my ego persisted in making me get her back.

I was not a good person. I see that now. At the time, I only saw what I wanted to see—that after a breakup, I missed her and would do everything to get her back into my life, without stopping to consider if this was good for her.

The old saying sums it up. I didn't want her but didn't want anyone else to have her. I even found out she was seeing an old flame and managed to stick a wrench in it. I wanted her available to me should I ever bother to make up my mind about her.

Somewhere in tangles of my ego was the idea that the perfect woman would come along and my choice would be made crystal clear.

Then I met that woman. She was twenty-seven. Beautiful and smart. A dentist. Yes, I met her going in for a cleaning. We began dating casually even though I was still living with June. I don't know what I was thinking, Cintra. I won't try to defend myself.

Her name is Samantha. I was flattered that such a young, attractive woman who had Ivy League degrees, who came from a wealthy family, wanted me. Samantha found out about June and dumped me. So I dumped June, and moved out again.

I was forty-three and the urge to pass on my DNA was becoming stronger. Samantha seemed like right bet. I asked her to marry me.

Soon after, June found out. She sent me medical records showing she'd had a miscarriage a few weeks after I'd moved out. She ended up having a procedure to take out the fetus and something went wrong.

She claimed she was told that getting pregnant again would be extremely difficult, especially at her age. In her mind, I had ruined any chance of her having a child. She blamed the miscarriage on me, saying it was caused by stress from the breakup. I'm no doctor and couldn't tell you if that's true. What I can tell you is that I felt terrible.

Samantha became pregnant almost right away after the wedding. We had twins, a boy and girl. Nikolas and Jasmine.

Cintra, for the first time in my life, I knew what love truly was. That real love was putting my needs, wants, and desires aside for the sake of someone else.

Then I realized that Jasmine could grow up to meet a man like me. A man who could manipulate her out of her chance of having a family, a partner, my grandchildren. I know it's despicable that I only fully compre-hended my behavior with June once I had my daughter, and knew that her heartbreaks would be mine.

I sent June a long email apologizing. All she'd wanted was a family. I'd taken that possibility from her, and now I had my own. To my shock, she wrote back saying she'd forgiven me. That to hate me would only poison herself. I didn't realize she was baiting a trap.

Although I'd matured with the birth of my babies, I hadn't matured enough. Jasmine was born with a congenital heart defect that would require two surgeries. She came through the first, but there was constant stress. Samantha stopped practicing so she could be home with the babies. A few months later, I was laid off—again. It had taken me a year to find another job the first time I was laid off, which was when I was with June. The only way Samantha and I survived is that her parents helped us.

But the worry was tremendous. Samantha and I began arguing. Meanwhile, June had become sort of a confidant, a friend. We would email several times a day. She seemed to understand exactly what I was going through. At the time, I had no idea that a mutual friend was filling her in on everything I was telling him about my marriage.

Now I will tell you some things I'm not proud of in the slightest, worse than what you've heard so far.

The stress of the babies, Jasmine's condition, and my unemployment broke me down. I began to get my validation as a man from the one person who seemed willing to give it to me. June. She became my escape, as

Samantha had once been my escape from the realities
June wanted to settle upon me.

Our emails became more flirtatious. In my mind,
this was harmless fun. I convinced myself it was good
for June too. I was propping up her ego so she could go
out there and find another, better man. You're probably
hoping this awful man—me—will hurry up with his
story.

For months, June and I continued this email relationship, sometimes reminiscing about our former sex life,
and dancing around the idea of bringing the past into
the present. I had no intention of leaving my family. Or
even having sex with June. These emails meant no more
to me than an amusing way to pass the time. But I knew
my wife would be devastated if she read them.

Then the day came. The trap snapped shut. After
one of my usual complaints about stress and arguments,
June wrote, "We should run away together." She put a
unicorn emoji next to the sentence. It was an inside joke
of ours. In the past, if we texted something outrageous
like, "We should move to Bora Bora," we'd put a
unicorn emoji next to it. I wrote back, "Yes, we should!
Come get me!" and put a unicorn emoji next to it.

Those two short sentences doomed me.

June knew my wife was away for a few days with the
babies to visit her mother. I was doing yard work when
two attractive women walked by on the sidewalk. They
called me over, saying they were lost and asking directions to a street.

Something strong and ammonia smelling clamped
over my nose and mouth. My shirt went up, and there

was a sharp sting in my side, like a needle. My legs melted, I had no control over my body.

Cintra's phone rang and she nearly jumped out of her skin. She was about to turn off the ringer when she saw the call was from Elliot.

"Cin? Are you coming?"

"Oh my God, oh… what time is it?"

"Eleven-fifteen."

"Oh my God, I'm…" She wiped hot beads of perspiration beaded along her hairline. "I completely forgot."

"Well, are you coming?" he asked, irritated.

"Elliot, I can't. I'm… doing something."

He blew air into the phone. "I was going to invite you to spend Halloween with us, and my birthday, but it sounds like you have other things going on."

Boston was on the phone. "You're not coming?"

"I can't today, sweetie. I don't feel well."

"Oh."

"Can you put your Dad back on the phone, please?"

"Yeah?" Elliot practically growled.

"I'm not feeling well. I need to stay in bed today. Can I call you tomorrow about Halloween?"

"Whatever, Cin," he said. "Feel better." And hung up.

She stared at the phone between her knees. She had lied to them, broken her streak of honesty. But what was she supposed to say? That she was reading the craziest letter she'd ever read, one she wasn't even sure was real?

She turned off the ringer, pushed a pillow behind her back, and sat up with the notebook on her thighs, searching for where she'd left off.

...NO CONTROL OVER MY BODY.

I woke up on the metal floor of a van, my hands and feet zip tied, a ball gag in my mouth. I was still so sleepy I could hardly move, but someone sat me up. The four people in the van wore black masks, but I would learn their genders from their voices. A man was driving, and there were three women.

One of them showed me my wallet. They showed me my phone, a winter coat, a couple of my gold chains, my laptop, and a bag of my clothes.

I could not understand why, if they had what they wanted, I was tied up in a van. The fact that they'd taken clothes seemed strange, but I wasn't thinking clearly.

They told me what was to happen. I was being taken in revenge for what I had done to June. My emails with June would prove she and I were having an affair and had run off together. The emails had been forwarded to my wife.

I was told they knew where my wife was at all times, and they named her parents' address in Rochester. They named the Y where she swam, our grocery store, our regular coffee shop, our park. They named the hospital where Jasmine was getting her treatment. I was told if I resisted, they would kill Samantha, and text messages they'd sent between my phone and June's phone would spell out that I was considering hiring a hitman to cash in on my wife's insurance policy.

They told me they'd taken out an insurance policy on Samantha recently, and it would look like I'd taken it out. I was told the texts between June's phone and mine would show that while I wanted to have my wife killed, June was trying to talk me out of it. This way, if it happened, it would all be on me.

I'll spare you my state of mind during what seemed a very, very long ride. On some level, I still thought this was all a horrific joke. June would eventually appear, laugh, and have her revenge. I vowed to be a better man from that second on. But it was too late, Cintra.

When the van finally stopped, one woman injected me again. I was extremely disoriented, but when they untied my feet, I could still walk.

My winter coat was put over my shoulders to hide my tied hands. Two of the women and the man walked me into a building, what I know now is the building we're both in. There was a quick turn and then we were in an elevator.

It wasn't until I was inside of a room, the coat was off and my hands untied that I realized I had a large black watch on my left wrist. One of the women told me to go ahead and try to get it off. I couldn't.

They pointed to the iron mesh on the windows, saying the windows were also glazed so that no one could see inside. There was nothing inside of the room except a box spring and mattress with sheets and blankets, and in the bathroom, a bar of soap, deodorant, and toilet paper. I was told I would be locked inside of the bedroom, and if I screamed, it would be useless, as the room was soundproofed. There's drop ceilings and wood panels all along the walls. I recognize a sound insulation job when I see one.

But I don't know why they bothered, as they told me if I screamed, my wife would be killed. Then they'd send police an anonymous tip leading them straight to the text messages and the insurance policy.

I was brought into the bathroom and my head was shaved. That was because they didn't want the watch getting wet with hair washing. The women shaved me while the man stood in the doorway. They kept their masks on the entire time. They told me I could use one hand to wash myself in the tub, no shower. If I tried any nonsense with getting the watch wet, they'd instantly know, and Samantha would pay the price.

They said the watch was equipped with GPS and sound monitoring. They would be able to track my whereabouts and listen to me at every moment. To show me this was true, they told me to very quietly speak a word. Then they left and closed the door. I tried to say something they couldn't easily guess. A few moments later, they came in. One of the women said, "Bitch." That indeed was my word.

They weren't done yet. I was told the watch could be remotely detonated, and would blow off my hand. It would look like an expensive computer watch that had malfunctioned.

I was told the apartment and my room was locked by combination and all the windows glazed, sealed, soundproofed and hurricane force resistant. It would do no good to scream, bang, or try to open or throw something through the windows. The watch I was told has an app that monitors my heart rate. If it spikes, they'll assume I had done or was about to do something to June and my wife would get it.

I was told their gang could go anywhere—mountains, deserts, jungles, cabins and boats in the middle of nowhere.

This is when I finally saw June, who came into the room.

"Niko, you have been sentenced to one year's captivity," she told me. "Then you'll be released. I think that's fair. You took seven years of my life. I'm only taking one of yours."

The look in her eyes was like nothing I had ever seen in her before. It was as if she was a completely different person than the one I had lived with all that time. I knew there was no point in trying to talk with her. If anything, I should say as little as possible.

Once my time was served, June said I could crawl back to my wife and beg for forgiveness. Since I had been so good at getting her back all those years, I shouldn't have much trouble with my wife. She told me they weren't animals, and I wouldn't be hurt or starved. What I would be is denied my children's first birthday, their first words, their first Christmas. I would be left for a year to imagine what my wife was feeling believing I'd abandoned her with two babies. In short, the torture would be all in my mind.

After I'd be set free, they said nothing could be traced back to any of them. A kidnapping tale would appear the ravings of a man trying to win back his wife. If I knew what was good for me, I'd get on with my life and keep my mouth shut.

Cintra, I agreed this was fair. One year of my life in exchange for wasting seven years of June's life. But I told her that my daughter had a heart operation coming up. All I wanted to know was if she survived it.

"I don't care about your daughter's heart, Niko. You never cared about mine," she said.

The first day of my imprisonment, I was put into the van again and blindfolded. The stop and start of the van, and loud horns, made me feel we were in a city.

The blindfold was removed. June brought me to a cash machine on the street and stood out of the way of the ATM camera. I was given my ATM card and told to take out the maximum. I was made to do this four days in a row, always at different machines. I assume this was so anyone who looked at my bank statements couldn't pinpoint my location. The withdrawals were to show that I'd taken out cash to pay a hitman, should the need arise.

It was on the fourth run that I had my first hint as to where we were, as a man talking near us had a distinct New York accent. June also finally told me we were in Brooklyn, but where, I don't know. I can see outside but I overlook the wall of another building. I've also never been here before. When you mentioned Prospect Park at dinner, that's the first real clue I've had.

It was also on the fourth day of my being brought to an ATM that I saw you in the hallway. June had told me people in the building were working with her. I wondered if you were one of them. When June brought you and Pedro to dinner, I had to assume the possibility that both of you were part of the gang. But as you talked, I became convinced this wasn't the case. You seemed too good.

I think she brought the two of you here as witnesses that she and I behaved like a normal couple. You could testify to that in court if needed, that I acted normally and not like I was being held against my will.

And I think she enjoyed it. Showing me off as a wonderful husband, all while knowing I wanted to alert you to what was happening, in case you weren't part of them, and couldn't. One of her little tortures. I think that's the real reason why she shaved my head too. She always said I was too vain about my hair.

Cintra, I have no TV, radio, books. She lets me out a little bit here and there, and when I'm out I'm so brain starved that I ask Leo any question I can think of, but my mind is muddling and sometimes I feel I'm losing the ability to speak.

Early on, I got the idea to try meditating. If I could learn to slow my heart rate down, then I could attack June from behind if I needed to, without my heart accelerating and tipping them off. I knew they would hear me, but how could they have a problem with meditation?

But June caught me meditating and put a stop to it. She may have had an inkling what I was trying to do. It was a ridiculous idea anyway, attacking June wouldn't be worth the risk. But in those first few days I clung to little ways to try to get control of the situation, even if just to calm my mind.

I began thinking if I could get your attention, then you could go see my wife and find out if Jasmine is alive. Especially after you said you were a crime writer who would pay attention to the little signs. But I didn't think it would occur to you in a million years that a man had been abducted, so I tried to make you think it was Leo at first. I hoped you'd pay attention to a literal sign.

June gives Leo pens and paper to draw on, then is careful to lock them back in a box. She counts the pens to make sure I don't take one. I have never seen anything else to write with. I'm let out a little in the morning, so that Leo sees me occasionally, and perhaps so I don't go completely mad. But one morning after Leo had been drawing, he was running around and stubbed his toe. He began to cry. June was distracted with him, giving me enough time to take one of his papers, which said "Up." I was able to hide this under my shirt, and then my mattress.

They were running late, so I trusted she wouldn't pay much attention to what Leo put up on the door. Even if she noticed what it said, there was no way she could connect it to me. I hadn't written it, Leo had. Maybe she would assume he'd stubbed his toe before finishing his message.

Cintra, I feel it was divine intervention that Leo happened to write, "I'm being held up," and if I took one of those papers, the message changed to "I'm being held" and could get your attention. It's hard to keep faith right now, but I suppose He threw me a bone.

So far as I can tell, everything with Leo is true, though Callie isn't June's sister. I guess they consider themselves sisters, being part of this gang that goes around punishing men for whatever emotional crimes they've committed.

June told me the couple who'd lived in this apartment before us went wrong. The man's imprisonment was revenge for his having a wife and family somewhere, and his girlfriend found out the day before their big wedding.

But the gang didn't vet the girlfriend well enough. The moment they had sex, their use of the apartment ended with gang members showing up. Sex isn't allowed. The gang didn't know how much the girlfriend would tell the man about the building and Callie, so Callie left the country to be on the safe side.

June told me the former hostage had come inside of the building a couple months ago, and confronted you, thinking you were part of everything. That made the gang "take care of" him. I'm pretty sure that means they killed him. Made it look like a drug overdose or accident or robbery gone wrong, who knows.

Callie didn't want to take Leo with her to wherever she's hiding, so he's left in June's care, if you can believe it. Gradually, June told me about Leo, how he used to be named Leonara. I took a huge risk calling him that in front of you, but June believed it was an honest mistake.

June will not hurt Leo. This is about punishing me. I want to ease your mind about the child.

I guess being the ringleader of an avenging group doesn't come with a salary, so Callie sublet the apartment to you and Pedro. Why they'd risk having people so close, I don't know. Maybe it was a financial necessity. Maybe they want both of you for future reference, to testify that I sat calmly at dinners and didn't ask for help.

The day I saw you in the laundry room, June was sick, to the point where she could hardly move. I was locked in my room all day. When Leo came home from school, I heard him complaining that he had no clean clothes.

June finally came in to give me food, looking horrible and shaking. I convinced her that I could do the laundry. I would not do anything to risk having my hand blown off, getting my wife killed, and being put in prison for her murder.

I think I got her at a moment when she was not herself. Maybe she was concerned Leo would complain about his dirty clothes to Callie. She worships Callie, you see. Still, I didn't expect her to agree. June stressed if I made one wrong move, the plan would go into effect.

Downstairs, I pretended I couldn't figure out the card machine. I knew she didn't have a card because she'd previously complained about losing it. I got permission to ask for your help. I had no idea if you'd even be home, but I had to try. First I went to my room, saying I needed to use the bathroom. I got the paper and was able to put it inside of Leo's pants pocket once I was in the hallway.

All this writing is extremely tiresome. June keeps me in the room while she showers, but I'll get the notebook into the jacket while she's making coffee. She has the jacket in the living room. It didn't fit Leo, so I think she's going to return it later.

Cintra, I don't want you to try to save me. If June truly means to keep me for one year, I can live with that if it keeps my wife alive. Please do nothing to put yourself or my wife in danger. Do not call the police!!! They're no match for these women.

I ask ONE thing. Find out if Jasmine survived her operation. I'm beside myself wanting to know one way or the other. If I can know this, then I can stay here for as long as June wants. Without knowing, I'm afraid I'll do something terrible even if it means the death of Samantha and myself.

Her name is Samantha Vasquez. The address is 601 Chestnut Street in Cold Springs. You can pretend you're a former student at Samantha's high school, Rochester High. Make up a common name. She won't remember. Pretend you recognize her, start a conversation.

Samantha is about five foot five and weighs about 130 pounds. She has long dark brown hair, light brown eyes, and a beautiful smile, like Julia Roberts.

When I see you again—if I do—let me know if Jasmine is alive by telling me about your novel. Say you've finished it if she's alive. If she's not, say you haven't. And so I know that you've read this when I ask, rub the tip of your nose.

My hand is aching. The sun's rays are creeping into the sky. I need to dress and hide the notebook under my shirt.

Cintra, if you feel this is too dangerous, don't do it. You have your own family, and I understand not wanting to risk yours for mine. Please don't put Samantha in danger by telling her about my predicament. If you decide not to do this, rub your nose when I ask about your novel, but say nothing. I will understand.

Niko

## Chapter Thirty-Two

*O*ne part of her thought, no, this can't be real. June and Niko are messing with her, getting back at her for butting into their business about Leo. Or maybe they're nuts.

But so much of it lined up. Someone had been meditating; she'd heard it through the wall. Niko couldn't know she'd heard it. And she suspected the first time she'd heard noise, it *had* been crying. Niko crying. Either the soundproofing job wasn't as adequate as June thought, or she was lying about it to him.

Niko's shaved head lined up. Cintra knew it was shaved because she'd seen the old photo of him with thick, ornery black hair. He couldn't know she knew that either.

Niko. The "future faker" from June's past.

Ettie Brightman. Niko hadn't mentioned her, but Cintra had little doubt. The gang of women—and at least one man—who'd kidnapped him and brought him to June. Ettie Brightman had something to do with all of it. It couldn't be a coincidence that Callie was the administrator of her fan site, and June was holding a man hostage in Callie's apartment.

One of the fans must be hosting "Liz from Colorado" in Brooklyn. Cintra wasn't sure if Ettie was involved with the gang in a methodical way, or was merely its muse. But a GPS watch rigged to explode on command sounded suspiciously like a modified ankle monitor, possibly smuggled out of prison by a guard or released prisoner. Ettie had cash for bribes thanks to all those donations.

Prison would be the perfect networking opportunity for a vigilante gang. Who couldn't you meet there? Everyone from murderers to bomb experts to hackers. If they all worked in concert, united in one passionate belief, motivated not by greed, but by principle, they'd be almost impossible to beat. Money easily tore people apart. Shared outrage? The bond would be strong as steel.

Then came the realization that the gang had targeted closer to home as well. They must have been behind the voice disguised phone call to Brittany. But how did they know her name? Did they have Cintra wired too? Suddenly paranoid, she patted down her body, ran her fingers through her hair, and scratched at her scalp. She wouldn't use her computer until she could have it scoured at the computer shop, they may have managed to remotely plant spy software.

She went to find Pedro, who was on the living room floor in skin-tight leggings, doing leg stretches.

"I'm going to stay with Elliot and Boston for a few

days," she told him. "It's Elliot's birthday and Halloween and they invited me."

"That's great," he said, deepening his V-formation. "Things getting back to normal?"

"Normal?" she snorted. "Listen, don't share this information with June, okay?"

"Why would I?"

"I don't know, but from now on, don't tell her a thing about me. Nothing."

"You know what, Cin?" he said, sitting up straighter. "I'm a little tired of this. One minute it's, 'I was so wrong about June. June's getting me a house. I'm giving Leo a jacket.' The next, she's evil, and don't tell her anything. Make up your mind!"

"It's made up. Don't tell her anything about me. Not one single thing. I'd suggest you not tell her anything about you either."

"Okay, Cinderella," he said, rolling his eyes and going back to his stretching.

She went to her room and began packing, enough for a couple of days. She'd lied to Pedro, but she had to. Lives were on the line, including possibly Pedro's and her own. Who knew what June was capable of, with her cadre of pals who had a tinted-window van, incapacitating drugs, ball gags, apartments with soundproof prison cells, exploding watches that could record your every move… what was a few lies compared to all that? She was pretty sure Dr. Grace would give her the thumbs up to lie. And to hell with her if she didn't.

She'd also stop off at the phone store in Park Slope,

and buy a new phone before heading to Penn Station, not daring to check the train times to Cold Springs on her current one. Jotting down Samantha's address—601 Chestnut Street—on a loose sheet of paper, she tucked it into a flap pocket inside of her travel tote.

## Chapter Thirty-Three

*O*n the Amtrak train, Cintra took a few minutes to gaze at the beautiful passing scenery, the cold blue sky, the cerulean serenity of the Hudson River fringed with fall foliage of crimson, orange, and gold.

Then she got to work. She emailed Mavis, telling her she was sick and would not be coming to work on Monday. She also told her she'd still not heard from any other Ettie fans. Perhaps True Crime should plan on a special without them, unfortunate as that was.

Out came her Kindle. She went back to the book she'd started a couple of weeks ago but now had even more interest in reading: *'Till Death Do Us Part: The Ettie Brightman Story*, which had been the basis for the tele-movie *A Woman on the Verge* starring Megan Walsh.

The book, an exhaustively detailed account of the rancorous and mutually spiteful divorce of Ettie and Montgomery "Monty" Brightman, had been published five years after the killings. But it had been updated a few years ago with new interviews and information. The book had never been out of print and still ranked high in the true crime category. Deadly endings to seemingly perfect marriages were always a topic of fascination, and the sad saga of Ettie and Monty continued to draw new generations of readers.

Ettie had been a beautiful, intelligent woman who'd spent most of her twenty-year marriage pregnant or nursing babies. Her twenties and early thirties were spent working long hours as a waitress, perfume counter girl, and babysitter, all while raising five children, to support the family while Monty attended Columbia University's medical school and completed his residency.

All the while, Ettie dreamed of the day she and her husband would be financially secure and he could spend more time with the family. But soon after that day arrived, it was snatched away from her by a much younger woman, Paige Livingston, who'd worked in Monty's hospital.

Monty and Paige had started an affair shortly after meeting. Although Ettie had her suspicions, Monty heat-edly denied it. Not only denied it, but gaslighted Ettie, insisting she was paranoid and delusional, and forcing her into therapy "for the sake of the children." This went on for not one, not two, but three years.

When Ettie finally demanded Monty end the affair or they get a divorce, Monty made his choice. Fortu-nately for the handsome heart surgeon, his best friend, Stanley Steelman, was the go-to divorce lawyer for most of the East Coast's wealthy set, and was willing to take his case for practically nothing. And very fortunately for Monty, he'd once operated on, and saved the life of, the very judge who would oversee his divorce case. Unbelievably, despite Ettie's lawyer's objections, the judge got away with not recusing himself from the case.

Ettie refused to slink off quietly into the night. Wasn't that what a used up, middle-aged wife was supposed to do when her husband decided it was time for her to go? But if that's what Monty had expected, he'd married the wrong woman. Despite coming of age in the "free love" sixties, Ettie's worldview was remarkably conservative. She truly believed that if she married the right provider, had the right amount of children, took care of husband, children, house, and pets, that she would be taken care of in return, not tossed out to fend for herself once her husband decided he wanted a younger model.

If she couldn't have her marriage anymore, Ettie at least wanted one half of their marital assets, and not one penny less. But when Monty fought tooth and nail to make sure this didn't happen, Ettie's mind and behavior deteriorated into frightening places.

She snipped the blooms off all of Monty's prized roses in his circular driveway. She papered the town of Belle Cove with his face and the words, "Dr. Brightman is a DOG who left his family for a BIMBO." She made hundreds of harassing phone calls to his home answering machine.

Then came the worst incident: For fifteen years, Ettie had kept the ashes of her and Monty's stillborn child. One day, she broke into Monty and Paige's new house, and dumped the ashes on their bed, leaving behind a note: "Your dead son wanted to meet the slut."

A detailed accounting of Ettie's disturbing behavior was used against her to strip her of custody of the children.

Monty too could be a master of tit for tat, but he was much more sly about it. Ettie had been desperate to retrieve their silver wedding platter, a gift from Ettie's grandmother. But Monty claimed it was lost. After his death, the platter was found wrapped up in his closet with the words "The fat bitch doesn't get this" on it.

And it was a stunning display of pettiness that directly preceded the murders: Monty sent his ex-wife a Christmas card with a photo taken inside of the Lake Champlain cabin that Ettie no longer had rights to, the same cabin where the family had always taken its Christmas photo. But that year, Paige was standing in the spot where Ettie used to stand.

"He had replaced me, literally," Ettie testified in her trial. "Bought a younger model. No stretch marks from birthing his children. No wrinkles from the stress of raising them and supporting him. No belly fat from six pregnancies. He didn't even have the decency to find someone who didn't look like she was my younger sister."

Cintra was deep into the book when she saw the name "Calista Bates." Grasping the train's armrest, she stared into the Kindle, unsure for a moment if she was imagining it.

*"Ettie has been enormously wronged, first by Monty Bright-man, then by the judicial system," said Calista Bates, co-founder of STOMP (Stop Torturing Our Mothers Please), a group fighting for reform of the no-fault divorce laws, which it feels*

*unfairly benefits men. "Monty would be alive today if he'd played fair. He thought he could take everything, including Ettie's own children, and move on with another woman who'd done nothing to earn the lifestyle to which Ettie was fully entitled, the lifestyle that Ettie allowed Monty to achieve by supporting him while he went to medical school. Monty not only drove her to an act of deadly self-defense, but the judicial system did as well. Many of us see her actions as justifiable homicide."*

The author of the book went on to say that Calista knew all too well what Ettie had gone through. Calista told the author that her ex-husband had also taken the majority of their marital assets after breaking up their ten-year marriage. He'd moved to Texas to "become a cowboy," leaving her with their one-year-old daughter.

Harry Bates was a real estate magnate who owned properties all over the world, yet because these properties were in the name of an investment company, a judge ruled they weren't marital assets, leaving Calista Bates with a tiny percentage of what she felt should have been hers.

Cintra had a good idea what Callie had done with her small settlement—bought two apartments in Brooklyn.

She put the Kindle on her lap, rubbed her eyes, and stared out the window at the glassy Hudson River streaming by. The train came to a shuddering stop and an older woman sitting next to Cintra struggled to get her suitcase out of the overhead compartment. Cintra helped her, then sat down again.

Somewhere along the line, Callie had founded or joined a female-led vigilante group that punished men for things the legal system didn't consider punishable offenses: Lying, cheating, "future faking."

Joseph was lucky he got off as easy as he did. It was obviously June and the gang who'd hacked into his work account and found out about his "shifting money around." Those astrology charts June had made for Poppy—an excuse to get Joseph's name and birth date. With that, they could easily trace where he worked and who his clients were. As for June telling Poppy the exact time to give Joseph her "We should go our separate ways" spiel, that must have been so the gang would know when to start threatening him. When he suddenly changed his mind about wanting to get married, and began acting so different, Poppy would think it was because of the "astrology." It wouldn't hurt that Poppy would be grateful to June, in case the gang ever needed her for anything.

Cintra didn't believe Poppy had been recruited by the gang, not with how astonished and insulted she'd acted when Joseph finally confessed what had spurred his change of heart. Impressive how dedicated June was to her cover—she even had an astrology chart hanging in her apartment. Or, rather, the gang's apartment.

Now Cintra knew why the apartment had looked so lived in, why the turquoise and beige sofa pillows matched the walls, though she hadn't seen any painters coming in and out of apartment 3D. June hadn't decorated the apartment. Only one thing that mattered came with her from Cold Springs—Niko.

Thankfully, Cintra's antennae had gone up when June wanted the same information about her and Elliot for more supposed astrology charts. But the gang had figured out who Brittany was anyway and made that threatening call. As if Cintra wanted their warnings to keep her husband in line. She could issue her own warnings, thank you very much.

Cintra was in awe at the scope and organization of the gang. And that they hadn't been exposed yet. She didn't know how long the gang had been active, but it smacked of quite a while. For sure, June and Niko weren't the first couple in the gang's wheelhouse, given that a different couple had been in apartment 3D before them.

Cintra could barely let herself ponder whether Niko deserved his punishment—whether any of the men did. She herself had had pretty good luck with men. Her father had raised her from the time she was fourteen. He'd been a good dad. Her stepfather, though she didn't know him well, seemed like a decent guy. And her marriage problems stemmed from her issues, not Elliot's.

But she knew it wasn't like that for everyone. Poppy had been complaining about Joseph's lack of commitment for years. Liam had been busy impregnating a woman while living with Pedro. There were, of course, the female friends, acquaintances, and friends of friends who'd suffered sexual assault. She'd had her own share of scary incidents. All you had to do was read the news to see what men were capable of. Maybe the world needed some women willing and able to turn the tables.

But was captivity the way to go about it? Niko's payback had an unsavory ripple effect—he may have missed the chance to say goodbye to his daughter; his wife was trying to deal with young twins, one of which was sick or who had even died, alone. Samantha and the twins had nothing to do with what had happened to June. However many revenge kidnappings had been perpetrated, most probably had similar unintended consequences. People didn't generally live as islands.

Right now, foremost in Cintra's mind was a father who was desperate for information about his baby girl. She also felt the weight of responsibility for a mother she'd never met. Getting information to Niko about Jasmine would hopefully prevent him from going mad and hurting June, which could spur the gang to retaliate by killing Samantha.

After that, Cintra would think deeper on what, if anything, she could do about Niko's situation, and whether it was worth the risk not only to him and his wife, but to herself and her family.

She put her Kindle in her tote under the seat, pulled her cable cardigan tighter around her shoulders, and hoped for a bit of sleep before the train chugged into Cold Springs.

## Chapter Thirty-Four

*T*he reflection staring at Cintra was almost comically not her. Her long shiny black hair was an orange-tinged veil of dry straw. The box of hair dye had said "Butter Blonde" but whatever this was, it wasn't butter. Last night, she'd cinched her hair into two ponytails and slashed off four inches on either side, leaving her with the worst haircut imaginable. She'd opted for dye over a blonde wig, worried her long dark hair would make it too easy for stray hairs to poke out. Besides, natural-looking wigs were exorbitant. Now, at eight in the morning, she tried to conceal her choppy cut with a ponytail.

On went the ten-dollar prescription-free tortoise-shell glasses she'd picked up at the same pharmacy as the hair dye. Then came the matching mauve angora sweater and beret, gifts from her mother on some long ago Christmas. She didn't want to wear all black. An all-black ensemble might alert a savvy spy to her city dweller status.

She had no idea if the gang knew who she was. But she was taking no chances. Anyone keeping an eye on Samantha hopefully wouldn't realize the orange-haired, bespectacled lady in a mauve sweater and hat was the same raven-haired, black-attired woman who lived next door to June and Niko.

Disguise complete, she left the bathroom of her studio in the quaint bed and breakfast located right off Cold Springs' main drag, and sat on the bed. On her phone, she went back to the pages she'd started researching last night: A few public Facebook groups for Rochester High School class members of the years Samantha must have attended, given her age.

Cintra didn't want to take someone's real name, worried Samantha might know the person. So she picked out a woman with the first name Lynn (nice and generic) and combined that with a last name that was common in the town, as popped up several times: Coba.

Lynn Coba.

She figured that would sound vaguely familiar to Samantha. Cintra knew about lies: The best ones had an element, no matter how small, of the truth.

She hoped Samantha wasn't going to want to talk about high school or mutual friends. Niko's "She won't remember" led her to believe Samantha had not been too involved with her classmates.

"Lynn Coba" would live in Manhattan, but was visiting Cold Springs for a break from the city, where she'd moved shortly after graduation. Lynn Coba couldn't live in Rochester. Cintra only knew enough about Rochester to answer the most basic questions. She didn't want to risk saying something wrong about the place.

Cintra hoped that Lynn Coba looked in her late twenties, not Cintra's age of thirty-eight. She also had to hope that Samantha hadn't moved; and that she was home. Being that it was Sunday, if she still lived at 601 Chestnut, the chances were good she'd be around.

Cintra pulled the rental car into a parking space a block past the address, but on the opposite side from the house. She did again what she'd done the entire five minute ride there, scanned the vehicles nearby to see if any drivers were paying her particular attention. Spotting a white van with a dark circular back window and tinted side windows parked across the street from 601 Chestnut, she palmed the little opera glasses she'd found in Callie's apartment and peered through them. The van's front seats were empty. That didn't mean spies weren't in the back of the van, watching the house that Cintra was going to watch.

The Chestnut Street house was a charming ranch with yellow and red brick siding, black shutters, and a red brick chimney. Canary yellow leaves blanketed the lawn, as if no one had had time to rake them. Cintra swerved the opera glasses to a mailbox with a black iron horse for a mail flag. On the side was a gold-tinged name plate: "Garcia/Vasquez."

Garcia. Yes, that was Niko's last name. The name June had adopted on her Facebook profile. She should have just deleted the profile. But Cintra imagined June had gotten too much of a twisted thrill changing her name to Niko's, and watching the reactions of her friends. She'd probably wanted Samantha to find it—solidifying the fiction that the two had run off together. Not very smart.

Allowing Niko to go to the laundry room. Allowing him to come into Cintra's apartment. Yes, June had gotten complacent or overconfident or had simply not pegged Cintra as someone she needed to be on guard about.

One side of her lips slid upwards as she luxuriated in the idea that she'd outwitted her neighbor. Then she tamped the sense of triumph down, telling herself not to make June's mistake of hubris. This was far from over, and June had extensive assistance.

She'd considered various scenarios and decided the most plausible one was for "Lynn Coba" to "bump into" her old classmate. Chestnut Street was a short walk from the main drag, so it wouldn't seem suspicious that Cintra was wandering around the area.

If Samantha was anything like Cintra had been when Boston was a baby, she'd want to get her twins out of the house while the weather was still good, before winter closed in. It was a nice day out, the biting chill of early October had retreated in favor of mild temperatures in the high sixties, with a pale sun and gossamer ribbons of cloud. Luckily, it wasn't raining.

Cintra had nothing to do but wait. She couldn't read. Her eyes had to remain on the house. She couldn't even drink coffee, worried that would result in a full bladder and nowhere to relieve it. She flipped through

Sirius stations, settling on music from the seventies, and ate a chocolate croissant.

It was 8:52 a.m.

\* \* \*

ABOUT AN HOUR LATER, during "Go Your Own Way" by Fleetwood Mac, a woman emerged from the house who fit Niko's description. She wore white running pants with a blue stripe down the sides, a black windbreaker, and had on a white cap with dark, billowy brown hair spilling from underneath it. And she was maneuvering a stroller down the step from the porch to a stone walkway.

The stroller clinched it. The woman had to be Samantha.

But Cintra's heart went into free fall. There was only one baby. That meant Jasmine hadn't survived her heart operation. Cintra would have to tell Niko that his baby girl was gone. He hadn't been able to say goodbye to her. He hadn't been able to comfort his wife. What would he do?

Maybe she should tell him Jasmine was alive. That would get him through the next nine and a half months. But when he learned the ghastly truth, he might be furious with her for tricking him. So far, her lies had done nothing but make people unhappy with her.

She couldn't decide which was worse—spending months believing your child was alive only to abruptly find out this wasn't the case; or to spend months mourning the death of your child while in solitary confinement.

There was no more time to contemplate it. Samantha was power walking, and already halfway down the block. It was essential that Cintra come at her from the front, so she could pretend to recognize Samantha's face, not her back.

She got out of the car, didn't bother locking it, and walked quickly in the same direction as Samantha. When Samantha came to the cross street and stopped to check for cars, Cintra hooked into the road. Then she slowed, trying to appear out for a casual stroll.

One car passed at the stop sign, and Samantha pushed off the curb, looking poised to start jogging. Cintra had to act.

"Samantha?!" she yelled out, tone a mix of surprise and uncertainty.

Samantha didn't seem to hear her, kept going. Realizing she had headphones on, Cintra increased her pace until she was almost across the street, and tried again, louder. "Samantha?!"

This time, Samantha stopped. Looked around at the trees before zeroing in on the source of the call. Cintra was only several feet from her.

"Are you… Samantha Vasquez?" she asked, cheerily, trying to look harmless.

Samantha grimaced and instinctively moved the stroller to her side, as if to shield her baby from this stranger. "Who are you?" she asked, amber eyes flashing. Niko had said she had a beautiful smile, but Cintra could see no evidence of that right now.

"I'm sorry. I didn't mean to scare you. You look so much like this girl I used to know named Samantha from Rochester High School."

"I'm Samantha," she said, pulling her earphones down to her neck, eyes still flashing suspiciously. "Who are you?"

Cintra pressed her hand to her mauve sweater. "Sorry, I'm Lynn Coba. I don't think we were in the same class, but I'm good with names and faces."

"Oh," Samantha said, her hand loosening its grip on the stroller's handle. "Lynn. Yeah, I think I remember. I'm terrible with names."

Cintra twisted around, touched her ponytail. "And my hair is a weird color. The dye job didn't quite work." She hoped that left it open as to whether Lynn Coba had been brunette or a more normal shade of blonde in high school, giving her persona a broader range of people she could have been in Samantha's mind.

"Right," Samantha said. "You were a class ahead of me?"

Cintra nodded. "Anyway, I'm here from the city looking around. Taking a weekend holiday. Was even considering moving to a place like this. It's so beautiful and peaceful."

"I suppose," Samantha said, looking as if she wanted to wrap up the conversation and get on with her exercise.

"This your little one?" Cintra asked, chin out towards the stroller.

Samantha, seeming to realize she'd been unwelcoming, moved aside, and notched the stroller's hood back a few inches. "Yes, this is Nikolas."

The baby, with jet-black hair down to his ears and wide dark eyes wondrously taking in the world, gave one of those beatific baby grins and kicked his legs in glee. He looked about eight months old.

"He's so cute," Cintra said, waving at him and making a goo goo face.

"He is," Samantha said, relaxing more. Out came the Julia Roberts smile Niko had mentioned. "And he knows it."

"Well, I didn't mean to bother you. But I saw you and… you like it here?"

Cintra didn't know why she was continuing conversation. She had the information she needed and should get the hell out of here in case someone was watching. But another few minutes of prying couldn't hurt.

"It's quiet and a nice place for a family," said Samantha. "I'd prefer the city myself, but it would be hard raising two kids there."

"Two?" Cintra asked.

"Yes, Nikolas has a twin. Jasmine."

"Oh! Jasmine!" Cintra burst out, too excitedly. "She's…" Cintra wagged her head from side to side, as if the baby was somehow concealed from her there on the sidewalk.

"She's in the house with my mom. My mom's foot is bothering her, so I'll take them out separately. The double stroller slows me down."

"I see. That's great to know! I mean, great you have them."

"Yeah, you know what? I'm being rude. Want to come inside for tea? Looks like the whole day will be nice, so I can take them out later. I don't get to talk to people my own age much in person anymore."

"If it's no bother," Cintra said, too invested in wanting to know how Samantha was handling her situation to do what she should do, which was leave.

## Chapter Thirty-Five

The inside of the house was pert and clean with arched doorways, sparkling light wood floors, and large windows that gazed out onto an emerald lawn bordered by a kaleidoscope of flaming red, burnt orange, and lemon yellow trees.

On the large brown couch surrounded by various toys was a heavy-set older woman in a mint green house dress, with black hair pulled into a bun. The woman was reading a magazine but looked up as they entered, and struggled to stand. Next to her was a baby in an elephant-patterned lounger. The baby was thin-faced, pale, and asleep, with lighter hair than Nikolas'. She was smaller than him too.

"No, Ma, sit," said Samantha, wheeling the stroller into the living room near the couch and angling it outwards. Nikolas cried, his face turning red as the leaves outside, then settled down as Samantha rubbed his chest. "I met a friend on the way out and thought we'd have some tea instead. Ma, this is Lynn. We went to high school together."

Cintra stretched out her hand and the woman shook it, still looking as if she might get up any moment.

"I'll make the tea," the woman insisted.

"No, Ma! Sit. Rest your foot. Lynn, this is my mom, Rosetta."

"Well, hello, Lynn, dear," Rosetta said, canvassing Cintra's face with lively brown eyes. "We must have met."

"Quite possible," said Cintra.

Samantha took off her cap, fluffed her dark chestnut hair, and waved Cintra into an easy chair. "I'll put over the water. Back in a sec."

"Lynn, Lynn," said Rosetta, looking reflective. "Yes, of course. Lynn, what is your last name again, dear? I've forgotten it."

"Coba."

Rosetta clapped her hands together. "Coba, of course. I know you and your mother. Laura, right?"

Before she had time to consider the risks, Cintra had nodded. "Yes, that's right."

"How is Laura? I haven't seen her in ages. Now, wait. I saw her at Dom's Supermarket last month."

"She's well," Cintra said.

"And your brothers. Pete? Is that right? Who's the other again? The handsome one?"

"Uh," Cintra shrugged. "They're both handsome."

"Three, right? Pete and…"

Cintra helplessly looked towards where Samantha

had disappeared, then tried to distract Rosetta by nodding at the baby in the lounger. "Is this Jasmine?"

"Oh yes," Rosetta said, turning her attention to the baby, her face glowing. "Isn't she a doll?" But she snapped her fingers, still grappling with her memory. "And Brad. Brad, and…"

Samantha came back into the room. "Any kind of tea you prefer, Lynn? I have green, cinnamon, Earl Grey…"

"Anything is fine," Cintra said, wondering what she could say to leave. This was getting a little too hot for her.

"Brad, and… wait, it's on the tip of my tongue. Sammy, she's Brad and Pete's sister. And who was the other brother, the handsome one?" she asked Samantha.

Samantha shook her head. "I don't remember all those boys."

"The Coba boys, Sammy. Brad, Pete, and… You're not going to make me guess, are you?" Rosetta asked, twinkling her eyes at Cintra.

"It's fun listening," said Cintra, giving an exaggerated palms-up shrug. Just her luck there might have been an actual Lynn Coba at Rochester High, though she suspected Rosetta was confusing her with someone else.

Rosetta adjusted Jasmine's white flowered headband. "I'll have to tell Laura I saw you. What's brought you to our neck of the woods?"

"Just visiting."

Samantha sat down on the couch and turned her attention to Jasmine, pulling her little white sweater over her chest, kissing her delicate head.

"She's adorable," said Cintra. "They both are."

"You're maaaarried," said Rosetta, eyeing Cintra's wedding ring. "To that boy? The one from school? I remember him. The tall boy. Wasn't he a Bianchi?"

"No, I got married in the city. But I kept my maiden name." Cintra's history of lying was coming in handy. In fact, the lying felt good and familiar, like catching up with an old friend, though it was the type of friend that, while fun to be with for short periods, would eventually bring trouble.

"I hope he's a nice one," said Rosetta. Suddenly, she scowled. "Nicer than the one my daughter married."

"Ma!" snapped Samantha.

Cintra laughed awkwardly. "He's nice, he is."

"That's good. Can't be too careful. I told Sammy, you haven't known this man long enough. He's so much older. Any man that age who isn't already married, something wrong with him." She crossed her arms disdainfully, then grumbled, "Should have married a Coba boy."

A teakettle whistled and Samantha got up. "Ma, don't bore her with gossip," she instructed, leaving the room.

"Can I help you?" Cintra asked Samantha, half-standing, hoping to get away from Rosetta.

"No, I got it," Samantha called back.

"Your grandchildren are so beautiful," Cintra said, returning to her seat.

"Yes, but this little one here…" She reached over and lightly poked Jasmine's belly. "She's had some problems. Hopefully it will all work out. She has a heart condition and needed an operation nine days after she was born." She clutched the beads hanging around her neck and brought them to her lips.

"I'm sorry to hear that. She's doing well?"

"We hope so. She needs one more, and then she's done. Was supposed to get it a month ago, but…"

Samantha came back into the room with three mugs, handed Cintra one, and then carefully separated the other two and handed one to her mother. "Lynn, I forgot to ask if you're okay with milk."

"Yes, that's fine," said Cintra, taking a sip.

"Ma, what are you blabbing about now?" asked Samantha.

"I was telling Lynn about Jasmine. She had a heart operation and needs another."

"I hope she's okay?" asked Cintra.

Samantha sipped her tea and stared off out of the window behind Cintra. "She was supposed to have the second procedure last month, but the doctors didn't feel she weighed enough. So we waited."

Nikolas squalled and Samantha said, taking him out of the stroller, "Do you mind?" and lifted part of her shirt.

"Go right ahead," said Cintra. "I have a son myself, so I know how that goes."

Nikolas latched on eagerly, sucking and gulping, his meaty little fist resting on his mother's breast. "I fed him an hour ago, so I don't know what his problem is. I only wish Jasmine ate as well. I bottle and breast feed and sometimes she gets the feeding tube."

"When is her operation?" Cintra asked.

"The seventh. I'm… I'm very nervous about it. She had some complications with the first surgery, fluid around her lungs."

"I pray for her every day, seven times a day," said Rosetta, fingering her beads. "God will get us through it. The seventh, that's a good sign."

"It is," said Cintra.

"And He'll punish that bastard," Rosetta added.

"Ma…" said Samantha, under her breath. "She's talking about my husband. We're separated."

"Separated?" Rosetta screeched. "That bastard ran off. Ran off on his babies!"

"Oh, I'm… so sorry," said Cintra. "Is… is he… he's not anywhere?"

Samantha looked down at the suckling Nikolas. "He was having an affair. He took off with her. That's all I know."

"Leaving her here with these babies!" cried Rosetta. "His daughter! Who's so sick! Lynn, dear, how is your father?"

"He's good," she said.

"Because I heard he had cancer."

"That's… better. It's better."

"Oh? I'd heard he was on his way out. No hope at all."

"Maaa…" Samantha warned.

Cintra was halfway through her tea and running escape plans through her mind. She cleared her throat. "Your husband… you haven't heard anything?"

"Nothing!" Rosetta cried.

Samantha shook her head. "No. I still can't believe

it. Leaving me, fine. But them? And Jasmine? He loved them, I—"

Nikolas began fussing, scrunching up his face, so Samantha slung him over her shoulder, firmly patting his back. "I'd like to get him more on the bottle, but he prefers the boob," she said. Cintra heard an impressively large burp. Samantha kissed his fat cheeks and put him back inside of the stroller. Jasmine was waking up, yawning, eyes flickering tentatively.

"I hear you," said Cintra. "I nursed mine until he was eleven months." She paused, and silence engulfed them. Even Rosetta seemed to have run out of things to say. "Could there be any way your husband, um… maybe something happened to him?"

Samantha shook her head, shoulders sagging. "No. He definitely went off with an ex-girlfriend. I have proof of it. It's so… I never would have thought… "

"He's scum!" shouted Rosetta.

"Do you know this ex-girlfriend?" asked Cintra.

"Not really. Only her name. June Cross. I tried to look her up online, Facebook, things like that, but couldn't find her. One of Niko's—that's my husband—one of his friends brought me to her house, but she doesn't live there anymore. A woman rents it, said she came through an agency and doesn't know who owns the house. I guess if he wants nothing to do with us, then fine, but…." She looked from one baby to the other, incredulous. "I can't believe they won't have a father."

"We need to call a lawyer," insisted Rosetta.

"Ma, please," said Samantha, putting up her hand.

"Not right now. We'll get to all that when Jasmine is better. I can't handle anything else on my plate."

"He's got to pay child support. We've got to get custody. You can't bury your head."

"I'm not burying my head. I can only deal with so much."

"What if—" said Cintra, setting her mug of tea on a side table. "—he ever came back?"

"Came back?" Samantha looked appalled. "What do you mean?"

Cintra leaned on her knees, and her pharmacy glasses, which had slid to the end of her nose, clacked onto the floor. With a guileless look, she picked them up and replaced them on her nose. "What if he ever came back and had a good reason for what happened?"

Samantha cackled sharply. "Would have to be a damn good reason."

"What if it was? Would you forgive him?"

"Never!" said Rosetta, clutching her beads.

"I can't imagine what reason he could possibly have," Samantha said. "But if it was something, I don't know, like he'd fallen, cracked his head, and gone insane?" She seemed distantly amused with this outside chance.

"Yes, something like that."

"I might be open to a discussion if he could *prove* it."

"Never," pronounced Rosetta. "He's a *liar!*"

Jasmine was making *heh-dahh heh-dahh* noises, and Samantha plucked her out of the lounger and hugged her up on her chest. "It's a very serious operation. I don't know if she will... I only wish he'd *call*."

"Tell me about the town," Cintra said, wanting to ease the conversation away from Niko, then make her escape.

Samantha said Cold Springs had a nice Y where she used to swim every day before the babies were born, was safe and quiet, and had good schools, so she'd heard. She was a dentist, and hoped to go back into practice as soon as Jasmine recovered.

"Or she can move to Rochester," said Rosetta. "Or I can move here. And Dad too."

"You know Dad doesn't want to move his practice," said Samantha. "Dad's an attorney," she told Cintra.

"He'll do what I tell him," Rosetta smiled, nodding at Cintra.

About five minutes later, Cintra said she'd better go, she wanted to get some things done, and didn't want to take up their entire morning. She shook hands with Rosetta, who said, "Give Laura my love and tell your father I'm so glad he beat that darn cancer. Do you mind if I call and ask your father to speak at the church? He's a miracle."

"I'm sure he'd love that," said Cintra.

Samantha walked her outside, shut the door behind them. "Nice running into you," she said.

"You too. I'll be thinking about you and Jasmine. I'm not much of a praying type, but I'm going to do it."

Samantha smiled, but her eyes narrowed as she inspected Cintra's face. "Everyone called me Sammy in high school," she said.

"Yes, I know," said Cintra, nodding.

"But you called me Samantha."

"I wasn't sure which you preferred these days."

The side of Samantha's full lips twitched, she put her hands on her hips. "Sorry about my mom. She has no filter."

Cintra looked into Samantha's honey brown eyes. "I hope it works out. With your husband, I mean. I have some issues of my own going on. It can be hard. Marriage."

Samantha gazed off towards the street. "If I was able to get a message to him, I suppose I would tell him..." She turned to Cintra, her bottom lip quivering. "That I need help. I don't want to do this alone. We don't have to be a couple, but he made these babies with me and he has a responsibility." Then she looked back towards the street, almost searchingly.

Cintra could not move for a few moments. She wanted to touch Samantha's arm, but instead she stepped off the little porch and waved goodbye before her face would reveal what she felt Samantha suspected —that "Lynn Coba" was in touch with Niko.

Worried that Samantha would keep an eye on her, she knew getting into a car parked so close to the house would seem suspicious. So she kept walking, intending to go around the block and double back, giving Samantha enough time to retreat into the house.

But halfway down the cross street, two women approached from the opposite direction. They were both brunette, somewhere in their late twenties or early thirties, in dark, nondescript jogging gear, with black caps pushed down over their foreheads.

Hyper-alert to any women in the area, Cintra

decided her best bet was to get back to the car. She turned straight around and picked up her pace.

Inside the car, her fingers traced the inside of the cup holder by the radio, but her key wasn't there. Isn't that where she'd left it?

The women turned the corner and seemed to be looking straight into her car windshield. She felt desperately around the floor under her seat for her key, then pushed a lever on the door thinking it would lock it, but instead the window glided down. As a city dweller, Cintra hardly ever drove. Cars were like big steel alien creatures she had to reacquaint herself with on the rare occasions she rented one, and the purposes of their buttons and levers seemed to change every few years. She flicked the lever and the window slid up.

On the sidewalk, the two women walked closer and then, to her horror, stopped a few feet from the car, chatting to each other, their words garbled through the window. Cintra realized she was biting her lower lip hard as she tried to calm herself and remember where she'd stashed the key before jetting out of the car to follow Samantha. Grasping the steering wheel with one hand, she peered up through the window at the women. They looked at her briefly, which stopped her breath.

Remembering that her yoga pants had side pockets, she patted down her legs, felt the key, yanked it out, and started the car. That's when the women kissed each other on the cheeks and went in separate directions, one woman passing her car without a glance, the other headed in the opposite direction. Cintra felt hugely relieved, but also ridiculous.

Checking behind her for cars, she pulled out, and saw Samantha staring at her from the sidewalk, her mouth forming the unmistakable words, *Who are you?*

Cintra pushed the gas pedal hard and panicked through a stop sign as another car slammed on its brakes and horn. Heart flapping in her throat, she whipped around a corner towards the main drag.

\* \* \*

AT NOON, after changing clothes, she had a Niçoise salad, side order of french fries, and a glass of sparkling water at an Italian restaurant connected to the bed and breakfast. She didn't dare venture too far, worried about running into Samantha.

Then she walked a block to a hair salon, where she'd made an appointment to clean up the disaster she'd inflicted on her hair with the dye and pharmacy scissors. The salon was small, with only one front window. Cintra asked the hair stylist if they could sit at the last chair in the back.

She wanted to get back to something resembling her natural color before she checked out of the bed and breakfast. Arriving as a brunette and departing as a blonde could draw the wrong kind of attention, and she absolutely had to fix the cut before seeing Pedro or even running into June.

The hair stylist, encasing Cintra in a black nylon cape, looked dismayed at the butcher job, asking what on *Earth* she'd been thinking. "I was going for a

Halloween thing, but it didn't work out," Cintra said, staring at herself in the wall-wide salon mirror.

"This is scary all right." The stylist shook her head and snapped her sharp-pointed scissors.

Two hours later, Cintra was almost back to her natural color, only a reddish tinge remaining, her hair fanned in neat, blow-dried layers around her shoulders. Goodbye, Lynn Coba.

"Never do that again," said the stylist.

On the way out, Cintra remembered she'd told Elliot she would call him today. It was almost five o'clock. She left him a message, then went to a gourmet coffee shop next to the salon, got a latte to go, and sat in the small yard behind the bed and breakfast, enjoying the prismatic spectacle of fall foliage. Elliot called.

"Yes, I'd love to spend Halloween with you guys," she said.

"Happy birthday to me."

"Ugh, I'm so sorry, Elliot. My mind has been all over the place. Happy birthday. I'd like to do something for you. Dinner?"

"Cin, is something going with you? I'd really appreciate some honesty. That's what this whole separation is about, isn't it? Honesty."

She paused, watching a couple at one of the yard's little wrought-iron tables as they entwined fingers and passed murmurs of affection. "There's lying and then there's not telling. I'm going through some private things."

"Private things you can't share?"

"That's what private means, Elliot."

"I know, but… Cin, are you seeing someone?"

"No! It's not about that at all."

"Because I—"

"Look," she said, keeping her voice low, "you've been having drinks with a young coworker you admittedly want to sleep with, and you didn't tell me about that, but now you need strict honesty in that department. If you want to hear I'm dating someone so *you* can date someone, then go do it. I'm not dating."

"I'm not either. But you're acting so mysterious."

"What about Halloween? I want to see my kid. What costume did he choose?"

"Chucky. Totally out of left field." He sighed. "But you didn't call, and I didn't know what was going on, so he made plans to go out with some kids from his class."

"Then I'll go with him."

"*With* him? He's thirteen. You'll make him a laughingstock, mom tagging along with his friends."

"Then I'll stop by before he goes out."

"They're leaving pretty early. About six-thirty. Will you be around by then?"

"I'll really try. I want to see him." She had work that day but would do whatever it took to get out on time.

They talked for about ten more minutes, then wrapped it up, agreeing that Cintra would get to the apartment at six p.m. on Wednesday, so she could take a few pictures of Boston and send him on his way. As for Elliot's birthday, they never got around to that.

In her room, she undressed and, despite the early hour, collapsed into the slightly bumpy bed and slept dreamless the entire night through.

## Chapter Thirty-Six

*B*y Tuesday, the sun had vanished behind gray, vertical coils of mist, the air smelling of damp, crushed leaves. But it was still warm enough that Halloween costumes wouldn't have to be bundled under a coat.

Pedro was surprised to see Cintra upon her return the day before, saying he'd assumed she was staying with her family through the holiday. She explained that as she'd slept on the couch, she'd only wanted to stay a couple of nights, enough to celebrate Elliot's birthday and take Boston to the early Park Slope parade. Pedro complimented her hair, both new cut and "those auburn undertones."

In the afternoon, she went to Halloween Haven in Greenwich Village to look for a costume. The place was almost as big as an airplane hanger and every inch was crammed with costumes and Halloween paraphernalia: spiders, spider webs, ghosts, goblins, gravestones, giant bats.

She found a witch costume that she liked. It was, of course, all black, the material silky with front buttons, a bodice with long, fitted sleeves, a ragged-edged skirt that hung to her shins, and a tall, pointy black hat. Then she found a black cloth crossbody bag decorated with white skulls.

The bag is where she would store the switchblade knife she'd bought at the Swiss Army store.

SHE PLANNED to attend June's Halloween party, having a feeling it wouldn't only be real estate colleagues there, but some of the Ettie Brightman gang. She didn't know how she would be able to identify them, but her writer's curiosity wasn't going to let her sit this gathering out.

Besides, she had to try to get a message to Niko. In a crowd would be the best place to do it, as she didn't know if she wanted to be alone with the couple ever again. Only she wasn't sure how to tell him that Jasmine was alive, but that the operation had been postponed. The code he'd given her in the notebook hadn't covered these gray areas.

She wondered if it would be too risky to flash him a note. She couldn't jeopardize Samantha's safety. Not to mention what the gang might do to her and Niko. No, a note would be too dangerous. She could say, "I plan to finish the novel in a week" or "I've postponed the novel." Would he have a clue what that meant? Even if he did, it wouldn't ease his mind about Jasmine, and could instead inflame it. June watched him too carefully.

She knew him too well. Even a flicker of something unusual in his eyes could spell disaster.

There was another problem. On the train ride back to the city, Cintra had researched Harry Bates, Callie's ex-husband. His body had been found on his Texas ranch five years ago, his death ruled "combined drug intoxication."

But friends in articles about his death were quoted as saying they had never known Harry Bates to do drugs. Of course, addicts are experts at hiding their addiction. But Cintra wondered if the gang had gotten to him.

According news stories, the once very wealthy real estate magnate had died near penniless after bad investments and settling several major lawsuits. Perhaps Callie had him dispatched for ruining Leo's chance at a large inheritance. Cintra didn't know how much Harry Bates had been a part of Leo's life, but given that Bates had lived several states away, she doubted it was much. Ending up poor after being an absent father might have been enough to seal his fate.

Did June *really* intend to let Niko leave the apartment after a year and walk back into his former life? Given that the gang may have also killed the former hostage in 3D, Cintra feared Niko was in much more danger than he knew. The plan could be to mentally torture him for a year, and then…

She needed to do something. But what? There were so many things to consider and any one of them could end badly, not only for Niko and Samantha, but herself and her family.

As for the former hostage, Cintra now realized that

his *breaking apart families* referred to his *own* family—the one he was trying to keep hidden from a duped fiancée. In his mind, it was the *gang* who was the problem, not his penchant for bigamy. But Cintra tried not to think too badly of him, knowing he might have paid the ultimate price for his sense of entitlement and stupidity.

She didn't expect any trouble from June at her Halloween party. If June had seen the notebook, it wouldn't have made its way back to Cintra inside the jacket pocket. But she wanted a knife with her.

If June gave her any serious problems, Cintra would have no qualms about using it.

## Chapter Thirty-Seven

On Wednesday, Halloween day, Cintra went to work as usual. Mavis came over to ask if she was feeling better, and she said she was. "We're filming the special," Mavis said. "Too bad about those fans. Wonder why they were so skittish."

Cintra had no doubt why. Callie must have told them all to keep their mouths shut. Janet had apparently gotten the memo late and then made up that story about her husband. Doubtful everyone on the site was involved in the gang, but enough probably were that Callie didn't want them drawing attention to themselves.

By 5:45 p.m. Cintra was in her old building in Park Slope, and took pictures of Boston in his Chucky costume. He told her Chewbacca had been too hot, and the Velociraptor too bulky. Elliot was polite, but cool. His costume was a simple Phantom of the Opera mask, and he had several oversized bags of candy ready for trick-or-treaters.

She walked Boston downstairs so he could meet his

friends at a nearby brownstone. On the sidewalk, they passed clowns, monsters, superheroes, princesses, insects, even an F train. "Now *that's* scary," Cintra said to the child in the subway train costume, who looked at her sluggishly, not appreciating her joke about the line's poor service.

A small crowd of young teens waited by the brownstone, and Boston made his greetings as they hooted over each other's costumes. She kissed her son on his forehead as he looked pained, not wanting motherly affection in front of his pals.

"Have fun and I'll see you Saturday," she said.

"See you then, Mom. Thanks for coming."

The kids urged him on, and soon he was walking away from her. She watched him go, and was stabbed by the sudden conviction that she may never see him again. She opened her mouth, wanting to call him back, to hug him tight to her. But she didn't want to embarrass him even more.

At eight p.m., Pedro came into the living room with his claws, his fangs, and his vaguely werewolfian costume of scraggly fur vest and matching leg warmers. Cintra had her witch costume on, but was planning to add pea-green face paint and a brown mole to the tip of her nose.

The switchblade was in the bottom of her skull-dotted crossbody bag. As she was depositing it, she'd remembered the pepper spray stashed in her tote bag.

On a whim, she'd put that into the crossbody
bag too.

She and Pedro shared a glass of red wine in the
kitchen, not wanting to be early arrivers to June's party.
Pedro was only planning to stay an hour or so before
meeting up with some friends.

"I've been too hermity lately," he said. "People are
starting to ask if I'm alive."

"I noticed that. I've been worried about you. Do you
plan on any more auditions?"

"I suppose," he sighed. "It's what I do, and what I
love. But I'm looking into other things as well. Teaching,
that kind of thing."

"You'd be great at that."

She still didn't want to bring up Liam's marriage
and impending fatherhood; if Pedro didn't know about
it, the knowledge would crush him. If he did, he clearly
wasn't ready to discuss it. At eight-thirty, they decided to
head to June's and went into the hallway. Pedro turned
and locked the door.

"I don't have my key," she told him.

"You want to go back in?"

"Nah, this will give me an excuse to leave with you. I
don't really want to stay long either." She didn't want to
tell him that she was uneasy about being at the party
without him. "Just don't forget me."

Cintra could hear noise from apartment 3D, a loud
clamor of people. She buzzed the door and within
fifteen seconds June answered.

"Helllllooooo!" she cooed, brandishing a pink wand
capped with a sparkly gold star. She was in a silky pink

gown with roundly-puffed sleeves, her blonde hair in ringlets topped by a plastic, gold crown. "I'm Glinda, your fairy Godmother. Your wish is my command."

"Grr," said Pedro, slashing at her with his claws.

Cintra thought it ironic: here she was dressed as a bad witch, and kidnapper June was dressed as a good witch. Truth was indeed stranger than fiction.

June led them to the dining room table. It was piled with Halloween-themed cupcakes, chocolate-dipped strawberries, raw vegetables and dip, cheeses, cold cuts, and bottles of wine, champagne, and vodka and juices. There was an ice bucket nearby, and slices of lime and lemon on a plate.

"Help yourself," said June.

Cintra poured herself a plastic cup of champagne, dipped a carrot into some dip, and ate it. As casually as possible, she asked, "Where's Niko?"

"He went to his room to email someone about a job, he'll be out in a bit."

*His room.* And emailing someone about a job on Halloween night? June needed some practice with her lies. Cintra wondered if he was going to be let out tonight; it would look awfully strange if he never made an appearance.

Soon, Pedro was on the opposite side of the living room, looking through a collection of vinyl records near a media console. Michael Jackson's "Thriller" was playing.

Cintra introduced herself to a pair of women who were by the table filling their plastic cups with white wine and inspecting the cupcake selection. One woman was dressed as a "killer bride," with blood tears streaming down pasty white cheeks. In her hand was a large, red-splattered fake knife. She said her name was Maressa and she worked with June at Barton's.

"Killed your groom, did you?" Cintra asked, sipping her champagne.

Maressa mugged, playfully stabbing the air with her knife. "He deserved it. Was five minutes late to the altar."

The other woman had a furry cat mask covering her face; the mask was so furry, she was drinking her wine out of a straw. She said her name was Wendy and she was "in insurance."

Insurance.

*The texts would spell out that I was considering hiring a hitman to cash in on my wife's insurance policy.*

*They told me they'd taken out an insurance policy on Samantha recently, and it would look like I'd taken it out.*

June touched her arm and said, "You remember Liz?"

Cintra turned and was staring into the almond-shaped green eyes of Liz. Or Ettie Brightman. Her breath stuck in her throat and she could barely get her hand up to shake Liz's hand.

"Hello, again," Liz said. She was dressed as a flapper, her plump body wrapped in a black beaded dress. A silver headband with a long white feather sticking out of it circled her bobbed gray hair.

"Hi," Cintra managed. She couldn't help being starstruck. Under other circumstances, she wouldn't

have minded talking to the murderess about her crime—
if she'd ever admit she was Ettie.

"Love your costume," Liz said. "Very… witchy."
They made small talk for about fifteen minutes. Liz
enjoyed Brooklyn but would soon be traveling. There
were places she wanted to see: the Grand Canyon,
Yellowstone, Redwood Forest.

"Oh? You haven't seen those places already?" Cintra
asked. "I mean, living out West…"

"I never got to do much traveling. Raising kids,
taking care of a home, the time flies."

"How many kids?"

"Two. But they were quite a pair." She smiled
ruefully. "It was all worth it though. They settled down,
are quite successful. My daughter has her own business,
my son is a data analyst."

"What are their names?"

"Names?" Liz looked mystified at Cintra's nosiness.
"Stacy and James."

Not the names of any of Ettie's five children. "Liz"
had her story down pat.

"I'm sorry," Cintra said. "What was your last name
again?"

"Smith," Liz said, without missing a beat.

Smith. The nerve of this woman!

As Liz turned to layer a slice of cheese over a
cracker, Cintra nonchalantly studied her profile. Ettie
had a model-like sloping nose, which Cintra had noticed
after examining more pictures from her trial. Liz had a
similar sloping profile, but the nose seemed bigger in her

face than Ettie's had seemed. Perhaps a shifting of her features from age and losing weight in prison.

They had different voices though. In her media interviews, Ettie's voice was disarmingly girlish. Liz's voice was a bit raspy, that of an older woman who'd done her fair share of smoking. She could have taken up the habit in prison. Was there any chance Liz wasn't Ettie Brightman after all?

Liz ate her cracker, and Cintra noticed a few of the party guests were casting sidelong glances, as if they wanted to approach Liz, but were too intimidated to do so. Finally June, who'd been talking with another woman, turned and asked Liz about her upcoming travels.

Cintra kept an eye out for Niko. One hell of a long email he was writing.

But then he entered the living room from behind a hallway wall. She couldn't believe her eyes. He was in a black and white striped prisoner's uniform. At first, he didn't see her, making small talk with a few guests.

And it began to dawn on her. It hadn't been obvious earlier because of the dim lighting, the masks and makeup, but it seemed like most of the revelers— perhaps *all* of them—were women. No, wait, there was a very large man over by Pedro, dressed as an executioner, with an ax in his hand that Cintra hoped was fake. His face was covered by a black leather hood, but the body shape and height—*had* to be a man.

Was he the only male here besides Pedro and Niko? Her eyes darted around worriedly. There were about fifty people in the room. A cold pit of nerves gathered in her stomach.

Niko was making his way to her through the crowd. "Ha," she said, indicating his prisoner costume. "That's interesting."

"Isn't it?" he asked, blinking at her. He had a black chain metal plate hanging around his neck, emblazoned with white lettering that said: PRISONER 1313.

Then June was next to them, with Liz beside her. "Liz is going to head out," June said. "She was the first one here."

"Afraid this old gal can't party like she used to," Liz said. "It was so nice meeting you," she said to Niko, then turned to Cintra. "And you. Again."

Niko and Cintra said their goodbyes, and June walked Liz to the door. Cintra glanced around the room, and that's when she knew it beyond any doubt. Liz was Ettie. Because even behind their masks and their makeup, she could tell by the direction of their heads. At least half the people in the room were watching Liz leave, as if she was a God who had passed among them.

Cintra lost track of June and Ettie through the crowd, then she looked down at Niko's wrist, at the watch. The listening watch.

"Great party," she said, trying to read his face.

"It is," he sighed, and turning to fix a vodka with soda water. "How is your new novel going?" he asked, his dark eyes on her over the lip of his cup.

Very slowly, Cintra reached for her nose with one finger and rubbed the tip of it. She still hadn't quite worked out what she was going to say. Niko held his cup an inch from his mouth, his gaze deadlocked into hers.

"The novel. Well, it's a bit complicated…"

June was back. Tapped Niko's black and white striped arm with her pink wand. "They let you out for the night, did they?" she trilled. "What are you in for? What crime?"

"I'm innocent," he said. "Was set up."

"Are you?" She looked at Cintra. "Why don't I believe that?"

"Maybe it was all a misunderstanding," Cintra said.

"He looks guilty to me!" June said, waving her wand.

The big man who'd been near Pedro earlier stood next to them. He was elephantine, maybe six foot five. Must have easily weighed three hundred pounds. The black leather hood, the ax. Queasiness pitched Cintra's stomach. She put down her empty cup. Reached for a celery stalk, hoping to calm her gut.

"Cintra, this is Rocky," said June. "He looks danger-ous, but he's a pussy cat. Rocky is a veterinarian up in Cold Springs."

Cintra nearly choked on her celery. A vet. A vet could easily have access to drugs. Drugs that could inca-pacitate a man. "Sorry," Cintra said, coughing, patting her chest with her palm.

"Let me get you some water," said Niko, leaving.

"Hi, Rocky," said Cintra. They shook hands. "I have a cat who licks his butt a lot. Could that be stress?"

"Could be lots of things," he said in a deep, gruff voice from behind the hood. "I couldn't diagnose him without an examination."

"No, of course not."

Niko was back and handed her a glass of water. She took a long sip. "So you came all the way from Cold Springs?"

"I'd do anything for June. She got me a great deal on a foreclosed house." He nodded down at June as she basked in his admiration. "Besides, not much going on up there. Got a hotel and will head back tomorrow. You ever been there?"

"Never."

"Nice place, you should check it out sometime. Come for the weekend. Cute little bed and breakfasts up there."

Feeling even sicker, Cintra nodded and drank more water. Her lips were suddenly parched and her tongue felt too thick for her mouth.

She'd missed her chance with Niko. She should have gone after him into the kitchen, told him that she planned to finish her novel in a week. She didn't want to say it in front of June in case this news caused his face to register something June didn't like.

"Would you excuse me?" Cintra said, certain her tone betrayed her burgeoning panic, but hoping her expression did not. "I'm going to hit the bathroom."

She shuffled off to the bathroom. Locked the door. Took long, ragged breaths, looking in the mirror at her pea-green face, and her brown nose mole, which had smeared when she'd rubbed her nose. Her pointy hat was off kilter and she straightened it.

This was feeling very dangerous. What had she done coming here? She despaired at the idea that she'd done the very thing she'd vowed she wouldn't do: become complacent. But how else could she have gotten a message to Niko? She couldn't possibly have risked it while alone with him and June. She should have waited until Pedro was with them. June wouldn't try anything in front of Pedro—would she?

Thank God she had worn a "Lynn Coba" disguise up in Cold Springs. Rocky, or any one of them, could have seen her there and recognized her here, even under her witch costume. But she hadn't had the disguise on every minute.

For all she knew, the woman who'd checked her into the B&B was inside the apartment, wearing a costume. For all she knew, the woman was right now telling June the green-faced witch at the party looked like a woman who'd just spent a couple of nights at her bed and breakfast.

Rubbing the switchblade knife through the fabric of the crossbody bag, she decided to get the hell out of the apartment. She'd get a message to Niko in some other way. And she'd ask Pedro to leave with her. He shouldn't stay here alone.

## Chapter Thirty-Eight

*a* knock came at the bathroom door. Cintra's throat pulsed hard as she turned to it. Calm down, it's someone who needs to pee.

"Cintra?" called a woman's voice. June.

"Yes?" Cintra called back, a quaver in her voice that she couldn't control.

"Sorry to bother you, honey, but one of my fake lashes fell in my eye. Can you look for me, see if you can see it? Ooh, it's painful."

Cintra slowly pushed up from the sink, and stood staring at the door. "Ahh, I'm kind of…" she stalled, hoping June would take the hint, go find someone else to help her. "I'm a bit… not feeling well."

"I have some soda water with me. Let me in, you should take a sip."

Cintra looked back in the mirror. There was no way June could know about the notebook. No way. She wouldn't have let Leo return the jacket with the notebook inside if she knew about it. And she wouldn't do anything with Pedro in the apartment. The women in the apartment… they couldn't *all* be from the gang, could they? Besides, what was Cintra going to do? Stay in the bathroom all night?

She fingered her knife through the bag. Then she reached inside and hit the button that snapped the blade open.

"Hold on a sec," she called, flushing the toilet for effect. Taking a deep breath, she opened the door. June stood holding up a plastic cup of fizzy clear liquid, looking concerned.

"I switched to soda water myself. Take this." She fluttered her eyes. "Oh, damn this lash. Can you help me look for it?"

Cintra took the soda water, sipped, then placed the cup on a nearby mounted shelf. June was holding one eyelid open, white eyeballs staring up at the ceiling.

"I think I see it," Cintra said.

"Let's move into the light," June said, pressing farther inside.

"I saw it. Did you want me to poke my finger in there?"

"Yes, if you could wash your hand first."

Cintra went to the sink, squirted some soap into her hands, and ran them under the faucet. She'd pluck the damn eyelash out and get the hell away from this party. Turning, she looked for a hand towel. The door was shut and June was blocking it.

"He forgot to give you the pen back," she said.

Cintra's heart beat loud in her ears. *Thump. Thump. THUMP.*

"The what?" It came out a tiny gasp, almost a squeak, and with that, she knew the game was over.

"The pen," June sighed, as if bored. "He gave you the notebook, but not the pen. Of course, that got me thinking. How would Niko get a pen? One thing had come in and out of the apartment recently. So I went to your place, and Pedro said you weren't there. I told him Leo might have left a notebook in the jacket by mistake, and he needed it. Pedro went to look in your room. He found this."

June reached behind her, and brought out the notebook. Cintra realized June had had it tucked into the thick pink belt around her waist.

Cintra's heart was slamming so rapidly against her chest, her mouth hung open to accommodate her quick breathing. How could have been so stupid not to see the pen was missing?

"June," she said, trying to dip her wet hand into her crossbody bag, but her hand was shaking so violently, she missed the opening. June put the notebook on the shelf and reached behind her waist again.

A gun was pointed at Cintra. It was small, silver, and looked like a toy, but she knew it wouldn't be a toy. She'd never seen a gun in real life. She almost laughed from shock.

She felt as if she'd frozen, gone completely paralyzed, and yet she must not have, because June said, "Cintra, please stop reaching for that bag, or I'll have to use this."

June was in a wide stance, both hands on the gun as she'd demonstrated during that long ago dinner. Cintra backed away, her calves hit up against the toilet. "How can you kill me with all those people outside?" she asked, absurdly.

"Those are my people," June said. "Ettie's people. I'm sure you've figured that out."

"I don't know Ettie and I don't know your people. I only know that Niko has a baby girl who is very sick and he wanted to know if she was alive. That's all. I'm a mother, June. I had to find out for him."

"That's very heart wrenching, but now you know too much."

Cintra thought about screaming. Would Pedro hear her over all the noise out there? Someone had turned up the music, it was much louder. Even if he did hear her, she was certain June would have locked the door. Would a scream only startle and enrage June, make her pull the trigger?

"I don't know what's going on with you and Niko, and I don't care," she said, a divine force giving her voice an authoritativeness she didn't feel. "If you want to hold him hostage for some kind of revenge, that's your business. I only wanted to let him know about his baby."

"Revenge?" said June. "That's what you think we're doing? It's justice."

"I understand that." Cintra softened her voice. A hope rose within her that she could reason with June— woman to woman. "And I feel for you, I really do. Everything Niko did to you. It was wrong. But a gun isn't the way to handle things. Think of Leo. Do you want him coming back to murder?"

"Leo is fine. He'll stay with his friend's family, then he goes to his mother for the holidays."

"But June, listen—"

"Shut up!" June reached behind her, opened the door, and wagged the gun. "Get," she said. "And keep your hands up, like in the movies."

Cintra cautiously walked out of the room, June backing away from her, the gun pointed. A few women were standing in the hallway outside the bathroom and, seeing what was happening, began to back away too.

Cintra had the frantic idea that one of the women would help her, would attack June. But none of them did. Instead, as she followed June into the living room, the crowd parted as if choreographed, as if they'd expected all of this. Someone turned the music down slightly.

The big man, Rocky. He could disarm June, couldn't he? But the hard truth was there; she just didn't want to face it. He was part of it. He'd supplied the drugs. Probably had driven the van with Niko in it, too.

Pedro. He was her last hope. He knew Krav Maga. Maybe he could get the gun from June and force her to open the combination lock. Please God that he hadn't forgotten about her and left the party.

The costumes moved in sync, crowded behind June on one side of the room. Watching, that's all they were doing, watching. A coven around the dining room table, around the plates of food, under the spiky gold chandelier.

"June, what the hell?" she heard. Pedro's voice.

"Ped!" Cintra glanced around anxiously. Found him, to her right, standing completely still, as if he'd been hit on the head.

"I said I was taking care of her," said June.

"I thought you were going to talk to her. Not this."

"Oh, shut up," she said. "You're the reason we're in this mess."

Cintra gaped at him, felt as if her face was melting. How appropriate. The melting witch. Pedro shook his head and looked down.

Then it all came to her. Everything.

Pedro lived in apartment 3C because he was one of them.

He'd given them Brittany's name. He'd told June about Cintra's suspicion that Callie was dead; that's why there had been a video-call. Liam had never even lived in the apartment; they'd broken up before that.

"Oh God!" she wailed. "You're in on this!"

"I—look. I didn't know a gun would be involved."

Cintra didn't see Niko. They must have locked him up while she was in the bathroom.

"Well, it is now! Why, Pedro, why?" But she knew why. Liam's unsettled face flashed before her, along with his pretty, blonde, and heavily pregnant wife. "It was Liam?" she said.

Pedro took off his fake claws, set them on the media console. "Yeah. Fuck that. I was so angry. I was ranting all over Facebook about it. You'd know that if you were on Facebook. He got married to a woman who lives in California, who has no clue he was living with a man when they met. He just erased me. Didn't even have a talk with me, nothing. Just—" He snapped his fingers. "Gone." He sighed and rubbed his face, then continued, "Callie got in touch and we were plotting ways to get back at him." He folded his arms protectively around his shaggy fake fur vest. "But I couldn't do it. It's out of my hands. I just hope he treats her better than he treated me. Then Callie offered me the apartment and… it's a free apartment. I needed something fast. And Callie has lots of theater connections. You know how it is, Cin." He blinked innocently at her. "All I had to do was stand by to help June if she needed it."

No wonder he was always in the apartment. He wasn't going on any auditions. He had to be nearby in case June needed his help for any reason. But he also wanted a roommate for money, because he wasn't working. Who better to move in than Cintra? In case she saw something unusual, who could a compulsive liar tell and be believed?

"You didn't care a man was being held hostage?"

He shrugged his shaggy shoulders. "They said they would let him out soon. Just a little punishment for how he'd treated June. I was in that mood, where I knew what it was to be tossed out like trash. And it didn't seem like they were beating him."

"All right," snapped June. "You've filled her in. Now we need to figure out what to do with her."

"Kill her!" boomed a woman's voice. "She knows too much."

"Yeah," came another woman's voice. "I'm in line

for the apartment next, and I don't want that messed up."

"Wait, wait!" Cintra pleaded, backing towards the wall. "You're going to fire a gun in a building? Someone will call the police."

"We're going to call them ourselves," said June, smiling. "Lulu, get Niko out here. Cintra, keep those hands *up. Up.*"

Cintra looked desperately toward Pedro, but he had wandered farther away, she could only see the back of his shaggy werewolf vest. Was he really going to let them kill her?

Why hadn't she hugged Boston when she'd had the chance? Her intuition had been right. That was the last time she would ever see him. How could this be happening? She thought she might retch from fear.

Niko was brought out by a woman who was dressed as a pirate, giving the appearance of walking Niko, the prisoner, to the plank. The crowd parted on either side of them.

"I'm so sorry, Cintra," he said, looking as if he might cry. "I shouldn't have got you involved."

"No, you shouldn't have," June said, as calmly as if Niko had said he shouldn't have used so much salt. "You should have taken your punishment like a man. But you've never been much of a man, have you?"

He hung his shaved head. Cintra could see he was emotionally beaten, completely beaten. He would be no use to her. And Pedro. He was a traitor! How could she die knowing her best friend wanted it? How could she die not having hugged Boston one last time?

"Cintra, I need you to turn to the wall, then go into your bag, slowly, and take out whatever you have in there," said June.

"She needs to take off the bag first!" one of the women called. "And kick it over."

June shook her head. "No, she needs to leave it on. The bag has to be on her, and if we try to put it on her later, we might get blood on us. Cops have these things that can show blood even after you've washed it off. I know what I'm doing. Cintra, turn to the wall, and take out what's in there, very slowly. Don't make any sudden moves. You won't be faster than a bullet."

Cintra's entire body was lit with starburst tingles, her jaw trembled uncontrollably and her knees were shaking. More than shaking. Practically knocking into each other. Terror had no dignity.

She had to get control of her body. Her only hope was getting control of her body. And to do that, she had to get control of her mind. Concentrate, *concentrate*!

Facing the turquoise wall with the astrology chart on it, she got her bag open with one hand, and made a split-second decision to withdraw only the knife.

"A knife. Perfect. Open your fingers and let it fall. Right at your feet."

Cintra let the knife tumble to the floor with a flat thud.

"Now you can turn back around," June said.

Cintra did, her left arm still straight out at her side.

"Here is how it will go," said June. "You've been obsessed by this idea that I kidnapped Leo. People at his school saw you stalk him. You started accusing me of kidnapping him, jabbing your knife. Pedro told me you've been in therapy for all your craziness, so it's believable. I had to shoot you in self-defense. And because Niko will blab his head off as soon as I let him out of here, he has to go too. Niko, you jumped in front of Cintra, and I shot you by accident. Maybe you two were having an affair, who knows."

"Jumping in front of the second bullet? That's the defense Ettie tried to use!" yelled Cintra.

June smiled. "But I've got dozens of people to back up my story, and Ettie didn't." She stood with both arms out rigid, back in that gun stance. "Rocky, bring Niko over here by Cintra."

The immense black leather hooded man moved towards Niko and grabbed his arm. He forcefully shoved him next to Cintra. Light glinted on the ax in his hand and that's when she knew it was real.

"I didn't want to do this, Cintra," June said. "I liked you."

"Wait!" she screamed, her palms spread out pathetically before her, as if they could stop a bullet. "I'm a liar. You must know that. Even if I told, no one would believe me!"

"Maybe not tonight, and maybe not tomorrow. But eventually, someone will. Besides, you work at that crime network. You could put reporters on us. They'd love this story."

The gun was aimed directly at Cintra's face. She was paralyzed, as if a false move would end her life quicker.

One thing was in her mind: Boston. Boston. No, no. He couldn't grow up without her, he couldn't.

Suddenly, her vision of June was blocked. She could only see the black and white prisoner stripes of Niko's back and his shaved head. "June!" he barked. "This has nothing to do with her. Let her go and put me back where I was. Or kill me. But let her out of here."

Cintra's hand recognized this chance before her brain did. With Niko blocking June's view of her, she pulled the bag to her center and dipped into it with her left hand. Gripping the pepper spray, she slipped one trembling finger under the plastic flap over the nozzle.

She had to get past Niko, get closer to June. How? And then what? What were the odds she could spray June in the face and get the gun before gang got her? They were everywhere. She was going to die. There was no way around it. But she'd go down fighting. And if there was any justice in the world, she'd take June out too.

"You always were an idiot, Niko," said June. "If you want to go first, that's fine by me."

"Wait, June, wait!" Cintra slipped the pepper spray up out of the bag, and quickly poked the tube past her right wrist and into her sleeve. "I don't have my key," she said, putting her arms up so the tube wouldn't fall out of her sleeve. "My apartment key. Why would I come here to threaten you with a knife but have no way of getting back in my apartment? It makes no sense! Cops will see that."

Cintra could see June over Niko's shoulder, and

something about her expression said she was finally unsure of herself. "Where's your key?" she asked.

Cintra said nothing.

"How were you going to get back in?"

Cintra said nothing. Niko stood his ground in front of her. She had to get around him.

June turned to look to her left. "Pedro?" she asked.

Cintra didn't dare turn her head to find Pedro, but she heard nothing from him.

"Pedro, go give Cintra your key. Put it in her bag. Slowly." For a moment, she swung the gun to her left, then brought it back. "Now!"

Cintra turned just enough, looking back towards the sitting area with the media console and speakers. Pedro must be behind some people. She couldn't see him at first. Then she spotted his shaggy shoulders. He was moving towards her.

June swung the gun again towards Pedro, and Cintra brought her hands down and reached into her sleeve, sliding to the left of Niko until she had a clear path to June.

She had just drawn the spray completely out of her sleeve when, in the periphery of her vision, there was a blur, a running brownish furry blur and a scream, "Run, sis! Ruuuuunnnnn!!!"

A sound like a firecracker cracked, and June was down, a mass of tufty brown fur on top of her. Cintra couldn't move, but felt herself yanked out of where she was standing. Chaos ensued. She heard yells and saw bodies running and leaping. She was being dragged, pulled with one hand, while her other pushed and shoved at arms and chests.

Niko was in front of her, and they were at the door. He was punching his fingers onto the combination lock.

Cintra looked behind her, saw a ghost white bride with blood tears and blood-soaked wedding gown moving down the foyer, a large knife in her hand. That had to be real too.

More costumes were behind the killer bride. They moved in sync down the foyer like a gruesome graveyard of ghouls who'd escaped from their coffins. The pepper spray wasn't in her hand. Dropped. Damn it!

Cintra got into her boxing stance, knees bent, and balled her fists. Terror had been replaced by fury. She bounced on her feet to keep her balance like she was taught in boxing classes, moved forward offensively, smacked the killer bride's knife down with her left arm, and popped a right hook at the bride's nose. White gown and veil and black wig reeled back and dropped.

"Come on, come on!" Niko shouted, grabbing her hand.

They rocketed down the staircase. But on the second floor landing, she hung down, almost sitting on the floor, free hand clinging to a metal banister. "Pedro!" she wailed.

"It won't help him if we're dead too," Niko yelled. "There's too many of them."

"Pedro!" She tried crawling back up the stairs but Niko was too strong for her.

He grabbed her face, his mouth inches from hers. "We need to get help. You can't help him. Let's go!"

Down the stairs they clattered, not even trying the doors. Who knew who lived behind them. How he'd opened the combination lock, she had no idea, but now was not the time to have a discussion about it.

Out the side door, they careened down the small side street, Niko squeezing her hand so tight it was painful. She yanked back, shouting, "My shoes. Niko!" and yanked and yanked until he stopped. She took off her heels, tossed them.

They ran to the first building, a condo next door with a brightly lit front. Through the locked glass doors, Cintra saw a desk where a doorman might be, but no one was there. Niko banged on the door buzzers.

"Do you have a phone?" he yelled at her.

"No, no!" She tugged at his arm. "They'll be coming. We're too close to the building. We need to find a cop. The park isn't far, there's usually a ton there."

The small side street turned darker by the shuttered horse stable. A crowd of older kids came towards them in costume.

"Do you have a phone?" Cintra hollered at them.

Even behind all their makeup, the kids looked terrified and backed away.

"Call 911!" she screamed at their stunned faces.

"We don't have time for this." Niko grabbed her hand, pulled her to the side of the horse stable, and into a small hay-smelling enclave. A horse whinnied and snorted from behind the brick wall. "Give me that thing," he breathed, trying to rip her bag over her head. "I need to wrap this watch. They're listening to everything. They could blow it up."

Cintra worked with him to take off the bag, and it tore at her hair. Somewhere in the madness, her pointy witch hat had fallen off.

"Wrap it," he ordered. "Tight as you can."

She wrapped the large part of the body bag around his wrist, then tied the sling in a knot around that. "I don't think they can blow it up. June said the room was soundproof and it wasn't. I heard you and her. She lies about things. She was brainwashing you to be obedient."

"That's a chance I can't take," he said. "Don't get on this side of me in case it blows. We need to get to cops before they kill Samantha. They could be doing it now."

"The park," she said. She cupped her hands around his ear and whispered, "There's a police substation."

She ran alongside him barefoot, hands holding up her ragged skirt so her legs were free, her feet slapping against the damp pavement, pressure pounding her knees. At the traffic circle abutting the park, packs of kids and adults roamed in costume.

"The GPS," he panted. "They'll track us. They've got cars. They'll shoot or drug us. They don't give a shit who sees them, they're all disguised."

She pointed. "Park is straight ahead. We can go in there, and get off the street."

Several cars zipped along Coney Island Avenue, going through a green light into the traffic circle. Cintra impulsively ran and banged her open palm on a car's dark driver window.

"Help!"

The car tore off through the circle, almost flattening

her bare feet. Another car was behind it. Cintra stood in the street, waving her arms. The car stopped, and she ran to the driver window, but that car too zoomed past her and through the circle.

"Goddamn it!" she yelled. "Where's the humanity?!"

Niko grabbed her hand. "They're not going to stop, Cintra, we look insane. We need to get to cops. They can call the cops in Cold Springs and send them to Samantha. I don't know her phone number by heart. Anything else will take too long."

They ran across the street, lights shining in the mist, making everything hazy and glowing.

"How did we get out? The lock," she panted as they ran. "This way, this way," she said, as she saw him looking around, confused.

"I've been listening to how she puts in the combination into the lock on my room. Which numbers they might be from where the sound lands on the pad. I thought I figured it out, then guessed the other lock would have the same one. Three-five-four-eight."

"Do you know what the number means?"

"No," he panted. "But we'd be dead if I was wrong."

They passed the tennis courts; a bubbled tent loomed like a giant white hunchback in the mist, and they ran past a mini-marble Parthenon towards a street that led into the park. It was a pedestrian and cyclist street only, as civilian cars were banned from the park. But that didn't mean the gang couldn't ignore the ban and come after them in cars. Laws didn't seem to bother them.

Cintra hadn't seen one cop car. It occurred to her that most of them were probably at the Halloween parades. She and Niko would have to get to the substation farther northwest.

"We need to get off the street," he said.

"This way." She pointed to a lawn. They ran to that, then hooked a right onto a path that led to the lake.

## Chapter Thirty-Nine

The thin, paved path was flanked by trees. Civilization peeled away behind them, their surroundings grew darker, mistier.

They slowed, winded, and jogged at a steady pace. Cintra was grateful for her frequent gym visits. But her feet were chilled and throbbing as she pounded over twigs and broken pieces of pavement. Niko was slightly ahead of her, then he veered off the path and bent forward, groaning.

"What?" she called to him. "Did you step on something?" No, unlike her, he had shoes on.

His other hand went to the cloth bag wrapped around the watch. "Ahh!" he groaned. She could tell he was in pain. Oh Jesus, the watch was going to blow. The women hadn't been lying about that.

"It's burning up!" He struggled to get the bag off with his other hand.

She ran to him, digging her nails in to find the

cloth's knot. If he kept yanking at it, he'd only tighten the knot around his wrist. Behind them a gulf of darkness shimmied with silver ripples, a few white swans huddled together on the shoreline: The lake.

"Niko! The lake!" She pushed him. "Get in the lake!"

Niko staggered, still fighting to get the cloth bag off his wrist. Cintra had done a better job of tying it than she'd thought. The goal had been to smother both the gang's ability to hear them and a blast. But neither of them had counted on Niko's primal desperation to try and remove a skin-burning watch. He fell forward, plunging into the lake with a splash. There were loud pops, a hissing, and the surface of the water bubbled as a small plume of acrid smoke rose. Niko cursed loudly and splashed around. Cintra's instinct to help him overruled her desire to keep away from the watch, and she dragged herself into the lake, her bare feet sinking into slimy sludge and algae.

"Are you okay?" she breathed.

"I think my hand is gone. I can't look."

He stared out blankly at the fat, white moon hanging over the ring of tree-tops, as if in complete shock. Toes buried in grotesque slime, she waded to him, feeling around under the water, trying to steel herself for the discovery of a bloody stump.

"No, it's there. I've got it," she told him. Geese barked harshly from out of the dark, as if cheering her find. *Ruh ruh!*

He didn't look at her, his profile and bald head lit by the high moon. She bent his fingers, tried to make him look at them. "It's there, see?" Even with only the moon-light and a lone street lamp near a lakeside bench, she detected a nasty, gauged burn mark on the top of his wrist. The watch was somewhere in the lake. She found the cloth bag floating on the surface, rung it out, and wrapped it around his fire-branded wrist.

"The watch is off," she said, hoping to bring him out of his catatonic state. "You're a free man."

"They're killing her," he said.

"No, they won't do that. They can't pin it on you anymore, because you've got me."

She got the cloth tied in a knot around his wrist. He turned to her, his face checkered with shadow and moonlight. "Is she alive?" he asked.

Jasmine. She'd forgotten all about her.

"Yes," she said, rubbing his arm. "She's alive. The operation was postponed. I saw Samantha and Nikolas and Jasmine. They're good, Niko, they're all good."

She watched as he deflated with relief. Then he laid his head on her shoulder. She patted his back for a few moments, and said into his ear, "We'll take the hiking path to the substation. It's right up ahead. Let's stay off that street. We've got to go. This is the last place they would have seen you and could be coming."

Up the dirt path that led into the woods, Cintra, who'd never been in the park past dusk, saw it was very, very dark. The canopy of trees, getting thicker by the moment, was blotting out the glow of the moon. Her skirt was soaked and sticking to her legs, slowing up her movements. Hiking the skirt up as high as she could, she tied the front of it in a knot, so it hung to her knees.

She knew from past hikes that the trail was pretty straightforward, up, up, and over a hill to a big, sloping lawn on the right, on the left more paths, then they'd find a stone staircase leading to the pedestrian street. If they kept walking westward from there, they'd reach the substation.

But the vast majority of her hikes had originated in Park Slope, so her trajectory had been from the opposite direction. Between that and the dark getting darker, her internal compass was failing, making her disoriented. She'd lived in the city for so long she'd forgotten was true night was like.

Niko, who'd never been in the park, would be no help. And people kept to the paved pedestrian paths after dark, didn't come traipsing into the dirt paths licked by thick, overgrown brush and dead-felled trunks from various storms. Prospect Park wasn't Central Park with its tidy, trimmed grid of well-lighted pathways. Prospect Park was wild, untamed, made for nature, not well-heeled tourists.

Her bare feet were battered from numerous sharp, unidentifiable things, including what must have been a bur, causing her to cry out and hop around on one foot, then plop to the ground with her muddied sole turned up in her lap. She carefully pinched it out with two fingers. Regrets were crowding her mind but there was no bigger regret than not wearing flats to the party.

Maybe coming to the park had been a terrible idea.

But she didn't know what alternative they would have had. From her years in the city, Cintra knew police response time was sketchy at best. Calling 911 and waiting for cops to arrive while standing mere blocks from the building would have been a death sentence for them both given Niko's GPS tracker.

But what fifteen minutes ago had seemed the quickest, safest route to help now seemed, in retrospect, impossibly stupid.

They should have gone down Coney Island Avenue, found a store, gone inside and asked for help. But they would have been tracked for sure. Those crazy bitches would have come right into the store and grabbed them. Was one cashier supposed to save them from an armed gang of fifty women? And with the city's strict gun control, the cashier probably wouldn't have had a gun.

The park had seemed the best way to lose them, but Cintra realized with mounting anxiety that she and Niko might be lost as well. But what if they hadn't come to park? Niko could have lost his hand, or even his life, without dousing his wrist in the lake.

She couldn't stop thinking about Pedro, back there with them. The pop-crack of the gun going off. Whether the bullet had hit him. Yes, he'd been trying to make her think she was crazy all of this time, but he didn't deserve to die for it.

Now she and Niko could be lost and Pedro might be dead. She should have split from Niko, got someone to call 911 and sent police to apartment 3D. But it had seemed essential to stay with Niko, who didn't know his way around.

This had all gone very wrong. She was glad her face, which she knew displayed her rising panic, was hidden from Niko in the dark.

Cintra pointed up the hill to a circular path that wound around a small field of twisty ivy, shrubs, and bamboo stalks behind wire fencing. If she was correct, there was a stone staircase behind it. They could take that to the paved pedestrian street ringed by a dirt horse path and trees, and follow the lighted street while staying on the horse path to be better hidden in case the gang came into the park with a car.

If the stone staircase wasn't behind the hill, then she didn't know what they would do. Her heart fluttered crazily at the thought of them stuck in the park until daybreak, not knowing if Samantha and Pedro were alive or dead.

"Up here, I think," she said. There was no running up the hill, they were trudging. Trudging like Lisa had trudged in the silver quartz monzonite trails in the bog. The only sounds were their heavy breathing, the crunch of leaves, the *eep-eep* of birds, and traffic whooshing in the distance like a rolling ocean. An airplane droned overhead.

Her ankle caught, banked sharply, and she fell sideways, smacking the side of her head on something hard and thick, like a tree root. "Ow!" she erupted, a solid block of pain connecting with the side of her skull.

There was a familiarity to the pain, to where it landed, the pancake roundness of it, and the quick, hot spread of pain through the side of her skull.

"Cintra!"

She remembered another fall. One on the front steps of her building in Park Slope, with Elliot reaching for her, or no… grabbing her. Grabbing her arm, and her ankle had twisted, like it had twisted now. She'd fallen back, catching a split second glimpse of his frozen face. Elliot's frozen face.

She lay on the ground in the dark woods, the white and gray mottled moon staring down at her, wondering when this had happened, this memory. She was sure it had happened, but when?

A flash of running from their bedroom, after reading something. Reading…

Niko was squatting before her, sitting her up. "You okay?" he asked.

She could only see the dark silhouette of his body, the glowing white of his pinstripes, and she could feel his breath on her face.

Could feel Elliot's breath on her face. "You okay?" Elliot was squatting next to her, on the sidewalk, the high-up lighted windows of their building staring down at her. The bang-slap of her head on the side-walk, and trying to staunch the spreading pain with her hand.

She had read something. An email between Elliot and a woman.

"I do care about you. But I love my wife. I don't regret what happened, but we can't continue. Brittany, you're in college. You're an intern. If anyone finds out, I'll be fired. And honestly, baby, it's not fitting to be fucking in your dorm."

She choked out a sound. Where was she? In the

woods or on the sidewalk in front of her building? Who was with her, Elliot or Niko?

"You damn bastard!" she cried. Ran, ran through the living room. Boston's look. His face like stone, his mouth open.

*That night you and Dad had the big fight?*

"Cintra, please! It's over, it's over!"

She opened the door to the staircase exit, ran down the musty stairs, footsteps pounding behind her, got to another door, opened it to the dark outside, and a hand was on her arm. She violently threw the hand off, and was losing her balance, falling...

"Cintra," Niko said, softly. "Here, sit up." His hand was on her back.

His hand was on her back. Elliot's hand. She had bang-slapped her head on the pavement. A couple of strangers were murmuring to Elliot. Did they need to call an ambulance?

No, no, I'm fine, she said.

The next thing she remembered, she was on their bed. With muted pain hot in her skull. The last thing she remembered, she'd been at the gym. How had she gotten home?

"I think I hit my head at the gym," she told Elliot, who was sitting next to her, his face grim. "I was using pulleys for my arms and I bent over. I think a metal bar came down."

"We should get you to the hospital," he said. "You could have a concussion."

"Cintra?" Niko whispered.

She held the muscle of his arm, Niko's arm. "I'm okay."

"Sit, rest."

"We need to get going. I'm okay. Because I remember it all, Niko. My husband is a fucking asshole. He let me think my head injury happened at the gym. But it was because of him. I remember it all."

## Chapter Forty

They wound around the circular path, holding onto each other, trying to walk as fast as they could, but in agony knowing how slow they were being.

The canopy of trees had opened into a vast violet-hued sky above them, and the moon gave enough silverlight to see silhouettes of paths and forest, but not enough to feel they could run safely.

Every few seconds came a cymbal-loud crashing, like boots chomping through the leaves and brush. But it was animals having their nightly gambols: squirrels, birds, chipmunks, raccoons and who knew what else. Each time she heard it, Cintra held her breath and dug her fingers into Niko's arm.

Then came the throaty wail of a baby crying. *Waahh waahh.* They stopped. She gripped Niko's arm tighter, stunned at the sound. *Waahh waahh.*

"Oh my God," she breathed. "Someone abandoned a baby in the woods."

They stood immobile, not knowing what to do, or

which way to go. A small, white animal face bucked against the wire fencing and they jumped back, letting out screams. The white face, the big white nose, bucked again and retreated. Cintra almost doubled over with relief.

"A goat," she told Niko. "They put goats in here to restore the woodlands. I read about it."

"Sweet Jesus," he muttered.

They continued along until a huge tube-like black mass lay horizontal in front of them. She reached out to touch it, felt rough bark. A massive tree that had fallen into the pathway. They clambered over it.

Tiny drops of peach-colored light trickled through the trees. The teardrops of light told her they were close to the other side of the circular path, where there was a stone staircase. The staircase led to the lighted pedestrian street, and a short way beyond that was the vehicle-trafficked street with the police substation.

"The steps must be coming up," Cintra said, feeling saved. There would be an end to this nightmare. Soon, they would be in a police station, sending help to Pedro and Samantha.

At the bottom of the steps, they started to run again, but Cintra was lagging with her throbbing head, her numb, battered feet, and her wet, knotted skirt. "Niko," she panted. "Don't worry about me. Run up ahead, across the first street, and through the lawn. There's a small paved path to a street right along basketball courts with the station."

"We'll get there," he said, slowing down and holding her hand.

It wasn't significantly lighter with the streetlamps of the pedestrian street about two hundred feet from them, but it looked light as day compared to the death-black of the woods.

Niko suddenly hunched down, pulling her with him. "Van," he said. On the street below them was a dark van moving slowly. They crouched lower behind a slope.

"Could be parks department," she whispered.

"Could be them."

They watched the van idling along the pedestrian street. A small group of people in costume walked by it, laughing and talking.

"Niko!" she heard, a man's voice, low and gruff. She recognized the voice as Rocky, the veterinarian slash executioner. "Cintra!"

Cintra grabbed Niko's arm. They lay flat on the dirt, heads up like turtles, watching.

"Niko! Cintra!" A woman's voice.

"Not June," she whispered.

"Niko! Cintra!" The man's gruff voice again. "We've got Pedro here! He's good for now but won't be for long!"

"All we want is for you to stop the Ettie special!" the woman called. "She's got nothing to do with anything! She's done her time! Leave her alone!"

"I can't do that," Cintra hissed in Niko's ear. "I don't have that power. Maybe I should pretend I do, but only if they give us Pedro."

He shook his head, light gleaming off his scalp. "They're just trying to make us to come out. They'll take us and keep him too."

Cintra didn't know what to think. If they truly had Pedro, then he was alive. If they were lying, where was he?

"Niko! Cintra!" The woman again. "We know where Elliot and Boston live! We know where Samantha lives!"

Niko's hand gripped around hers so tight it hurt. She tried to twist it away. A big part of her was urging a run at the van. She would reach right into the window and grab the woman, tear at her face, dig into her eyes, for threatening her son. The only thing that stopped her was the idea of stupidly getting killed and depriving Boston of a mother because she couldn't control herself.

A beam of light shot out from the van, lanced the trees, and swept towards them. Cintra lay her face flat in her arm so the witch-black of her costume would fuse with the dark. She smelled Earth, inhaled specks of dirt.

"Nikoooo!" called the woman. "Come out, you coward. You user and future faker! Don't make Samantha and Cintra pay for your mistakes like June had to!"

He grunted lowly, and the pressure on Cintra's hand multiplied until she seriously worried he would crush its delicate bones.

"That's it. If they want only me, I'll go," he told her in a normal voice. The pressure was off her hand, leaving it limp. The next thing she knew, he was standing. She grasped at his fingers with her working hand.

"Get down!" she whispered furiously. "They won't do anything to them. Not with us out here and me to backup your story."

"Really, Cintra?" he asked, his body tensed and tilted towards the street. "Will anyone believe you?"

Of course he knew about her problem, thanks to June. And June knew about it thanks to Pedro. She snaked an arm around his ankle, weighing him down with everything she had. "I'll take a polygraph. If they're still threatening everyone, that means they haven't done anything yet. Get *down*."

He stood rigid as the van continued its leisurely drive along the pedestrian street and the beam of light bobbed away. The van rose up a hill, and dropped below its crest, the streak of light triangled on a tree before it disappeared.

"*Now* we go," she ordered, pushing herself up.

They trotted down the slope and hit the pedestrian street and ran across it, ran north on a lawn, and past a children's playground until they came to a small paved path. A water fountain was at the entrance. Cintra couldn't stop herself from hobbling to the fountain and gulping at its cool stream. Niko took a quick turn after her.

"This way," she said, waving him towards the left. Cintra was limping, clasping Niko's arm.

A shadow emerged from a tree in front of them, and Cintra thought it was a stranger, until the shadow stepped under the streetlight and she saw the pink, frilly gown, the blonde ringlets, the glint of the silver gun. She opened her mouth, but no sound came out.

June moved closer, the gun pointed. Behind her was a white dress, seemingly disembodied, until it too moved under the streetlight and a knife gleamed in the woman's hand. The killer bride. June had lived here long enough to know there was a substation in the park. She and her pal had simply gone to the pathway nearest to it, then waited for Cintra and Niko to come out of the woods. Cintra wanted to smack herself in despair. Would she never get a step ahead of this lunatic?

"Don't move," June said.

Niko thrust his arm out and pushed Cintra behind him. "June, stop this," he said. "Leave Cintra alone. No one knows anything. Take me and we'll go on as before."

"I know you think I'm an idiot, Niko. And I guess I was. An idiot for you. All those years, hung around buying your nonsense and lies while you shopped for someone younger behind my back. Seven years, and you moved on like it was nothing. Left me to miscarry on my own. Deal with it on my own while you made a family. I get death and you get life. But I'm not an idiot anymore. Let Cintra go? As if she'll keep her mouth shut. What a joke."

Cintra wanted to yell out that she would keep her mouth shut, but she couldn't speak, as if her throat and tongue had forgotten how to form words. She despised how fear clutched her in a straightjacket of uselessness. A scalp-tingling screech came from behind her, and she turned. The van. It was parked on the pedestrian street. The massive leather-masked man jumped out and lumbered towards them.

"Ladies! The party's over. Time to haul ass."

"We have to get rid of them," June said.

"June, please!" Niko pleaded. "I'm so sorry for the

way I treated you. You're right about everything. I was selfish and stupid. I regret it more than anything. And not just because you're holding a gun on me."

Cintra watched as he slowly advanced on June. Was he trying to get close enough to her to take the gun? She wanted to warn him, tell him to stop, but the pair were on their own track. She had no power here.

"I'm sorry, June. I apologize. I said it by email but never to your face. And I should have. What can I do to make this right?"

"Make this right?" June's voice was high-pitched and out of control in a way Cintra had never heard before. "How dare you! There's no making this right! I had a chance to have a family, and now I don't! And you—you get whatever you want."

"These people with you, they're like family, aren't they? I know it isn't the kind of family you planned for, but June… Please. We loved each other once. In some strange way, maybe we still do."

Cintra couldn't see June's face clearly in the glow of the streetlight, but she felt it—felt that June had grown hesitant. The gun even dipped down slightly. Niko's words had gotten to her. Cintra wanted to add something that would appeal to June's humanity, which must be still in there somewhere. But she didn't dare. This was between June and Niko. If anyone could turn her around, it would be him.

"Please," Niko breathed. "Take me back if you want. I deserve it. We should have spent this time talking about everything. I'll do that for as long as you need. But let Cintra go." He was halfway to her. "June, listen," he begged, holding up his hands. "I'm so sorry. I was a fool. Forgive me."

"Yes, Niko," June said. "You *are* a fool if you think I'd fall for your lines again."

A loud crack split the air. Niko hit the ground, his white and black pinstripes lifeless on the pavement. Cintra heard a far-away scream, and thought it was June screaming. But no. It was herself.

She staggered to Niko and slid down next to him in what seemed slow motion. She needed to do something. CPR. But she was trembling too badly to keep her mouth on his. His eyes were open, staring glassily. A slick disc of blood seeped through his chest and she tried to press her quaking hands on it, to keep the life in him, but her hands were too trembly to do much good.

She shouldn't have given him a notebook. Shouldn't have visited Samantha. Shouldn't have gone to the party. All the things she shouldn't have done, and any one of them would have kept him alive.

"For fucks' sake, let's go!" she heard Rocky's gruff voice.

Cintra tossed her neck back and wailed into the dark. "Help! Help!" Her voice was hoarse, it barely made any sound. No one would hear her.

A woman's voice, somewhere near her, harsh and urgent. "Leave her. Leave her. She's not what we're about. Not what we're about."

Cintra's cheeks were stiff with tear trails, saliva drizzled from her open mouth as she pressed down on Niko's chest. She couldn't leave him here and have him die alone on the ground with his killer standing over him. If there was any chance he was still alive, she had to stay with him. Didn't anyone hear the shot? Wouldn't anyone come help?

"Niko, Niko," she breathed, trying to still her shaking hands, wet with his blood.

"I'm not here to kill women, Cintra," June said, her voice incredibly close, the edge of her pink gown in her side vision. "But he worked for years to turn my love into hate, and he finally got his wish. Go home and teach your son to be a good man."

A primal instinct stormed Cintra's body, leaving her with no rational control. Flinging her arms out ragingly, she caught June around the ankles, toppling her down to the ground. The pop-crack of the gun sizzled overhead. She clawed fists full of frilly gown, only wanting to get the gun and use it to smash June's face to pulp, smash off that pert smile forever. Then a force had her by the arms, and was dragging her back, yanking her up to her feet. She bucked and kicked back at the force, but her bare, soft feet landed harmlessly on thick boots and hard shins.

June sat wide-legged on the ground, her blonde hair snarled around her face, both arms straight out and the gun aimed at Cintra's chest. A bullet was going to shatter her heart. She hadn't escaped death, only postponed it, and now it was here to take her from her son.

"Boston!" she screamed, a primitive roar. She wanted that to be her last word.

The silver of the gun. Tapping noises, *tap tap tap*, metal against metal. She flinched over and over, but felt nothing. *Tap, tap, tap.* Big hands on her arms hurled her down, shearing her forearms on the pavement.

There were voices, a clap of yells, and white sneakers came into her line of vision. Someone said, "Holy shit, call 911," as tires squealed out in the dark.

## Chapter Forty-One

*C*intra looked up to see a small crowd gathering around them. In the usual New York fashion, the people seemed calm, almost unaffected. A couple of them were on their phones. A man was saying "Prospect Park" and looking around for a location. "Ambulance. Southwest. Across from the pizza place. I don't know. He looks dead to me."

Cintra searched out the face of a woman who was staring down, a small white dog at her feet. Something about the woman said she was good, solid, and helpful. Cintra shakily stood and asked the woman for her phone.

*We know where Samantha lives. We know where Boston and Elliot live.*

She managed to still her hands enough to text Boston's number, grateful he happened to have one easy to memorize. He would never pick up a call from a strange number, or even bother listening to a voicemail.

*Boss, it's Mom. I don't have my phone on me. If you're out,*

*go to a friend's house, please! I'll explain later. I'm coming home.
If you're home, lock the door. Don't let anyone in.*

Cintra handed back the phone, and the woman looked steadily at it, a strange, almost revolted, expression on her face. Cintra realized the phone screen was fingerprinted with Niko's blood.

"Will you do me a favor?" Cintra asked her. "I need to go check on my son. There's a chance the people who shot this man might go for him next."

The woman looked shell-shocked, as if she hadn't understood a word Cintra had said. Then she came back to herself. "You go," she said, authoritatively. "I'll stay with him."

"And please call 911." Cintra told the woman the address of her apartment building. "They need to go to apartment 3D, as in David. There's been a shooting there. A man could die. Apartment 3D."

The woman nodded. Woman to woman. She understood.

Cintra took off running.

She calculated it. The police substation? She'd get stuck trying to explain to some desk person that a vigilante gang of women might be after her son. The desk person would think she's high on drugs and spend precious minutes telling her to calm down. Maybe they'd even haul her to a psych ward. The subway? Forget it. Car service? She certainly wasn't going to wait for one and she had no phone or money anyway, and wasn't going to hope the driver would be charitable. Hitchhike? Hardly.

She was going to run home. She was almost at the

end of Prospect Park Southwest, and from there it was a straight shot, only three long blocks to Fifth Avenue, and five short blocks to her old building. She'd be there in fifteen minutes, tops, as long as she kept running.

She had to get home, home to Boston. Chances were the gang would get the hell out of town, but she wasn't going to count on that. She'd make sure he was safe and that police had gone to Pedro, and then she'd find out which hospital Niko had been taken to. It occurred to her that Niko had no identification on him. She'd call nearby hospitals asking for a man in a prisoner's costume who'd been shot.

She felt guilty leaving him, but her mothering instincts had taken over. She'd almost been taken from her son twice tonight, and seeing his face was not a choice, it was simply something that had to be done. Niko would have told her to go. Sometimes knowing your child was okay was the only thing that mattered. That's why he'd risked his and Samantha's life to find out the same about Jasmine. He would understand.

She wound around Bartel-Pritchard Square and kept running, dodging people on the sidewalk. The pain in her feet was almost unbearable, but there was nothing to be done about it.

But past the square, her energy flagged dramatically. Adrenaline was only going to get her so far. She began to steadily jog. Then her lungs tightened and rebelled, and she had to stop, bending over and sucking in loud, heaving breaths. It wasn't that much farther. Two more blocks and she'd be on Fifth Avenue.

They wouldn't come for Boston, would they? That

had just been a threat. To get her and Niko out of the woods. Then she remembered Samantha. The gang could be headed to 601 Chestnut, or even there right now.

She had to hope the gang had enough brains to call off any additional murder plans, knowing Cintra would point the finger at all of them, not only for what June had done to Niko, but for anything that might happen to Samantha.

All along she'd suspected that the gang had used threat of harm to Samantha to keep Niko in line, and they wouldn't really kill a mother with two babies. But after seeing what June had done to Niko, she wouldn't put anything past her or her pals. And, oh God, Niko. She could barely think about it. Two babies would grow up without a father. Samantha would find out what had happened, and how if only Cintra hadn't given him the notebook, he'd be alive.

She had to call 911 and try to get police sent to Samantha.

A couple strode down the sidewalk and she limped to them. "Please," she breathed. "Can I use your phone? There's someone in trouble, real trouble, and I lost mine."

The couple stood staring blankly at her, and it was then she realized how horrific she must look. Green face paint tear-smeared all over her face, a skirt knotted up around her thighs, blood-stained hands, bare, muddy feet. She was shocked they stopped for her at all.

"Please," she said, almost crying with desperation,

something she worried would frighten them, causing them to leave. "I just need to call 911."

"Ahh," the man said, slowly, feeling around his pockets as if he wasn't sure if he had a phone, or was reluctant to hand it to her, worried she was making up some kind of story to steal it. Damn New Yorkers and their suspicious minds. She wanted to screech at him to hurry up, but didn't dare.

Finally he found it, tapped at it a few times, and handed it to her. He pointed at the call icon and she opened it, and once again, her maternal instincts seized control. Instead of dialing 911, she texted Boston's number.

*Boss, it's Mom. Pick up from this number. Emergency.*

She dialed Boston's number. *Burr burr burr.*

"Uhh, Mom?"

"Boston?!" She exploded, almost dancing with relief. "Are you okay? Did you get my message?"

"Yeah, just now."

"Where are you?"

"Getting ice cream."

"I need you to go to a friend's house. Understand? Anyone. Whoever you're with."

"I'm headed home."

"I'd prefer you to go a friend's house. Where's Kenny?"

"What's wrong?"

"Just do it! Go to Kenny's or anyone else from your class. No dawdling around."

"She's saying go a friend's house."

"What?"

"Yeah, I don't know. She sounds all whacked out."

"Whoever you're talking to, go to their house."

"It's Dad's friend."

"What? Who?"

"Dad's friend. Dad sent her to get me."

"Dad's friend who? I need a name."

A pause. The man whose phone she'd borrowed looked at her impatiently. She didn't care.

"Answer me! Who are you with?"

"Hello, Cintra." A woman.

"Who is this?"

"Elliot's friend. Boston is fine."

"Elliot's friend who?" The voice. It sounded familiar. Not June familiar but… familiar.

"There's more apartments in this city than 3D, you know. Lots more."

Cintra's heart crashed right to the bottom of her cold, numb, battered feet.

"Keep away from him!" she yelled. Her hand was shaking so badly she worried she would drop the phone. "Hello? Hello?"

The man rocked, looking impatient. The woman next to him stood quietly riveted.

"They have my son!" she screamed.

## Chapter Forty-Two

*G*etting ice cream. It had to be the ice cream
shop on Fifth Avenue. There would be
nowhere else to get ice cream this late.

"God!" she thrust out from her throat as she ran.
"God!"

But calling out slowed her up. No more of that. Just
run, run. That's all. Shut up and run. God, God, God.
Why did they want Boston? No, this couldn't be happening. It's happening.

Her brain stormed this way and that. Was there
anything else she could do? Any way she could get to
him? The cars were all passing down the one-way street
in the opposite direction. Even if she managed to get a
car to stop and take her to Fifth Avenue, the person
would have to drive in the opposite direction and then
turn down another one-way street. And they'd hit traffic.
No. That would take too much time.

Her feet, her shins, her knees. Please, please let them
hold up! The pain was getting excruciating. Her ankles

felt ready to shatter and the block seemed as if it would never end. She was making noises she'd never heard before—guttural, animal cry-whines. More people ambled down the sidewalk, coming from Fifth Avenue. She dodged around them.

"God!" she hollered again, despite herself. "No!"

The lights got brighter. She turned right onto Fifth Avenue, Boston's old middle school on the opposite side of the street. The people. They were walking so casually, so nonchalantly. Her world was ending and no one knew it. No one cared to know it.

Now she came to a side street where the traffic was moving. She thrust out her arm to try to stop the cars. But this was Brooklyn. Traffic stops for no one. "God!" she screamed again, raging at the cars. "Move!" She saw an opening in the line of cars and dashed through it.

The ice cream shop. Only a block. Maybe he would hear her.

"Boston!" she screamed out into the street, to anyone. "It's Mom!"

The people on the sidewalk, some in costume, mostly ignored her. A mother calling her son wasn't anything that would draw attention in New York, no matter how crazed she looked.

"Boston! Where are you?" She doubled over, completely winded, and drew several choking breaths.

"Wrong state," a man sniped as he passed.

"Are you okay?" a woman asked, sympathetically, and Cintra wanted to collapse on the woman and plead for help. Please help me find my son. But that was impossible. She ignored the woman and kept running.

The ice cream shop. Its red, blue and white awning. Its brightly lit front. Where was he? Which direction would he have gone in?

Cupping her hands around her mouth, she screamed out, "Boston!!!"

"Mom!"

Yes, yes, he was here. A sob of gratitude bubbled in her lungs. She heard him but didn't see him. She looked around frantically.

"Mom!"

A man moved down the sidewalk, and behind him she recognized the spray of orange curls, the blue jumpsuit and multicolored long-sleeved shirt of her son's Chucky costume.

"Boston!" She held up both her arms, waving hysterically.

Then a woman was near him. She had brown hair almost to her shoulders. The woman turned. She looked so familiar. A woman from the party? No, she wasn't in costume. She had on all black clothes—black pants, a black zipped-up hoodie, a black cap.

Cintra threw both her hands in front of her. "Boston! Come to Mommy! Get away from that woman!"

Why wasn't he moving?

Then she saw it. The woman had something in her hand. And her hand was sticking straight into Boston's side. The woman was saying something to him as he held his ice cream cone high. He looked bewildered, confused. So confused.

"Get away from my son!"

The woman looked around, and then she and Boston began moving towards the sidewalk.

"Don't come near me!" the woman yelled.

A black car pulled up to the sidewalk. The woman and Boston moved towards it. A few people around Cintra stopped, watching, unsure what was happening. Someone slammed into her shoulder and she reeled back for a moment.

"Get away from my son!" she screamed, pointing. "Someone stop them! Stop them!"

Boston and the woman moved towards the black car. He was going to be in it in a few seconds and Cintra would never see her son again. The woman turned. She had a gun pointed at Boston's side. A small, black gun.

"Back off, Cintra!" the woman ordered.

The fuck she would. She walked purposefully, hands spread out before her.

"Just get away from him. I don't understand. He knows nothing. Take me!"

Boston's mouth hung open. She could tell he had no idea what was happening. She couldn't even tell if he knew there was a gun at his side.

"Your husband took advantage of me when I was nineteen," the woman said. "Now he's trying to get me fired. He wants me gone because of you. I got a bad review and it had to be him."

"Oh my God," Cintra whispered, as it came together for her why the woman looked so familiar. "Brittany!" she yelled. "Get away from him!"

Boston looked down at the gun, and then back up at Cintra. Now he knew, she knew he knew. She watched with awe as Boston's ice cream cone fell in slow motion to the sidewalk.

Without any thought, she rushed forward, towards the woman and Boston. She would take a bullet. This would give Boston enough time to run. Once the gun went off, Brittany wouldn't want to stick around and try to get him into the car. She'd leave.

A small explosion sounded and a white flash buried her vision.

She was in a white room of some kind. Everything felt calm and peaceful. So this was death. It was like they said. White, serene, infusing her with a feeling of warmth and unconditional love.

"Daddy?"

Her father was across the room. The father she remembered from her childhood—big, bulky, fleshed out. Not the rail-thin father with the hairless skull-head. The living skeleton he was in those months before he died.

He was close to her, and yet so far away. Something separated them, some kind of vast warp of time and space that was beyond her comprehension. Yet she saw every atom of his face and body, and felt his love in every molecule of her.

"Dad, I'm so sorry I lied. About the car accident. About those times I said Boston was sick and I couldn't visit you. I hated to see you the way you were."

"Cintra, I've forgiven you," he said, in that low, warm voice, the voice she hadn't heard in so long that she'd almost forgotten what it sounded like. "But you have to forgive yourself. That's what's most important, honey. Can you do that?"

She was sucked back to the present, to the people on the sidewalk scattering with more speed and precision than she'd ever seen a group of people move.

Brittany was splayed was on the sidewalk, a growing patch of dark liquid next to her. Cintra's hands flew to her mouth and she couldn't take her eyes off the sight.

In a moment, Rocky, the executioner, was there, his leather hood still over his head. He hauled Brittany into his arms like she was nothing but air and carried her to the dark van parked near the sidewalk behind the black car, its back door open. The killer bride was peering down near a sidewalk planter, as if she'd dropped something. She found the black gun, casually picked it up, and got into the van's passenger seat. All that remained behind was the blood puddle and the lonely black cap.

"Cintra!"

Cintra looked towards the voice. The blonde snarl of hair. The pink, frilly dress. June was standing next to the open door of the van, a black gun in her hand.

"Just her leg," she said. "We turned her down, but her ride has been keeping tabs on her for us. Picked a fine night, didn't she? We'll drop this problem at the ER and she won't bother you again. See? I'm not so bad. Now, if you know what's good for you, you'll consider this over."

She smiled, that smile Cintra knew so well, the smile of a woman who wanted to be a friendly neighbor. The black car rolled slowly into the street, then blazed up the bus lane. June got into the van's back door and it slid shut. The van vroomed loudly and it too shot away, then took a quick turn and vanished, leaving behind the gassy fumes of an overtaxed engine.

Cintra looked around desperately for her son. "Boston!" she yelled. "Boston!"

He came out of the ice cream shop, orange wig gone, looking more stunned than she'd ever seen a human being look. Her baby. She staggered to him and threw her arms around him.

"What the freak was all that?" Boston asked.

Cintra laughed maniacally. Laugh-cried and didn't hug her son but devoured him with her arms. Grabbing his cheeks, she said, "That woman wanted to do something very bad, and the woman in the pink dress helped us. My neighbor. Ex-neighbor." And then, half-delirious, "In 3D." She hugged him more.

"Girls are crazy," he murmured, as police sirens howled in the distance.

## Chapter Forty-Three

_I_ t was a sparkly April afternoon. Cintra was in
the outdoor box garden, planting seeds of
kale, broccoli and cauliflower, which she'd read could be
planted this late, and marigolds, which she'd read
discouraged pests. Hopefully, these things were true.
She'd never planted anything in her life.

It was fairly warm, mid-sixties, the sky lucid blue,
and she wore a planting outfit of wrinkled blue jeans,
black t-shirt, and light Nylon jacket, with her big
gardening gloves and her hand shovel, rake, and spade.
Her hair, mostly back to its natural raven color, was in a
ponytail.

Boston and his friend, Noah, were kicking an orange
soccer ball around the yard. She wasn't sure what had
happened to Kenny, who hadn't made an appearance in
a few weeks; these days, it was all about Noah.

A quick spurt of horn honks came from the front of
the house, and she put down her tools, took off her
gardening gloves, and jogged to the front. A dark

minivan was pulling into the driveway. Cintra bobbed on her feet, waving the van closer to Poppy's car. It stopped, the engine cut, and she waited what seemed an agonizing time for the door to open.

Niko emerged, smiling. They greeted each other with a long hug.

The bullet had pierced Niko's prisoner's ID plate, then charged through into his sternum. But the plate, though made with cheap metal, had miraculously slowed the bullet down enough that it traveled only millimeters into his body, stopping short of his heart. Police had found it on the ground, splintered in half. By the time an ambulance arrived, Niko had come back to consciousness and was even sitting up. Within a week, he was released from the hospital and had gone back to Cold Springs.

Cintra and Niko separated from the hug, and she spontaneously kissed his cheek. His hair had grown back, black and thick, curling down a little past the tips of his ears. He was in jeans and a brown suede jacket, looking quite handsome, she had to admit, leaving her a little embarrassed at her dirt-smeared outfit. He'd caught her unprepared, an hour early thanks to light traffic.

He retrieved a cooler out of his trunk that contained two pies (cherry and pumpkin) and other foodstuffs he'd offered to bring for the Easter Day meal tomorrow.

In the kitchen, Boston came in with his friend, and he greeted Niko with fist-bumps. The boys left to bike ride around the tree-fringed streets, with Cintra calling after Boston to be careful and not to go on traffic-glutted Flatbush Avenue, the things she always called after him.

She changed clothes, then sat with Niko sat on the swing bench on the porch, iced tea (with a bit of rum mixed in) in hand, enjoying the fresh, spring day. A cotton-candy pink cherry blossom tree in the front yard perfumed the air.

"Thanks for inviting me," Niko said, clinking her glass. "You've got a little slice of heaven here."

"I'm glad you could come. Though I'm sure you'd rather be with the twins."

He waved. "They're fine. The grandparents wanted them, and Samantha understood that I wanted to visit you. She'd like to come down too when the twins are a little easier to handle."

"Have you memorized her phone number yet?" she teased.

He cleared his throat and took a sip of tea.

Cintra had met Samantha at Methodist Hospital, where Niko had been taken for surgery, but things had been so harried that they hadn't spoken much. "I'd love to meet her under better circumstances. And I'm so happy Jasmine is doing well."

She and Niko had been in touch by email, through encryption software. No sense letting the "gals" know what they were discussing, in case they were still interested.

He had revealed a shocking symptom of his captivity—the visual monotony of staring at bare white walls for most of the day had resulted in the occasional hallucination. He knew what was happening because his father had been a long-distance trucker who'd experienced the same. One time, he saw a child in medieval robes who appeared at his bedside before walking to the door and sliding underneath it like a vapor. He also said his hearing had become acutely sharp, which is how he began to distinguish where June's finger was landing on the combination lock on his door.

He'd also told her that, at first, Samantha was thrilled he'd survived June's murder attempt, and relieved that he was back in her life. But as his condition had improved, her mood deteriorated. She hadn't yet dealt with her feelings of betrayal over Niko's flirtatious emails to June, especially as they'd complained about Samantha and their marriage. The couple was in marriage counseling.

"How's it going with Elliot?" he asked, nudging her with an elbow.

Their attention was momentarily drawn by Cintra's neighbor, who was banging on the side of a little wood-shed in her picket-fenced backyard with a hammer. Cintra had only said hello a few times to the neighbor, a middle-aged woman with short, auburn hair and a chipper manner. Looking off into the cobalt sky, Cintra noted traces of clouds that looked like pinwheels.

"He usually does some groveling when he comes to pick up Boston. He insists that he hadn't been with his coworker since she was an intern at his job four years ago. Whatever." She wiped down one leg, as if she'd forgotten to change from her dirted-up garden jeans. "Maybe I could forgive him for the affair. But not for the lying, which is ironic, considering how I used to lie to him."

"Yeah, but your lies weren't like *that*," he said.

She was silent. The family-splitting lie she'd told Boston was still so brutal on her psyche that she couldn't bring herself to tell Niko about it. "He claims because he caught me in a few lies about where I was, he thought I was having an affair," she said. "Once, he told me I was turning him into a person he didn't want to be. I think what he meant was that I'd already turned him into that person."

"You can't blame yourself," Niko said.

That was another thing she was working on. "Dr. Grace says this disorder is often too much for marriages to handle." She sighed at him. "Anyway, I'm fine living with my son and cat."

What she didn't tell Niko was that it had taken her weeks to return to Dr. Grace, as she'd begun to wonder if the young psychologist was involved in the gang too. All that talk of bubble baths and meditation was a perfect way to make Cintra feel she was losing her mind. But she finally realized if that had been the case, June would have bragged about it while holding the gun on her.

She and Niko swung a bit more in silence, Cintra a touch lightheaded from the rum, then she asked, "Have you heard anything from Detective Morales lately?"

"Nope. You?"

"Only that last time, when was that? February? He'd said 3C and 3D had been sold, one shell company to another shell company."

Detective Morales was a chatty type who'd been willing to answer Cintra's emails, telling her more about the case than he probably should have. Such as that Callie had been tracked to a tiny island in Greece and claimed she knew nothing of her tenant, June, holding an ex-boyfriend hostage. Police couldn't track the owner of the Ettie Brightman fan club site's URL, which was registered in India. The IP address was hidden with a VPN. After a few phone calls with Detective Morales, Callie had hired a lawyer who'd told him to either charge Ms. Bates or leave her alone. But there was one person the detective wouldn't discuss: Leo, since he was a minor.

"But I finally got it through a friend of a friend who teaches at The Science Center that Callie arranged to take him out to live with her," said Cintra.

"I hope the kid is okay. Sometimes I think they kept him there to keep me in line too. He was another reason I couldn't think about doing anything to June. I had no idea what would happen to him if I..."

She watched the side of Niko's face as he stared at his feet, then gently touched his arm. "You don't have to justify it. I would have done the same. Anyone threatening my family? I would have done whatever they wanted."

He nodded almost imperceptibly, then gazed in the direction of the neighbor's reinvigorated hammering. "How's Pedro doing?" he asked.

Glimpsing a long silhouette behind the screened door, Cintra raised her hand. "You can ask him yourself. Ped! Get your ass out here. Niko's here."

Pedro emerged on the porch with a shy, conflicted grin. As Niko stood, Pedro said, "Careful," indicating his left shoulder, the one that had been shot. Niko greeted him with a gentle handshake on his good arm. "Good seeing you, man," Pedro said, then looked down, then back up. Contriteness was all over his face.

"Cin, I'm off to the gym," Pedro said. "Then headed to the pharmacy. Need anything?"

She said she didn't need anything, and they watched him walk down the porch, and to the street. "He feels bad," said Cintra.

"He should," Niko said, with an exaggerated frown. "But I appreciated his email. It sounded genuine and remorseful. I don't know any of us who haven't made mistakes. Big ones."

Niko had refused to press charges against Pedro, who was cooperating in the investigation. After the gun had gone off in the apartment, hitting Pedro in the shoulder, chaos had reigned, and he'd staggered out to apartment 3C, locking himself inside to call police. But by the time they'd arrived, the partygoers had vanished.

"I never asked you how he knew I had the door lock combination, or at least thought I did," said Niko.

"Oh, he didn't. He panicked and thought he could wrestle the gun from June. Wasn't very well thought out. Between you and me, I suspect his Krav Maga training was a bit of an exaggeration."

In one of their emails, Niko had speculated to Cintra that the gang hadn't used a camera monitor on him because they had members who knew how easily those things could be hacked. Everything they'd set up gave them plausible deniability, but video of Niko locked alone in a room would not have. But thanks to the absence of a camera, Niko had been able to write in the notebook without being seen.

In the kitchen, they filled their glasses with rum iced tea, then Cintra showed Niko where he'd be sleeping. It was a room she'd fixed up in nautical style, with seafoam walls, bleached driftwood furniture, and lighthouses and scenes of Cape Cod framed on the walls. He put down his overnight bag, and Cintra gave him a tour of the rest of the house, the same foreclosed house that June had shown her. Because the home's real estate agent had disappeared, the auction had been pushed back. And thanks to Poppy's solid income, the house was theirs.

Cintra wasn't sure why June had showed her the house, except she probably thought Cintra was getting too nosy, and having her move out of apartment 3C wouldn't be a bad idea. The house showing had also worked embarrassingly well to defuse her suspicions and warm her to June.

Cintra wasn't concerned that the gang would figure out she lived in June's old listing. She and Niko felt they had no other choice than to live normal lives. Were they and their families supposed to live life on the run? They had to hope that the gang would leave them alone as it was in enough hot water already. The media had inadvertently helped out in that respect. Several days after Niko's shooting, a photo of his "cell" was leaked to the tabloidy *City Post*. A frontpage headline had blared: EX-NAPPED!

A warrant was out for June. If she had any brains, and Cintra knew she did, she'd stay gone.

As for "killer bride" Maressa (if that was her real name), there were several women with that name, with various spellings, who worked at Barton's, both in Cold Springs and in Brooklyn. Cintra couldn't identify any of them from photos, thanks to the woman's "killer bride" ensemble.

The gang had picked the perfect night for their confrontation—the one night of the year when it was completely normal to wear a disguise.

As for Ettie Brightman, Detective Morales said she was living with a niece, checking in with her parole officer, and had admitted giving out a fake name to people she didn't know. She'd said she was aware of the fan site, but knew nothing of a so-called vigilante group.

Over the winter holidays, Cintra had been busy renovating; helping Pedro, who'd still been wearing a sling; and having teary scenes with Elliot. In the end, they'd decided to stay separated. Boston, who was keen to live in a house with a backyard, would stay with her during the week, with Elliot on weekends and alternating holidays.

Poppy, who'd broken her engagement to Joseph, was usually either at work or out with her new boyfriend, a twenty-eight-year-old building contractor from Bay Ridge whom she'd met during renovations. It was Poppy's boyfriend, Tony, who'd explained what Cintra hadn't been able to figure out: how she heard Niko meditating through a soundproof wall.

"They probably used mineral wool," Tony had said.

"If there was an air gap, low frequencies would have gone straight through it. In the right spot, ya'd hear it. Not as easy to soundproof a wall as ya would think."

Cintra was working on her novel. Its plot, much like her life, had taken some unexpected zigzags.

Lisa (Cintra could never bring herself to rename her) had morphed into a woman who'd divorced her manipulative, hotshot lawyer husband, and won custody of their thirteen-year-old son, Ditmas. Then Lisa's ex-husband steals Misty, the one-eyed terrier mix Lisa had adopted from a shelter, and disappears into the New Hampshire wetlands. Lisa and her son, utilizing his obsession with a people tracking video game called I Know Where You Are, embark on a dangerous and soggy journey to rescue the mutt. Working title: *Dog in a Bog*.

## Chapter Forty-Four

---

*A*fter Boston went to bed, and Poppy went out with her boyfriend, Niko and Cintra had hot tea on the porch swing bench, chatting about anything but June. She told him the full story of "Lynn Coba" and they laughed over the situation comedy aspects of her conversation with Rosetta. But then the inevitable topic reared up.

"This is going to sound crazy," he said, rocking the bench a little. "But sometimes…" He stopped and couldn't seem to continue. She nudged her sneaker up against his, saying, "Go on."

"It makes no sense. After everything June did… " He trailed off again, looking down at the white burn-scar on his left wrist.

"Yes?"

"I remember the June I knew before all of this. The girl at the beginning of our relationship. She was so sweet and happy. I feel like I made her the way she ended up. All of this guilt about it."

He stopped again, staring off into the night. She waited, not wanting to press him. Finally, he said, "Then I think about her in prison. And how there's a part of me that doesn't want that. Maybe she needs help instead."

Cintra nodded, she wasn't sure what to say about that.

"Is that wrong?" he asked, turning to her, the porch light slanting down his cheek.

Cintra was back on the no-lying track. But one thing she had learned was that the truth or fiction of words didn't matter as much as the intention behind them. When Boston had asked why she and Elliot remained separated, she didn't tell him about Elliot's affair, or his lying to her about her head injury. She didn't want her son to look at his father differently. So she'd told him a different form of truth—that she and Elliot would always love him, and would always be his parents, but were no longer sure they wanted to be married.

And right now, she thought it was wrong Niko didn't want June in prison. At one point, Cintra had had sympathy for June. But not after she'd tried to kill Niko, and Pedro, and tried to take Cintra from her son. But she didn't want him to feel even guiltier. So she said, "No, it's not wrong, Niko," and squeezed his knee.

Just then, Cintra's neighbor emerged from a side door and stood on her porch. She looked over at them and waved. "Nice evening, isn't it?" she asked.

"Sure is," Cintra said, irritated with herself for not having asked the neighbor's name the last time she'd seen her. She was about to call over an introduction, but the woman faded into the shadows.

Soon, Cintra showed Niko to the guest bedroom. In hers, she got undressed and went to her computer. She liked to look at the fan club site occasionally, hoping for anything that might give her a clue as to what the gang was up to these days. She'd figured out that the combination on the doors—three-five-four-eight—was Ettie's birth date.

Lately, there hadn't been much of interest on the site, which had settled down after Ettie's release. But tonight Cintra saw one thing had changed: EttieAdmin's avatar. Shortly after the shooting, the avatar had been switched from the boat on clear blue waters to a generic photo of a rose. Now it was different. She clicked into the avatar and hit the enlarge button several times.

Three women, their backs to the camera, their arms around each other. All were wearing skirtinis, each in a solid color, one yellow, one red, and one bronze. They stood looking out into an expanse of breathlessly blue water undulating with silver ripples below an azure sky.

Cintra knew she was looking at Callie, Ettie and June. Where they were was anyone's guess, there was no landscape to give a better idea. The caption on the photo said, "Three amigas!"

She spotted a shape in the corner, and hunched towards the computer, staring at it. The edge of a palm tree. High above the curved trunk, a few palm fronds waved carefree in the wind. Cintra took a screenshot for Detective Morales. But several minutes later, she still couldn't bring herself to send it to him.

*See? I'm not so bad.*

No, June was worse than bad. Because if she was *all* bad, Cintra would be able to forget about her.

Around three a.m., she came out of a dream about a dog that was tied up in a yard, howling. Gradually, she realized the sound was rooted in reality, and she gingerly displaced Dumps, who was curled between her legs.

She went to the window nearest where the distant, howl-like sound had originated. The window was open a few inches and Cintra shoved it up farther, squinting into the moon-drenched night. The sound had stopped. Then it started up again: low, remote, and eerie. Her neck prickled.

The sound was coming from her neighbor's woodshed.

## About the Author

**C.G. Twiles** is a longtime writer who loves Gothic, mysteries, cemeteries, traveling, ancient history, animals, and old houses.

Thank you to my wonderful beta readers: Frances White, Julia Byrd, Jenna Beatrice, Amna Naseer, Madelyn Monaghan and Megan Easley-Walsh. A big high-five to literary agent Carly Watters for invaluable feedback, and to the kids next door for writing strange (and inspirational) notes on their front door.

If you enjoyed this book, please leave a review. Reviews are the life-blood of an author.

Visit CGTwiles.com to keep in touch and sign up to learn more about near-future releases. Also follow me on Facebook or Instagram for the latest promos.

facebook.com/cgtwiles

instagram.com/cgtwiles

bookbub.com/profile/c-g-twiles

# Also by C.G. Twiles

The Best Man on the Planet: A Modern Gothic Romantic Thriller

For an excerpt of *The Best Man on the Planet*, keep reading.

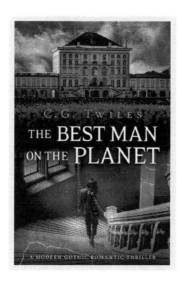

## Chapter 1

*I*t wasn't the kind of place you'd expect to see in the middle of Brooklyn.

Looming like a fortress over a delicate side street fringed with yellowwood and sweet gum, the Venetian Gothic *palazzo*-style mansion should have been a heartbeat from the Grand Canal, not within shouting distance of Flatbush Avenue, with its dollar stores and rumbling delivery trucks.

Casey dug out her phone and pulled up the address in street view: 555 Sterling Avenue. This was it. She'd assumed the interview would be in an office building and was disoriented with the mismatch between assumption and reality.

A swirl of icy wind deposited hair into her gaping mouth as she took in the five stories of ruddy brick and terra cotta, the balcony with columns sprouting quatrefoil carvings, and the bell-shaped windows capped with stained glass and hung with jowly lion-creatures. A frieze of pilgrims shuffled along a third-floor loggia and a verdigris belvedere brightened the roof.

Compared to the earthy brownstones on all sides, the mansion was an architectural Zeus flanked by second-tier Gods.

At the top of the steps, the grimacing face of a beastly devil on the black iron knocker confronted her. The demon looked as if it might bite the hand brazen enough to grab hold of its nose ring, so she pressed the doorbell. The engraving to the side read: "Foster House 1889."

As she waited, the cold seeped into her boots, numbing her toes. Casey wondered if there'd been a miscommunication. Maybe her contact—Miss Brock, she couldn't forget a name like that—had sent her the wrong address. Maybe she should be on Sterling Place or Sterling Street. It wouldn't be the first time a mix-up like that had occurred.

*Seeking resourceful and compassionate researcher. Journalism experience preferred.*

The salary had caught her attention first, the word "compassionate" second. *Savvy, dynamic, detail-oriented.* Those were the usual words in researcher job ads.

She toyed with the bell's surface, ready to try again, when the door drew back. An older woman, possibly in her sixties, penetrated her with a look of deep annoyance, as if the ringing had roused her from a nap.

"Miss Brock? I'm Casey Matos. I have an appointment at four."

The woman's expression didn't alter into a

welcoming one, but she stepped aside. "By all means, so you do."

Casey entered a mosaic-tiled foyer the size of her apartment. Despite windows spanning the length of one wall, stained glass filtered the light from the low-slung sky, leaving the foyer with the dim, melancholy feel of hanging inside a cloud.

Miss Brock ushered her into a side room with turquoise walls, and indicated she should sit on a settee with long slashes along the front, as if a cat had laid claim to the fabric. The room smelled piquant and subterranean, like fresh cement.

"This is a beautiful house," Casey said. "Not at all what I was expecting."

"I imagine not." Miss Brock sat and fixed her with round, silvery-tinted eyes, like small mirrors. Her reddish hair was pulled into a neat bun, accentuating steep cheekbones.

Casey imagined the woman's face must have been a burden in life, stirring up a riot of attention. She preferred her own more tepid features—dewy brown eyes, permanently flushed cheeks, dark caramel-colored hair to the plateau of her shoulders—which allowed her to put story subjects almost instantly at ease. Sometimes, if she got lucky, these subjects forgot she was there and said all kinds of things in front of her.

"The house is modeled on the Ca' d'Oro in Venice," Miss Brock said. And then, indicating small talk was over, "My employer is Mr. Samuel Foster. He placed the ad. Did you understand it?"

Mr. Foster. Foster House. The mansion must have been built for his family. No wonder the job paid so well.

"He's looking for someone to do research on crimes?" Casey glanced at the reporter's notebook inside her tote, more to avoid the woman's reflective stare than to jigger her memory. "Victims of crimes? It didn't say much more."

"Precisely. Mr. Foster is retired and runs a charitable foundation for those affected by violent crime. He'll tell you the specifics. He prefers a full time person. No vacation. Sick days and weekends, of course, but he'd like to have this finished sooner rather than later. And he'd like someone who can start as soon as possible. He believes when people need help, time is of the essence. Does this sound like something you'd be interested in?"

"Definitely. It sounds interesting. He sounds like a good man."

The blatant flattery failed to loosen the woman's reserve. "Then let me take you to Mr. Foster," she said.

Casey followed her through a main room with elaborate cave crown molding, like tiered wedding cakes, and two monster chandeliers raining hundreds of crystal tear drops. The dark staircase rhythmically grunted with their footfalls.

Visit CGTwiles.com to sign up to receive notice of the publication of her next novel.

Made in the USA
Middletown, DE
15 January 2021